BOKURU

By

Jon C. Hall

authorHOUSE™

1663 LIBERTY DRIVE, SUITE 200
BLOOMINGTON, INDIANA 47403
(800) 839-8640
WWW.AUTHORHOUSE.COM

First published by AuthorHouse 06/22/05

ISBN: 1-4184-6870-3 (e)
ISBN: 1-4184-4190-2 (sc)

Printed in the United States of America
Bloomington, Indiana

This book is printed on acid-free paper.

DEDICATION

To those individuals who possess

that rarest of human attributes,

the open mind.

8-12-03

Jon C. Hall

ACKNOWLEDGEMENT

This book would not have been possible
without the generous and untiring support of my sister,
Barbara D. Hall, whose personal encouragement,
willingness to listen to the story and concepts,
assistance in developing my computer skills,
and editing of the final manuscript,
made this book a reality.

8-12-03

Jon C. Hall

TABLE OF CONTENTS

CHAPTER ONE: *THE LANDING*

Out on the broad African savannah, vultures pecked noisily at the remains of an abandoned kill that lay on the top of the bank of a small stream. To the south, a distant rumbling grew louder as a giant cloud of dust loomed ever closer, slowly blotting out the horizon. The vultures gave a last stab at the carcass, and then rose seeking escape on a thermal updraft.

The first of thousands upon thousands of wildebeest galloped just ahead of the swirling dust cloud, reaching the edge of the stream below where the vultures had been feeding. They stopped, hesitated momentarily, and then plunged into the water, splashing across the shallow river, and scrambling up the opposite bank. Pressed by those charging behind them, the leaders galloped out onto the open plain in their annual northerly migration. Looming far ahead in the hazy distance was the gray cone of a long dormant volcano.

The reverie faded as Jim Henderson gradually became aware of his surroundings in the plane. The "Fasten Seat Belt" sign was flashing overhead. Most of the passengers were sleeping. The flight across Africa from Lagos, Nigeria had been a long one. The voice of a stewardess gently gave them their landing and deplaning instructions.

"We are in contact with the tower at Nairobi International. We should be in our landing approach in a few minutes. Please fasten your seat belts. Be sure all foldout tables are in the upright position and all loose objects are properly secured."

Jim was a long way from his apartment on North Dearborn Avenue in Chicago, Illinois. Since graduating from law school three years ago, he had been employed as an attorney at the small law office boutique of Grayson, Grayson, Phillips & Myers. He remembered his meeting about this case with David Grayson, the senior partner in the firm. That first meeting was why he was on this flight half way around the world.

Jim had been called in just before noon, five days ago. When Jim stepped into the office, David Grayson was not sitting at his desk. Instead, he was standing by the large east window, stooped forward, looking through a brass telescope mounted on a solid mahogany tripod by the drapes. Through the window, he could see the blue waters of Lake Michigan. The thirtieth floor provided a broad, open view that encompassed the park, the harbor, and the open lake. The normally placid surface of the lake was stirred into a chop of white-capped waves by a stiff wind coming out of the north. A single sailboat could be seen about a mile offshore.

"Jim. Come on in. Put your pad down for a minute and have a look," said David Grayson.

Jim put his legal pad and pen down on one of the leather guest chairs and went over to the window where his boss was looking through the telescope. Jim's own office was around the corner and down the hallway where the view was restricted to the adjoining office building. David Grayson stood back so that Jim could look through the telescope. The sailboat was focused in the center of the eyepiece.

"Is that who I think it is?"

Jim peered through the eyepiece. "I see it, a *Sparkman* thirty-seven. Yes, I recognize it. It's *Sea Serpent*."

"I thought it might be. How can you be so sure? I couldn't read the name on the back of the boat at this angle."

"I can see the logo. It's on a pennant flying from the spreader."

"A pennant?"

"Yes, sir. He always flies a black pennant with the head of a serpent on the spreader. It's very clear, sir. I know the boat." Jim stepped back so that David Grayson could take another look.

"So it is, Jim. So it is. It's Sonny Chesterson," Grayson muttered softly, almost to himself.

"Yes, sir."

"Is he in trouble out there? I can't tell what's going on. It looks like one sail is down in the water." He stood back so Jim could have a second look.

Jim studied the boat for a moment. "They're not in trouble, sir. It's a botched sail change. They had a spinnaker up, and they are in the middle of putting up a jib. They're practicing for a race, sir. This is a workday. He has new crewmembers on board. He uses weekdays to break them in before the weekend races. He's getting ready for the last race of the season this weekend," said Jim, again stepping back from the telescope.

"You sound like a man who knows Sonny fairly well."

"Yes, sir. I've crewed for him a few times."

"I knew you worked with him pretty closely when we handled the back room for him on the Stillson case. I heard he invited you out for a sail after the trial was over, but I didn't know you had any personal contact beyond that. He's one of the premier commercial litigators in Chicago, and I understand one of the better sailors around here, too. He's a busy man."

"Yes. He works hard, and he plays hard."

"Well, he was very complimentary of your efforts at realigning the evidence and exhibits for him when the case took that surprising twist."

"Thank you. I was taking sailing lessons at the yacht club on small skiffs on the weekends. The class finished, and we were putting the sails away late one Saturday afternoon, when he came ashore. He recognized me immediately. We had a few drinks together at the yacht club bar. That was when he invited me to come out with him as 'ballast.'"

"Ballast?" David queried.

"Yes, sir. He often takes a novice on as a guest when he goes out. He calls these guests 'ballast' because they don't have any assigned sailing responsibilities. They can just enjoy the sail or help out when there's a gust or squall, but it is up to them to decide if they want to participate. They have no obligation to do anything."

"But you went back. You sailed with him?"

"Yes, after the first trip, he invited me to join the crew. I had to go out on a day much like this one with strong gusts of wind."

"That's an honor, Jim. You're cementing a contact with an important legal firm. I'll bet it's not easy sailing with him. If he manages his crew like he manages a trial, he's got to be a tough taskmaster."

"They call him Ahab at the yacht club. He is driven not just to finish, but also to win every race he enters," Jim replied.

"I can believe that. That would be true to his character. He has quite a reputation on and off the water."

"His boat is feared by many of his peers," said Jim. "He won the Mackinaw once and finished in the top ten in two other years. He was ahead in class and fleet last year when he lost his mast in a bad storm."

"It seems he is up and running again," said David Grayson, looking again through the telescope, then standing back for Jim to confirm his observation.

Through the telescope, Jim could see the boat moving through the water, heeled over about 30°. "He's on a beat now. He'll sail a couple of miles then change sails and direction on command. He'll repeat the process until the crew gets it right," said Jim. "He won't stop until the sun goes down or they get too cold."

"I can imagine it gets pretty chilly out there at this time of year."

"Yes. Some days are pretty nippy."

"Well, stay with him, Jim. You'll learn a lot from that man. He's a good contact to maintain."

"I'll try. I've accepted an invitation to crew with him in three weeks for what they call the "Frostbite." It's the last race of the season. It's just a local club race. He could win his class by default."

3

"By default?"

"Yes. At this time of year, most everyone else has hauled their boats for the winter just in case there's a bad blow."

"You don't sound like you have any problem sailing with him."

"Not really. He's tough, but he's fair. There are only two things he does not forgive."

"Oh?"

"If you sign on as crew, and you screw up on a race, that's a sin to him. If you accept an invitation for a certain date, and you don't show up, that, to him, is the second unforgivable sin."

"What happens?"

"In either event, he will never call you back. The secret to a top racing boat is a good list of dependable, qualified people available for crew on a moment's notice. He says if you have to cancel, call a week in advance so he has enough time to find a competent replacement. Personally, I think the only real way to be sure of remaining on the list is to always show up if you are called."

"Well," posed David, as he straightened up and stepped over to his desk. "Have a seat. I didn't call you to discuss sailing."

"No, sir, I didn't think so," said Jim as he slid into one of the leather guest chairs.

At fifty-five, David Grayson had a full head of wavy, white hair. He was tall and thin. He was dressed in his standard dark blue three-piece suit. As usual, he did not wear his suit coat once he was in the office. His suit coat was draped over the back of his chair. Jim admired the solid look of cool detachment and overwhelming authority when Grayson put on his reading glasses and peered over the tope of the rims with his steel blue eyes, looking directly at Jim. "This is a bit awkward, Jim," he started, looking down momentarily at the open file on his desk. "What we want to do is trade you and Sid around for a while now. You need some trial exposure, which we promised you when you first came on board, and Sid could use some field experience. That was our plan, but we did not select the project I have here on my desk this morning. It seems that fate has stepped in and decided things for us."

"The client controls," said Jim, knowingly.

"Yes. Let me ask you a question first. Jim, how is your schedule right now? I mean your personal schedule. Could you handle another trip out of the country?"

"I'm open, sir, as long as we can cover my current office work. There are a couple of things that need some attention here."

4

"Sid can back you up. Please speak up if you have any personal objections. I know we have taken advantage of your single status in the past."

"I have never felt any imposition to your requests," Jim replied honestly and openly. "I've been to some places I would probably never visit on my own," Jim smiled remembering some of the off-track places the firm had sent him on assignment.

"Well, fine. Good." David paused before continuing, collecting his thoughts. "I'm allocating two weeks for this case, although you may be able to wrap this up in eight to ten days, as long as there are no glitches."

"Yes, sir."

"Since you are open to travel, how do you feel about going to Africa? He asked, peering intently over the top of his bifocals, directly into Jim's eyes.

"Africa? I've never been to Africa," said Jim. "It's a big place."

In the past, David Grayson had called special meetings to bring Jim into special projects. This meeting now was not without precedent. The office did work for some of the largest Chicago firms, where the Grayson's provided the investigation and evidence preparation and maintenance work on commercial litigation cases. A small firm with lower overhead was often economically more viable for collecting and organizing detail evidence before a trial than using the manpower in larger well-known firms.

While he and David reviewed his work schedule to free up his office time, Jim was not surprised when asked about the present status of his passport. Jim had been sent out of the country on several prior cases. Business trips had taken him to Canada, Venezuela, Mexico, Aruba, and the Bahamas. The firm tried to use local counsel and local detective agencies as much as possible. Normally, it was far more economical to use the local professionals than sending an attorney who had to be taken away from other cases to cover what the locals could do. In cases when actual physical contact by the firm was essential, Jim, as junior associate, was usually selected as the field man to make the trip.

However, when David Grayson mentioned Africa, Jim's initial reaction was one of surprise. He had no prior contact with Africa or any country there. In fact, Jim had never even traveled across the Atlantic Ocean on assignment. For Jim, Africa was still the "Dark Continent," a place he knew nothing about, other than what he read in the newspapers or saw on television. The one thing he was sure of was that this case had to be very important. The fact that the use of local personnel had been eliminated assured the seriousness of the case. The extreme importance of sending an actual representative from the firm underscored the importance of this assignment.

Gradually, as the meeting progressed, it dawned on him that he should have anticipated this African assignment. Actually, he mused, he had been forewarned. Three days ago, he had received a fax at home that should have tipped him off.

"You know we have an important retainer with the Midwest Museum of Natural History," David offered.

"Yes, I'm aware of it," said Jim. He knew the firm had a retainer with the museum and was cemented by the fact that the Grayson family made large annual contributions to the museum.

"The museum is one of the most significant clients we have. Our relationship goes back many years."

Jim had worked on many of the cases for the museum, but always under the umbrella of one of the Grayson's.

"I'm sure you have heard of Dr. Edward Bronston, the internationally known paleo-anthropologist," he continued.

"Yes, sir," said Jim automatically. Jim not only knew the name, but also personally knew Dr. Bronston's daughter. Nancy worked in Chicago for the museum as Assistant Director of Finance. She was the one who had sent Jim the fax from Africa a few days ago.

"Dr. Bronston has been doing field work in Africa for many years, and is known internationally for his discoveries of fossilized bones of what are thought to be our ancient ancestors," said David Grayson. "I'm assuming you don't have any objections to archeological work on human ancestors on religious grounds?"

"No," said Jim, thinking more about the fax he had received from Nancy. She had sent the fax from Nairobi, Kenya.

"Good."

"I'm familiar with Dr. Bronston," said Jim, being as non-committal about what he really knew about the Bronston family as he could. He was not sure what relevance his relationship with Nancy would have on this assignment. "I've read about his discoveries. He is very well known."

"What you may not have been aware of is that Dr. Bronston's work was financed by the museum. In fact, Jim, they have sponsored Dr. Bronston for over ten years now."

"I didn't know that," Jim responded honestly.

"Senior management at the museum purchased a one million dollar life insurance policy on his life to cover their investment in him."

"I see," said Jim. "I was unaware of the financial relationship."

6

"Well, Dr. Bronston died suddenly, out on the plains of Uhuru at his field camp about 150 miles north of Nairobi, Kenya."

Actually, Jim was already aware of the death of Dr. Bronston from the fax he had received from Nancy a few days earlier. She told him three things. First, she informed him that her father had died suddenly, and she had gone to Africa to arrange the funeral. Second, she instructed Jim to immediately revise his resume to include his amateur archaeological background and fax it to Keith Kendall at the Chicago museum. Third, she asked Jim to come to Africa as soon as he could, a request that, at the time, he dismissed as pure fantasy.

"Our client made an application for payment of the claim as beneficiary under the terms of the life insurance policy right away. Here, you can see for yourself," Grayson stated as he pushed his open file folder across his desk so Jim could look at it.

Jim picked up the folder and examined the contents.

"The only document I see is a copy of the death certificate," said Jim as he looked up at Grayson, puzzled by what he saw. "The death certificate is issued by the Department of Vital Statistics and Health Services in Elizabethtown, Uhuru."

"Good. What else do you see?"

"The date of death is October 18 and it is signed by the Deputy Coroner."

"And the cause of death?"

"The cause of death is given as 'probable suicide,'"

"Yes. Now you see the crux of the issue."

"There is one other thing I noticed," Jim added.

"Oh? What is that?" Grayson responded.

"There appears to be a certification stamp on the face of the document. This is only a fax copy so it is not clear, but I think someone obtained a copy from Vital Statistics and then went to the trouble of having the copy certified. Is the authenticity of the document being challenged?"

"No one is challenging the death certificate. Dr. Bronston died on the date stated at a remote archeological field camp. The event is not being questioned, nor is the validity of the death certificate. Actually, the insurance company made a preliminary denial of coverage on the basis that the death certificate has been issued showing the cause of death listed: suicide. Suicide is an absolute exclusion within the first four years of issuance of the policy."

"I see. That's pretty standard for life insurance policies, isn't it?"

7

"A suicide exclusion is common. The exclusion usually applies from two to five years. Apparently, Dr. Bronston died from a self-inflicted wound from a small caliber handgun. Anyway, all we have here in Chicago is a fax copy of the death certificate."

"The file is pretty thin," Jim noted.

"Yes, we'll need a lot more documentation for you to work with. I should have a copy of the insurance policy and letter of denial here this afternoon. No one, Jim, is questioning the basic document. What concerns our client, the museum, is that they do not believe the cause of death to be suicide."

"They don't believe that he took his own life?"

"No. Their position is understandable because they have lost one of their most valuable and well-known associates and assets. As things stand now, they will not recover this loss under the insurance policy. To make a long story as short as I can here today, senior management at the museum wants and on-site investigation. They have pointed out that there was no inquest and no autopsy conducted locally."

"It doesn't sound like there is much to work with. I didn't know how he died," said Jim, feeling inept, but not knowing what else to say. He didn't want to disclose his relationship with Nancy, or that she had already told him about her father's death. Certainly, he did not want to disclose the request she made for his revised resume to be sent to the museum, or that she had requested him to come to Africa personally.

"The insurance company has issued policies on most of the senior museum staff, and, I might add, on some of us here at the firm as well. So, things are quite cordial at this stage. The policy is less than four years old, so the suicide disclaimer provision in the policy looks enforceable at this time. I'll have a full copy of the policy later today for you to look over. Let me know what you think of it after you look it over," Grayson instructed Jim.

"Thank you. I will review it and get back to you," Jim responded.

"The museum and the insurance company have met, and they agreed that a follow up investigation needs to be completed before a final decision is made under the terms of the policy."

"I see," said Jim. "So the challenge is not of the document but on the conclusion stated on the document."

"Exactly. Dr. Bronston was apparently found slumped over his worktable in a tent at his archaeological excavation. The insurance company and the museum mutually agreed to send an outside investigator from Chicago on a fact-finding mission to Africa. The insurance company was caught short. They have no available field

8

people to send to Africa right now. Apparently, they have no local contacts in Africa that they are willing to trust to investigate this important case. It seems that the local detective agencies in Nairobi and Elizabethtown have no one with any background in archaeology, something everyone here decided was relevant to any investigation conducted on Dr. Bronston's death. All agreed that Dr. Bronston's career work might be relevant to the investigation of his death. They were also concerned that since he died in a remote region of Africa, that someone should actually go there and look around. They were afraid of hiring an armchair investigator who would simply write up a report in some air conditioned office, far away from where it actually happened, and let it go at that."

"Their concern makes sense," Jim nodded in agreement.

"The bottom line is they didn't know anyone qualified to send. In any event, what brings us here today is the fact that the museum put in a specific request for you to be the hands-on investigator for Dr. Bronston's death."

"Me?" Jim nearly jumped out of his chair.

"I am not sure why they asked for you specifically, Jim, but they are our client. I promised them I would talk to you on their behalf. Subsequently, the museum representatives have met again with the insurance company representative assigned to the claim. The museum representative convinced the insurance company's claim adjuster that you are the best qualified person to represent both parties, at least as far as making the fact-finding investigation and writing up the report of your findings."

"I don't know what to say. I'm flattered."

"Needless to say, the firm has acquiesced, subject, of course, to your acceptance of the assignment."

"I don't think I'm qualified. I'm willing to go, but I have never been to Africa before. I don't know the culture or the language. I have no experience in conducting a suicide investigation either. That's a big difference from commercial litigation," observed Jim.

"You know evidence, and you are an excellent observer of details. Your analytical detachment will serve you well. Don't underestimate your abilities here. I am confident that you will uncover the facts surrounding Dr. Bronston's death. The museum will pick up all of your costs and expenses. You will report directly to their people while in Africa."

"Yes, sir."

"Frankly, my initial reaction was against the idea, Jim. I mean I agree with your comments. You've never been to Africa. I'm aware that you don't know the customs or the native languages, and you don't have any local contacts. The investigation will be a new twist for you, but I don't doubt that you will handle it well. There will be qualified contacts for you who do speak English and will help facilitate your investigation. Besides, the museum people insisted that you are the most qualified to handle the investigation so I am sure they will provide you with whatever you need to wrap this assignment up."

"I feel a bit overwhelmed."

"That is understandable. If it's any help, they did tell me that most of East Africa was once a British colony. So, English is the language predominantly used by the professional and business communities there. That means you will have little difficulty with communication while you are there. Once you arrive at the excavation site, there will be personnel who can help you communicate with the workers there."

"That's a big relief," Jim responded.

"Dr. Bronston's daughter works for the museum. The museum representatives tell me she will be in Africa while you are there. We have been cautioned that she may be a bit emotionally distraught right now, but everyone agrees she may be of some assistance to you also. In addition, the museum is arranging for a local contact to act as your guide. Apparently, the man they have in mind is a college professor and personal friend of the Bronston family."

"That makes me even more comfortable with this assignment. It could also help me a lot with the investigation," said Jim.

"By the way, Jim, I didn't know you had a background in archaeology."

"Oh, that," said Jim, laughing lightly, then suddenly remembering how he had revised his resume in response to Nancy's request in her fax. "I joined the state anthropological society, and I am a member of the local archaeology association. I have gone on a few weekend excavations, but just as an amateur. I have no formal training. It's an interesting hobby for me."

"Well, I did not know what to say when the museum people told me. There was nothing in your personal file here at the firm about this hobby. Frankly, they caught me by surprise."

"I'm just an amateur."

"Certainly any relevant background will help. How did the museum know about your interest? I had to find out from them."

"The local archaeology group holds its meetings at the museum, and some of the staff are members," said Jim, not speaking an untruth, just not telling all of the truth to protect Nancy. "I'm sure word gets around in small circles."

"Well, however strong your background is, I think it may have played an important role in your selection for this job. The insurance company had no one with matching credentials, and the museum was quite insistent in our asking you to take the assignment. In any case, this firm is flattered that one of our attorneys was specifically requested to do the investigation. It is certainly a feather in our cap and reinforces our strong, professional tie with the museum as a client. Your background in preparing admissible evidence for trial certainly qualifies you to make factual investigations, even though you have no prior experience in personal injury or violent death cases. This should not be a difficult assignment for you. Everything sounds pretty straightforward. I understand you will have full cooperation form the local authorities. The local contact I mentioned arranged to help take care of all of that."

"I don't know what to say," said Jim. "I just hope I can live up to everyone's expectations."

David Grayson paused before he continued, underlining the change in topic. "The reason I asked about your passport is that they are anxious for you to begin as soon as possible, while the trail is hot, so to speak."

"We have reviewed my work load," said Jim. "I have no personal conflicts with this becoming an immediate assignment." He remembered Nancy's request that he come right away.

"Then it's settled." Grayson summed up the situation, as he stood up to shake hands with Jim, signaling that the meeting was over. "See my secretary, Agatha, on your way out. She will coordinate whatever shots and paperwork you will need to make the trip. The museum will arrange your airline tickets and hotel reservations."

"Thank you, again," said Jim.

"Oh, good luck. You'll be our first emissary to Africa."

"I probably will have some questions once I have some time to think about all this, but right now my mind is blank."

"You'll do fine, Jim," said Grayson, still standing behind his desk. "Your experience and intelligence will serve you well. Frankly, I don't know what you will find. It really doesn't look promising for our client, but if you can throw something in to muddy the waters, we could work out a compromise, if necessary. Unless I miss my guess, the museum will be happy if they get some sort of settlement from the insurance company. The facts do not appear favorable for them right now."

11

"Yes, sir. I'll do what I can."

"Just do a good job, Jim. We can ask for no more. I will call them and let them know you are available and have accepted the assignment. I'll tell them they have our permission to call you directly immediately. Your contact here with the museum is Keith Kendall. Do you know him?"

"I've heard the name," Jim responded.

"He will be your immediate supervisor for this project even though he will remain here in Chicago. He will give you all of your instructions directly."

"Fine, I understand," Jim agreed.

"Oh, don't worry about time sheets. The financial arrangement is set so you can concentrate on your tasks and not take the time keeping track of your hours. It's a per diem assignment."

"That will help a lot," said Jim as he turned to leave.

"Oh, yes, one final thing. My secretary found this business card on the floor in the lunchroom. She showed it to me, but I don't recognize the name. I thought it might belong to you," he said, handing the card to Jim.

Jim looked at the name on the card, puzzled for a moment. "It is mine. I must have dropped it when I was in the lunchroom today. Steve Chandler from BK's Bar and Grill just off Division and Rush Streets gave it to me. I know him personally. He's been soliciting some tax work lately. I think he needs corporate returns for the last two years for his business. I'm supposed to call him back today," Jim explained.

"Any complicated limited partnerships?"

"No. I don't think so. He said it would be pretty straightforward."

"Go ahead, Jim. Do it. You might run it by my brother before you release anything, but you need to develop some clients of your own. Just remember that tax work is not our specialty."

"Thank you. I'll be careful," said Jim, as he turned to leave.

As soon as he was out the door, his initial reaction was that Nancy Bronston had more clout at the museum than he thought. She was his only contact with the museum. In the past, he had met a few people at the museum fund-raising functions, but only by simple introduction through Nancy. They could not possibly have remembered him any more than he remembered them. He was aware that Dr. Bronston had made many of the important discoveries of the human archaeological artifacts found in the museum. He mulled over the fact that Nancy told him in her fax that her father had died suddenly, without any apparent warning. She told him her father had been working at his excavation site north of Elizabethtown, the capital of Uhuru. Those things he knew, before his meeting with David Grayson. What Jim had not known was that Dr. Bronston was reputed to have taken his own life. Nancy had stated nothing to indicate how her father had died in her fax. All she asked was for Jim to come to Africa quickly. If Jim were now to be the investigator in the case of her father's death, he would need to know all the facts. Obviously, a lot of information was missing. Jim was also uneasy about his being selected as the investigator, based on his amateur archaeological experience. Knowledge of archaeology could be relevant, but he felt it should be far more extensive than what he had to offer to review the scene of a death.

Agatha Stein, David Grayson's secretary greeted him when he stopped at her desk on the way out of the office. "Here's a folder with a medical information sheet from Uhuru, Mr. Henderson. Take it to your doctor. I need it back tomorrow afternoon. Your doctor has to certify that you have taken the shots listed."

"Thank you," Jim responded as he accepted the folder from Agatha.

"The rider page is for you. It provides the other requirements needed to obtain a visa for Uhuru and the information you need for a travel visa for Kenya, since you land there first."

"It looks complete," said Jim. "I think the rider explains the requirements clearly for me."

"Mr. Kendall from the museum is making all of the flight arrangements for you. He will contact you directly when the details have been completed. He will be very pleased that you have accepted the assignment. We all are. Mr. Kendall has been pushing for you to accept the assignment from the first they heard of Dr. Bronston's death."

"Great." Jim didn't know what to say.

"Just don't let it go to your head. He told us the insurance company approved you also, but only on condition that they would not be bound by your findings. He said the insurance company agreed only to review your report and take it under advisement. They reserved the right to order their own separate investigation if they are not satisfied with the results in your report."

"Well, I will do my best," Jim promised.

"Mr. Kendall also said the parties agreed the relationship between the museum and the insurance company is not adversarial, and you are the best qualified, even thought you work for the law firm that represents the museum."

So much for conflict of interest, Jim thought to himself.

Jim was sure Nancy Bronston was the one who had recommended him to serve as investigator for her father's death. He was also convinced that her influence was the exclusive reason for his selection.

Two days later, on the way to the airport, he learned that his assumptions were wrong. It was true that Nancy was his primary contact at the museum. She sent her fax to prepare him for his meeting with Grayson. While he did revise and send his resume as she instructed, he had otherwise forgotten about her fax. Later, the same day as his meeting with David Grayson, she sent a second fax, which included details of what to pack. She also provided him with the name, Dr. Arturo Umbawi as his African contact, once he arrived in Elizabethtown. Jim later received a copy of a resume for Dr. Umbawi, as well as one for Dr. Rumundo Tubojola, the Minister of the Interior of Uhuru. Both were faxed to him from Keith Kendall at the museum the following day. Nancy's fax included detailed instructions for his trip to Africa. She told him not to use hard suitcases, to wear one light suit and pack everything else in duffle bags. She was very precise in what she itemized for him to bring. She instructed him to include only the necessary clothes listed, to travel light, and not to bring excess baggage.

Jim had attended college at Great Lakes University in downtown Chicago on a scholarship. He met Nancy Bronston in a class on American literature in their senior year. They started spending time together that semester, but, on graduation, Nancy went on to graduate school in Michigan, under what she called the non-technical MBA program. Meanwhile, Jim enrolled in law school at Great Lakes. When Nancy graduated two years later with her MBA, she returned to Chicago with a job at the museum where the Bronston name assured her of a secure career. She told him the museum had urged her to obtain a graduate degree and had paid part of her tuition. When Nancy had returned from Michigan, Jim still had two semesters to go at law school. A few months after her return to Chicago after graduation, she had called him to invite him to attend one of the monthly meetings of the amateur archaeological association that was held in the museum. He accepted her invitation even though he knew nothing about archaeology. That meeting led to a renewal of their relationship, and introduced him to the world of archaeology. At the time, Jim had no other hobbies or outside interests, so the association filled a void in his life. After attending meetings for a year, the association invited him to join, which he did with Nancy's encouragement and approval.

For Jim, the weekend excavations, which took place in the suburbs northwest of Chicago, were fascinating. He looked forward to reading the monthly state association magazines as well. So, Jim had maintained his membership in the society. At the same time, he also escorted Nancy to museum fund-raising functions. Suddenly, out of the blue, she sent him that fax from Africa with instructions for him to update his resume, specifically adding on his archaeological memberships and a detailed summary of his field excavation digging experience.

Prior to receiving the fax, he had not known she had left the Chicago area. He learned the real reason for his selection as investigator on his trip to the airport for his flight to Africa from Keith Kendall. Two days before he was to leave, Keith called him and offered to pick him up and drive him to O'Hare airport for the trip. Jim instinctively detected some urgency in Keith's voice so he accepted the offer.

Keith Kendall was a dapper, well-dressed man, a few inches over five feet in height. He drove a big, black Lincoln and lived in Evanston, a nice suburb immediately north of Chicago. They had traveled in silence until they were about half way to the airport. "Look, Jim," Dr. Kendall started abruptly. "We know they found Dr. Bronston, gun in hand, slumped over his worktable. At least that's what the police report tells us. We are told he died instantly from the gunshot wound. We're having trouble disputing the facts, but there was no note, no warning, and, more importantly, no foundation for such extreme action. We believe that suicide was more than a bit out of character for Dr. Bronston. I might add, Nancy agrees. She must be in terrible shape over there in Africa all by herself."

"I agree," Jim responded.

"Part of your responsibility, while you are there, will be to look out for her when you get there."

"Yes, sir. My pleasure." Jim smiled gently, thinking about Nancy.

"Look. We're not expecting a miracle, Jim, but no one is going be at ease about this unless we can understand why he would do such a thing. There has to be a clue there somewhere."

"I'll do what I can," said Jim. "What if he didn't do it?"

"Then find out what happened. Nancy needs you right now. She has been like a voice in the dark asking for you. At least today, I could tell her you are on the way. She needs answers, Jim. We all need answers."

"Well, I'm on my way."

"Finding a reason for what he did is your primary assignment, of course, but whether he intentionally took his own life due to some despondency or whether the gun went off accidentally, is only part of the equation. Don't get me wrong, it's important to Nancy, and it's important to us. We know the coverage under the insurance policy is certainly significant. It's a million dollar question. But there is more to our need for you to go to Africa," he said, pausing for a moment to allow what he was saying to register with Jim.

Jim waited, expectantly. There was nothing for him to say at the moment.

"Since you are familiar with Dr. Bronston's work, have you heard of the skull referred to as Uhuru Man?" Dr. Kendall continued.

"Yes, it has been around for some time. I think Dr. Bronston discovered it about 15 years ago. The news was published in all the major publications, even internationally back then. I remember reading about it, vaguely. I was not really up on African archaeology at that time."

"Most people aren't. It was truly a miracle find," Keith continued. "The skull was found on the surface of the ground in what was then the Uhuru Territories, but it had been crushed into hundreds of pieces by roaming cattle. It took months to find all the fragments and to reassemble them into the famous skull. It's the only skull of that particular species of hominid. No other skulls or even pieces of the same species have ever been found since. It is truly, one of a kind."

"I didn't know any of the details since it was discovered before I developed an interest in archaeology," Jim admitted.

"Uhuru was a lawless and dangerous place back then, run by nomads, cattle herders, and bandits. In those days, an archaeologist claimed his trophies, packed them up and raced back to the security of his own native country to report his finds. Our deal with Dr. Bronston back then was that he was paid for his costs of operation, a small salary and a finder's fee for major discoveries. However, all the fossils he collected belonged to the museum. We own Uhuru Man to this day. For some time, the skull was displayed in a special case in the museum in Nairobi. We loaned it to the museum in Elizabethtown when they first opened several years ago. That's where it is today. You may see it in the museum when you are there. The file is on my desk. My point is, when I was cataloging all our important assets just last week, I checked each one to be sure we had them insured. What I found was that Uhuru Man is not insured."

"What! Why not?" Jim was astounded. "If it is so important, I think you should have it covered. That only makes good business sense."

"The problem is that it has no value. There is no way we can establish a value for Uhuru Man."

"No value?" asked Jim.

"It's not what you think. We simply cannot obtain insurance coverage because there is no way to assess its actual value. Ancient fossilized hominid skulls are so rare, they are not capable of being given ascertainable values."

"I didn't know that. Insurance is not my specialty."

"This ancient man business is no fluke, Jim. I cannot even estimate how much we receive in donations and entrance fees just to see the plaster cast of the skull of Uhuru Man here in Chicago. I mention this one skull solely as an example of one rare exhibit. You have to understand, every time we bring in a new archaeological discovery of the past, our donations and entrance fee receipts go up."

"I never thought of hominid fossils as so valuable," said Jim.

"They are, Jim. What I was trying to lead up to is that we have heard rumors that Dr. Bronston was on the verge of another significant find at the time of his untimely death. If that is true, and his remote excavation site contains an important discovery, then it is even more important to have the Bronston name tied to it. The Bronston name is synonymous with that of our museum as sponsor. Today, original discoveries belong to the country where they are found, but first rights to make casts and to publish reports belong to the sponsor or the museum. This makes them quite valuable, almost to the same extent as if we had the original fossils. Frankly, our bottom line depends on new discoveries and new exhibits to draw in more people and continue growth of receipts."

"So, in some ways, your museum operates like any other business," Jim responded.

"In some ways, yes, that is true, Jim."

"I really don't know much about how a museum runs. I never thought about it."

"Most people don't. We will explain that to you, but it is not that relevant. With your background, you should grasp the fundamentals quickly. Nancy can help you with any questions while you are in Africa."

"Right now, I don't know what questions to ask," said Jim.

"The questions will come to you as you proceed," he paused for a moment and then changed the subject. "We need a special favor from you, Jim."

"The firm will do anything it can to help," Jim gave his professional endorsement.

"The firm be damned, Jim. What we need is a personal favor from you. That's why we wanted you."

"What can I do?"

"Look. You know Nancy personally. We know that. She made it very clear to us that she trusts your advice. The Director of Antiquities of Uhuru, with our encouragement, has asked her to step in and manage the excavation, to basically replace her father there."

"She shouldn't have a problem with that," said Jim.

"That's just it, Jim. She has been noncommittal, even somewhat evasive, when we ask her. She is aware of her father's reputation and experience, but she doesn't think she can step into his shoes in the field. She has told us she does not feel qualified for the job."

"Oh," Jim was surprised.

"The Minister of the Interior of Uhuru has asked for our help to convince her to step in as site manager at Bokuru. He is quite satisfied with her qualifications."

"I think she could do it, too," said Jim.

"Good. We were sure you would agree with us. Because you know her so well, it's going to be your job to persuade her to stay on as site manager. Look, the museum will pay her salary and expenses. The Antiquities Department in Uhuru can do the detail work separating and cleaning any fossils, so the science angle is covered. They can also deal with any bone reconstruction and assembly work. They have a well-trained and qualified staff for performing those activities and functions. Nancy would not have to do exactly what her father was doing. We know anatomy is not one of her strengths so she would not have to do any reconstruction, either. The university would supplement her weaknesses in archaeology with local help, right in Elizabethtown. Basically, we need her in charge of the site. We think she can hold onto the existing field staff, too, since she knows them personally. Those workers have been with her father for years. She knows them from her visits to the site over the years."

"Continuity of staff is important. I understand that."

"Right, and her daily work would not be too strenuous. She has a good business background from her graduate studies. The staff would handle the physical labor."

"It sounds like she would be a figure head," observed Jim.

"Perhaps, in a way, that is not too far from the truth." Keith appeared uncomfortable with Jim's comment. Jim had hit the nail on the head. Keith continued, "But we do need a qualified manager on site. We really don't want a stranger in there, or some one new. We can't allow one of Dr. Bronston's archaeological discoveries to be snatched away by someone else, especially when we have paid for all of the work to excavate it up to now."

"I understand."

"I think you understand your role. She can do whatever detail work she is comfortable with. Where we need your help is to convince her to step in before the government gives up on her and assigns the site to someone else. Right now, they are on our side. They are working with us, but we can't expect them to wait for her decision forever. For some reason, she is stalling."

"I see. You know she is headstrong and intelligent. She will do what she thinks is right, for herself and the excavation."

"Yes, of course. That's precisely where you come in. She will listen to you. Oh, one more thing. Be careful. Don't overdo it. We don't want her to adopt her father's profession permanently. We want her to finish the site, but we don't want her to decide to become a field archaeologist, wandering all over the African hinterlands in search of needles in a haystack. That kind of work takes special skills. Besides, field people have to live and work in some pretty rugged, and I might add, dangerous environments. There are plenty of field archaeologists qualified for that type of work."

"I'll talk to her," said Jim.

"Good. We understand your role is going to be sensitive. You will have to walk a thin line. Find some way to motivate her to finish this site, but that's it. Her future is here in Chicago, not out on the African savannah. She is very good at what she does here in Chicago. We want her back in the museum in Chicago."

"I'm sure she appreciates your confidence in her."

"None of us can possibly understand her loss, Jim. Her father is gone. He was all the family she had. He cannot be replaced, but it would be wrong for her to decide to select a career in the field. We are all afraid that, alone in a foreign country, under emotional stress, she could make a bad decision in the memory of her father and his work. She might want to be close to where he worked and substitute for him. You must dissuade her from that."

"I understand my role. I will do what I can," said Jim.

"That's what we wanted to hear. We have complete faith in you. I have only two additional comments before I drop you off," said Keith. "First, what we have discussed here today should not be repeated, ever. Keep it confidential."

"No problem," Jim promised easily.

"Good. Then, finally, if you find Dr. Bronston's excavation site is a dud, and there is nothing there of value, cut our losses and get out quickly. If there is nothing there, close up shop, Jim. Pack Nancy up and bring her home. This site has been different for this part of Africa because nothing was found on the surface. Instead, they saw only geological evidence of an ancient cave system exposed by erosion. Dr. Bronston talked us into funding an excavation of this site on his hunch that he would find something significant there. We were thinking of a small trench, but he elected to excavate the whole cave. It has been a very risky undertaking from our standpoint. His crew spent months excavating down from the top of the cave, merely on his professional best guess they would find hominid bones. As a result, we have spent large sums of money on what could turn out to be just a fishing expedition."

"I see," said Jim.

"This whole thing could be nothing more than a wild goose chase."

"So, you don't know exactly what he found, if anything?" Jim was surprised by Keith's admission about Dr. Bronston's excavation.

"It is more than a little embarrassing, Jim, but we have absolutely no idea what, if anything, was found at the site. The excavation has been going on for a long time and has been expensive for the museum. When you are out there, if you find that Dr. Bronston made a significant discovery, we want Nancy to stay with it. But, if all you find is an ancient hyena lair or something like that, leave it to others to complete. Get her out of there. Do I make myself clear?"

"Absolutely," said Jim. "I understand completely."

"Great. Just remember what I said about the Territories. Uhuru is a separate nation now, but it is still a dangerous place. Please be careful."

"I promise, I will."

"Oh, you'll see in your information folder that you will be staying in The Grand Hotel in Elizabethtown. It is close to all the people you will need to interview in town. All your costs there are already covered. Your signature will be the authorization for the hotel to invoice us directly. You will not be billed for your stay there. For your cash needs, use the Uhuru National Bank. You will find the bank office diagonally across the street from the hotel. There's an account there already set up in your name so you can draw on it as needed."

"Thank you. You seem to have thought of everything," Jim was impressed.

"We had no idea how to estimate what your cash needs will be. The only thing we do know, for sure, is that when you go out to the field camp, it will be difficult to spend any money. There is nothing there and all the supplies are laid in."

"I've gone on other trips out of the country, and there were always unanticipated expenses to pay," said Jim. "Some travel expenses are hard to anticipate ahead of time."

"Yes, but this part of your trip will be different from anything you've ever done before. As I understand it, there is nothing around the camp for over a hundred miles in any direction."

"Oh, that is remote," Jim responded.

"Yes, it is. Just remember, we are putting all our faith in you, Jim."

"I'll do my best. I understand what you are asking for me to do. It is not just the investigation of Dr. Bronston's death."

"Look, Jim. You may think we don't know you at the museum, but we do know who you are."

"I've been pretty much behind the scenes," said Jim.

"Do you remember the Big Bob case?"

"Yes," said Jim. "It was a big dinosaur, a brontosaurus, as I remember. I think it was discovered in Wyoming."

"Yes, it was unique. I won't bother you with the technical name, but it was the largest specimen of that particular species ever found. We were interested in buying it, but there were three different parties claiming ownership. You were the one who said we should deal only with the owner of the land and let the finders and others work out their problems among themselves."

"I remember," said Jim. "I didn't know you were aware I was the one doing the work on that case."

"Your employer gave you credit for what you did. Well, you defined the issue very clearly, and insisted that a survey be made of the property to determine ownership of the land."

"Yes, the original government surveyors never properly staked in all the required government corners, so we still did not know who the land owner actually was," said Jim.

"No, but you looked up the law on establishing lost corners, so a survey could be completed," added Keith. "In the end, we found who owned the land, and a settlement was reached quickly. Good legal representation made it possible. When we went to bat to bring you in for this trip, we knew who we were asking for. Ancient man is big time. It has far more significance than the dinosaurs that get the kids all excited. This gets the big kids all excited. We need to be sure we have the right representation at all times."

"I appreciate your confidence in me."

The rest of the trip to the airport was completed in silence, but Jim knew then that there was much more than Nancy's need to find out why

21

her father died in this assignment to Africa. Nancy and the museum each had their separate reasons for selecting Jim to go to Africa.

Again, the overhead light flashed. This time, a soft gong sound accompanied the flashing overhead light. Jim mused, his trip had been a long one. The first leg had been from Chicago to Lagos, Nigeria, and the second and present one from Lagos to Nairobi. He was patient. He knew why he was here. It was important when on assignments away from the office to avoid the many distractions involved in travel. He knew he had to maintain a solid grasp of his specific, assigned objectives. He had learned that it was all too easy to lose track of your goals when in a foreign environment.

For a moment, he recalled those years when he sat on the couch beside his mother in the little bungalow that had been their home in Carbonwood, Illinois. He was a junior in high school. His father lay dying of cancer in the bedroom. His mother held Jim's hand and spoke to him in a way that she had never done before.

"Let me tell you what I don't want you to do, Jim. You keep telling me you want to go to law school. That's a pretty high objective for a boy still in high school. I know you are not trying to impress me. I have seen your grades and your test scores. You have a gift, son. If that is your goal, hold onto it no matter what happens and no matter what we do now."

"Yes, Ma."

"I don't know where your aptitude comes from. You did not inherit it from either your father's side of the family or mine. Both our sides of the family are filled with stories of early pregnancies and lost dreams. No one on either side ever graduated from college before, never mind anyone going on to graduate school. Don't lose your focus."

"I promise I won't, Mom."

"It's going to be difficult, Jim. The doctors say your father will be gone soon. He only has a few weeks, at best. I am ready to accept it, now. There is no other alternative. We have exhausted all of our savings on medical bills and painkillers. We even used the proceeds of a second equity mortgage on this house. You have to understand, we will lose the house, Jim. There is nothing left."

"No, we can save it, ma. It's our home. I can help." Jim remembered blurting out, "I can get a better job. We can save the house, I know we can."

"That's exactly what I don't want you to say or do. Let the house go, Jim. You have an offer to stay at the studio apartment over the hardware store from Mr. And Mrs. Davis. You can keep working for them until you go to college. Just stay with the part time job. Above all else, keep your grades up in school. If you do, you will get a scholarship for college. I am sure of it."

"What will happen to you, ma?"

"I'll move in with Mrs. Strantham, the widow down the street. She wants me to care for her full time in exchange for living space. I can work at the hospital part time, too. I will get by, Jim. There is little I need in this world now. My dream is to see you graduate from law school. Be the first one in our family to do something meaningful. Let me live my life through you, Jim. Your dream will be my dream. If you drop out of school and marry that Benson girl you are seeing now, you would have to give up your dream and get a full time job to support her. We would both lose. I would be disappointed, Jim. Do you understand?"

"Yes," he replied meekly looking down at the floor.

"Wealthy people don't have to make these kinds of tough decisions, but you do. An early marriage and getting an education are not compatible for you. Do you understand?"

"Yes," he said nodding his head, at a loss for words.

"The next few years will be difficult for you."

"I won't give up, mom. I promise you."

"I don't think you will either. Mr. Davis has a brother who owns an apartment building in Chicago. It's right on the main bus routes. They have told me they have an apartment there for you. If you can get accepted up at the university, you will have an inexpensive place to live there, but you must keep your grades up, Jim. For us, there is no alternative."

"I understand," Jim said feeling uncomfortable.

"We could only stay together at the expense of your goal. Let the dream control, Jim. Make me proud," she pleaded with her son.

"I will. You know I will," he responded.

"He still remembered the strength of his conviction, all these many years later. That had been her pep talk. It had scared him, and matured him at the same time. It had also cemented his resolve to hold on to his goal.

When the day came, years later, and he graduated from law school and was sworn in before the court, he drove the seventy-five miles to Carbonwood to share his moment of triumph with her. He knew she had Alzheimer's. He knew that it would only get worse. She had been admitted to the Carbonwood Nursing and Convalescent Home and had been moved to the assisted living wing, but it had been almost four

23

months since his last visit. Final tests and the bar exam had kept him away, involuntarily. She was there at this very moment, while he was high over the African continent. On that triumphant day, he had brought a bottle of sparkling cider for their celebration of his achievement. He did not know when he drove into the parking lot of the nursing home in the cold and snow that he would never open that bottle or share it with his mother.

The four months of studying for the bar exam had been a lifetime for him. She had changed for the worse. The disease had ravaged her brain. When he sat down on the couch beside her wheel chair and looked into her eyes, he knew. His heart sank. She no longer recognized him. She would never know they had accomplished their dream. She had sacrificed her life for their goal and now the disease had stolen not just her past, but also her identity and the awareness necessary to celebrate their victory. She had enjoyed his visit. She still liked to be with people. She simply no longer knew one person from the other. His greatest moment of exhilaration was his greatest moment of despair. He was torn by the terrible injustice of it.

He stood out in the cold winter evening in the parking lot, the paper bag with the bottle of sparkling cider still unopened, trying to adjust for the long drive back to Chicago. He would never forget that moment, he thought, as he looked around the cabin of the plane. She would never have believed he would be here, an attorney, high over the African continent on a special assignment for a client. He smiled briefly at the bittersweet memory of that uncelebrated victory.

The soft gong that accompanied the flashing seat belt sign brought him back to the present. Jim's briefcase was open on the fold out table in front of him. He reached in and retrieved an 8 X 10 glossy photograph. The picture was that of a dark faced African native man in his mid-sixties. The man had large, wide, wire-rimmed glasses and a receding, white hairline that gave him a particularly distinguished, owlish look, and every bit the appearance of a teacher, which, in fact, Jim knew he was. The man's name was handwritten on the back of the photo, Dr. Arturo Umbawi. Jim studied the picture of the man who was scheduled to meet him on his arrival at the airport. He had inadvertently left the doctor's resume on his kitchen counter in his apartment in Chicago, but he remembered some of his background. Dr. Umbawi had been educated at the university in Nairobi and stayed on as a professor, teaching archaeology, anatomy, and philosophy. Jim remembered reading that the doctor lived in Nairobi with his wife of many years.

The plan was simple. They had exchanged photographs. They would each be wearing beige suits with white shirts and ties. Each would also wear a name badge on their lapel. Jim was to step through the custom's door into the main lobby of the terminal, then move a few feet to his right and wait. With badges and cross photos, they were sure to find each other. Jim had the phone number for the hotel where he was registered to stay in Elizabethtown, an emergency number for Nancy Bronston at her friend's house in Nairobi, and numbers for Dr. Umbawi's office and home, just in case they missed each other at the airport.

Dr. Umbawi had promised to pick Jim up at the airport and drop him off at The Grand Hotel in Elizabethtown that evening. Jim put the photo back into his briefcase, retrieved his name badge, and then closed the case and slid it under the seat in front of him. He folded the table back into the seatback and tightened his seatbelt as instructed for landing. He would attach the name badge to his suit coat when he retrieved his coat from the overhead bin as soon as they landed.

The sign overhead continued to flash: "Fasten Seatbelts." This time it stayed on. The voice came back on the intercom: "We are in our final descent for Nairobi. Please stay in your seats until we have stopped moving and the airplane doors are open. We should be on the ground in approximately ten minutes."

Prepared or not, his adventure in Africa was about to begin.

CHAPTER TWO: *TRIP TO UHURU*

Forty-five minutes later, Jim stepped through the doors of the customs section of Uhuru airport. The main terminal was bustling with a sea of mostly dark faces. He took a moment to get his bearings, then stepped to his right, and walked out of the doorway. He scanned the crowd that was gathered around the custom's exit. Dr. Umbawi was nowhere to be seen. Jim recalled again that the doctor was a short man, only five feet five inches tall. Still, Jim did not see him in the crowd. There was no one in a beige suit, white shirt and white tie. The plan had gone awry. He set his bags and briefcase down on the concrete floor, straightened his name badge, and looked around again hopefully.

This time he saw a cardboard sign held high above the crowd. His last name was crudely printed on it in bold letters in black ink. Someone was waiving the sign as they worked their way forward in his direction. At the same time, he heard a young, male voice shouting his name into the crowd. Within moments, the young man, about eighteen years old, broke through the crowd and approached him.

"You don't know me, but I'm here to pick you up and take you to Dr. Umbawi. My name is David Johannson," said the youth in perfect English, extending his right hand. "I'm lucky to have found you."

David's skin was white, almost pale and was of obvious Nordic descent with blue eyes and long, unkempt blond hair. He sported an unkempt beard that was as unruly as his hair. Jim noticed immediately that his handshake was limp and clammy. David was about the same height as Jim, who stood five feet ten inches tall. It was David's attire, more than anything else that set him apart from the others who had gathered at the custom's door in the airport. He was wearing a monk's robe of a deep, rich, burgundy colored cotton fabric. The attached hood was tossed back off his head and hung down below his shoulders. The robe was tied with a sash around his waist, leaving it open at the top and bottom, revealing jeans, tee shirt, and tennis shoes underneath.

"I'm Jim Henderson, as you have figured out."

"Sorry for the confusion, Mr. Henderson. Dr. Umbawi was delayed. He had mechanical trouble with his car in Elizabethtown. The hotel bus isn't scheduled to come out here until ten o'clock this evening, so he sent me to pick you up."

"I'm glad you are here," said Jim, relieved to see someone here to greet him.

"Dr. Umbawi will meet you at your hotel in Elizabethtown. That's where I'm supposed to drop you off."

"Isn't that a long way from here?" Jim asked. "You've got to be going a long way out of your way."

"Not at all. Our temple shares space here in Nairobi with a food for peace group out of Paris. I was at the storefront earlier today. Just before I left for the temple, Dr. Umbawi called. Apparently, he knows a couple of the followers out at our temple. I came here to Nairobi early this morning to pick up supplies. We buy our rice from the food for peace group. They have the best prices in this part of Africa. I was just loading the bus when the call came in. Our temple is located north of Elizabethtown, about fifty kilometers outside, along the Bokuru River. I have to drive right through downtown Elizabethtown to get back to the temple, so your hotel is right on the way for me. No trouble at all."

"I see. That is convenient for me," said Jim.

"We were lucky that the call came when it did. Coming here to the airport was convenient for me because it kept me out of the downtown traffic. I painted this sign in a hurry before I left. I hope I spelled it correctly. I just got here when you came through customs."

"Your timing was perfect," said Jim. "I had just set my bags down."

"Dr. Umbawi gave me a brief description of you and told me where you would be standing. He also told me what you'd be wearing. He was right on the money," said David, smiling, and proud of his accomplishment.

"I was only here for a couple of minutes before I saw your sign," said Jim.

"I was worried that I might be late. I knew if I was delayed, you'd move, and I would probably never find you. Anyway, I'm here," he said, reaching down and grabbing one of Jim's duffle bags.

Jim quickly grabbed the other one, along with his briefcase.

"Follow me. We need to take advantage of all the daylight that's left." He turned to head for the exit doors to the terminal. "Dr. Umbawi wants to meet you for dinner. We don't want to keep him waiting."

"I'm right behind you," said Jim.

"The bus is right outside. I'm in the first lot right across the street."

"Great," said Jim.

"I understand you came all the way from Chicago. Let me warn you about the humidity. Today will be hot and sticky in Nairobi because we had a shower this morning. The heat and humidity outside will shock you when you leave this air conditioned terminal."

"I'm ready," said Jim, trying to keep up with David, who quickly dodged through the crowd to the exit door.

David was right. The outside air was oppressive. For a brief moment, Jim found it hard to breathe, but he kept up with David who was now walking briskly towards the nearest parking lot.

"It's not far. I parked in the third row," David explained, pointing ahead.

Jim saw the small bus before they reached it. The bus stood out in a sea of compact cars. The converted school bus had been painted, or, Jim thought, more descriptively, whitewashed to cover most of the original bright yellow school-bus paint. The chassis was mounted on a small truck frame and was originally designed to seat less than twenty passengers. The white paint was so crudely applied that it looked like it had been brushed on. The shape of the lights and exterior mirrors revealed the original use of the bus, in spite of the change in color. The size of the bus was similar to the one Jim remembered riding when he was in grade school in Illinois. As they neared the bus, Jim could see an enormous eye painted with black paint on the side just below the windows. The eye stood out in stark contrast to the white paint. David followed Jim's gaze.

"The all-seeing eye of the Creator," explained David, as he put Jim's duffle bag down and struggled with the catch on the door.

"It certainly stands out," said Jim, staring at the eye.

"There's one on the other side too. They're supposed to match, but they are hand painted," said David.

"So I see," said Jim.

"I know you were expecting an East African. I'll bet you didn't think you would meet someone from Minnesota," said David.

"I was expecting Dr. Umbawi. You are right though, I was surprised to be met by an American."

"There is an old African saying that, when in Africa, always have a back up plan," warned David.

"It seems to be very appropriate," commented Jim.

"There are three or four other temple groups with retreats in Uhuru. They are all based in Europe or the States. The Government of Uhuru is quite liberal when it comes to these groups. They leave us alone. I'm staying with the Temple of Tessan. The home office is actually in San Francisco, but they only have one temple in Uhuru," David informed Jim.

"Tell me about it," Jim responded as they stepped up into the bus. David had finally released the door latch to the bus. David slid into the

28

driver's seat and Jim took the passenger seat on the opposite side of the aisle.

"I am, what the temple calls, a neophyte. I don't know how to explain it. Look, did you ever go to camp when you were a kid, Mr. Henderson?"

"Sure," said Jim, putting both duffle bags on the seat behind him and setting his briefcase down on the floor in front of him.

"My grandparents saw an advertisement in a magazine that was a solicitation for teenagers in trouble. The temple runs that ad all over the states. Their pitch is to the parents of troubled teens. The temple offers a place out on the remote plains of Uhuru to cleanse the mind of the troubled youth. They promise a retreat away from the outside influences of society, where the kids have time to readjust, mature, see the light, or find the creator. They say the desert is supposed to be a spiritual purifier. Anyway, my grandparents signed me up for an eighteen month program."

"I see," said Jim.

"As I said, it's like going to camp. Your folks sign you up for a set period of time and pay the fees. You simply show up and follow instructions. You start out at the bottom level, that's what they call the neophyte. The temple assigns you a counselor or big brother to keep an eye on you, and you do all the basic upkeep functions to keep the place going. The neophyte just follows the curriculum, and goes home when their time is up," David explained.

"Just like camp," Jim commented.

"You've got it. Look, take off your suit coat. It's out of place out here. Besides, there's no air conditioning in this bus, or should I say, it's conditioned by air. We'll be fine while we're in motion, but you will be uncomfortable until we get out on the open road."

Jim took David's advice and removed his suit coat. He draped it over the seat behind him. Soon they were underway. David was silent until they were out of the airport and on the main road.

"I guess I was a hothead back home, Mr. Henderson. I saw a lot of things I did not like about the world. I was brought up in a fundamentalist environment. My grandparents think everything about the world is what the Creator planned. I don't agree, I think we can alter things. Sometimes, we even have to take drastic action. We can do something about the way things are," said David.

"What do you specifically find wrong with the status quo?" Jim asked.

"I was concerned about my grandparents," said David.

"How is that?" Jim asked.

"My grandparents have always lived on the farm. My grandfather inherited the place from his father. They are like millions of others in the States."

"How so?" asked Jim, encouraging David to continue.

"They are broke. The small farmers can't make it anymore. Did you ever hear of NAFTA?" David asked. "I think it stands for North American Fair Trade Agreement or something like that," he said, glancing momentarily over at Jim as he drove through the outskirts of town.

"Yes," said Jim. "I don't know much about it, but I'm aware of the treaty."

"The American small farmer was already in trouble before NAFTA. You know, America went from ninety-four percent of our population living on the farm around 1800 to five percent by the 1960's. Low income, bad weather, high costs were always risks, but big business and taxes destroyed the small farms. Some farmers had a chance if they were disciplined, but they also had to be lucky. Then along came NAFTA. It was really designed by the eastern establishment. They were scared that fifteen million people living in Mexico City were about to uproot and seek greener pastures across the border in America. Can you imagine seeing fifteen million people, one sunny morning, on the Mexican border? Well, anyway, they came up with NAFTA to create jobs in Mexico to stabilize the population. It did work, but the successes were mostly agricultural. The result is that the US is flooded with cheap products imported from Mexico," said David.

"I thought there were a number of countries involved," said Jim.

"Yes, but Mexico was what it was all about. Anyway, that was the final blow. Every month, hundreds of small American farms go out of business, while the fat cats with all the money buy up the land and turn it into subdivisions. It's the end, Mr. Henderson. The economics of big scale are the only competition against cheap Mexican farm goods. The small farm is headed for extinction," said David.

"And you blame it on NAFTA?"

"Small farms have been dying for a long time. NAFTA just finished them off. Anyway, I could see what was happening. I decided to do something about the plight of the small farmer."

"What did you do?" asked Jim.

"I joined the militia," said David proudly, glancing over to Jim.

"You mean the National Guard?" asked Jim.

"No, the militia. They are the radicals against the government, not part of it. They want to stop interference by the government in their lifetime. They want to put an end to taxes, gun control, foreigners, everything. I thought the militia would be able to help me. I thought they were pro-active, but I was disappointed."

"You were disappointed with extremists?" asked Jim.

"Yes. All they do is play war games on weekends. They're just a group of good old boys who don't know what to do with their spare time. They are losing their farms and their jobs. All they can do is complain about international conspiracies," explained David.

"All I know about the militia is what I read and see on television. From what I can tell, they are basically anarchists," said Jim.

"You're right, but all they do is talk among themselves. Anyway, I became what you call outspoken. After a while, I got on a local radio talk show. I said it might take the militia to blow up a government agricultural building to draw attention to the story of the small farmer."

"That was one way to do it," Jim stated.

"I guess I was out of line for them. Within days, federal agents showed up at the farm asking my grandparents questions about me. They also showed up at the militia, which didn't go over very well with them either."

"I'll bet," said Jim.

"My grandparents decided to send me here. The militia didn't want the kind of attention I was bringing to the group. They thought I was too radical."

"What happened?" asked Jim.

"They threw me out. They told the Feds they wanted nothing to do with me. Now, here I am in this remote wasteland, halfway around the world in East Africa, because I was in the militia, when in fact, I was thrown out. Have you ever been out beyond Elizabethtown?" David asked abruptly.

"No. This is my first trip to Africa. I have never been here before today," responded Jim.

"Let me give you a hint, Mr. Henderson. Don't go out there unless you absolutely have to. It's all scrub desert, except for the Bokuru River, which isn't much more than a small stream at this time of year."

"I assume you'll go back home when your time at camp is up," Jim observed.

"The Temple priests watch you," David continued, ignoring Jim's comment.

"What denomination are they?" asked Jim.

"None. The priests think they are the modern version of the Essenes."

31

"The Essenes? I've never heard of them. Who are they?" asked Jim.

"The Essenes are the Sons of Light. They are the ancient group that lived in the dessert of Israel and wrote the Dead Sea Scrolls," David informed Jim.

Jim said nothing. He had read about the Sons of Light, and he didn't like their views. He had learned to avoid discussing certain issues and to drop the subjects when they came up in conversations. Religion was one of those topics.

"As I was saying, the priests pick off one or two neophytes each year and invite them to become what they call followers. The followers are the next higher level above the neophytes at the temple."

"What are the qualifications for becoming a follower?" asked Jim.

"They have to show the proper level of consciousness. The priests at the temple are not bad. The temple is not a cult or anything like that, at least not at the neophyte level. If they like you and think you have promise, they promote you. If you are asked to stay, they pick up your costs. After two or three years, if you reach the next level of mental awareness, you may become a priest," said David.

"Is that your goal?" asked Jim.

"Neophytes like myself seldom even see the priests. In my case, I have no future here. I will go back home when my time at camp is up. My grandparents are fundamentalists, Mr. Henderson. I had a hard time when I first got here. The temple says the Bible is not a sacred book."

"Really? Not a sacred book?" asked Jim, shocked.

"They say it's man's view of the Creator, and it is so full of the biases of man that the vision of the Creator is clouded by misconception. They say the Creator rules other worlds, too. In their view, it is man's arrogance that says humans were made in the image of the Creator."

"And, that is wrong?" asked Jim.

"The temple believes you can only find the Creator by listening for his message inside yourself."

"They seem to have a different view of things than most conventional religions," said Jim.

"I'm not a member, but I think we each have a purpose on this earth, and we are placed here to carry out that assignment. The temple says to find your purpose, and to know the Creator, you must use meditation and prayer. To them, the key is to be patient and listen for his inner message."

"But you don't believe them. You're going home," said Jim.

"I'm beginning to think, in some ways, they are right. I guess my only criticism of the temple is that the priests spend too much time seeking the highest level of consciousness so they can be close to the Creator."

"What's wrong with that?" Jim asked.

"Nothing. It's just that they use mind altering substances to do it."

"You mean drugs?" asked Jim.

"No, not marijuana, cocaine or heroin. I don't mean that addictive stuff. I think they are into some sort of cactus or mushroom they get from Central America."

"They're trying to escape from reality," observed Jim.

"Not really. They are not trying to escape from the Creator. They are trying to find him. They smoke the stuff and they mix it in their tea. I think they just run this camp to get funds to support their effort to find the Creator. Do you know what I really think?" David asked.

"No."

"They're too far out, Mr. Henderson."

"You may be right," said Jim, seriously stifling a deep-seated chuckle. Here was the radical, calling the religious sect he was affiliated with too radical, just as he had with the militia.

"I don't know much really. I'm an outsider here. Neophytes are not allowed into the inner court or the prayer rooms. We aren't even allowed to talk to the priests."

"So, the followers are in charge?" asked Jim.

"Yes, they run the day to day operations."

"That's good. Don't give up your own opinions just to conform to those of others," Jim warned David. "You've got to be your own person."

"Did you ever hear of the Dead Sea Scrolls?" asked David.

"Sure," responded Jim. "Who hasn't? Has your group read the interpretations?"

"I haven't, but the priests have."

"Didn't they say you have to be clean of body and spirit to appear before the Creator?" asked Jim, violating his rule of avoiding the subject of religion. Somehow his curiosity simply got the best of him, and he was curious about David's views.

"Yes, they are the ones. Only the truly pure can appear before the Creator. The temple priests try to model themselves after the Sons of Light. In reality, they live off the fees for taking us wayward teenagers in for camp. Anyway, that's what I believe. I mean, what does it cost to keep me out here in the desert?"

"It doesn't sound expensive," said Jim.

"Neophytes do all the work to keep the place going. The priests don't do anything, as far as I can see."

"Could I go out to your temple for a visit?" asked Jim.

"Sure. They welcome everyone, but there's not much there to see. The whole compound consists of mud huts. There's no big meeting room or anything. We don't even have sermons. All you would see is our living huts and our vegetable gardens."

"So, what's the attraction?" asked Jim.

"Basic communal living. You have to be a true believer to appreciate the place. If you want solitude, now, it has that, but don't expect much else. I think I told you, when my time is up, I'm out of here. You can have this desert. The sand gets into everything."

"You keep talking about your grandparents," said Jim. "What happened to your parents?"

"They owned a small farm, but it went under. My father became depressed about it. He got up one morning and shot my mother, then he killed himself."

"I'm sorry," said Jim.

"I moved in with my grandparents. The bank got the farm. My grandparents are getting old now. They are pacifists. I'm different. I think we have to stand up to save the small farmer. All the farmers need to unite. I'm just too radical for them. Hell, Mr. Henderson, I was too radical for the militia."

"I'm really sorry about your parents. I had no right to pry," Jim apologized.

"Don't worry about it. You couldn't have known. Besides, I'm used to it. I've adjusted. I know my grandparents are the only family I've got. They've been good to me, and I know it."

"You shouldn't be too harsh on their politics," said Jim.

"They do their best. You know, I probably didn't have to come here to Africa, but when my grandparents first told me about this place, it actually sounded interesting. Besides, they scared me. The said if I stayed there, I was going to be charged with trying to overthrow the government," said David. "And, I believed them."

"That is serious," said Jim. "Maybe leaving the country for a while wasn't such a bad idea. Scaring you to come here sounds like it could have been in your best interests."

"I think so. Yeah. My grandparents were scared, too. I think they actually thought I was in big trouble. They put some land into a reforestation program that paid them up front just to plant seedlings. They used part of those funds to send me here. My grandparents meant well, but they were scared. You know, that's one of the things we're fighting," said David.

"What is?" asked Jim. "What are you fighting?"

"Fear. Those good old boys in the militia can see what is happening all around them. They just don't know what to do about it. They're afraid they won't be able to cope. I mean, farming is all they know. The farms are going under, and their towns are dying. My grandparents are scared like everyone else, Mr. Henderson."

"I don't want to interrupt, but I have been traveling for almost two days," said Jim. "What time is it here? I've totally lost track of time. I need to reset my watch."

"It's a little after five o'clock now, but to tell you the truth, I don't wear a watch, and the clock on the dashboard doesn't work. I mean, that's one thing the temple teaches out here, and I agree with it."

"What do you agree with?" asked Jim.

"Look at yourself. You say you need to know the time. Even if I tell you the exact time, what would you do with it? We'll get to Elizabethtown when we get there. There's nothing you or I can do about it. If you're early, you're early. If you're late, you're late. You get there when you get there, period."

"You have a point," said Jim. "I never thought of it quite like that."

"Yeah. We just use a sundial out at the temple. They made one just like the one the Essenes used long ago."

"Out here, that's probably all you need," said Jim.

"Modern society is all numbers. They teach young kids that the sun is ninety three million miles away. Tell me, Mr. Henderson, what kid is going to have any idea what that number means? It doesn't have any meaning to them, and it has no impact on their lives. It's a meaningless number."

"I have to agree with you," said Jim.

"Here's another example."

"Okay. Go ahead, I'm ready."

"They told me as a kid, the world is 4.5 billion years old. Now, I ask you, what does that mean to a little kid, or an adult for that matter? Even if you could comprehend it, which you can't, what are you going to do about it? It's another meaningless number, Mr. Henderson."

"You're right, but numbers are everywhere," said Jim.

"Half of the material you see in newspapers and on television is a mumbo jumbo of numbers that have no significance to the lives of anybody. Everyone gets all excited about numbers that have no meaning," said David.

35

"So, what is the answer?" asked Jim.

"Drop them. We don't need to memorize numbers that don't mean anything. The temple tells us to follow the sun. You know when it comes up, when it's noon, and when it sets. That's all that really counts out at the temple. People all over the world are filling their heads with information they don't need."

"There's a lot of truth in what you say," said Jim. "I noticed that all the seats in the bus have been removed, except for the first two rows. Is that so you can use this bus like a truck?"

"Yes. That's what we use it for mostly. You probably think that the back end is full of all sorts of exotic foods since we are here in Africa. But what you see in back are the same things you have at home. I have a number of fifty-pound sacks of white rice, four bags of yellow rice, fourteen big bags of potatoes, six bags of onions, all sorts of fresh vegetables that we don't grow in our gardens at the temple, boxes of canned fruits. You name it. There's nothing in back that's exotic, Mr. Henderson. You'd recognize everything there."

"I'll bet your temple is strictly vegetarian. I didn't hear you mention meat."

"You got it. How's that air?" asked David. "I'm afraid it's the best I can do. Just be thankful the sun is getting low. We try to avoid driving this bus in the middle of the day."

"I see," said Jim. "It's not too bad this late in the afternoon."

"You know, some church group in the States donated a lot of old school buses to be used by the local village schools here in East Africa, but the locals don't know how to repair them. On top of that, parts are next to impossible to get here, never mind paying for them. A local school district here in Uhuru just gave this one to us. Some of us spend a lot of time working on it to fix it up."

"At least your temple is enterprising."

"Many of the neophytes are from the United States. We know how to obtain the service manuals and order the parts needed. The temple has enough money to cover the maintenance expenses, so it winds up being one of the few sources of reliable transportation around," said David.

"That's a good thing then. I bet it gives you neophytes some good experience in auto maintenance and repair."

"There's a lot of school buses out in the territories just rusting away, stripped for parts and abandoned. Sometimes donations are not carefully thought through, especially out in the territories north of Nairobi. The whole commercial world you take for granted in America just doesn't

exist out here. Anyway, I have all the windows open so we have the
maximum circulation this bus can give," said David.

"I'm fine. What else can you tell me about your temple?"

"Well, you said it. We're vegetarians, whether we like it or not.
The temple believes the problems of mankind today started when man
began to kill animals for food. If we want to get back to our true nature,
we have to stop such violent practices. But look, don't pay attention to
me," said David. "I'm just talking. Look around. We just passed the
outskirts of Nairobi, and it's sheer poverty. You won't see much until
Elizabethtown. To understand Africa, you have to understand poverty in
the cities."

"I couldn't miss it," said Jim, looking out the window.

"Do you know what we need the most here?" asked David.

"No. What do you really need most?"

"Not us, Mr. Henderson, the native people. They need medicines.
They have diseases here that we haven't seen in the States for a hundred
years."

The city and its dense population thinned quickly once they turned
onto the Outer Territories Road. The Outer Territories Road ran north,
away from Nairobi, towards the border with Uhuru and its capital,
Elizabethtown. The air was no longer humid, since it had not rained
this far out of town. Jim was glad they were in motion. He realized that
David was right. The bus would be impossible to bear under the steady
rays of the midday sun.

"You'll have to excuse our roads, Mr. Henderson. This road to
Elizabethtown is still mostly dirt. They are still working on it. They
spray tar on it from time to time to keep the dust down, but it's mostly
unpaved and dusty. It's been under construction since I came here."

"I can see it's still just a dirt road. Traffic must stir up a lot of dust,"
Jim observed.

"They plan to fully pave it by the end of next year. Right now, it can
be a bit rough in places, especially after a heavy rain and ruts develop
with the traffic," David complained.

Nairobi, or that part of it along the outer loop road, was mostly lined
with simple, shanty structures that thinned out the farther they traveled
away from town.

"Do you have all the papers you need to enter Uhuru?" asked David.

"Yes," said Jim. "I have all my documents right here in my
briefcase."

"Good. We will only have a brief delay if you have everything in
order. Elizabethtown is not much further beyond the border. It's about

three kilometers from here to the border, then another 15 to town. See, I did it myself."

"Did what?" asked Jim, preoccupied, looking out the windows at the sandy, red soil along the side of the road.

"Numbers. I just gave you all those numbers."

"You did, but I think they are useful ones," Jim answered.

"I see you looking out the window. If you are looking for wildlife, you won't see much here."

"You mean, there's no hope?" asked Jim. "I'd like to see the big five before I leave Africa."

"I don't want to disappoint you, but most of what you'll see along this road are cattle, chickens, and pigs. I've seen wildebeest, gazelles, antelope, dik-dik, duiker and some others, but not in large numbers. They are few and far between in this part of the country, and they spook easily when man is around. Do you know the only reason you still see wild animals out here?"

"No," said Jim.

"Ebola," said David.

"Ebola?"

"Yes, scientists found that the natives get Ebola from eating wild animal meat."

"That's good to know," said Jim. "Listen, I do appreciate you picking me up and providing this guided tour. You have really been helpful. I'd like to ask you a question though."

"Sure."

"You have a pair of sunglasses on the dashboard," said Jim.

"Oh, yeah. I do."

"Well, why don't you use them? Don't you want to protect your eyes from the bright sun? Wouldn't they help?"

"The sun is getting low now. To tell you the truth, I don't wear them because they are a symbol of evil," said David.

"Sunglasses, a symbol of evil? You must be joking." Jim was astounded.

"They are a symbol of distortion. I mean, why do people use them?"

"To reduce the glare from the sun, to protect their eyes from ultra violet rays," Jim answered.

"To distort reality. You can't handle the real world. It's too harsh, too bright, so you distort it. You make it more pleasing, more acceptable by putting on the glasses. You turn the real world into one of your own creation."

"I see," said Jim, mulling over David's revelation.

"Do you? You have to take off your sunglasses if you want to see the real world."

"I'm glad I don't wear sunglasses," said Jim.

"Sure you do. You wear them every day."

"I do?" asked Jim.

"Yes. You call it culture."

It was a loaded statement. Jim did not answer. He could not predict where the conversation would go. He instinctively knew this topic was something to avoid with David. "Well, I do appreciate your commentary as well as the tour," said Jim.

"Think nothing of it. The lecture is free," said David. "It's on the house. I'm just happy to talk to someone not associated with the temple for a change. Sometimes those people drive me nuts. They just say the same thing, over and over."

He drove on in silence for another kilometer.

"Can I ask you a question?" asked David.

"Sure," said Jim.

"I'm just curious. Dr. Umbawi didn't say what brought you here to Africa."

"I represent an insurance company. I'm here to investigate the death of Dr. Edward Bronston. Have you ever heard of him?" asked Jim.

"Sure did. I used to work out at his camp, part time. He found all those extinct animals that lived out here, millions of years ago. Africa must have been quite a place back then. His camp was only a few kilometers down the river from the temple. We heard he committed suicide. You know, it's a shame," said David.

"That he took his own life?" asked Jim.

"That they had to close down Bokuru," said David.

"Bokuru?" asked Jim.

"Yes. That's the name of the excavation site where Dr. Bronston had his camp. It's named for the Bokuru River that runs right by it. Eric and I could always pick up spending money by working out there as day laborers."

"Eric? Who is Eric? You haven't mentioned him before."

"He's my big brother at the temple. He's a follower. I talked him into going out there and working with me at the excavation. We could always use a couple of bucks when we go into Elizabethtown or Nairobi. My grandparents were willing to send me to the temple, but they have been more than tight with spending money. I'll miss that extra work. I'd tell you to go out there and see the place for yourself, but I think everyone is gone now," said David.

39

"I don't think they closed the site permanently yet," said Jim. "I think they are trying to get his daughter, Nancy, to open it up and finish the excavation work. In fact, she may need your help since you have experience."

"Oh, I didn't know," said David. "I thought they closed it down when Dr. Bronston died. I haven't been back or anything, but I thought it was abandoned since he died." David was visibly surprised.

"Well, maybe so," said Jim. "At least temporarily, you may be right. Maybe all the fieldwork is done, and all that remains is paperwork. All I know is that she's been asked to wrap it up. I have another question for you."

"Go ahead."

"I don't understand how you would be willing to work out there. I know you're not a member of the temple, but if you were brought up as a fundamentalist, you must have some reservations about working at an archaeological site," Jim spoke honestly, pondering the puzzle and realizing he was crossing a dangerous line. His curiosity urged him to go ahead.

"Neither Eric, nor I had a problem working out there. Even the priests at the temple had no objections."

"They didn't?" Jim was surprised.

"They said the more we find out about the past, the closer we will be to the Creator. Dr. Bronston was known for finding all sorts of different extinct creatures, but he didn't preach that they changed into each other. That's what other people did with his work. The temple believes there were lots of creatures that are gone now," said David.

"I only asked the question because I thought an archaeological site was the last place a true believer would want to work," said Jim.

"We saw no conflict in what we did, but I will say one thing," David continued.

"What's that," Jim queried.

"It's hard work," said David. "We earned every dime they paid us."

Jim chuckled then got very serious. "I may need to talk to you and your friend in more detail as part of my investigation," said Jim.

"Certainly," said David. "You can reach us at the temple anytime."

"Miss Bronston may want to talk to you about coming back to work," Jim added.

"Sure. Just let us know," said David. "Do you think she will take over, and open the site up again?"

"I don't know," said Jim. "That will be her decision, but I'm going out there with her the day after tomorrow. We're going to drive out early in the morning. I'll let her know you're still available for work."

"I'll tell you one other thing," said David.

"What is that?"

"You won't need that suit out there."

"You're right," Jim chuckled again. "I need it tomorrow for a couple of meetings, but after that, I plan to leave it at the hotel. Nancy Bronston is the one who told me to bring these duffle bags instead of a suitcase, and she did say to leave my suit in Elizabethtown. Did you ever meet her?"

"No, but I've heard a lot about her. I didn't start to work out there until after her last visit, and I haven't been out to the camp since Dr. Bronston's death. You may want to dig out your documents, Mr. Henderson. That's the border station just ahead."

"Yes, I can see it. I'm ready."

"Welcome to Uhuru, Mr. Henderson."

CHAPTER THREE: *DINNER AT THE GRAND*

David Johannson dropped Jim off at the curb outside the front entrance to The Grand Hotel in downtown Elizabethtown precisely at 6:00 PM local time. The hotel was an old, three-story, stone building built back in the glory days of the British Empire. The exterior had been sand blasted, the masonry redone, and the wood trim repainted, all within the last few years, giving the building the appearance of being old, yet somehow new at the same time. It was one of the more imposing structures in downtown Elizabethtown, in contrast to the outlying residential area where a sea of dilapidated, weatherworn shacks of corrugated iron, aluminum and wood packing crates cluttered what would, in more prosperous cities be considered the suburbs.

Dr. Umbawi was waiting in the main lobby. He was seated in one of the overstuffed chairs reading a newspaper. Jim recognized him at about the same time Dr. Umbawi looked up. As the doctor rose to greet him, Jim noticed that he wore a beige suit, white cotton shirt, and tie. His name badge was pinned to his coat pocket. He looked exactly like the photograph in Jim's briefcase. Jim grinned. Dr. Umbawi had kept the agreement and dressed as he had promised for the airport.

"Dr. Umbawi," said Jim, putting down his bags and extending his right hand. Dr. Umbawi grasped Jim's hand in an iron grip, and they shook vigorously. Dr. Umbawi was grinning also.

"James Henderson, at last," said Dr. Umbawi, smiling broadly. "I apologize for not being able to meet you at the airport as we planned. Unfortunately, I ordered replacements for all the rubber hoses in my Land Rover, and they just arrived yesterday."

"That was thoughtful planning," said Jim, as Dr. Umbawi motioned for him to take a seat in the stuffed chair opposite his own.

"We do that sort of thing here every three years." Said Dr. Umbawi, as soon as they had both settled in the soft chairs. "We find it wise to take precautions here in the territories. Well, anyway, I had to make an appointment with a mechanic. The whole thing was arranged through Dr. Tubojola who recommended a shop here in Elizabethtown. Good mechanics are few and far between anywhere in this part of Africa, and their schedules are overbooked. We must take advantage of their availability when we can get it."

"It sounds like you did the right thing," said Jim.

"It seemed that way this morning. This was a good day for the work to be done. I was invited to a breakfast meeting at the museum here in town. My mistake was that I had no idea how long the repairs were going to take. Unfortunately, my Land Rover was still in pieces when it was time to leave to pick you up. The problem was, what the shop estimated as a couple of hours to do the job, actually took the rest of the afternoon," said Dr. Umbawi.

"That wasn't your fault. You couldn't have anticipated the delay," said Jim.

"I knew the hotel bus runs late tonight, so I took the liberty of calling the temple in Nairobi, and they were able to put me in touch with the young man from the temple who picked you up. He was loading supplies for the trip back here. Thankfully, he was able to swing by the airport."

"You called at exactly the right time," said Jim.

"By the way, where is he? I'd like to thank him for his help," said Dr. Umbawi.

"Well, thankfully, everything worked out, lucky as it was," said Jim. "My driver, a young man named David Johannson, just dropped me off out front. He said he wanted to make it back to the temple before dark, so he did not stay. He was running late. I hope he made it," said Jim.

"That's a shame. We could, at least, have offered him a refreshment before he went on. I wanted to thank him personally."

"He was anxious not to lose any more time," said Jim.

"That's unfortunate, but enough of my excuses. Tell me about your trip from Chicago," said Dr. Umbawi.

"There's not much to say. It was long, physically tiring, but thankfully, quite uneventful."

"You didn't see any lions in the jungle on the way from Nairobi, did you?"

"No, there's no jungle between Nairobi and Elizabethtown," said Jim. "It's pretty barren."

"That's a local joke, Jim. Even if there were jungle on the way, you would not have seen lions. There's a common misconception that lions are found in the jungle, even in these so-called enlightened times. The truth is that lions are found out on the open savannah, not in the jungle."

"That's a bit embarrassing. I think I should have known that, but I'm not sure what my perception was before you raised the question," said Jim.

"You have no idea how glad I am to meet you at last," said Dr. Umbawi. "Nancy has told me so much about you."

"I hope it was all good," said Jim smiling.

"Believe me it was. She apparently thinks very highly of you. However, I do have a confession to make."

"And what is that?"

"First, an apology, then a confession. When Nancy first arrived, she was already set on bringing you here as soon as she could. Who was I to question her? I thought if she wanted her boyfriend here, she was entitled. After all, she was dealing with the shock of losing not just her father, but also the last living member of her family. To me, it was perfectly natural to seek the emotional support of someone she felt close to."

"I understand your thinking," Jim commented.

"Actually, I paid no attention to anything she said about you. I don't even know what my mental picture was of you at that time."

"I was actually hired by the museum."

"Yes. Well, obviously, I was elated when I received your resume by fax."

"My amended one?" asked Jim.

"I received the one with your archaeological background," said Dr. Umbawi, smiling.

"I'm not a detective. I really have no background in suicide investigations," Jim admitted.

"No, but your legal background is a good fit. We are dealing with an archaeological mystery, Jim. Why would one of the best paleo-anthropologists in East Africa take his own life? That is a real mystery," said Dr. Umbawi, looking seriously at Jim.

"So, do I fit your mental picture of what a suicide investigator should look like? My brain is empty of any hypotheses at this time."

"Actually, I think I pictured a taller, thinner, more scholarly looking man, maybe a few years older. However, that does not matter. Your background fits what I feel is required for this investigation. Nancy could not have picked a more qualified person for the task."

"I was under the impression that you had something to do with my selection for the job," said Jim.

"Yes, I did jump onto the bandwagon once I saw your resume. I envisioned you as the perfect person to solve our mystery."

"Thank you for the confidence in me. I still have my doubts."

"Look, Jim, here comes the bellman. Go ahead and sign the guest register at the front desk and pick up your room key. You're pre-registered. Let them take your bags up to your room. In fact, why don't you take a few minutes to freshen up? When you are ready, we'll have dinner together in the restaurant right over there," said Dr. Umbawi, nodding in the direction of the double oak doors across the lobby.

"Fine, if you're willing to wait. I'd appreciate a minute to freshen up from the trip. It was a hot, dusty ride here. I'll only take a few minutes."

"Just remember, you cannot take a shower now, at least not a hot one. There's no hot water in this hotel until 7:00 AM Even then, I understand, they cut it off around 9:00 AM You might want to check with the front desk on the times, just to be sure you don't miss out in the morning," said Dr. Umbawi.

"I'm sure I'm a bit dusty from the bus ride in from the airport," said Jim. "I'll wash the grime off my face and change my shirt. A quick shave and some after shave lotion will do, and I'll be as good as new. I won't take long. Are you sure you're willing to wait?"

"Don't be silly. I have my paper. I'll meet you in the restaurant. There's a table reserved in my name. Ask the maitre'd. He'll help you find me when you come back downstairs."

"Thank you," said Jim, standing to leave. "I'll be back in a few minutes."

"I see you have your briefcase. You can leave it in your room, but you may want to take some notes later, so bring a pen and notebook back down with you."

Half an hour later, Jim entered the restaurant. Dr. Umbawi was seated at a small table against the back wall. Jim took the remaining seat. "Thank you for waiting. I do feel much better," said Jim.

"No problem. By the way, this is my favorite table here. It's away from any entertainment they may bring in, so it's quiet back here. If you notice, we're not directly under any of those ceiling fans either. I don't like sitting under a draft."

"This is just fine," said Jim.

"I think you know, I live and teach in Nairobi. What my resume didn't show is that I am also on retainer with the Uhuru museum and also with the Department of the Interior. I'm tenured at the university, so I have a ready reserve of graduate students to handle my lectures. I'm here in Elizabethtown on a regular basis under one or the other of my retainer agreements. My dining experience has led me to decide that the best food in Elizabethtown is right here in this hotel. Over the years, I've become a regular customer. They hold this table for me unless the place is full," said Dr. Umbawi.

"This is a nice, private spot, and quite comfortable."

"Then let's order a glass of wine and celebrate your arrival in Africa. I'm a Chablis man, myself. What would you like, Jim?"

"That's fine with me. Make it two," said Jim.

"In that case, I'll just order a whole bottle. I'm sure both of us can do it justice," said Dr. Umbawi, turning to address the waiter who had appeared, as if on signal. "Don't worry about the bill, the museum in Chicago pays a flat fee for a room here at the hotel, year round, which also includes breakfast and dinner for two."

"Yes, the museum personnel told me about the arrangements. I didn't want to take advantage of their hospitality. This is my first trip for the Chicago museum. I want to make a good impression, but if you say this is their on-going arrangement, I guess we should take advantage of it."

"I understand your feelings, but it doesn't matter, either, what we order. The museum gets a wholesale flat price on everything. In exchange, the hotel is assured that at least one room is fully paid for year round. People who come to Africa usually travel in groups. One room is seldom enough to accommodate the visitors, so it is a good deal for the hotel," Dr. Umbawi explained. "So, order whatever you like, you don't have to worry about the tab."

"When their wine arrived, Dr. Umbawi proposed a toast. "To you, Jim Henderson, and to a successful investigation."

"To you and your help, Dr. Umbawi," Jim reciprocated the toast. "I'd be lost in Africa on my own. I would not know where to start. You have provided me with a hospitable beginning."

As soon as they ordered, Dr. Umbawi continued. "Here's my business card. I have added my home phone number, and I have penned on the back, the number where you can usually find me at the museum here in Elizabethtown. I also added the number for the front desk here at the hotel. The phone service is not the best in this part of Africa, but having the hotel number may help in an emergency. Use the hotel to find local transportation and that sort of thing. I think you will find the staff very helpful. Now, you have all your necessary phone numbers on one card. Just don't lose it."

"Thank you," said Jim as he accepted the card and tucked it into his shirt pocket.

"Nancy and I discussed at length how we could best help you while you are here in Africa. We decided that I would act as your host and guide. That's why my job was to meet you at the airport. She is, like you merely a visitor here in Africa. On the other hand, I was born in Kenya. I have lived and worked in East Africa all of my life. I also speak the local languages of Kikuyu and Swahili, if they are needed. Since most everyone here and at the site speak English, I don't think you will find the need for a translator. But if you do, let me know." Dr. Umbawi paused and shifted his thoughts, "I should add that Nancy was concerned that she was too close to your investigation to be of direct help. I agree. Both of us shared the concern that you must remain as objective as possible in conducting your investigation of Dr. Bronston's death. As a related party, she is too emotionally involved. We decided that I am, shall we say, more objective," said Dr. Umbawi, smiling lightly.

"Well, I appreciate your help. Your local insight will be invaluable," said Jim.

"I will do what I can. There are a couple of things you should keep in mind at all times. First, always remember who I am. Teaching is my primary profession. When the student is a young child, a great deal of factual teaching in involved. When the student is older, the teacher's role becomes one of providing orientation, guidance, and motivation. Students at the college level and up are really self-taught. They learn what they want to and are interested in. What the adult needs, is to learn to think on his or her own."

"Are you saying that you can't teach adults?" asked Jim.

"Adult students are introduced to reading, writing and arithmetic at a young age, but their education has usually been short-changed on reason as a legitimate discipline. Anyway, just keep in mind, what I say and do comes from a teacher's point of view," said Dr. Umbawi.

"I'll try to remember that," said Jim.

"Secondly, keep in mind that Uhuru is now a separate country. This is a Kikuyu nation. Elizabethtown is the capital, just as Nairobi is the capital of Kenya. The two countries have different laws. I am a Kenyan citizen. Thus, I am like you, a visitor here in Uhuru. You will meet Dr. Tubojola tomorrow afternoon. I have arranged the meeting for you."

"Great. He is on my list of people to interview."

"He is a citizen of Uhuru. He lives and works here in Elizabethtown. He is first and foremost an administrator, a bureaucrat. As Minister of the Interior, he is one of the top officials in the country, and ranks just below the President in power and authority in the country. Dr. Bronston, on the other hand, worked here under a visa as a foreign national. He is buried here in Uhuru as a special adopted son by act of the government, but his nationality will always be American. Oh, I think it was very gracious of Nancy to realize that his heart was here in Africa, not in the States, and his burial here was most appropriate."

"I agree," said Jim, nodding in affirmation. "I understand he spent most of his life here."

"You need to be aware of the basic differences in cultures as long as you are here. Understanding these differences may help you understand why people act as they do and deal with the situations reasonably."

"I appreciate your advice," said Jim.

When the meal arrived, they both ate in silence, savoring the best food in Elizabethtown, as Dr. Umbawi promised. As soon as the table was cleared, Dr. Umbawi ordered after dinner drinks for both of them. "I've looked over your resume. Your archaeological background is especially remarkable, Jim. I was elated to see that type of experience in the investigator selected for this assignment."

"I think my weakness is that you really need a detective, not an attorney. I don't know anything about suicide cases, other than what I read in the common press and see on television. My firm responded to the demands of our client, the museum. They were quite insistent on my being the right person for this assignment. No one else in the law office has any experience in this sort of thing. The only reason the museum was pushing for me was that I had, at least, some archaeological experience, and I knew Nancy. The museum people are worried about her being over here alone. They want her back safely, and since she kept asking for me, they sent me. So, briefly, that's why I'm here."

"I think your resume shows us that you are the person we need right now. I have a feeling your archaeological experience may be just enough to help you in your investigation. There are detectives here in East Africa, but they do not have any knowledge of archaeology, and that may come to be very important," said Dr. Umbawi.

"I hope you are right about my background. If you are, all I have to do is apply my knowledge and skills," said Jim.

"The important issue is that you can read an archaeological report and understand it. This skill will help you when you are out at the site. When you are there, Jim, take your time and look at everything, every detail."

"Ill do my best," Jim promised.

"You may want to take some notes, since this is the first interview in your investigation."

"Actually, I think I already blew my first interview," said Jim.

"Why do you say that? We didn't set you up with anyone else today."

"I talked to David, the young man who picked me up at the airport."

"Why would you want to interview him?" asked Dr. Umbawi.

"Well, David told me that he worked part time as a general laborer for Dr. Bronston. He said he and another fellow from the temple, both worked at the site part time. I think the other fellow's name was Eric."

"Eric? I wasn't aware of these two young men working at the site."

"He did not give me Eric's last name. He just told me there was another guy from the temple who worked at the site part time," said Jim.

"What did David tell you?" asked Dr. Umbawi.

"He caught me short. I was surprised when he knew Dr. Bronston and had worded at the site. Frankly, I didn't know what to say or ask. I didn't expect to meet someone so important so soon," said Jim.

"I'm not familiar with your friend David, and I have not heard of anyone at the temple named Eric, but that's not important. Actually, I only know a couple of the followers out there. I did not know that anyone from the temple was working out at Dr. Bronston's archaeological site. He may have told me he brought in some part time help, but if he did, I assumed they came from town and stayed out at the camp."

"Oh," said Jim.

"I'm just a little surprised he picked up help from the temple. I would never have guessed Dr. Bronston would have found laborers there."

"I don't know how they met, but I'm certainly glad you found David. He was right on time," said Jim. "I had just come out of customs when he arrived."

"That arrangement was sheer luck, Jim. I called on the remote possibility that someone might be coming back to the temple. We just lucked out. No one would have guessed that the person we intercepted also had experience at Dr. Bronston's site."

"I see," said Jim. "In any case, it worked out."

"Perhaps it is a good omen, and your luck will hold for the rest of your investigation," said Dr. Umbawi.

"Well, I didn't do so well in the interview process because I was caught off guard," said Jim.

"Don't worry about it," said Dr. Umbawi. "I'll contact the temple and set up a formal interview, either at the camp site or at the temple. You need to have the time to conduct an official interview with everyone who has been employed at the site."

"I appreciate your assistance."

"Did David tell you anything useful?" asked Dr. Umbawi.

"Yes, I learned he is from Minnesota, and I learned a lot about the temple. I asked him if he knew why Dr. Bronston would commit suicide, but he said he had no idea. I do remember he thought the site was now abandoned, after Dr. Bronston's death. He was not aware that Nancy was considering taking over for her father. Oh, I did ask him if he knew what they found out there," said Jim.

"And what did he say to that?" asked Dr. Umbawi, looking intently at Jim.

"He said, when they reached the bottom of the cave they were excavating, they found a few scraps of fossilized bone. I think he said Dr. Bronston thought they could be hominid in origin. That's all."

"So, that was it?" asked Dr. Umbawi.

"Oh, yes, he did ask why I was here in Africa."

"What did you tell him?" asked Dr. Umbawi.

"I told him I was here to confirm Dr. Bronston's cause of death, and I was representing an insurance company."

"Well, that's close enough," said Dr. Umbawi.

"That's all we talked about," said Jim. "The rest was just small talk."

"Remember the old saying, when you are talking to people, be careful, especially when interviewing," said Dr. Umbawi.

"What saying is that?"

"Loose lips sink ships."

"Yes, I remember that one. I think it came from World War I."

"Yes, it did. Well, it still applies today. Remember, keep your interviews on the issues, and do not say too much. You never know when you might be influencing your investigation," said Dr. Umbawi. "You have to keep focused and particularly avoid leading questions. Don't give the person you are interviewing the answer that you want."

"I'll remember that. You know, I did ask him one important question though."

"And what was that?"

"I asked David how a true believer could work at an archaeological site looking for the remains of ancient man."

"You asked him that question? asked Dr. Umbawi, amazed. "That's a good one."

"Yes, I thought so. I asked because it bothered me."

"As well it should. I'm curious, how did David respond?"

"He said the temple had no conflicts with the archaeological investigation. In fact, he said the temple did not believe in a literal interpretation of the Bible, and the more we found out about the past, the closer we would be to the Creator. He distinguished Dr. Bronston from other scientists."

"Oh, really? That surprises me."

"Yes, he said Dr. Bronston did not preach evolution. He said Dr. Bronston would just report what he found and would leave the interpretation of the significance of the finds to others. Is that true?" Jim asked.

"There are two schools of thought, Jim. One says the field archaeologist should simply report the details of what they find, and do nothing more. The other school thinks the world will never gain any useful knowledge if reports of mere numbers are published in some obscure journal. They believe the field archaeologist has a duty to interpret what is found in the field, even if it is only a theory. This second school believes the field archaeologist is in the best position to make interpretations of what they find," said Dr. Umbawi.

"That makes sense," said Jim. "So, Dr. Bronston was in the first school."

"Yes. Well, David was right. Dr. Bronston was definitely noncommittal. He reported his results and let others do the interpreting. He would announce his new findings, but he let others figure out the classification and significance. He often said that was the only way to stay unbiased when doing field work."

"I see," said Jim.

"You need to understand, Jim, when they first began to find what appeared to be our ancestors, some people began to shout that *Homo sapiens* descended from killer apes, and that explained who we were and why our history is so full of violence against our own kind. That argument elicited a response that threatened to turn science backward, and lead to a denial of any inquiry into our past. That school of thought scared one group of scientists, who were a lot more mainstream in their thinking. They saw a threat to true scientific inquiry. This school rallied with a more moderate view that said that true survival of the fittest by the strongest follow with the biggest club was not accurate. Man, they said, would not have survived in that kind of environment."

"That's interesting. They had a different view?" asked Jim.

"They claimed that man evolved and survived only because he had culture, social cooperation, compassion, love, understanding. Their position was that those characteristics had prevailed and were the reason for our survival."

"That sounds plausible."

"Well, that position was like balm on an open wound. A lot of the religious institutions came around and accepted our natural history, reserving the realm of the soul as their domain. As a result, most mainstream religious organizations have accepted that perhaps we were a bit more hairy, at least a long time ago. They have made peace with the past."

"That may explain the temple's position," said Jim.

"Well, I think science has come a long way with acceptability of the historical findings with a majority of people in western civilization. I'm just hopeful we do not have another black eye like Piltdown," said Dr. Umbawi. "That could really set us back."

"Piltdown. I've heard about it, but I don't have a good handle on the details of what it was all about," said Jim.

"The Piltdown forgery was an unusual event in archaeology and the study of early man. What happened was that someone altered a real fossilized human skull to make it look older than it really was. That person also did the same thing to a jawbone from an ape. The skull and the jaw bone were planted together in old sediments in England along with similarly altered, ancient animal bones brought in from Africa. They deliberately planted them along with flora and fauna to make up an assemblage that appeared to be over half a million years old."

"So, that was Piltdown?" asked Jim.

"Yes. Before the hoax was uncovered, the human skull and the jaw were estimated to be between half a million to a million years old, based on the sediments where they were found along with their proximity to the other altered animal bones."

"It sounds like someone went to a lot of trouble," said Jim.

"Yes, and science did not have modern dating techniques back then to detect the error. That estimate made Piltdown the oldest human remains ever found."

"But they weren't. The fraud was discovered, wasn't it?"

"Yes, but not for forty years. Piltdown represented two significant clashes with the prevailing theory at the time."

"How so?" asked Jim.

"First, Piltdown showed man to be very old, when the thinking then and later substantiated, was that modern man was little more than one hundred thousand years old. Second, Piltdown showed the modern cranium with an ape-like jaw, which backed the popular theory then in vogue that the human brain led the way to the human body. Most mainstream scientists believed the opposite, and the human upright body that stood on two legs came first. The theory then, and later confirmed, is that the freedom of the hands to manipulate tools led to the increased brain size and our ultimate humanity."

"I think the brain came first," said Jim. "Of course, I'm no expert on such things."

"That's an old concept, Jim. Our distant ancestors, the Australopithecines, demonstrated that the brain of the apes with a capacity of six hundred fifty cubic centimeters existed in a totally upright walking body and the physical structure of a modern human. You see, the key to human emergence was not the big brain, but the pelvis, or more accurately, the muscles that control upright walking. That musculature was the key to the emergence of the lineage that led to modern man and the freedom to manipulate tools."

"I see," said Jim. "I haven't read much about what we know in that arena."

"We have learned from a study of the natural world that bone form follows function. Random favorable changes to the bone that facilitated the new use of those muscles led to where we are today."

"I can go along with that, but I don't understand the Piltdown forgery," said Jim.

"Let me finish. To begin with, as soon as they discovered that Piltdown was not as old as they originally thought, it lost its significance. Piltdown had no more meaning, and the fact it was faked was immaterial. It had meaning only if it was very old."

"But why?"

"What made it important initially was that it placed man on earth much earlier than the time established by the prevailing scientific consensus had. The damage to science was that it took so long to recognize that Piltdown was the most famous and well know fraud in the history of science."

"Do they know who did it?" asked Jim.

"They have a pretty good idea, but there never was a trial. The experts are pretty sure that the perpetrator, a well known professional archaeologist, had intended to disclose the forgery at some time, but died suddenly, before he had the opportunity."

"But why would someone go to all that trouble?"

"He had a hidden agenda. Actually, there are two theories. One says that all he wanted to do was point out how sloppy the professionals were. Primarily, he wanted to embarrass his peers and show up their short comings," said Dr. Umbawi.

"What was the second reason?" asked Jim.

"There are some who believe he supported the hypothesis that the big brain came first, and not the body. They say he created the fraud of putting an ape's jaw with a modern human cranium to support his school of thought."

"In which case, he really did not intend to expose his own forgery," added Jim.

"True. Unfortunately, he died and took his real intent with him to the grave. We will never know the real reason why he did it. We can only speculate."

"Well, at least now I know what Piltdown was all about. Thank you for the explanation."

"Scientists are human beings, Jim. They have all the weaknesses of our species. Some of them have religious convictions, even though they are steeped in the scientific method of analysis."

"That's hard to believe," said Jim. "They are supposed to be professionals."

"You should be aware that one of your astronauts, who actually walked on the moon, was such a strong believer that he lost his life trying to climb Mount Ararat in Turkey, near the border with Iraq and the Soviet Union."

"After he went to the moon?"

"After he went to the moon," said Dr. Umbawi.

"What was he doing in Turkey?"

"He was looking for Noah's Ark."

"You must be joking," said Jim. "If the Ark was real, it was made of wood and would have rotted away a long time ago."

"I wish I was joking. There are many more examples of purportedly scientific professionals running around being true believers. Sometimes professionals do not even recognize they carry a religious bias when they are engaged in what should be open-minded scientific work."

"It's still hard to comprehend," said Jim.

"We should not be over critical of scientists, Jim. They are, after all, human beings just like the rest of us."

"But they are supposed to be objective."

"When a human child is born, it perceives a universe that is centered around its own personal needs. The rest of its life is a process of realizing that the universe is not centered around one individual or its needs. Long ago, we had a difficult time accepting that the world was not flat. If the world were not flat, it would no longer be a stage with the almighty staring down from above. He could no longer look at everyone all at once. A round earth meant that some people were not in the Almighty's spotlight at any one time, and the Creator could not see everyone at the same instant. The concept of the earth circling around the sun was another blow to mankind's ego, denying us center stage. The problem is that we instinctively cherish our early perceptions."

"Come on, Dr. Umbawi. No one believes the sun revolves around the earth any more."

"We pay lip service to the concept, but we give up our early beliefs only begrudgingly."

"How so?" asked Jim.

"For example, we still talk in terms of sunsets and sunrises."

"Yes, of course we do," said Jim. "They are just convenient terms."

"Think about it. Those are the terms of our ancestors, Jim. The terms are misleading. We should have adopted a new language long ago, but our early myths and beliefs lie deep within us."

"I never thought of it that way. You are right. It is the spinning of the earth that creates the appearance of a rising and setting of the sun."

"Good, you see my point. Scientists are not alone in their innate biases. I didn't want to digress. Just remember that those who knew Dr. Bronston are going to say that suicide was impossible. They will say that he was so alive and had such a strong sense of purpose that he could not have undertaken such an act as suicide. Closure will not come to those people until you can show how this man would logically take his own life. They will provide little help to you to find a motive for suicide," said Dr. Umbawi.

"You used the term motive. This isn't a murder investigation."

"That's were you are wrong, Jim. Suicide is murder. It is murder of the self. You know who did it, you just don't know why. With any murder, you need motive and the whole picture falls into place. Look, you have a smoking gun. The pistol was found in his hand, but what you don't have is a note or letter or, I'm afraid, much of anything else to show what his motive was. Then again, that's why you are here, to dig in and find that little something that will give you the lead to solve the mystery of his motive."

"What about you?" asked Jim. "You say you knew him for a long time, and he talked to you frequently. Are you telling me he gave you no hint that he was about to take his own life?"

"As I told you, I'm in the same camp as everyone else. It hurts, Jim."

"It hurts?"

"Yes. I thought I was his best friend, yet he gave me no hint of his intent to commit suicide. He shut me out, Jim." Dr. Umbawi appeared sincerely disappointed and the sadness in his voice underlined his feelings.

"No one has told me what he found at the excavation, other than a couple of pieces of fossilized bone. Do you think that is all he found out at the camp?" asked Jim.

"As I told you, I have never been to Bokuru. On the other hand, you will be there the day after tomorrow. I think we will have to look to you and your investigation for that answer, Jim."

"If he dug for a long time and found nothing of significance, that could have triggered depression, which could have led to suicide," said Jim.

"Good. You are thinking. I can only say he was enthusiastic about the excavation when he talked with me. And, he did talk to me regularly, so I can affirm knowledge of his mental state about his work."

"Maybe it was disappointment. Maybe he had an expectancy that he would find something more significant than what he actually did find," said Jim.

"I can say this much, he was genuinely excited about Bokuru."

"Well, if he was on an emotional high, as you say, that would eliminate one motive for suicide," said Jim.

"Understand, I have known the Bronston family for over fifteen years, yet, as I said, I can't help you. As you know, Nancy first stayed at my home when she came here on this unfortunate trip. She went to visit a friend from her school days, just a couple of days ago. While she stayed at the house with my family, she didn't say anything about Bokuru or what her father may have found there."

"It seems logical he would be more lenient in applying his rule of nondisclosure with members of his immediate family, especially Nancy," said Jim.

"Not necessarily, Jim. She did tell me she didn't have a clue why he would take his own life. She is taking things quite well under the circumstances, but she is emphatic that he did not commit suicide. I'm sure she will tell you the same thing when you meet with her."

"If he was not telling anyone everything about his work, he might handle his personal problems the same way," said Jim. "Sometimes we find out that we don't know some people as well as we thought we did."

"You will have to prod her as best you can. She may know something she is not consciously aware of. It is possible he did not share the intimate details of his personal life with me," said Dr. Umbawi.

"I will do the best I can," said Jim. "I'll see her tomorrow."

"All I can do is tell you is that I am one of those who simply cannot accept that this particular man would resort to such extreme self-destructive conduct. I can't imagine a situation where suicide would be the logical means of solving some one of his problems, unless it was severe pain or something like that, which I did not know about. I can't conceive of a problem of such magnitude that he would have any difficulty solving," said Dr. Umbawi. "That's what stumps me. Of course, I could be missing some key fact because I am too close to the situation, which is why this is your investigation and not mine."

"So, when I write down the word motive, where do I begin?"

"Well, sometimes we have to find our answer by a process of elimination. Why do people commit suicide, Jim? Let's list the possibilities."

"Medical reasons are tops, I think," said Jim, writing it down on his note pad.

"Yes. Good. I don't know what the most common reason is for suicide, but certainly medical reasons would be right up there."

"I think there are two kinds of medical motivations for suicide," said Jim. "I'm writing down pain as the first category. Then I'm writing down disability to cover those who cannot handle being disabled and dependent and do not want to be a financial burden on others."

"Be careful of that category. I think you may be combining two. I think psychological reasons why people commit suicide are a separate category from medical for you to put down on your list. Depression, that sort of thing is separate from being dependent financially and wanting to end an obligation. I think you have to separate them, I would list each as a separate category," said Dr. Umbawi.

"Yes. I read an article once about what was called a psychological autopsy. I suppose that's what is really involved in looking into motivation. I understand what you mean by listing each possibility and then eliminating them one by one, instead of guessing."

"Well, what else do you have for categories?" asked Dr. Umbawi.

"I put down legal problems. Sometimes legal problems are so bad they drive people to suicide. Divorce and bankruptcy are examples that come to mind."

"Ah. Be very careful of bankruptcy. That's in a category I think of as financial. When you stock market crashed back in 1929, many people jumped out of windows. They could not face financial ruin. I think financial motives is a category in and of itself."

"You're right. I agree," said Jim. "Sometimes the death of another person, like a spouse or other family member can motivate one to commit suicide. That makes up another category of emotional distress."

"Yes, but let's put that in psychological reason as a category which we already have," said Dr. Umbawi. "I would list it as a subcategory."

"Fine. Things like depression will fit into that one," said Jim. "I've written them all down, but I think I'm just getting confused. These categories all seem to overlap."

"Don't worry about it. At least you now have a list that will point to the questions you must ask. Anyway, it's your investigation. This list may help you."

"Thank you, I appreciate your input."

"We have set you up to meet his doctor in the morning. You should address the medical issues first, especially the issue of physical pain."

"I think his doctor will be my most important interview."

"Next, you are scheduled to meet Nancy at the cemetery. It's only about a kilometer away from the doctor's office. Take a cab after you finish talking with the doctor. Everyone who lives here knows where the cemetery is. Nancy can help with the psychological area and personal financial issues as well," said Dr. Umbawi. "I know you and Nancy are personal friends, but you must stay focused on your mission here. You need to discuss psychological issues with his doctor, as well. I think those areas overlap enough to raise the issue with him as well as with Nancy."

"I will," promised Jim.

"As for psychological, legal and financial, you can also talk at length with Dr. Tubojola tomorrow afternoon about those issues," continued Dr. Umbawi. "Just review everything with Nancy before you make a final determination and write up your report."

"Of course. Tomorrow I'm scheduled to go to the camp with Nancy. I can talk with her then at length."

"Yes, that will give you an opportunity to meet all the people who work there. It will also give you a chance to inspect the crime scene. I know time has passed, but it may yield some clues, even now. Don't be afraid to poke around the camp."

"Yes, I agree," said Jim. "I understand why you think suicide is a crime."

"Good, because it is. Oh, I will get you a full copy of the police report so you can take it out to the camp with you to read. I'll bring whatever I can obtain to our meeting here tomorrow night for dinner. I would have obtained a copy today, but my schedule was thrown off by my transportation problems."

"Oh yes, a copy of that report should help me a lot," said Jim. "I understand there was no autopsy or inquest hearing, so the report might contain some lead."

"I understand the coroner just accepted the police field report at face value. At least you can look at that. To them, everything seemed straightforward at the time."

"That doesn't give me much to work with," said Jim.

"You are going to have to work with what they found, at least to start with." Just then, their after dinner drinks arrived. "Let's drink to a successful investigation," Dr. Umbawi raised his glass to Jim.

Jim picked up his glass and tipped it toward Dr. Umbawi's glass. "I hope I'm on the right track, but it doesn't look easy right now."

"Find out why he did it, Jim." Dr. Umbawi's expression was gently pleading. "We all need closure and answers. Right now you are the person who can discover the motive. There is no one else to do that."

"I think tomorrow morning should give me my answer," responded Jim.

"Whether it's tomorrow or not, I have faith in you. The investigation is in your hands."

"I will do my best," said Jim.

"To your success," said Dr. Umbawi as the two glasses gently touched and clinked.

CHAPTER FOUR: *A MEDICAL OPINION*

The next morning, as Jim put on his suit coat, he realized that if everything went according to plan, this would be the last day he would wear it before he left Uhuru. The rest of his stay was scheduled to be out at the remote field camp where Dr. Bronston died. The camp, he was told by Dr. Umbawi, was out on the dusty, open savannah an hour and a half's ride north of Elizabethtown. Nancy had told him to think of that part of his trip as camping without amenities. He had an omelet and coffee at the restaurant in the hotel, and then took a jitney from the hotel to Dr. Bhatt's office.

The doctor's office was only seven blocks away. He found the office in a two-story, wood frame building in an older section of the city. All of the buildings in this section of the city were either one or two stories in height, made of wood with most wearing a makeup of fresh, white paint to cover their age. There were two storefront offices in the building, each with its own entrance. A central doorway that opened into a stairwell leading to the second floor divided the two street level offices in half equally.

Dr. Bhatt's medical office was on the first floor to the right of the central staircase. A curtain was drawn across the inside of the storefront window to give privacy from the casual pedestrian's gaze. The sign in the window stated that the office was currently open for patients and posted the office hours as well. The door opened easily into a lobby where there were about two dozen chairs available for waiting patients. The back, interior wall of the room consisted of a closed door on the left and a sliding glass window on the right. Patients were already seated in the waiting area. A middle-aged, native woman with two small children, a tall middle-aged European man, and an elderly gentleman who looked Indian were seated in the waiting room. On the windowsill was a mechanical bell that operated by pressing the clapper on the top.

As soon as he pressed down on the lever and the bell sounded, an Indian woman dressed in a traditional Indian sari opened the sliding glass panel, smiled, and handed Jim a clipboard with a stack of patient information forms attached. A pen was attached to the board with a string.

"Good morning," she said in a strong, lilting Indian accent. "You must be a new patient. Please fill in one of our patient information forms and we will be with you soon. Have a seat in one of the chairs."

"Good morning. I'm not a patient. My name is Jim Henderson. I'm from America. I believe I have a business appointment with Dr. Bhatt for 9:00 AM. Dr. Umbawi made the arrangements." He handed the clipboard back to her.

"Oh, yes, Mr. Henderson," she responded apologetically, looking down at her large desk calendar which had penciled in appointments for the office schedule. "Yes, you are here in the book. Please do have a seat and make yourself comfortable. The doctor will be right with you, he is with a patient right now."

Jim took a seat facing the interior door, as she slid the glass panel back to its closed position. Within a few moments, she opened the door again and called out a name he did not catch. The woman with the two children stood and all three followed the receptionist through the doorway into the inner office. The receptionist closed the door behind them.

Jim was a bit anxious about his need to stay on schedule, but within a couple of minutes, the door opened again. This time a man, who was identified as Dr. Bhatt by the name badge clipped to the pocket on his white lab coat, stood in the doorway.

"Mr. Henderson?" he asked.

"Yes," Jim answered as he stood to greet the doctor.

"Please, come in." Dr. Bhatt was about 60 years old, Jim guessed from his demeanor, a small thin Indian man dressed in the typical, white doctor's jacket, matching white pants, and white loafers. He smiled when Jim approached. "Follow me," he said as he led Jim past the open administration area and back into his private office. Dr. Bhatt motioned for Jim to take one of the two chairs facing an old, wood desk cluttered with papers. The wall behind the desk was covered with medical certificates and plaques certifying the doctor's credentials.

"Please have a seat, Mr. Henderson," he said.

While Dr. Bhatt took his seat in an old leather chair behind the desk, Jim tried to make himself comfortable in one of the stiff, straight backed, wooden chairs that faced the desk.

"Thank you for waiting patiently," Dr. Bhatt said as Jim adjusted to the wooden seat. "My wife, Venubi, whom you met out front, runs the office for me. I told her to bring you right in, but no matter. I realize you have come a long way. I don't want you to have to wait long after you have made such a long trip to come here."

"Thank you," said Jim, taking out his pen and pad.

"Time will be your most valuable resource because you will have so little of it here. Dr. Umbawi explained to me why you are here. Your trip must have been very tiring? Watch out for jet lag. It may not hit you right away, but it will catch up with you, so be careful. You will be tempted to skimp on sleep to take advantage of the limited time you have here in Africa," said Dr. Bhatt.

"Both of my flights were very long. I had an extended layover in Lagos. I was able to sleep on both flights, and I had a nap in the airline lounge in Lagos. I had a good night's sleep at the hotel last night too," said Jim. "I feel well rested now."

"Good, but still be careful."

"I don't want to impose on your valuable office time. My schedule is flexible. However, I have to follow the schedule set up by Dr. Umbawi for me to talk to everyone I need to see to complete my investigation."

"Believe me, you are not imposing, Mr. Henderson. It is a pleasure to have you here. You are very lucky, you know."

"I am?" Jim was curious.

"Yes. This is the beginning of the month-long ceremony of the Diwali Festival."

"No one told me this was a holiday," said Jim.

"It is the Hindu New Year, which is also called the Festival of Lights. My wife wanted me to take some time off, but we will wait. There was so much to do right now, a vacation was out of the question. We had made no plans, so when we heard from Dr. Umbawi that you were coming, fortunately your visit has not interrupted anything. You have an important objective, which is of concern to us all, but first, please let me welcome you to Uhuru. Have you ever been here before?" asked Dr, Bhatt.

"No. This is my first trip to Africa. It's actually my first trip across the Atlantic Ocean. Dr. Umbawi met me last night at the hotel. He was my welcoming committee. And a very pleasant one as well."

"Yes, good. I've never actually met Dr. Umbawi. He was, I'm told, a close friend of the late Dr. Bronston. We spoke at length by telephone the other day when he called to set up your appointment with me today. He seems to be a very intelligent fellow. He is very disturbed about what has happened. I had heard his name before from Dr. Bronston, of course. I only spoke to him this one time when we scheduled this meeting. Perhaps I will have the opportunity to meet him one day."

"I assume you discussed the reason for my being here?" asked Jim.

"Yes, at length. We had quite a conversation."

"I know my task is not a pleasant one. I will have to ask a lot of pointed questions. Besides, one's death is never a pleasant topic," said Jim.

"Well, it is necessary. This sort of thing is, of course, a part of our daily life in this line of work. I must be prepared for it every day."

"Yes, of course," responded Jim.

"I suppose I should begin by telling you a bit about myself so you have an idea of whom you are talking to. I was born in Bombay into a Vaishyas class of business people. I was educated in Bombay. Fortunately, I was lucky enough to get into medical school by a fortuitous set of circumstances that I will not bore you with. I met my wife at one of the medical clinics where I worked during my internship. We left India to come here to seek better opportunities and to get away from the slavery system of India."

"Slavery system? I thought that was abolished world wide," said Jim.

"You Americans are so very naïve. We do not call it slavery in India. We call it our caste system. This is our custom of bonded servitude that keeps tens of millions of our citizens in a state of slavery for life. You are right. Officially, slavery is illegal as is the caste system in India. However, our constitution is not like yours. It is merely a piece of paper. It looks nice at the United Nations meetings, but the reality of India is quite different."

"I just thought slavery as a concept in actual practice was gone," said Jim.

"You Americans know little of the real world outside of your own country. I became a social radical when I was an intern. I had to spend time providing health services to the indigenous people of India. They are lower socially than the main castes. Religion and culture are so interwoven into our social structure, that it is impossible to overturn three thousand years of traditions. To really help the indigenous people, we need to overturn the existing caste system."

"I'm sure it will take time," said Jim.

"Child labor is also endemic in India. We have laws, but there are too many exceptions and the existing laws are often not enforced. Tell me, Mr. Henderson, have you ever been to Calcutta?"

"Calcutta?" Jim responded.

"Everyone from your country should go there for a visit. There is the future of human existence on this earth, unless we can come to terms with the problem of over population and our existing social structures."

"You don't think we will?" asked Jim.

"There are powerful economic interests working against change. Unfortunately, I pushed too hard for reform back in Bombay."

"Your ideas were not welcome?"

63

"I'm afraid not. I was threatened with arrest and beatings for helping the dalits, who have medical needs just like everyone else," explained Dr. Bhatt.

"Dalits?" asked Jim.

"Those are the people who are the lowest, below all casts. They are called dalits. When I became active for the oppressed, just because they needed medical treatment, I faced severe intimidation, and had my life threatened by those who seek to maintain the status quo. All people are equal under the law in India, but only on paper."

"That's a shame," said Jim.

"The only way for the people to fight the inequities of the current system is to organize and stand together. To rebel against the system, they must be wary. They must be educated, and that is where the struggle is being lost."

"How is the struggle being lost? Certainly change will come," said Jim.

"What can be done when there are over seventy million children working for under the minimum wage? They are not in school, Mr. Henderson. As we all know, the way to freedom is through education and knowledge. Perhaps there is some hope for the long-range future, but when I saw my wife worried about my safety, I began to share her concerns. It did not take long for me to be receptive to the advertisements in the Bombay newspapers for doctors to come here to Uhuru. I'm afraid India is a case history of oppression of its own people and change comes too slowly. I did not see how I could make a difference. The Uhuru advertisements were too tempting, so now, we are here. This is a small office, but we can see the results of our efforts working for improvements here. So my little practice has its rewards and is growing slowly."

"I admit I don't know much about India or Uhuru, for that matter," said Jim.

"You would have to go to India and stay for a while to see it to really understand. There is no other way. You know I am Hindi, Mr. Henderson."

"Yes, you told me."

"I am not always proud of what the Hindu's have done. They make up eighty percent of the population of India. The Hindu caste system dominates India and creates the inequities that exist. There are also Christians in India. Many people are not aware of this fact. However, even they have separate churches for the dalits. The Hindu caste system is wound very tightly into the very fabric of the country."

"I admit I'm ignorant of your country and its customs," said Jim.

"Once I became aware of the extent of the problem and how it denied the dalits even the basics of medical care, I could not stand idly by. This is just not my nature."

"What could you do?" asked Jim.

"That was the problem. There was little I could do as an individual."

"I read somewhere that there were extensive grassroots efforts to change the culture in India, to stop they way the under-privileged are handled."

"Perhaps, in time, they will have some success, but you cannot change three thousand years of culture overnight," said Dr. Bhatt.

"I understand."

"I did not mean to digress, but when I saw the ad in the paper for doctors in Uhuru, especially for the program of prevention, it was not a hard decision to come here."

"Prevention?" asked Jim.

"Yes, each citizen and resident is entitled to one government paid medical examination every two years. It is a system aimed totally at prevention of medical problems. Here, there is still a chance; there is hope. In India, I was being swallowed up in what I saw as an uncaring mass populace. If felt meaningless. I was insignificant. I did not feel that I was accomplishing anything. Here, I can make a difference. In Uhuru, my life has meaning," said Dr. Bhatt.

"A government sponsored maintenance program sounds like a good start," said Jim.

"Yes. It is a small success. This general medical office exists within that government program. I am not a specialist. They needed outside doctors when Uhuru became independent. I took advantage of the opportunity to be able to transfer my license from India with very little red tape. Unfortunately, I was not able to bring my equipment. Acquisition of medical equipment and supplies in Uhuru is difficult and expensive."

"I can imagine," said Jim.

"As I remember, Dr. Bronston came here a little over two years ago. He had just started to work here in Uhuru. One of the laborers he hired, when he started his field camp, had been here in this office under the prevention program. Dr. Bronston was referred here by one of his own employees."

"Was Dr. Bronston ill?" asked Jim.

"He thought he was fine. I'm afraid Dr. Bronston was not a man who had much use for medical doctors. I don't know when his last visit for a check up had been before he came to us. I'm afraid it was a long time ago."

"Something must have brought him here. Was it the free examination?"

"No, he did not have any particular affliction when he came in. In fact, he came here because the insurance company from America requested that he have annual medical checkups," said Dr. Bhatt.

"This is interesting."

"I remember his response, because, even though Uhuru would have paid for his annual visits, since he qualified as a resident, he insisted that he pay for his own visit. He brought a special form for us to fill in and send to his insurance company. I remember the form because it was long and quite intimidating," said Dr. Bhatt.

"They sent a form from America for you to fill out?"

"Yes. In my opinion, his first time here was well spent. The insurance company knew what it was doing, Mr. Henderson."

"They knew he had a problem?" asked Jim.

"My records will show he had two physicals. The first, as I said, was over two years ago, and the second just four months ago. He is actually a good example of the wisdom of the government program. Prevention is the key to good health, Mr. Henderson."

"Did you find something on his first visit?" asked Jim.

"Yes. I'm afraid we did. Thankfully, he came in when he did for that first examination."

"Why is that? What did you find?" asked Jim.

"Because, while he was in very good health, generally, he did have one condition that he was completely unaware."

"Was it serious?" asked Jim.

"He had very high blood pressure. In fact, his readings were off the top of the chart. We put him on a prescription immediately that he was to take twice a day. I think it may have saved his life. At least we brought his blood pressure down under control. Since that initial diagnosis, he took his own blood pressure daily. He kept a written record of the readings and brought in his first year readings on his second visit. We kept a copy here in the office."

"Maybe he just ignored his medicine," commented Jim.

"We know he took his medicine because his blood pressure readings showed the effects of the medication. His readings during the intervening year between visits were all in an acceptable range."

"Did you say his last check up was four months ago?" asked Jim.

"Yes. His last physical was a few days or so from being exactly four months ago. Oh, I guess I should say formally that we do protect the client's records in the country, just as you do in America," said Dr. Bhatt. "You know, I thought about it last night, Mr. Henderson. I realized that by meeting with you I had a dilemma."

"I know. I could sense it coming, doctor-patient privilege," added Jim.

"Yes. As an attorney, I'm sure you understand. Well, I wanted to cooperate with you in any way I could, but I had to be concerned with patient confidentiality, too. I decided to walk the line to balance both needs by telling you anything you want, but at the same time, I won't release my internal files. I will however sign any statement you want to prepare that summarizes what we discuss. I can do that if you will prepare it," said Dr. Bhatt.

"That's fine. I'm taking notes now, as you can see. That may be all I really need."

"Did they give you copies of the reports?" asked Dr. Bhatt.

"What reports?" asked Jim.

"The reports for each of the last two annual exams. I had to fill in rather exhaustive reports on his medical condition. As I said, the insurance company furnished the forms. Of course, in our limited facility, we could not do all the testing they wanted, but they accepted the reports without comment. I sent them in each year, and I never heard back from anyone. If I recall correctly, I had to send a copy to the museum as well. As their investigative representative, you should have received a copy of each of them," said Dr. Bhatt.

"I wasn't told about any reports," said Jim. "No one told me about any annual physicals or of the existence of written reports."

"That is typical, I'm afraid, Mr. Henderson. Bureaucracies are impossible. You know, the left hand never seems to know what the right hand is doing, even when they sit right next to each other. Don't worry. The reports were released to your principals, so they should be available to you as well. My wife will give you copies before you leave today."

"I would appreciate that," said Jim. "Thank you."

"Let me do this as well. I can also give you a copy of his blood pressure readings over the intervening year, between his first visit and the last one, just a few months ago. The copies of the blood pressure readings were attached to the last report as an exhibit. I'm sure we have his figures here in the office. Since they were attached to the report, they would also be available to you."

"Thanks again," said Jim. "Any medical information will help me."

"Just keep in mind that his blood pressure readings taken from his last visit here up to the date of his death would be out at his camp, unless of course, the police picked them up. We do not have those records in this office."

"That would be fine," said Jim. "I've marked my notes as a reminder to look for the recent readings when I go the field camp."

"You should have them for your records, although, again, the ones we have show readings in the normal range. Dr. Bronston was instructed that if the figures reached a certain level, someone was to drive him to the hospital here in Elizabethtown immediately. High blood pressure significantly affects the way the brain functions, Mr. Henderson, and can have serious affects on the liver and other soft organs. Immediate medical assistance can prevent serious damage to the patient."

"I've heard that it is something to be careful of," said Jim.

"I have to tell you, we had no such emergency ever with Dr. Bronston. These modern drugs do wonders. While you are writing things down, you should also note that he took his blood pressure condition very seriously."

"What makes you say that?" asked Jim.

"He lived at the camp which was remote from any major civilization. Getting supplies of medicine and batteries for his blood pressure device was not a five-minute ride to the drug store. He had to be sure to keep a supply on hand that would last several months for both his medicine and the batteries. Medicine and batteries were the items he could not run out of. He had to take the time to plan well ahead to obtain them. That's why I think you will find he kept daily records of his blood pressure for the last few months."

"What you are saying is that, in your opinion, he was taking his medicine twice a day and recording his blood pressure once a day regularly even after his last visit four months ago?" asked Jim.

"Yes. Well, let me qualify that. I cannot be one hundred percent certain that he did take his medicine since his last visit, of course. I am sure he did take the problem seriously. He was no fool, Mr. Henderson."

"You're not painting the picture of someone who was about to commit suicide," said Jim. "I mean, he appears to have been seriously concerned about his health. Why would he turn around in such a short period of time and suddenly commit suicide?"

"I can only agree with that observation, Mr. Henderson. You should be aware that other than his high blood pressure problem, he showed no other medical problems according to our examinations and records. He had no complaints, and expressed no symptoms of any problems.

We found no evidence of anything such as cancer, heart failure, kidney problems, or anything else that I could test for in our office, or at the local lab from a blood sample diagnosis. I should add, just for the record, that we do not have the facilities to do a lot of what, in your country, would be considered routine, standard tests for a thorough annual physical. On the other hand, I saw no reason to send him to Nairobi for more tests. Some would say because he may have had high blood pressure for a long time before his first physical, we should have required an MRI. But, again, he showed no signs of damage from prior strokes, and we do not have the facilities yet to have an MRI done in Uhuru."

"So nothing more was done?" asked Jim.

"I saw no need to further inconvenience him. As I said, he would have had to go to Nairobi for any further testing. I did not find anything to justify further testing on a professional, medical basis. You might note that it is possible he had strokes due to the high blood pressure before he came for his first visit. However, he showed no symptoms that I could detect of any damage from prior strokes. I saw no need to look for anything deeper."

"If he had no symptoms of damage, there was no need for concern," added Jim.

"I should add that it is possible, although I think it is remote, that he had any brain damage, or that he was judgmentally impaired due to such strokes. But, again, I have no way of telling whether that was true with our rather modest facilities. Even the blood lab here in Elizabethtown is limited in what it can do," said Dr. Bhatt.

"But you saw no symptoms?"

"Precisely."

"Is it possible he had prior strokes that impaired him so much that he would have been driven to commit suicide?" asked Jim.

"Well, you should write that down as an open issue. In my opinion, strokes do not affect decision-making in that way. There is no known case showing a stroke to caused someone to develop such a deranged mind to the extent of driving the patient to intentional acts such as suicide. The affect is usually much more limited than that. If there were a serious mental problem, there would have been visible signs of altered behavior. You could ask the others with whom you come in contact that very question. Perhaps some outside opinions on his behavior would augment your investigation. I have only what I have studied in my medical training. I have no real experience on the matter."

"I'll try to remember to ask," said Jim.

"I mention the prior strokes issue simply because of the possibility. Stroke victims have burned down their own homes accidentally under conditions of judgmental impairment, given away all their money, but not undertaken acts such as suicide, that I know of."

"I see."

"As for other matters, you will see the reports. They will show that he was in remarkably good health for a person his age. Most people in their mid to late 70's would willingly trade places with him on the health issue," said Dr. Bhatt. "Could I interest you in a cup of coffee? I apologize. I should have asked when you first came in."

"No, thank you. I'm fine," said Jim. "I came here thinking I would find a medical motivation for suicide," said Jim, thinking out loud. "So far, nothing is showing up."

"There was no medical basis for suicide whatsoever. His high blood pressure was the only medical issue I could find, and that has been under control for some time. In modern medicine, we are learning that we have to deal with the whole person, not just the medical problem at hand. It has not been so with your western medicine. I talked to your friend, Dr. Umbawi, about that."

"About what?" asked Jim.

"About Dr. Bronston's whole psychological well being. Medical problems often arise out of other problems that cause stress, fatigue, and mental depression, that sort of thing. There is a very good practitioner in the diagnostic treatment of pain upstairs in this building. He uses acupuncture and has an exceptional record of success with his treatment of pain. I understand acupuncture is now just beginning to be recognized as an acceptable course of treatment for pain in your country."

"Yes. It has been around for a long time, but you have to seek it out. Did Dr. Bronston ever receive such treatment? Did he complain of undiagnosed pain?"

"No, he had no such needs. I just wanted to point out to you that there are alternatives to what is often referred to as western medicine available here. The other office upstairs deals in pain of the spirit and works with hypnosis. People come here also to seek their purpose in life through hypnosis, or to cure diseases we cannot treat in a conventional way. Dr. Bronston needed no such treatment. He knew his life work. My real point was that we, as doctors, must learn to treat the whole person, Mr. Henderson. The physicians here often cross-refer patients in this building. All the doctors here try to treat the whole person, mentally, physically and spiritually," said Dr. Bhatt.

"I think I'm trying to conduct what is called a psychological autopsy," said Jim. "I'm trying to discover what his total psychological state was at the time of his death. It's similar to what you are saying about treating the living as a whole person, not just medical symptoms."

"Yes, that is good. You are looking in the right direction. Everything in the body is interrelated. These interrelationships are not as easily pinned down under close scrutiny as your western medicine would like, but your whole psychological state interrelates with your physical condition. We now know in some ways that the brain generates activity that produces substances that help fight diseases. We know the interrelationships are there, but we have a long way to go to show them at the provable microscopic level that modern, western medicine calls for. It takes faith to accept our way of looking at medicine," said Dr. Bhatt. "Faith, unfortunately, is not yet a part of western medicine."

"I understand what you are saying," said Jim. "But how do we relate this to Dr. Bronston's death? I'm here to investigate a suicide."

"That's the problem," said Dr. Bhatt. "Dr. Bronston had another thing going for him."

"And what was that?" asked Jim.

"He was a free spirit."

"A free spirit?"

"Yes. He had his work. At his age, he was very much full of life. He had goals. He was doing all the things that he wanted to do. His work affected all of mankind. His life had meaning and he was genuinely excited about his excavation work. What he did was more than a job. It was his dream. He committed his life to it at all costs. What I am trying to say is he had no age related ceiling that kept him from going on to do what he wanted. The average person faces forced retirement, and that affects the psyche. To have good health you must find joy in your work. Dr. Bronston had that. He was in an enviable position. We now know that those who retire after many years at the same job face a high potential for heart attack within the first year of retirement. That is a time when people lose their lifelong goals, their life purpose, and their sense of self-esteem. They work all their lives to reach retirement, only to discover it is not what they had thought it would be, and it destroys them psychologically," said Dr. Bhatt.

"I understand. I've heard about that. Even in our culture, we are aware of the problem. I don't think we are doing anything substantial about it, but we are aware of it."

"Before you can have effective treatment, you must first have awareness," said Dr. Bhatt.

71

"Yes, I agree."

"To understand health, you have to understand the whole person. We are increasingly aware of these things in medicine today. However, in Dr. Bronston's case, he was free from the psychological barrier of retirement."

"Yes. I can see how that would be important to psychological health."

"That's why I was shocked as much as everyone when I heard that he committed suicide," said Dr. Bhatt.

"What about personal, financial issues, political, those kinds of problems?' asked Jim.

"They're way beyond the limits of my office. I'll leave that to you to investigate. All I know is that he told me he had an older sister and brother, but they have predeceased him by several years. His wife died a few years ago as well. He seemed to have recovered from that. He has a living daughter who is in good health, as far as I know. No, I don't think there is any related person who could affect him psychologically to any extent to make him take his own life. I really can't help in that area. Outside his line of work, I didn't know much about him. I only had contact with him when he came to my office for his required examinations for the insurance company."

"Can you think of any other area that he may have told you about, even casually, that might have some bearing on his motive for suicide?" asked Jim.

"Not really. In all honesty, I just didn't know that much about him personally. Of course, he is famous. I read all the articles and headlines like everyone else here did, but that did not give me any additional information that would help you."

"I see,' replied Jim.

"You have a clean bill of health from me as far as conventional medicine is concerned for Dr. Bronston."

"Well, that's important to know," said Jim. "I had to rule out medical reasons."

"I wish there was something I could suggest to you that could point you in the right direction, Mr. Henderson."

"What you have done is very helpful. You have helped me eliminate possibilities."

"I'm afraid I am not providing the answers you want or need in your investigation."

"On the contrary, I can a least stop looking for a medical motivation for suicide," said Jim.

"I have encountered suicides before, but there was a clear tie to a serious adverse medical condition. The motive was obvious."

"Finding Dr. Bronston's motive has been elusive so far, but I'm just getting started. I have to eliminate the possibilities as I go. That's all I can do. In time, I'm sure something will come up."

Jim knew the interview was at an end. He stood up to take his leave. They shook hands again. He had taken too much of the doctor's valuable time. He also had his schedule to keep.

"Follow me up front. Let's get you copies of those reports on your way out. Perhaps they will help," said Dr. Bhatt.

"Thank you," said Jim. "I'm sure they will."

"I wish you well in your search. Please let me know what you find. I, too, am curious about why he would do such a thing. I am here if you need help in any way."

"Thank you again. I will remember your offer," said Jim. "Right now, I'll just keep my nose to the grindstone. There's an answer to why Dr. Bronston took his own life here. I know there is. I just have to find it."

CHAPTER FIVE: *THE CEMETERY*

The cemetery was on the west side of the inner city. It consisted of a two-block area completely surrounded by a high, wrought iron perimeter fence. Inside the fence was a thick ring of trees and tall shrubs that provided total privacy from the outside world. According to Jim's cab driver, the founding fathers and early settlers were buried here. Now space was limited for only the rich and famous, and then only by special permit. The taxi driver also explained that the general population now used a newer cemetery several kilometers out on the east side of town. This older cemetery was only a few blocks from downtown.

When Jim passed through the tall, wrought iron gate and entered the cemetery, he noticed that most of the graves were located in a large, open, grassy area in the middle of the grounds. Around the perimeter, within the ring of tall trees, was a well-worn path. From this path, there were short side trails that ran back out into the main open area like spokes on a giant wheel. The graves were located along the perimeter path as well as along the side trails. Jim had no idea of where to look for Nancy. There was no guardhouse with a map nor had Nancy provided him with a map. He simply assumed he would have no difficulty locating her in a small cemetery. He had nothing written down with instructions for finding Dr. Bronston's grave.

When he did not see her out in the open area, he started walking along the perimeter path beside the shade of the tall trees. Here there was little direct sunlight, so he was protected from the strong, hot rays of the sun. Inside the shadow of the trees, beams of sunlight streaked through the occasional openings in the leafy canopy. A tribe of wild monkeys chattered noisily high up in the trees. Along the perimeter path, the graves were overgrown with plants and vines that had been neglected for some time as evidenced by the dense growth. Here Jim felt more like being in a garden than a cemetery.

When he finally saw Nancy, she was on one of the side paths leading back out to the central, open graveyard. Luckily, he noticed her kneeling down at the gravesite on the path since the shrubs and overgrowth were dense in that area. Fortunately, it had only taken him a few minutes to locate her.

As usual, Nancy was dressed perfectly for the occasion. She was wearing a light gray pantsuit with a crisp white blouse topped off with dark gray gardening gloves. She was kneeling by the freshly turned earth on the grave, carefully planting the last of four pots of leafy, green ferns.

The empty pots lay scattered by her knees. The grave was at the edge of the shaded area under the cover of the thick overhead canopy of trees and just at the edge of the open grassy area of the main cemetery.

She must have heard his approach, because she looked up just as he turned down the side path. He felt his heart skip a beat. Suddenly, he realized this meeting might be awkward. "Nancy," he said, as he approached her. His voice was dry and a bit raspy.

As she looked up in his direction, she smiled and stood to greet him, taking off her gloves and leaving the flowerpots and trowel on the ground. Before he had time to figure out what he was going to say, she had embraced him and gave him a solid kiss on the cheek. She was just a few inches shorter than he was. He had not known what to expect, but the intensity of her greeting caught him off guard. She had the natural good looks of a model accentuated by the way she was always impeccably well dressed for every occasion. It was her pixie-like smile that always disarmed him. At museum functions, she attracted men like a magnet, but she was no flirt. She handled men very carefully. Her subtle aloofness and obvious intelligence kept them at bay. Yet, they were still attracted to her. She was very charming in public, a characteristic that made her ideal for her position at the museum. He knew that she was the museum rainmaker, the one who was responsible for bringing in the big donations.

"Jim," she said. "You have no idea how glad I am that you are here."

"Well, I made it," said Jim, awkwardly. "I came as fast as I could."

"So I see," she said.

"It's good to see you, Nancy."

"How are you? How was your trip?" she asked

"Long and grueling. I still feel as if I'm in a hazy dream. It's hard to accept the fact that I am actually here, in Africa. It just doesn't seem real yet. Everything happened so quickly."

"Well, if you're in a dream, you need to come to grips with reality. Dreams are not going to help you in Africa," she said.

"You're right," he said.

"Have a seat," she said, guiding him over to a wrought iron bench that was located a few feet down the path. They sat down together. She put her gloves down the bench beside her. "You need to come to grips with where you are, Jim. I need you to be sharp now that you are here in Uhuru. You probably thought my invitation was a joke, but I was and still am very serious about it."

"Obviously. Nothing really sank in until David Grayson called me into his office. That's when I knew it was real and very serious. I

75

followed your instructions, though. I redid my resume and faxed it to Keith Kendall at the museum, although I admit I thought your request for me to come to Africa was a bit unrealistic. I had already used up all my vacation time for this year, which I thought you knew. Besides, I could not afford the cost of a trip like this on my own. I won't have my law school loan paid off until next spring. Even though I really wanted to come and help you, it just didn't seem practical. I had no idea David Grayson was going to send me here."

"You should not have been surprised. I knew what I was doing. I already had the museum convinced you were the one to do the job. Well, you are here, and that's what counts. You don't look the worse for wear, after such an exhausting trip," she said.

"I'm still not so sure I'm the right one for this investigation. I feel a little out of my league, and a long way from home," he said.

"I understand how you feel, but don't worry. You'll do fine."

"I'm flattered that you went to all the trouble to bring me here," he added.

"The truth is, Jim, you are the best qualified person to do the investigation."

"I don't know what to say about your father's death. I want to say I'm sorry, but that just seems so inept, so empty."

"You don't really need to say anything. What is important is that you are here." She hesitated, and then continued. "After I got the call, I was so busy making arrangements, packing, getting my ticket, taking a cab to the airport, it was easy to hold my emotions in check."

"I'll bet."

"I was too busy then, but it was a long flight from Chicago to Lagos," she said.

"That's for sure. Personally, I thought it would never end," said Jim.

"Once I was on the plane, all my feelings of shock, loss, and grief overcame me. I admit I lost it up there at 30,000 feet, Jim. I'm glad you weren't with me. You would probably have panicked. I would have totally embarrassed you, but I had plenty of time up there to think all by myself and pull myself together for what I had to do when I got here."

"It wasn't fair that you had to make that journey alone," said Jim.

"Life isn't fair, Jim. I was by myself in a way I had never known before. I felt pain and loss I had not felt since I lost my mother. But there is a difference now. Back then, I still had my father. He was my cushion, my security blanket," she said.

"And now he's gone."

"I think I cried all the way across the Atlantic, Jim."

"I'm so sorry. I didn't know you had left until I received your fax."

"I didn't tell anyone outside the museum. Thankfully, the plane was only half full, as they are these days, so there was no one in my row of seats. No one saw me breakdown."

"I wish there had been someone with you. Mr. Kendall was concerned about you, you know, about you being here alone," said Jim. "The museum people were very helpful. They went out of their way to help me catch the first available flight. They really are very supportive and extremely concerned about you."

"I understand that, and I appreciate their concern. I really do, but by the time the plane landed in Lagos, I had struggled out of my grief and pulled myself together. I finally realized I was not the only one who ever had to endure a personal tragedy of this kind. I made up my mind that when I got to Nairobi, I was going to call and ask you to come to Africa. Reality had settled in when the plane landed," she said.

"I'm flattered that you thought of me at a time like that," said Jim.

"I have no one else now. You have to understand, once I made that decision, even before I got here and realized the true situation and how the facts made no sense, my feelings of helplessness were gone. I felt a new purpose, a new sense of meaning seep into my psyche. I had to find out why he died," she said. "I knew you could help me do it."

"I don't see how I could be responsible for all that," said Jim.

"You were, but I think I simply overcame my feeling of grief by doing something about my situation. That one act of deciding to call you helped me refocus."

"Good," said Jim. "I just hope your confidence in me is well placed."

"Just making that small decision started me on the road back to reason."

"You look fine, especially after all you have been through," said Jim.

"That's because I am beyond grief and despair now. I have accepted the fact that my father is gone. I know it will be a long term struggle to fully recover, but I am over the big hurdle."

"That's good to hear," he said.

"Once I can find the answers then I will be able to make peace with his death and I'll be ready to start life anew."

"Well, I'm here to help," said Jim.

"I have to do what is needed here to wrap up the past, then I have to look to the future. I'm willing to stay as long as it takes, but my future is not here," she said.

"You may not be your usual self," he said, "but you look fine on the outside."

"Thank you. The real problem initially, Jim, was that it was just so sudden. One day he was over here doing fine. The next day he was gone forever. There was just no warning."

"That's got to be especially tough for you," said Jim.

"I know he was not a young man, but he was someone I knew was going to live well into his nineties. There is just one thing you must understand, Jim. I have adjusted to the fact he is gone, but I am never going to accept suicide as the answer, no matter what they say," she said, looking sternly at him.

"I don't know if you have seen it yet, but I have a copy of the death certificate. The coroner used the words 'probable' suicide," said Jim.

"That's a cop out, Jim. It's like being a little bit pregnant. I won't accept it. It does not fit. I'm having trouble with the coroner's conclusion. Dr. Umbawi sent me a copy of the death certificate when I was still in Chicago. That death certificate is the real reason why I asked you to come to Uhuru."

"Well, it has been certified and issued. Challenging it now will be an up hill struggle," he said.

"Yes, but I'm having trouble with that cause of death statement. It's the one thing that bothers me. It bothered me in Chicago, and it bothers me even more here in Africa. Something just isn't right. Call it a woman's intuition, or call it whatever you want, I can't deny my feelings about it," said Nancy.

"What do you think happened? Do you have an alternative hypothesis?" asked Jim.

"That's just it. I don't, but suicide just doesn't make any sense. You never met my father," she said. "If you knew him, you would understand why it doesn't fit. He would never do such a thing."

"I have to look to you, Nancy. I didn't know him. What they gave me in Chicago before I left wasn't much. I need to know more about him and his life if I'm going to unravel the cause of his death. I need to know all about his normal day to day behavior. I have to look at his habits and do a victimology study. They call it a psychological profile. I need to put his death in an overall perspective, especially since it is suspicious," said Jim. "I'll have to get inside his mind. I need to think the way he thought on his last day."

"That's exactly what I wanted to hear you say. You are on the job already. I knew you could handle the investigation."

"Well, it's the truth. I may not have any experience, but that's what I've got to do," said Jim.

"My father was born in a small farming community about seventy miles south of St. Louis, Missouri. His father was a prosperous farmer there, but Dad never had any interest in farming. It took too much time away from his real interests."

"What did he like when he was in school?"

"When he was young, he was small for his age. He did not participate in athletics. Reading, studying nature, and looking for Indian artifacts were the things he loved to do most."

"I'll bet he did well in school," added Jim.

"He did very well. In fact, he excelled. He grew up in a Presbyterian household and was steeped in a biblical background. He got a scholarship and went to a top university in New York."

"That would have been quite a culture shock for him, going from such rural country to the big city," Jim observed.

"That's where he developed his interest in the human past and specifically archaeology. I think his early college years were a bit troubling because of the conflict with his religious upbringing, but he worked it out in his own way. He took a teaching job at a college in Chicago after he graduated."

"He could have had a pretty easy life just teaching college. How did he get into field work?" said Jim.

"Things changed when he was invited to go on an archaeological expedition to Ethiopia. One of his former professors back in New York invited him to go. The invitation came after his first year of teaching, and that was it."

"That was what?" Jim asked.

"He was hooked on field archaeology. He literally fell in love with Africa and archaeology on that trip. All at once, his teaching career was over."

"So he left and went to Africa," Jim added.

"Yes. My mother and I accompanied him on his first three annual trips, but we lived in a rented house in Nairobi while he went out in the field during the week. Kenya was born out of a violent revolution not that long ago. We were concerned that there might still be some strong anti-white sentiments," she said.

"Things have changed."

"Yes, we did not know much about Africa. Neither of us had caught the archaeological bug like he had. We didn't really care for roughing it in the primitive conditions he had to endure to do his work. When

79

my mother's health started to fail, and he increased his involvement in Africa, he moved the family from Chicago back to St. Louis where my mother had friends and family. We were not rich, but my father was a good provider. We never had any financial problems. My memories of my youth are that we were comfortable, not rich and not poor, but comfortable. The only problem for my mother and me was just that he was always so far away. He was rarely there for us physically or emotionally, actually more like never."

"Africa is half way around the world," Jim added.

"Right. When I was young, we traveled throughout Africa. Whenever he came home to St. Louis, we always took a trip to the museum in Chicago."

"The museum has sponsored him for years. How did he find his sources of funds?" Jim asked.

"The first year he went to Africa as a member of someone else's expedition, but he wanted his own expedition. He didn't like the politics and the personality clashes that are inevitable on someone else's expedition. He found funds through grants at the university where he taught in Chicago. I think someone at the college made the contact with the museum, and helped bring the museum in as a co-sponsor the subsequent year. When my father started to produce significant finds, the museum stepped up their support and became his primary sponsor. It was one of the smartest things they ever did," she said.

"Smart for them or for your father?"

"The museum was able to leapfrog over the more well known museums on the east coast with first rights to casts, exhibits, and the ability to participate in the public exposure that came with the important discoveries. Their tie to my father gave them an inside track to Africa, which the other big American institutions did not have."

"I see," said Jim. "They each made each other's reputations."

"Yes. It was a trade off. My father had reasonably secure funding so he could concentrate on fieldwork instead of spending his time looking for funds. On the other side, they had exposure every time he made an important discovery."

"It always seemed to me from what I read, that your father had more than his share of the important finds," said Jim.

"That was a function of looking in the right area and having the eyes of Mobutu. The real key to his success was often dumb luck."

"Luck?" Jim asked.

"You have to be in the right place at the right time, often just after the rains expose something new."

"Your father helped you get your job in the museum, too," said Jim.

"My mother and I both loved the museum. When all my girl friends were falling in love with high school football players and rock stars, I fell in love, not with a boy, but with the museum. My dream when I was little was that I would someday have my own office in the museum. I never wanted to be just a housewife," said Nancy.

"Your dream came true," said Jim.

"Yes, and my father played the key role in seeing that it did. I know that. I have been lucky. I'm not anti-marriage; I'm just not the barefoot and pregnant type. The museum is my real life. You're right. My career is a dream come true."

"It's funny I should come all the way to Africa to have this conversation with you, but I think I understand you now more than I ever have before," said Jim.

"Your problem, Jim, is that you never asked much about me, and you were not a good listener either."

"You're right. Right now I need to understand more about your father so I will listen carefully to everything you say so that I can learn more about your father. If he was doing what he wanted to do and didn't need to worry about forced retirement, why would he commit suicide? There's still something missing from what you have told me."

"That's just it, Jim. He was so up, so motivated. He was busy and involved with his work. He had all the reasons in the world to keep on working and keep on living."

"That's what you keep telling me."

"Taking his own life is out of character. I know I haven't been here to see him for a few months, but he would never change on that score," she said. "He just didn't have the personality traits for someone who would commit suicide."

"I met with his physician first thing this morning," said Jim.

"Oh great. Dr. Bhatt?" she asked. "Dr. Umbawi mentioned his name and told me he had scheduled an appointment for you to talk with him. I've never met him."

"He was most cordial, a very dedicated professional man," said Jim. "And he was very cooperative. He gave me everything he released to the insurance company. I could not ask for more. It was interesting that I had to come here to Africa to find out the insurance company and the museum had required him to take an annual physical for the last two years. Dr. Bhatt filled in reports for them. No one told me a thing about his annual physicals."

"I didn't know about them either," she said. "Dad would have seen them as an inconvenience and big interference with his work. I'm surprised he showed up for his appointments."

"Well, the last one was only four months ago. Your father had a clean bill of health except for high blood pressure. Dr. Bhatt diagnosed it two years ago during the first examination."

"I think Dad may have told me that he was taking medicine for high blood pressure, but that's the extent of what he said to me. It seemed to be just a matter of course, no big deal."

"Well, you should know, the doctor did not find anything else, so I came away with no medical motivation for suicide. Dr. Bhatt said he was personally shocked just like everyone else. I remember him saying that most men your father's age would envy your father's good health," said Jim.

"Medical problems can be one of the more frequent reasons for suicide," said Nancy. "It's just that my father didn't commit suicide. What you are saying fits right in with my opinion."

"I think we can rule out medical causes," said Jim. "I still have to stick to suicide for the moment, because that's what the death certificate says. I'm going to have to rebut it for my client. I just don't know where to begin. Right now, I'm concentrating on finding a motive for his suicide."

"Just remember, the conclusion is wrong, Jim."

"Dr. Umbawi suggested that, when you don't know why something happens, you should follow the money, but suicide rules out the collection of life insurance. The money has not changed hands yet. The policy was in favor of the museum, so I asked myself on the flight, why would he want to hurt the museum? He loved the museum, and it provided his funding. There was no answer, so I'm trying to understand who would benefit the most from your father's death? I think that's the key question now."

"I don't think I ever told you, but I am the beneficiary of a hundred thousand dollar life insurance policy with another company for Dad's life. Dad placed it with them last year. I'm sure that policy will be lost, too, if the suicide determination holds up," she said, "So he would be hurting me, too, if suicide was the cause of death. I know in my heart he would never do that. He really discovered and loved me more after mom died."

"That's very interesting. I suppose you know there wasn't any inquest or hearing, either. They just used the police report to make their determination," said Jim. "I didn't know about your insurance policy, but you are right. You have the same problem. If he wanted to help you, he would not have taken his life and cut off the benefits of the policy. That doesn't make any sense."

"I talked to him weekly, but I don't remember him saying or alluding to anything unusual or out of character over the last month," she said. "I keep reviewing our conversations in my head, over and over again, but nothing stands out as unusual or different in his voice or manner."

"He didn't give you any hint of personal trouble?"

"I'm sure he didn't have any personal or financial crises. Don't get me wrong, we were not rich. He made maybe fifteen hundred a month under his agreement with the museum, over and above his costs and expenses. That's not much. Our small house in St. Louis was paid for and we didn't have any real expenses either. We were included in a blanket medical plan through the museum and they paid the premiums."

"That was worth a lot by itself," said Jim.

"The museum sent his checks by direct-deposit into a joint account with my mother in St. Louis so she could pay the bills. As you probably know, he could not be paid in Africa under the labor laws that restrict foreigners out of the labor pool. That sum was above the general operating costs for running his camp, so we always got by. They frequently wired money to him here in Africa for the operating expenses. He paid his laborers locally. What he earned may not sound like much in the States, but out here it was all savings. As long as she could, my mother paid the local housing expenses out of their joint account."

"I will need to look at all of his accounts, both personal and the operating accounts for the camp."

"Yes, of course. I'll make those records available for you. He also had the proceeds of my mother's life insurance policy, and he had the proceeds of the sale of the house in St. Louis after she died. He didn't have to depend on his pay for fieldwork at his age, although that was his life. He could have been a college professor or speaker and done quite well almost anywhere. He was well known internationally. He could have written a book about his life, but he loved what he was doing, and he did not like distractions from his work."

"So, he had a one track mind," Jim added. "Did he have any other interests at all?"

"No, Not really. He was not interested in material things. His needs were simple. Oh, he had an inheritance from his father too, but I don't know how much that was. When I get back to Chicago, I'll have to straighten out his estate. Right now, I don't have all the details," she said.

"Don't worry about that right now. I'm getting the picture. Dr. Umbawi also said your father's death didn't make any sense, but sometimes we find out we really didn't know people as well as we thought we did. He also said that if there were a motive, I would probably find clues out at the field camp," said Jim.

"That makes sense. The field camp at Bokuru was his life, so there isn't anywhere else logically to look. I have set up the schedule so that you and I are going out there tomorrow morning," she said. "My father spent all of his time out there. Lately he was talking about trying to keep Bokuru open through the rainy season that runs from January to the end of April, so that the camp would be open year round. If it didn't work out and the weather forced a temporary closing during the wet season, he told me Dr. Tubojola offered to put the whole crew to work at the museum here in Elizabethtown until after the rains, but my father had already decided to try to keep Bokuru open."

"Then he must have found something interesting," said Jim. "Or else he was pretty sure he was about to find something. Why else would he want to stay out here in the rainy season?"

"I don't know about that, and I don't know what to tell you to look for when we get out to the camp. There isn't really much out there. It may sound romantic and exotic to the uninitiated, but it's basically a place to eat and sleep out from under the strong African sun and rain. The excavation pit itself is just a hole in the ground. The living is rustic, to say the least. I hope you came prepared."

"That's why you had me bring everything in duffle bags," Jim reminded her. "The ones I brought are small marine bags I use for sailing, but I followed your instructions explicitly"

"Good. Dr. Umbawi may be right, but don't get any great expectations about Bokuru."

Jim looked over at Nancy and gathered his thoughts before he spoke what he was thinking. He began slowly, "We've never discussed the possibility of an accident," said Jim. "What if the gun went off accidentally?"

"That does not make any sense, either," said Nancy. "My father didn't own a gun. In fact, he hated guns and he prohibited them from his camps, against everyone's recommendation that he should have at least one around for security. I was scared to death of lions, hyenas, and snakes when I went out there. I wanted him to have a gun out there in case a wild animal became a threat."

"Lions?" Jim asked.

"They are out on the plains, north of the camp. Mobutu and my father always told me there were no man-eaters in the area. They said the local lions follow not just the wild animals, but also the herds of domestic cattle, sheep and goats. They said lions and other predators leave the camp alone due to their natural fear of man. The thing that always bothered me was that the Masai would bring their herds in close to camp when they bring them to the river for water and when the herdsmen drop in to the camp for medicine. That would place the camp at greater risk since the herds were so close."

"I didn't know your father was a medical doctor?"

"He wasn't. The camp is always stocked with simple things like aspirin, bandages, eyewash, iodine, alcohol and other over the counter pills and first aid items. I'm bringing some items with us to restock the camp tomorrow. It pays to be on good terms with our neighbors, and the herdsmen are the only neighbors out there."

"I didn't know you provided medicine for them."

"It is just simple stuff, Jim. In any case, my father would not have been playing around with a gun."

"What you're saying is that if he had one in his possession, it would have been a recent acquisition for the sole purpose of taking his life," said Jim.

"I suppose you could say it that way," she said. "I don't know where the gun came from. Just try to understand that he would not normally have brought a gun into the camp."

"A young man named Johannson picked me up at the airport. He told me he was part of a temple group that is out there somewhere along the river. He said he had been a member of the militia in Minnesota. He also said he worked for your father part time. Maybe he took a gun out to the camp," said Jim. "I would think he would be competent around guns with his training in the militia."

"I thought Dr. Umbawi picked you up?" she asked. "That was the plan."

"He was supposed to, but he had car trouble. He arranged for this temple group to send someone to help out. Dr. Umbawi was waiting for me at the hotel here in town once I got in from the airport. Do you know this Johannson kid who picked me up? He said he worked for your father."

"He was not around when I visited Dad at the camp six months ago. My father never mentioned his name. He must have been hired after I left," she said.

85

"I think he just worked part time. Anyway, the main issue we will have to deal with when we are out at the camp will be where the gun came from, and how your father came into possession of it."

"Just remember, my father was totally set against guns. I remember we had a neighbor back in St. Louis who shot his wife accidentally when checking out a burglary late one night. That was many years ago when I was just a little girl, but Dad never forgot it. The woman died from the injuries she sustained from the unintentional gun shots by her husband."

"You never told me that story before," said Jim.

"The point is, Dad did not like guns and avoided them."

"I feel a bit overwhelmed. On the flight from Chicago, I thought a suicide investigation would be pretty straightforward. Do you really think I'm the right one for the job? I'm not a detective you know," said Jim.

"Just remember who brought you here, Jim Henderson, and why. All I know is that my father is gone. Why, Jim?" asked Nancy. "I want to know why. That is the question for you to find the answer."

"Right now, it seems to be a pretty big question," said Jim.

"Remember, the death certificate is just someone else's opinion," she said.

"If it's the wrong cause of death, the real cause is not going to be easy to find," said Jim.

"You are going to have to look at every detail, Jim. It's not going to be easy, but I have faith that you are the one to do it. You are my only hope."

"Well, I don't think I'm off to a very good start," said Jim. "Dr. Umbawi is going to obtain a full copy of the police report for me, so I can take it with us and read what they found. Hopefully, that will help."

"I hope so."

"Well, whether the event was accidental or intentional, the first question is, how did he wind up with a gun?" asked Jim.

"Someone had to bring one out to the site," she said.

"And he had to find out about it and gain access to it," said Jim. "I'll have to ask everyone there about it. I need to trace the gun carefully. At least, I have that to work on. Just keep in mind, if he intended to commit suicide, he could have bought a gun here in town and brought it out to the camp himself without telling anyone. Once he made the decision to commit suicide, he would be looking for a gun no matter what his previous position may have been," said Jim.

"Talking to the people out at the camp will be a good place to start," she said.

"Yes, I agree. I'm curious about his recent blood pressure records, too. I'd like to see the ones for the last few months."

"Right now, Jim, there's only M'Bee, the cook and housekeeper at the camp; Mobutu, the excavation manager, plus the two native laborers, whose names I forget," she said.

"Plus the two part time day laborers from the temple. Don't forget, one of them was the guy who picked me up at the airport," said Jim.

"I don't know about them," said Nancy. "Remember, my father did not have anyone like that working out there on my last trip half a year ago," she said "You will have to find out about them and establish that there were actually two others from the temple working there."

"You haven't been back to the camp for six months?" asked Jim.

"No. Tomorrow will be my first visit since that trip. Remember, I will pick you up in front of the hotel at 8:30 AM tomorrow morning. And, don't bring that suit. Just bring the items I told you to bring. You're going to be camping out at Bokuru. It's really primitive out there," she said.

"Yes, you warned me. I did follow the directions in your fax carefully when I packed." Jim paused for a moment, deep in thought. "I still have to assume that your father pulled the trigger. Let's start with that for now. Why would he do it?" asked Jim.

"And that, Jim, is precisely why you are here, to answer that question. If you can't answer it, you will have to find out how he died."

"I'm with you, but right now I need a break. I need a lead to work on. I feel I'm going out to the camp empty handed."

"You think I can help you," she said, "but it is up to you to find the answer."

"Well, my strategy is to eliminate all the reasons I can think of so the one we are looking for is all that is left. For instance, were there any dramatic events with relatives that could have caused him to take such drastic action? I know your mother died several years ago."

"Yes. She passed almost five years ago, but he adjusted to her death, at least as well as you can expect someone to. I think he came to accept her death within the first year. No, that could not be the motivator that would push him over the edge. He would have done it a long time ago if that was his motive. Not now," she said.

"How about other relatives?" asked Jim.

"He had much older siblings, a brother and sister, but they both predeceased my mother by several years. He knew lots of other people who have died, but none of them was as close to him as Mom. I'm his only living relative, and I'm doing fine," she said, smiling.

"I'm not trying to pry. I'm just looking for some event that would motivate him to conclude that the only option he had was suicide, no matter how farfetched it may be. I think you have eliminated personal and family emotional causes. How about personal financial matters? Is there anything else you can think of to add as a possible motivator for him to commit suicide?" he asked.

"No. I think I have already told you what I know. His life was simple. His expenses have always been covered. He probably had three or four hundred thousand dollars in the bank. That may not amount to much in today's world, but his needs were nominal and I don't think he ever tapped that money. I grew up feeling secure during my childhood. There were no serious monetary crises. I know he got bonuses on big discoveries, and fees for speeches, articles and things like that, which also boosted his savings," she said. "I didn't know how much they were. We never talked about money at home. Financial matters were not of concern to me until it came time to go to college."

"I'm not hearing any personal financial crisis of a magnitude to cause him to want to end his life," said Jim.

"That's because there wasn't any," she answered. "He had plenty of job offers if he wanted to stop doing field work. He had his Land Rover here and an older car in storage in St. Louis that had almost no mileage on it. That was the car that he bought for my mother. I don't know much else about it. I have my own subcompact on lease in Chicago."

"I know. You're totally independent," said Jim.

"Yes. He would have been fine just doing a few speeches a year, if he wanted. He could have bought a condominium overlooking the lake in Chicago if he wanted."

"Did he ever gamble or get into drugs, alcohol, or anything like that?" Jim asked.

"Goodness, no," she laughed. "He was the original stuck in the mud tea totaler. He has worked out here in the savannahs of Africa for over fifteen years. He never went to Vegas and he had no gambling problem. Alcohol and outside women were not a part of his life. He had absolutely no interest there. His work was everything. Besides, there's no way he could get into trouble out here on the open savannah."

"I understand," said Jim. "I'm just trying to be thorough."

"I wonder if anyone can really understand," she said. "You know, I think his true dream, the one that kept him going, was that somewhere out here he was going to find, not just a fossilized bone or two, but a whole skull with a face," she said.

"A face?" Jim asked.

"Yes, a fossilized face of one of our ancestors. You know, fossilized skin, a true face staring back at us from a million years ago."

"That sounds a little far fetched," said Jim. "I thought only bones fossilized."

"It is possible, Jim. They have found fossilized skin from way back at the time of the dinosaurs. Anyway, I think that was his dream, the one thing that motivated him."

"That would really be something special," said Jim.

"It was a dream of a real tangible thing, not just a few bits of fossilized bone where creative artists try to put features on canvas. He wanted to see what our ancient ancestors really looked like. He would rather find something like that, than win a big lottery. Do you understand?"

"I think so," said Jim. "Anyway, I'm crossing off personal financial issues as possible causes from my list."

"Keep going, Jim," she said. "Just remember you are going to wind up where I did."

"Where is that?" he asked.

"With no answer." They both sat in silence for a while, letting those words sink into their minds.

"Was he in good shape with his grants and rights to dig?"

"You know, I am not sure," she said. "That's a good question for Dr. Tubojola to answer. He's the one person who would know the status of his permits and applications with the Department of the Interior. He is probably the only one who could answer those questions. All that information had to be on file with his application for permits to dig at Bokuru."

"I'll remember to ask it this afternoon when I meet with Dr. Tubojola."

"I know that Dad had plenty of sponsors. Everyone wanted to back him. They were lined up. His international reputation assured financial support for life. As long as he was in the field, he had the attention of the international press. Whenever he found anything, the world spotlight was immediately on him. Some people spend a lifetime seeking fame. He had it about once a year, and it would last for months."

"He was lucky," said Jim. "I read about your father when I was in school. He was famous even back then."

"He did not cherish the attention. He recognized that it was a necessary evil to get funding. You know, the museum and even the people here in Uhuru want me to take over this site and replace him. Everyone identifies success with the Bronston name," she said.

89

"That's why everyone wants you."

"That is the one thing that has held me back. I don't think I could handle it. I'm a private person, Jim. I think notoriety and publicity are my biggest fear," she said.

"I think all they want is for you to finish this one site," said Jim.

"Perhaps, but my fear is still there," she said.

"Maybe your father didn't find anything of significance at this last site, so there's nothing to worry about, " said Jim.

"You may be right," she said.

"Did your father ever say anything about what he discovered?"

"No, but my father usually didn't announce any discovery until the work was done, and he was sure of his position and the status of the findings. He never took me into his confidence about any of his findings until he was ready to publish and make his announcement to the press," she said.

"Well, maybe you'll get off easy."

"How's that?"

"Maybe there's nothing at Bokuru," said Jim.

"We'll see when we go out there tomorrow," she said. "We'll know first hand. Give me a day or two out at the camp, and I'll make up my mind if I am going to stay, but that's it, Jim. I have no interest in becoming a field archaeologist like my father. I love Chicago. That's my home."

"I was wondering about that. I thought maybe you'd get the fever and want to continue in his footsteps," he said.

"No way. I may stay, but it will only be to finish my father's work at Bokuru. After that I'm on the plane back to Chicago," she said.

"From what you have told me it seems that his life was uneventful other than for his archaeological discoveries."

"We only had moments of high excitement when he discovered something at one of his archaeological digs. He would be in all the magazines, on television, and in the papers. Then after a few weeks things would die down again while he looked for another site." she added.

"I see."

"You know, you have to meet Mobutu. He has been with my father for over 14 years. My father called him eagle eyes, because he's the one who actually found the first bits of fossilized bone exposed by erosion after heavy rains that led to the big discoveries. He can spot a small half inch piece of hominid bone separate from all the other rocks from twenty yards away. Once he spotted something, my father would then open a camp and excavate for months until they found all the other pieces in association with that first one. Then he would put the pieces together and try to reassemble actual bones."

"So the first pieces were right on the surface," Jim asked.

"Usually, yes. At least the first piece is. After the initial find, they would excavate and sift the area all around the one they found on the surface."

"I see. The key is the recognizing that first piece of bone they see on the ground as significant."

"Yes, but Bokuru is totally different," she said.

"Keith Kendall told me they didn't find anything on the surface."

"No they didn't. They didn't start Bokuru from a surface finding. What happened was that a geologist from the Department of the Interior found what appeared to be the top of a cave where the ridge above it had been worn away by wind and rain. Dr. Tubojola thought the cave was promising and asked my father to take a look. Dad decided to excavate down through the roof. He didn't even dig a trial trench first. They had no fossils to work with, but he decided to excavate the whole cave."

"So he just assumed they would find something significant?" asked Jim.

"Yes. Anyway, Mobutu is in charge of running the general excavation operation, and he is the one who looks for bits of hominid bone in every ounce of overburden they sift through."

"That sounds like a lot of work. Our Chicago excavations were always pretty small, not much work."

"You know, Mobutu doesn't get the credit he deserves. It's just only recently that he has been given some recognition in the press. He should get a lot more attention and credit than he has in the past. In many ways, he has really been the key to my father's success. They have been a good team together," she said.

"I am looking forward to meeting him," said Jim. "From what you are saying, he should be a lot of help."

"You are beginning to see the scope of your assignment," she said.

"Maybe your father's field notes out at the site will help, too," said Jim.

"Yes, that is a good idea to check the official record books. They could be very helpful in providing any information on what has been found. My father may not have disclosed findings to the press, but his field records would be accurate. In the meantime, perhaps Dr. Tubojola will have some insight for you this afternoon," she said.

"I'm looking forward to the interview. What can you tell me about him? All the museum people gave me in Chicago was a brief biographical sketch."

"I've met him on several occasions, mostly when I was little. He's an important man here in Uhuru. Not only is he curator of the national museum here in Elizabethtown, but he is also the Minister of the Interior, which includes being Director of the Department of Antiquities for the whole country. He's one of the top officials in Uhuru. Someday he'll probably be president. You were able to schedule an interview with him because Dr. Umbawi knows him personally," she explained. "Dr. Umbawi is a consultant here in Uhuru."

"That's exactly what Dr. Umbawi told me about Dr. Tubojola," said Jim.

"He should be able to help you, if anyone can."

"I was just thinking about Dr. Umbawi," said Jim. "You are both in the same boat with Dr. Bhatt. No one seems to know any reason why your father would commit suicide," said Jim. "You are all leaving me with no answers for my investigation and lots of questions."

"That's because my father didn't commit suicide," she said again. "I don't care what the coroner says, or what they put on the death certificate. My father did not commit suicide. There's no way he would do that. In a couple of days, you will reach the same conclusion on your own."

"Then how did he die? No one believes it was an accident," said Jim. There was an awkward period of silence. Nancy did not answer him. Jim did not know what more to say.

Nancy appeared lost in her thoughts for a moment.

"How's your mother?" she asked, breaking the silence.

The question was a total change of subject, and caught Jim off guard, to his relief. "Well," he responded, thinking slowly, remembering. "I suppose I should say she's fine. She's still there in the nursing home in Carbonwood, Illinois. She looks fine. In fact, she's much the same as when you saw her last, just a little older perhaps," he said.

"You seem to be holding back. You're not telling me something."

"You're right. You know she has Alzheimer's?"

"Yes, I knew she had short term memory problems," she said.

"Well, now it's much worse. When I go there, she doesn't recognize me. It's upsetting. She doesn't know who I am. She'll sit in her wheelchair, holding my hand smiling, but she doesn't have a clue as to who I am. She's just as happy with a stranger doing the same thing. I'm convinced she thinks Jose is her son," said Jim.

"Who's Jose?" she asked.

"Jose is the male orderly who is assigned to her at night. He sneaks her ice cream and cookies from the kitchen. He is always there for her," said Jim, feeling a tug of jealousy. "I can't compete with him."

"Jim, you don't have to," Nancy responded sympathetically. "He's just doing his job," said Nancy. "It appears he is doing it quite well, too. Things could be much worse. Relax, be happy she has Jose."

"I know you're right. It's just that going there is an empty experience. I don't get anything back from her. There's no essential response from her. It's a hollow exercise," said Jim.

"You know a little about my father, Jim. Just remember that he didn't even know he had a daughter until my mother died. I don't think he wanted children, but if he did, he wanted a son to carry on for him. It wasn't until my mother died that he really discovered me. My mother essentially raised me by herself since he was in Africa most of the time. All of a sudden, he realized that he had ignored me when I was young," she said. "Look at me, Jim. I'm the one who gets nothing back. My father is gone. He was all I had. Don't expect so much from your mother. The day you realized that she didn't know who you were was a day of real change in your life."

"It was?" he asked.

"Up until that time you went to visit her because of both her emotional needs and yours. That day changed things. You could not help her anymore and she could not help you. Just remember from then on your trips down to the nursing home have been for yourself, not for her, she doesn't even know that you are there," she said.

"I never thought of it that way."

"You are so lucky you still have her, and she is in a kind and caring facility. A lot of people don't have that. You'll be miserable unless you understand why you visit her now. When I leave Africa, I will leave his grave forever. I will only have memories. I won't be able to visit his grave whenever I want."

"You're right, Nancy. But it is still very hard when I realize she doesn't know who I am," said Jim sadly. "We take so much for granted until we lose it or something changes."

"Maybe now you can begin to let go, Jim. She has been your whole life. Even you admit you might not have graduated from law school but for her motivation and her sacrifice for you. She kept you going. Now you are on your own. You are like me. You must reach down inside yourself to obtain your own motivation. You can't borrow any of that energy from her. You have no wife and kids, but that was not possible while she kept you with your nose to the grindstone. No female could compete with her. There is life after work, Jim. You may not realize it yet, but there really is."

"I'm sure you're right," he said. "You have excellent insight."

"It's the story of the apple of knowledge," she said.

"The apple of knowledge?" he asked.

"Yes" she said. "You bit into the apple of knowledge. The innocence of life has been lost forever."

"So, the apple is my problem?" he asked.

"If you realize what has happened and recognize that you have lived an unbalanced life, perhaps then you have a chance. If you can see the apple, you can see the tree from which you picked the apple. Maybe you can see it for what it is," she said.

"You mean there's hope for me, yet?" asked Jim, trying to inject a little humor into their conversation.

"Sure, there's hope, but you cannot go back to innocence lost. You bit the apple. You can never go back. I don't mean that there is no hope for you. You can become a normal human being, if you can let your mother go."

"I thought you majored in business management, not psychology. As long as I am not hopeless, I feel better," he chuckled. "For the last year I haven't received any real emotional return from my work with the firm. Everything has been boring, a simple routine, at least until this trip."

"See what I mean? You have a chance. First of all, you need to think about your future after this trip."

"My future?" he asked.

"Sure. You're not going anywhere with the firm. They are a family of rich boys playing at being lawyers. They are really just coupon clippers," she said.

"Coupon clippers?" he asked.

"They already have their wealth. The firm is small. It's just an extended family. You can't grow or advance there because you're not family. You're an outsider, and you always will be. There is no upward mobility for you there. You have to develop your own practice; your own clients or you have to move on. You can do it now while you are young or you can do it later when it is more difficult."

"Well, you're right. It is a family business, and they have one real practitioner who is not family. No one is going to replace him," said Jim.

"Yes. See what I mean? I think you should consider tax work, especially advising the wealthy on how they should make donations. If I were you, I would go ahead and get an advanced degree in taxation. I could send you clients. We can't help them at the museum. I could send you referrals. You could build a business in that direction, if that's what you wanted to do," she said.

"That might be a good idea," said Jim. "I hadn't thought of that. That would help you get donations, too."

"I spend time building the confidence of potential donors, so I know they will listen to my referrals. There's a lot of estate work, too," said Nancy.

"That sounds interesting," said Jim. "I didn't think I was coming to Africa to discuss my career back in Chicago."

"I think I know enough about you to see that you need something more than just going to the office each day," she said. "You need something of importance and meaning to you. I'm just trying to come up with an idea," she said.

"My apple problem," he said.

"Yes," she said. "You need something. You just can't sit back and live a routine day-to-day existence. You don't seem to be into baseball or football and you don't seem to be the gardener type. I think you need to look for something that will hold your interest and give you a sense of purpose. In a way, you are like my father. He was fiercely independent. Oh, I know he wasn't a good father when I was young, but he was great after that. He became my mentor. Suicide would have been selfish, Jim. I don't see him doing anything to hurt me. One of those things deep down inside tells me that he didn't commit suicide," she said. "To commit suicide, he would have to make a drastic change in personality, and there is no evidence of that."

"I understand your point," said Jim. "I just don't know where it leaves me in my investigation. I need something other than your deep feelings to work on."

"You know, Jim, I think you would have married young if you and your mother had not jumped on your dream. You would have had a bunch of kids early in life."

"You think so?" he asked.

"Yes. Personally, I grew up without any pressure at all."

"So, where did you get your motivation to go to college?" asked Jim.

"I developed that direction myself. My mother was ambivalent about my future. I don't know where my motivation came from, except that everyone in school thought I was smart, and that I should go to college. Besides, I fell in love with the museum. I knew college was the only way I could get there."

95

"You were smart. A lot of parents push their daughters into early marriages. They want to be sure someone picks up the responsibility for their support and that some one will take care of them."

"My father's independence was a strong influence on me. My father helped me get the job at the museum. I know that. Being realistic, when I look at my own life, I think I'm more of a cold fish than you, so I apologize for anything I may have said about you."

"I've been pretty narrow in my view of things," said Jim. "What you said is true."

"All I can say is that life insurance policy tells me my father didn't take his own life. It would be such a callous uncaring thing to do. If you have to follow the money, think in terms of how it does not flow, Jim. I just don't buy suicide. My father would be cutting me off and cutting the museum off. He would not betray me or the museum that way," she said. "Do you know what he told me once?"

"No. What?"

"He told me not to marry a dreamer. He said I should look for an ordinary eight to fiver, an average guy who spent his weekends cutting the grass and watching football or golf on television."

"He said that?" asked Jim.

"He said dreamers are not reliable. In the end, they would get up and chase their dreams, like he did to my mother. He told me he knew what he had done to her emotionally by chasing his dream. When it finally dawned on him, it was too late."

"Maybe your father was right about you," said Jim.

"My father's death has been a real dilemma. I'm glad you are here. Now it's your dilemma," she said smiling. "At least you now see why I look you in the eye and say he didn't do it. Anyway, you now know why I wanted you here. You are the one to solve the puzzle," she said.

"If Dr. Tubojola can't give me a lead this afternoon, then Dr Umbawi will be right."

"How so?" she asked.

"My only hope for a lead will be out at your father's camp," said Jim.

"Let's hope so. No one is going to be satisfied unless you find a clear, understandable, rational reason why my father would do such a thing."

"But if he didn't do it as you say, then how did he die?"

"Find out what happened at Bokuru, Jim. Something happened out there."

"I'll do my best."

"Well, we better wrap things up here," she said looking down at her wristwatch. "We've got to get you to the museum for your interview with Dr. Tubojola. There is just enough time to grab a sandwich at the cafeteria at the museum if we start now. We can leave these things here. The groundskeeper will clean up. I don't want you to miss the appointment. Dr. Tubojola is a very busy man. I'm sure Dr. Umbawi had to use his best influence to get you in."

They stood to leave.

"I noticed that the headstone is blank," Jim observed.

"Right now, my father is the unknown soldier of African archaeology," she said smiling wanly. "There has been no time to do anything, Jim. Right now, I don't know what to put on a permanent stone, never mind selecting one. This one is just a loaner from the cemetery. I'm still shaken up inside. I'm putting my trust in you to solve this problem. I have no one else," she said.

"Why not, Dr. Umbawi?" asked Jim. "You know him very well."

"He's too involved. He is just like me in that respect. We both suffer from clouded vision."

"Clouded vision?" Jim asked.

"We were too close to my father. We need an outsider with a different perspective to do the investigation. Come. Let's go," she said. "We've got to keep you going, and something tells me you have a long way to go."

CHAPTER SIX: *THE MUSEUM*

At the information booth in the museum lobby, Jim was given a badge to clip to his suit coat pocket. The attendant informed Jim he was already cleared for admission by Dr. Tubojola. The badge was routine to allow him access to the third floor administrative offices. Dr. Tubojola's office, according to the attendant, was located on the third floor at the end of the hall. No one was allowed on the third floor administration area without one of the plastic laminated identification badges he now had clipped to his suit coat. When he exited the elevator on the third floor, no one was seated at the front security desk, so he took the initiative and walked down the corridor to the reception desk that served several offices at the end of the hallway.

Ms. Kenazu, the young receptionist, smiled, glanced at his badge, and pressed a button on a panel on her desk. The latch on the door to the inner office directly behind her released, and the door partially opened. "Please go right in, Mr. Henderson. Dr. Tubojola is expecting you," she said.

"Thank you," said Jim as he turned towards the closed door. When Jim pushed lightly at the door, it offered little resistance and swung open into Dr. Tubojola's office. The room was spacious and comfortably furnished. Dark paneled walls of rare, African woods circled the interior, making the room look very rich and expensive. A huge oak desk filled the floor in the center of the office. Behind the desk, set against the back wall, was a massive, matching combination credenza and bookcase. To his left, two large windows looked out over the city. The windows were covered by thin, almost transparent drapes that were closed to filter out the glare. Through the thin curtain, Jim could see that dark clouds were now gathering over Elizabethtown. It was about to rain.

A large landscape oil painting rested on a wood easel a few feet in front of the windows. Two matching, upholstered guest chairs faced the desk. Dr. Tubojola was seated in a high backed, leather, executive chair. It was swiveled around so that Dr. Tubojola faced a computer screen mounted on a small stand at the side of his desk. From the wrinkled lines on the side of his face, Jim guessed Dr. Tubojola was in his mid-sixties. The one thing that stood out over the arms of the chair was his completely bald head. He wore a white, opened collar, dress shirt, contrasting sharply with his dark skin. He did not look up, but remained hunched over his computer keyboard, staring intently at the CRT screen while he tapped at the keyboard. The soft light from recessed spotlights in the ceiling lit the room, and a banker's lamp with a green, glass shade on his desk added more focused light to the working surface.

Jim hesitated once he stepped into the office, since Dr. Tubojola had not looked up or acknowledged his presence.

"Come right in," said Dr. Tubojola, continuing to concentrate on the computer screen. He had a deep, confident voice. "Go ahead and close the door behind you. It will give us a little privacy."

Jim closed the door.

"Please take a seat. I'll be with you in just a moment," said Dr. Tubojola, still concentrating on the computer screen in front of him.

"Thank you," said Jim, taking a seat in the nearest guest chair.

"I'm just finishing a couple of editorial comments on the site report from Emil Ellington. Do you know of him, Mr. Henderson? He's the reigning authority on the giant hyena that wandered the savannahs of East Africa two million years ago."

"No, I've never heard the name," said Jim, weakly, feeling more than a little uneasy that his host had still not looked up to visually acknowledge his presence.

"Emil is from Eastern University in Ohio. Since you have some interest in archaeology, I thought you might have been exposed to some of his work on ancient East African carnivores. Unfortunately, his report needs to be completed and approved by my office today to be able to obtain his Ohio funding voucher for next year's excavation work. Emil needs to put some meat on the bones, so to speak. It's a shame really."

"A shame? Why?" asked Jim, still feeling a bit awkward.

"Dr. Bronston's site, where he died, was a cave site."

"So I have been told," said Jim.

"Everyone here was hopeful that the cave might have been used as a hyena den. I told Emil we might have an ancient midden for him. Unfortunately, poor Emil ran out of time and had to finish up his report. The problem was that Dr. Bronston died before he announced any findings or filed a report. Emil's university will not wait. His report is pretty basic, and a bit hastily done, but it will get by with a little touch up. I'm afraid Mother Nature has not been cooperative in yielding her secrets to Emil. Ancient hyena dens are truly rare. Ah, there we have it," said Dr. Tubojola, smiling broadly as he made a final tap on his keyboard.

Suddenly, the computer screen went blank.

"My secretary will be proud of me. I think I signed off properly for once. Emil will have a hard copy in time to make his flight."

Dr. Tubojola turned around in his chair to face Jim, and then stood to greet him properly. Jim quickly stood to face him. The doctor was an imposing figure. He had a heavy build and stood over six feet tall. When he extended his hand, Jim found his own suddenly swallowed by the grip. "Mr. Henderson," he said, smiling again. "Welcome to Uhuru and our new museum."

"Thank you," said Jim, smiling lightly as his hand slid out from Dr. Tubojola's firm grip.

"Please sit down. Feel free to take off your coat and tie if you wish," said Dr. Tubojola, returning to his seat. "Personally, I gave up on coats and ties years ago. They are such a burden. So few people seem to wear them these days."

Jim sat down but did not take off his suit coat.

"Please excuse my lack of courtesy. It was important that Emil have his report. Time is of the essence here, and I didn't want to lose what I had on the screen. At the same time, I didn't want to leave you out in the lobby after so long a journey to get here, so I had my secretary send you in anyway," said Dr. Tubojola.

"Believe me, I understand," said Jim. "I have the same problem at the office."

"Computers are everything these days. They seem to control what and how we think. They control our lives. It's amazing how we have become so dependent on them in the last 30 years. I'm sure, as an attorney, you have felt their intrusion as well."

"Oh, yes. They have their advantages and disadvantages," said Jim, feeling a little more at ease. "I certainly agree with you. We can't live without them. Yet, they are far from perfect."

"I guess I should welcome you to Africa, but I think Dr. Umbawi may have already beat me in doing so," said Dr. Tubojola.

"I met him last night. We had dinner at my hotel."

"Yes, of course," said Dr. Tubojola. " Now, tell me, Mr. Henderson, what do you think of our museum here in Uhuru? Does it measure up to your Chicago standards?"

"I haven't seen much yet, but so far it's very impressive," said Jim. "Frankly, I'm surprised to see such a modern facility out here in this remote part of Africa. It would seem that a frontier town like Elizabethtown could not support such a facility."

"Our goal is to attract the worldwide tourist and professional market, not so much the local citizen. If the museum looks up to date, it is because it is new. We designed this facility with the most current technology available. We have had the advantage of being able to learn from the mistakes of others around the world."

"Well, you appear to have done well," said Jim.

"I hope so. The shell of this structure is an old colonial administration building constructed by the British back in the 1800's."

"Just like my hotel," offered Jim.

"Yes, The Grand. I believe both structures were built around the same time. This building housed the offices for the government that ran the Uhuru Territories. When we took it over, we gutted the structure. We even dug out a basement, which now extends out under the streets."

"It's a good restoration. It almost looks new," said Jim.

"We blocked out all the windows on the two main floors, which you will see for yourself if you look closely when you go back out onto the street."

"Why would you block out all the windows?" Jim asked.

"The only functional windows are here on this third floor level. The third floor was transformed into offices to free up the exhibit floors. All the administration offices are up here. There are no windows on the exhibit floors and, of course, there are none in the basement."

"But why block them all out?"

"There are a couple of reasons. The curator of any museum will tell you that the most important asset he has is space, and that to me means no windows. Windows simply take up too much important wall area. Secondly, windows create reflections and glare. You cannot place a glass display case in front of an unblocked window. All you would see is reflections and uncontrolled light. Glass creates all sorts of haphazard visual interference with the displays. You need focused lighting for an effective exhibit. A good museum must control all interior light to provide the proper highlight for its exhibits. Outside light is the enemy of the curator, Mr. Henderson."

"What you say makes sense. I had never thought about it before. This is an attractive facility, although I have not had the time to go through any of the exhibits yet," said Jim.

"Your badge entitles you to free access to the main exhibits. You should take some time to see the main displays while you are here."

"I'll try to do that," said Jim. "Right now, I'm on a pretty tight schedule."

"We want every relevant seminar, every convention in prehistory to come here to this facility. We had to build an auditorium in the basement of this facility, which took up more valuable space because there were no large meeting rooms anywhere in Elizabethtown. Without an auditorium, we would not draw the conventions which bring in the scientists and tourists," said Dr. Tubojola.

"What about The Grand? It should have convention rooms?"

"The hotel has a lot of atmosphere, but it does not have the facilities to handle large conferences or meetings. It was built in a different era with different needs. The dining room, which is now the restaurant, is quite large, but the acoustics are terrible and don't serve large gatherings for speakers very well. We had to yield exhibit space to be sure we could attract conference and convention business to Elizabethtown."

"It must have been a difficult decision to yield exhibit space," said Jim.

"We must be state-of-the-art to attract conventions. Of course, you are quite correct, the most important issue for every museum is display space."

"You sound as if you have used up your display space already?"

"All museums, worldwide, have the same need for additional space. No matter how well they planned in advance, all have space problems. Most people do not realize that the majority of the museum space requirements are not in the exhibits. The exhibits probably represent around 10% of the museum's collections, and the collections are constantly growing. The facilities, on the other hand, are growing by unplanned expansion. We are not immune simply because we are new. We have already removed all our storage items from the basement and moved them to offsite facilities. The basement has absorbed our expanding exhibits. The problem is that no museum is shrinking, that I know of. In any case, our museum is one of the cornerstones of our plans for the economic growth of Uhuru."

"From what I have seen, you should be very successful," said Jim.

Dr. Tubojola paused for a moment, then picked up two sheets of letter size paper from an open folder on his desk. Jim recognized the resume he had amended and faxed to Keith Kendall back in Chicago a few days earlier. Obviously, his resume had been circulated in Africa before his arrival.

"I was wondering, before we start, if perhaps I could ask a couple of questions about your resume?" asked Dr. Tubojola.

"Certainly," said Jim, cringing a bit, well aware of his weaknesses.

"I am curious about your professional archaeological memberships."

"Membership in the local organization shown is open to anyone who is interested in archaeology, attends the meetings for a year, and pays the dues. There is nothing more to it than that, I'm afraid," said Jim, quietly.

"And the state organization?"

"Membership is required. When you join the local chapter, you automatically have to join the state association as well. They are tied together. The officers of the local chapter are usually professionals and graduate students. The senior officers go to the state meetings. Both organizations are run by the professional archaeologists and professors. My career as an attorney does not allow me the time to become involved enough to assist in the leadership of the organizations," said Jim.

"I see you have participated in some of the field excavations in the suburbs of Chicago."

"Yes, sir. All my field experience has been at Indian habitations and refuse midden sites northwest of Chicago. We're just one step ahead of the subdivision developers."

"How old were the sites?"

"The carbon 14 dates for all the sites where I worked dated from 500 to 1500 years ago," said Jim.

"Loose soil less than two feet deep?" asked Dr. Tubojola.

"Yes, sir."

"Who were you working under? Who was in charge of these excavations?"

"Overall supervision was by Dr. William Maywood, if I remember correctly, but he never came to the site when I was working. The other professors and students led the digs."

"Bill Maywood?"

"Yes."

"Well, good. He's one of the best in the business. If he was your supervisor and instructor, you have made up in quality what you appear to lack in quantity of experience. Do they have an organ?"

"An organ, sir?" asked Jim.

"A house organ. An internal publication where the graduate students can publish their work?"

Jim was impressed. Dr. Tubojola was thorough. He had completely dissected the archaeological section of his resume in a few questions.

"Yes. It's a state publication. It comes out monthly and is mailed to all the members of the state organization," Jim added.

"That means the publication is funded by your state dues. Tell me, do you read it?"

"Yes. Ever since I joined, I have read all the issues thoroughly. The articles are very interesting."

"Very good. My only comment on your legal experience is that it does not seem to be focused on personal injury or matters of violent death, but that, of course, is not my concern. I will leave that to the experts in such matters."

"My professional background is focused on obtaining and preparing evidence in commercial litigation cases," said Jim.

"Yes, of course, and that will be relevant here, I'm sure. In case you are wondering, I have personal reasons for asking questions about your archaeological background. I will come back to in due course. I think my only comment for the moment is that your experience appears to be adequate. You have to remember that I had no part in the selection of the investigator into Dr. Bronston's death. That is not my issue. Dr. Bronston's death is outside the scope of my department."

"I see," said Jim.

"I was given your resume as that of the person selected as investigator to be sent here by the insurance company. I was asked to cooperate in any way I could," he said, looking sternly at Jim.

"I admit my archaeological background is that of an amateur," said Jim, trying to recover from what he perceived as the damage that had been done.

"Yes, I understand, but you have been exposed to the basics. You know the terminology and the concepts. You can read a report and understand it. That should be sufficient here for what you have to accomplish," said Dr. Tubojola, putting Jim's resume back down on his desk. "Did Dr. Umbawi send my resume to you?"

"The museum in Chicago faxed me a copy. I read it. I know that you are the head of this museum, and you are the Director of the Department of Antiquities," said Jim, trying to recall the details of the biographical sketch he had left back in Chicago.

"You are right. I am Curator of this museum. In that capacity, I do report to a board of trustees. I am also Minister of the Interior of Uhuru, which includes the Department of Antiquities. I report to the president of Uhuru, whose responsibility is to the legislature. We are a small country so many of us public servants have multiple roles, at least for now. As you can see, I prefer to keep my office here in the museum. Although my roles are strictly administrative, I should be in the new ministries building, but there is no space for me over there. It is a modern, glass structure, but frankly, the facilities are much nicer here, and this office suits me just fine. I like the ambiance of this place."

"It's very nice," said Jim.

"Large, classical, stone structures are hard to find in East Africa. Due to the high costs, no one builds them any more," said Dr. Tubojola.

"You have to be able to live in your office. You spend a lot of time there," said Jim.

"Yes, and I am comfortable here. Your hotel has a long history as well. It has served as a hotel since it was first constructed. Even though they renovated it a couple of times, they managed, never the less, to keep the same old charm," said Dr. Tubojola. "My only criticism is when they did the renovation, they did not upgrade the facilities. They have no modern conference rooms. I have no idea where they got all the stone for these two structures back then. I know the stone was not quarried locally, because the stone is foreign to this part of Africa. I have a feeling a lot of our people paid a heavy price for the effort to settle the British Empire here."

Dr. Tubojola paused for a moment, then continued. "A look at your resume tells me why Miss Bronston was so insistent in recommending you for this investigation," said Dr. Tubojola. "I would not worry about your amateur archaeological status."

"I'm here to investigate a suicide, but I have had little to work with so far," said Jim.

"Perhaps we can help. I want to apologize again for being so rude when you came in, but I was under a deadline to finish my approval of that report."

"You'll have to forgive me," said Jim. "It looked like you were either grading a paper or writing it yourself."

"You'll understand my role better after you have been here awhile. We operate quite differently here in Uhuru from what you may be used to in the States. Well, anyway, that's done. Let's talk about why you are here. I think I can say I know who you are, and I am aware of your mission. You know who I am, and what my positions are. I think we have sufficient foundation for our meeting. Oh, there is one thing I might add."

"Yes."

"I am Kikuyu. I was born in Kenya and revoked my citizenship when Uhuru became an independent republic twelve years ago. I am a citizen of Uhuru. I think I often dream in Kikuyu although my education has been totally European, specifically British. I only say this to alert you to the fact that you and I should perhaps anticipate a cultural misunderstanding or two."

"I'll keep that in mind," said Jim.

"I might add that I know you are on a tight schedule, Mr. Henderson. I respect the fact that you have traveled so far to conduct your investigation," said Dr. Tubojola. "Right now you must be running on sheer adrenalin. If it hasn't hit you already, jet lag will catch up to you eventually."

"Thank you for warning me. I'm fine so far. "

"Before we begin, May I offer you some coffee, tea, or a perhaps a brandy? I can have them brought up here for our convenience. There is no problem," said Dr. Tubojola.

"No, thank you. I just had lunch with Nancy Bronston in your cafeteria downstairs in the lobby," said Jim.

"I asked myself before you got here, what could I do to help you? Why would you want to interview me, of all people? What could I possibly offer to the investigation that others could not?" asked Dr. Tubojola.

"Dr. Umbawi thought you would be helpful," said Jim.

"Perhaps I can. I came up with two reasons. First, I knew Dr. Bronston both personally and professionally for many years."

"I need to talk to everyone who knew him here," Jim added.

"Yes, and that is, in part, why you are here, with me right now. My position as Minister of the Interior and as curator of this museum also gives me special knowledge of some aspects of Dr. Bronston's life that you will not get anywhere else."

"Your perspective is important to me," said Jim. "I believe Dr. Umbawi thought you would be helpful to me also. Dr. Umbawi set up this meeting because he thought you would be useful in my investigation," said Jim. "Everything I know about you was provided on the brief biographical sketch that was faxed to me in Chicago. It described your formal positions in the government and your educational background. I'm dependent on your suggestions as to how you may help the investigation. I defer to your judgment. I only hope you don't mind if I take a few notes as we go along?" asked Jim.

"Please proceed. I have no objections," said Dr. Tubojola. "In fact, I have taken the liberty to press the recorder button here on my desk so that our entire conversation will be taped, that is, as long as you do not object."

"Not at all. That would be fine," said Jim.

"Good. Recording our conversation will give you two options in addition to your notes. You may take a copy of the tape or obtain a written transcript, at your expense. Of course, I might add, transcription here at the museum would be quite reasonable, depending on the duration of our conversation," said Dr. Tubojola.

"Fine. I may want to do that."

"Good. Just let me know your plans. The typing service is up to you. I think, however, that your transcription costs will be a lot less here than in Chicago."

"You are right about that," said Jim.

"Fine. Now, feel free to interrupt me at any time if you have any questions."

"Please proceed," said Jim.

"I thought I would be of better service to you if I took the initiative since I know what you are looking for, as opposed to you entering into a general fishing expedition, guessing what knowledge I might have," said Dr. Tubojola.

"Thank you," said Jim. "You're right. I'm on the short end of knowing what questions to ask."

"The key to your investigation is in knowing your subject. Stop by word processing on your way out. We have a dossier on Dr. Bronston here in our files. You passed the door to word processing on your way here. It is back down the hall. You'll see the sign."

"I'm sure I'll find it," said Jim.

"In addition, there is a good book on Dr. Bronston by Peter Chambers of Great Britain published about two years ago. Dr. Umbawi is meeting you tonight for dinner, is he not?" asked Dr. Tubojola.

"Yes, he is," said Jim. "We're going to meet in the restaurant at my hotel."

"Good. I asked him to bring a copy of Peter Chamber's book with him to loan to you. I think it will be good reference material. Dr. Umbawi told me you did not have any real time to prepare before you were rudely drafted into your investigation," said Dr. Tubojola. "That book might help you."

"Dr. Umbawi's right," said Jim. "I barely had time to pack."

"When you come back to Elizabethtown from your trip to the camp, I'd like to take you around to meet our staff and see some of the exhibits I think may be relevant to your investigation."

"Thank you for the invitation. I'll take you up on that," said Jim.

"For the moment, you should know that Dr. Bronston did not have a close relationship with anyone on the museum staff or with my department staff. He knew most everyone by name, of course, but he spent his time out at his excavation camp. I think it's safe to say that I was his primary contact both with the museum as well as the government, so I totally understood Dr. Umbawi's request to give you some time," said Dr. Tubojola.

"Dr. Umbawi has been very helpful to me so far," said Jim.

"He's from Kenya, but he's on retainer with both the museum as well as my department. We have a close professional working relationship."

"I know I'm imposing on your valuable time," said Jim. "I wish I was better prepared with specific questions."

"Please relax, Mr. Henderson. The one thing you can do here with us is to be at ease. We do understand your concerns. Please consider yourself among friends. We will help in every way we can. Feel free to contact us here at the museum at any time just as you would Dr. Umbawi."

"Thanks again," said Jim. "I think I'm going to need all the help I can get."

"I should add that you might not always receive such a warm welcome in Africa. There are those who may resent the fact that an outsider all the way from America has been sent to investigate the death of our Dr. Bronston. They will say there are plenty of qualified people here in Africa."

"I've wondered about that," said Jim. "It appeared to me that it would have been cheaper and perhaps more efficient to use a local investigator."

"The initial inquiries from the States about what happened and why did not yield positive results. Over here, we were all in a state of shock. No one had any idea why Dr. Bronston would take his own life," said Dr. Tubojola. "Chicago detected our uncertainty over the event and elected to send their own investigator."

"The death certificate reads *probable* suicide," said Jim.

"Yes. Outside of the police, no one here could accept suicide. I think you will find, if you have not done so already, everyone you encounter will concur. Not only are they having trouble accepting his death, but they do not believe suicide was the cause."

"That is exactly the reaction I am getting so far, and not just from Nancy," said Jim.

"Everyone in this museum and my department has reacted in the same manner. In any case, we did not instill any confidence in either the people from the museum in Chicago, or at the insurance company. I'm not even going to discuss the issues of cultural or racial bias that may have crept into the decision making of what we saw as a simple local issue. The important point is that Chicago sent you, and it is up to us to make sure you are most welcome," said Dr. Tubojola.

"So, here I am."

"Yes, of course. Miss Bronston, I might add, was most insistent that you were the one for the job. I'm sure you know her opinion is held in high regard over here."

"How well do you know Nancy Bronston?" asked Jim. "I know you recommended her to replace her father."

"I've met her on many occasions over the years. The first time I met her was many years ago when she was just a little girl. The last time we met was at her father's funeral. Those of us who have been here at the museum a long time have watched her grow up."

"You have recommended that she replace her father, the most well known paleoanthropologist in Africa. Frankly, her archaeological background is the same as what you see on my resume. We have shared our field experience as well. She chose a different career path than her father."

"Yes, but you do not give yourselves credit, Mr. Henderson. I know who you have been working with in the field. Your experience is of the highest quality, however, you do ask a valid question. I do not wish to dismiss it lightly. We know her strengths and her weaknesses. Archaeology was not her major in college, but it was a minor. Most of her courses were supportive of building the background she would need to run her own site. Some of the most significant people in the field here in East Africa do not have a formal education of the same caliber. What she lacks in field exposure can be backed up here at the museum. We know her father was one of the very best at reconstruction of fossilized bones. His only known hobby, if you could even say he had one, was in putting together jig saw puzzles. His knowledge of anatomy, past and present, was world class in American vernacular," said Dr. Tubojola. "He enjoyed the challenges of jig saw puzzles from the natural world. That was his passion, his life."

"I think Nancy is concerned about her qualifications in that area," said Jim.

"That was my point. We have Mr. Ernest Smythe on staff here at the museum. He is on loan from the Coroner's office in London and working on his doctorate here. He has excellent skills in the determination of cause of death by bone analysis. He is very promising and will one day be a shining star in his field," said Dr. Tubojola. "He is just one of our staff members we can make available to her. His knowledge of anatomy past and present is the best."

"I think you need to tell her that," said Jim.

"Yes, you are right. We plan to meet after you return from Bokuru. Our agenda includes all the issues involved. Everything will be on the table."

"Fine. I think that is what she needs," said Jim.

"Miss Bronston is well qualified although, as you point out, we also have good field people here in East Africa. However, she brings two things with her that put her ahead of the local competition."

"And what is that?"

"She brings the Bronston name, and she also brings the museum in Chicago with its strong financial resources."

"She is Assistant Director of Finance," said Jim, proudly.

"Yes, exactly. The Chicago museum has been the primary financial support for Dr. Bronston for years. They have also been responsible for sending many academics, students, and tourists to Uhuru with their American dollars, which our country so desperately needs."

"They are paying all my expenses," said Jim.

"Frankly, the Chicago museum's involvement is crucial to our small struggling country. We hope there are appropriate tradeoffs. They have a trump card over the big museums in New York, Boston, London, and Paris. Their close support of Dr. Bronston has kept them in the limelight, Mr. Henderson."

"But will Bokuru bring international attention?" asked Jim.

"Let me come back to that question in a moment. Try to understand, the Chicago museum wants Miss Bronston to replace her father at this site as much as we do. Having her do so makes sound economic sense for all of us. The Bronston name is an important factor for all of us."

"Yes, but again, you are assuming Bokuru is significant," said Jim. "If it is a dry hole in the ground, it won't matter to anyone."

"You're right. I will come back to that issue, but for now understand that the Bronston name is known worldwide. Having her step in will keep world attention on this site, if, as you say, it is important. My only point is that her name is gold in this business. We need her for her name, if for no other reason."

"I think that is one of her concerns," said Jim. "I don't think she wants to be a figurehead."

"You're right. That was a poor choice of words on my part. We need her as a manager. She will bring much to the excavation effort at Bokuru. The workers already know and respect her."

"That's a good point," said Jim.

"My real concern is that we can support her where she is weak."

"I agree. You don't have to convince me. You have to convince her," said Jim.

"I'd like to come back to her and to your question, but, for the moment, let me tell you a what we know about Bokuru. You should know that all living humans on the earth today are the same species, *Homo sapiens sapiens*. We evolved from a direct ancestor, *Homo erectus*, a hominid that was anatomically similar to us, and walked upright over two million years ago. The major difference from our ancestors was mostly that it had a smaller brain capacity. *Homo erectus* had a post- cranial anatomy that was almost identical to our own. *Homo erectus,* in turn, descended from *Australopithecus africanus*, a hominid more apelike than man, to make a long and complicated story as short as I can."

"Modern science has learned a lot about the ancient past from these ancient ancestors," said Jim.

"All we know about these ancient creatures comes from field people wandering around with magnifying glasses looking on the surface of the ground for bits of fossilized bones. That's where everything we know began, Mr. Henderson."

"Field people like Dr. Bronston," said Jim.

"Precisely. Whenever it rains, loose soil is washed away exposing small pieces of fossilized bone. When the archaeologist finds a bit of hominid bone, a grid pattern is marked out for excavation so they can look for more parts related to the exposed bone. The archaeologist then applies for a permit to excavate the identified grid. Oh, I should say that in South Africa ancient caves have been important archaeological sites, but generally surface observation of flecks of fossilized bone are what start the whole process, especially here in East Africa. Except, that is, for Bokuru," said Dr. Tubojola.

"So Bokuru is an exception?"

"Yes, but I'd like to back up a bit. I'm getting ahead of myself. I have the cart in front of the horse, so to speak," said Dr. Tubojola.

"That's fine."

"Uhuru is a young country, and we are poor with few natural resources. We were born more out of emotion than common sense. Every asset no matter how small is important to us," said Dr. Tubojola. He turned and retrieved a box of cigars from the credenza behind his desk. "Have a Petit Pierre, Mr. Henderson," he said, holding the open box out to Jim.

"No thanks," said Jim. "I don't smoke, but please feel free. I don't mind the smoke. I enjoy the smell of cigars. I just don't smoke myself."

111

"Thank you," said Dr. Tubojola, who took a moment to prepare to light a cigar for himself. "This brand is one of the best from Cuba. A gift from an important political visitor. Cigars are one of my few vices, a luxury of my position. We don't command the salaries you do in the States so we grab at the few perks we can."

Dr. Tubojola, first sniffed, then gently stroked the length of the cigar. After relishing the aroma for a brief moment, he carefully snipping off the end, and then unceremoniously lit it.

"I understand," said Jim, smiling lightly, as he thought of David Grayson back in his office in Chicago who also enjoyed cigars. He watched Dr. Tubojola pause again, for a few moments after his first puff, sit back in his chair, and puff again on his cigar. Jim was amused that both Dr. Tubojola and David Grayson shared the same ritual when handling a cigar.

"When you came to Uhuru, you had to show a drivers license, passport, evidence of medical condition, proof of required inoculations, and all the surrounding red tape, just to obtain your visa to enter Uhuru."

"Yes," said Jim. "It was quite an ordeal."

"Every foreigner who comes into the country must have a valid visa. What you need to remember is that all visas expire on a predetermined schedule," said Dr. Tubojola.

"Yes," said Jim. "My visa is for thirty days."

"We collect revenue from every source possible, Mr. Henderson. You have the standard tourist visa, but there are other classes. This brings us to the first area of questions you undoubtedly have thought of. Dr. Bronston, as a foreign national, also had to be here under a visa. His visa was under a special professional visa reserved for teachers and professionals involved in education and research. That category we also use for foreign archaeologists. As you may anticipate, that class of visas cost quite a bit more than your tourist visa, but it is issued for up to five years and can be renewed without a lot of red tape. What you need to know is that Dr. Bronston was only two years into his present renewal period at the time of his death. I realize this information is of no help in your search for a reason for him to take his own life, but may still be meaningful. What is important is that he was here legally and was under no threat to have to leave soon. He had no problems with residency."

"Thank you. That's the kind of information I need," said Jim.

"But it does not help give you your answer," said Dr. Tubojola. "Now, as I said before, you find fossils by wandering around looking on the ground. You must be licensed as an archaeologist under, what some people refer to as, our anti-pot hunter law even if all you do is explore the terrain looking for needles in a haystack."

"We do not have any strong national laws in that area," said Jim. "All we have are a few state laws without much teeth."

"Trust me, Mr. Henderson. Our laws here for archeological finds have teeth. Now, to get a license as an archaeologist, you have to pay a stiff fee and meet educational and professional standards. These requirements keep out the undesirables. This license is renewed annually to maintain control and standards. However, once obtained, the license is easy to renew, as long as you continue to meet the rigorous requirements. Also, for your information, this license is issued and monitored by my department."

"I see," said Jim, as he continued to take notes.

"Dr. Bronston was about three months from needing a renewal, but he would have had no reason to anticipate any problems with the renewal of his license."

"That's important to know," said Jim.

"You are just a tourist, Mr. Henderson, nothing more, nothing less. In our country, it's unlikely you will make any significant archaeological finds in thirty days."

"That seems to be an effective law," said Jim. "It's important for me to know that Dr. Bronston had no licensing problems."

"The next thing you need to be aware of is that, if you find a bit of fossilized bone you think is significant, even to pick it up, you need to set a grid and apply for a permit to dig that particular site. The regulations for excavation permits are even more formidable. There are more stringent requirements for an individual to qualify for such a permit."

"I understand," said Jim.

"In addition, the application for an excavation permit requires that you put up a bond to assure completion of the project and restoration of the land when the project is done. The national government has to be ready to step up to the plate in the event the archaeologist does not complete the promises made in the application. In addition, the applicant has to demonstrate that the financial resources are available to complete the project and restore the land," said Dr. Tubojola.

"You are thorough. We don't have that level of standards in the U.S."

"Yes. We are amazed that your resources are not protected, and private persons can establish private rights to what we have established legally as public property. Hopefully, we have learned from other's historically bad experiences. What is important to your investigation,

113

however, is that Dr. Bronston's excavation permit was in good standing. The archaeologist applies for the period of time he anticipates is necessary to complete the project. If that period seems reasonable and the archaeologist qualifies, we approve the permit."

"For a small country, you have adopted a very carefully structured law," said Jim.

"We think so, Mr. Henderson. Now, if the archaeologist needs more time, we allow permit extensions with only a simple, written explanation. The application process is not a heavy burden. What you need to know is that I sign and approve all permits and then they are managed by my department."

"What was the status of Dr. Bronston's permit for the site?"

"You may want to mark in your notes that Dr. Bronston's permit was only a couple of months from expiring."

"Oh?" asked Jim.

"Let me assure you, for his site, a renewal of the permit would not have been a problem. I would certainly have approved it. Such a renewal is just a matter of providing a revision of how much more time you need and why. It is not a big deal. I can say that I have never turned down a request for an extension, if that helps you," said Dr. Tubojola.

"Yes. Thank you," said Jim.

"I know, for example, that Dr. Bronston was digging down to the bottom of a cave. No one expected it to be so deep, so no one thought he would be digging for as long as he was."

"I see," said Jim.

"Once again, I know I'm not helping to find your suicide motive. I am simply trying to help answer the questions I thought you might have. Unfortunately, that's all I can do."

"You are way ahead of me," said Jim. "Your information is right on the money."

"For your investigation, you must know that Dr. Bronston was a most favored visitor here. He was welcome to stay as long as he wanted. We would have gone out of our way to assist him in any way we could," said Dr. Tubojola. "For your understanding of his state of mind, I am sure he was completely comfortable with his legal status here, in all respects."

"Thank you. That is important information I need to know," said Jim.

"Perhaps there is one more thing you might find of interest," said Dr. Tubojola. "We do recognize private rights in real estate, but the concept is a bit different than in your country. All real estate here is on long-term lease. We do not have fee simple ownership. In addition, all leases are for surface use only. You can build a house, a ranch, plant crops, run a farm, feed your herds, but you do not own the property, and you have no rights below the surface of the ground. All property below the surface remains the property of Uhuru, and that specifically includes our archaeological heritage. Dr. Bronston could have dug to his heart's content, but anything he found would have still belonged to Uhuru. He could not legally have kept it."

"I understand. Other countries are doing the same thing these days," said Jim.

"Yes. It's our third world anti-western approach to things we want to protect. We want to stop the rape of our cultural and antiquities from our cultural and natural resources by outsiders. The archaeologist can make casts, take photos, publish reports and take credit for any discoveries, but the original artifacts belong to us forever and must remain here in Uhuru. I might add, those artifacts are how we build the exhibits for our museum and develop traveling exhibits on loan to other museums around the world. This ensures that our economic strength continues to be generated by new discoveries."

He paused for a moment studying Jim as if to see if the impact of his words was being effectively absorbed. He paused until Jim stopped writing on his pad. Then he continued. "This is a Kikuyu nation, Mr. Henderson. The population consists mostly of farmers and cattlemen. Maize is our largest crop, and our soils are not especially suited even for that. If you want to study our fossil records you must come here on our terms."

"And bring money," said Jim, smiling.

"Precisely. My job is to maximize the value of our limited resources. The average tourist spends over $2,500.00 in American dollars in Uhuru, where, comparatively, our average citizen earns only around $150.00 per year. Our general population exists below subsistence poverty level, even by standards for Africa. We cannot look internally for a tax base at this time, so we first attract foreign businesses and money, then tax the outsider who has much deeper pockets than the native African." Dr. Tubojola paused to take another puff on his cigar.

"I see the painting of a lake and buildings on that tripod over there by the window. Is that a new hotel?" asked Jim.

"It is much more than that, Mr. Henderson. What you see is an artist's rendition of the proposed Lake Kamaju tourist area for the north basin of Karanga."

"Karanga?" Jim asked.

"Yes. Karanga is the name of our new wildlife park. I am surprised you have not heard about it. The marketing program is already underway. That painting is also close to what the South Basin Project looks like today."

"The basin project?"

"Yes. Karanja consists of over one million hectares of land that was just semi-desert a few years a go. With the advent of global warming of the earth, more areas are becoming desert each year. Modern science shows that the deserts in Africa are expanding. With an increasing human population, over the long term we are going to need to reclaim the deserts of this earth."

"That sounds like a major undertaking," said Jim.

Dr. Tubojola took another slow puff on his cigar. "What was once a broad green savannah supporting vast herds of wild animals became arid over the last two thousand years. No one wanted that land because it was so dry and unusable. As a result, there was no political opposition when we dedicated it for a park. The South Basin Project was undertaken first because it was the easiest part to do. It is both close to Elizabethtown and to the upper Bokuru River. We spent three years digging out the lake and sculpting it for different habitats, then we covered it with layers of old canvas tarps. The tarps were then covered with gravel, sand, and finally a base of river mud."

"Why not simply line it with concrete?"

"Good question, Mr. Henderson. We are funding the project with an International Bank loan, and the available funds are not sufficient to pay for the high cost of concrete and the labor to put it in. The tarps are actually thousands of surplus military tents from the World War II era. Our experts tell us they will last long enough for the lake to build it's own foundation, so when the tarps rot away years from now, the lake will hold its present level."

"That's ingenious," said Jim. "I'll bet the tarps were donated?"

"Yes, of course. The water area you see in the artist's rendition of the planned lake is located at the north basin site. The tourist centers at both ends of the park will be almost identical. I wish I had a good photograph for you of our progress at the south end, but I don't have one in this office."

"Could I go out and see the south entrance in person?" Jim asked.

"The south basin area is not scheduled for opening until March, I'm afraid."

"It looks inviting."

"Our goal is for the tourist to be able to visit one observation area and see the African big five, perhaps from the balcony of their hotel room. If you come back in March, I will provide you and your personal guests with courtesy entrance passes. We have hand planted over two million trees and plants especially grasses, and still have another million to go before the opening. The park will look even better then. We will have brought in much of the wild life by March. Unfortunately, we cannot relocate the wildlife until the area is ready. Hopefully, we can start that phase in January," said Dr. Tubojola.

"Your park has to be expensive, especially since it is built on such a large scale. I thought the International Bank only made loans? How will you ever pay them back?" asked Jim.

"We have, in a way, mortgaged a part of our future. The future revenue from tourist dollars that the park brings in will be used to retire the debt, but it is not as expensive as you might think."

"How so?" Jim asked.

"The land was free and the labor cost is low. Even a poor country like Uhuru has recessions. We are at the right period to bring in cheap labor now. My department is the largest employer in the country. Most of what you see in the painting was done at the south end by manual labor. The plants and animals are simply relocations, not acquisitions."

"The hotel complex in the painting can't be cheap," said Jim.

"You're right. It's not, but both the one already built and the new one planned for the north end, are being built by a Japanese consortium, using their own capital. We have simply provided the land under lease. The investors will be paid off from revenues the hotels generate, while at the same time the hotels will be creating a tax base for Uhuru."

"How about evaporation? With the extreme heat in Uhuru, won't your lakes simply evaporate?"

"The south lake is easy to maintain because we can control the water level and the massive sprinkler system we are installing by pumping water from the Bokuru River."

"You have undertaken a tremendous project, but one thing bothers me, Dr. Tubojola."

"What is that?"

"What you seem to be building is more like a modern zoo than a park. I mean, it will look natural, but it will be almost totally artificial."

"Good point, Mr. Henderson, but that is the way of the future. Zoos are no longer just for viewing. They are now becoming the nature preserves for endangered species. Zoos must promote breeding. To induce species to breed, zoos must look more like a natural habitat to make the wildlife feel at home. Wild animals do not breed under stress."

"Like the zoos in Miami and San Diego in the U.S. "

"Precisely, Mr. Henderson. At the same time, all parks are becoming more like zoos. For years all parks had to do was regulate the movement of their visitors. Now, they must control the environment and wild life as well, because mankind is pressing in on the park boundaries."

"Humanity is encroaching worldwide," said Jim.

"Yes. Let me give you an example."

"Sure."

"Are you familiar with your big park at the south end of Florida? The Everglades?"

"Yes, of course. I went there when I was a young kid in school."

"Then you are familiar with the wildlife trail at the entrance."

"Yes."

"Did you know that the whole area would have dried up many years ago because of man's manipulation and use of the water supply?"

"I knew water was a problem," said Jim. "I thought it was a quality issue."

"The water level there has been maintained artificially by pumping water into the Everglades for over forty years."

"I didn't know that," said Jim.

"If you went back today, beyond that area, you would understand why I call that part of your park the 'dead zone'."

"The dead zone?"

"Yes. I use that term because you won't see much until you go all the way down to the Gulf of Mexico. I know what I'm saying because I have been there. We hope to learn from your failures. An enormous park that once was home to millions of birds is now a desolate place as far as wildlife is concerned."

"I've read that they are working to restore it by pumping and regulating the volume and quality of the water," said Jim.

"My point, Mr. Henderson. They cannot bring it back unless they do so artificially. There is nothing natural about the Everglades any more. I'm not being critical. It is just a fact of life."

"I see what you are saying about parks," said Jim.

"In Uhuru, we have to build our future from scratch. We have very few resources. Wildlife and archaeology are both important resources here, Mr. Henderson. Our populace knows nothing of birth control. Runaway human population growth is our biggest problem, and is likely to remain that way into the foreseeable future."

"Your job as Minister of the Interior must be a difficult one. Where do you get the time to do everything?"

"I have a set schedule. I live a busy life. I have to fight to keep on schedule. Sometimes I have to deal with the interruptions. I like to be in control of my life, Mr. Henderson. I do not like the world controlling me. I do not like surprises. Changes in my schedule make me short tempered and irritable, but I have a way of dealing with side distractions."

"I have the same problem with such interruptions," said Jim. "I'd like to hear your solution."

"I have two answers. First, I try to define the source of the distraction and reduce it down to its most essential issue. I form a quick solution and act decisively to carry it out so I can get back to my regular schedule. I cannot allow side issues distract me."

"That sounds easy on paper," said Jim. "I always found the day-to-day distractions hard to deal with. They interfere with my long-term projects. They are annoying."

"What may seem to be little side distractions that are easy to ignore will become cancers that grow and destroy you if you are not careful. You must deal with them immediately. Right now, for example, we are digging out the contours of the lake for the north basin. We have been borrowing road-building equipment from the outer territories road project to complete the project. As a result, we are almost a year behind in surfacing and paving the road from Elizabethtown to the border with Kenya."

"Borrowing from Peter to pay Paul," suggested Jim.

"Exactly. I have been pushing to get the basic work done so we can move the equipment back to the road before the bank decides to make an inspection."

"I see your dilemma," said Jim.

"My present problem is that three days ago, they exposed parts of fossilized bones of what we think are from an extinct short necked giraffe. The archaeological people want to stop the basin project and open up a site. They want to dig up as many of the fossilized bones as they can," said Dr. Tubojola.

"That sounds like the right thing to do."

"Yes, I agree. Fossils of that particular giraffe are quite rare in this part of Africa. What I have learned is that an initial bit of fossilized bone is often not alone and the odds are that more fossilized bones are in the same area. We could be looking at a major excavation. At the same

119

time, we are most anxious to keep going because we need the equipment for the road project," said Dr. Tubojola.

"Your life is complicated," Jim observed.

"To compound the problem, I don't have an archaeologist available to put in charge of the giraffe excavation."

"I see," said Jim.

"I'd steal Mobutu Nyzeki from Bokuru, but we need him there until we know what Dr. Bronston found. Mobutu is being groomed for his own site, but I don't dare pull him if Bokuru is important. He has exceptional eyes for spotting fossils."

"You need to put him in the best place where his skills can be used," said Jim.

"I wish it was as simple as that. You see, Mr. Henderson, there are two kinds of archaeologists in Uhuru."

"Two different kinds?" asked Jim.

"Yes. There are those who are working on their advanced degrees, students actually. They either fund their own work or use grants from their colleges and universities. They don't have much money, but they do take care of their own financial needs and responsibilities. The second type of archaeologist is the professional who has completed an advanced degree and is here because this is their life work."

"Like Dr. Bronston," said Jim.

"Yes. They obtain their funding from sponsors, and they are attuned to the need to make discoveries that generate media attention. Headlines produce and maintain sponsor support."

"Publish or perish," said Jim.

"Yes, in a way you are correct. My problem is Mobutu Nyzeki. Have you met him?"

"No, but I will when we go out to the field camp tomorrow."

"Good. Well, he is qualified to handle his own site. I told you I would like to put him on the giraffe site, but right now he is paid by the Chicago museum, the sponsor of Bokuru. If we can influence Ms. Bronston to manage the excavation, the funding would remain in place and Mobutu would continue to be paid by the Bokuru project. If, however, I move him, we lose the funding for him. He does not have the international reputation to obtain outside funding on his own, especially for a major project that does not, how shall I say it, have the sex appeal of an ancient hominid site. We would have to look to our own meager budget in Uhuru to finance his excavation. On the other hand, seeking a professional outsider with private funding in place could take months if not longer," said Dr. Tubojola.

"I see your problem. You probably have to deal with crises like that every day."

"That is the nature of my job."

"Didn't you say you had two answers for handling crises?"

"Yes. The second is that I take off quality time each day. I just drop things. I take a period of rest and relaxation to stand back and put things in perspective. I call it dream time. I leave this office and go for a walk down through the exhibits. It is important to relieve the tensions of the day and drop things once in a while. The exhibits provide an escape for me."

"That is a good idea," said Jim. "All we get in Chicago is lunch."

"You need more time than lunch to relieve stress. Right after lunch is the best time to take off because that allows your blood to focus on digestion, and your brain can relax. I come back feeling refreshed and ready to tackle my problems, but I am curious."

"Curious, about what?" asked Jim.

"Yes. I'd like to know how others deal with distractions and how they manage the interruptions in their schedule to stay on time. I would be grateful for any insight you might have. As a busy Chicago lawyer, perhaps when you get back from Bokuru, we could spend a few minutes discussing your methods."

"I'm not sure I have any answers, but I would welcome the opportunity to meet again," said Jim.

"Good. I am like Dr. Bronston in some ways."

"How is that?"

"I am driven by a simple image in my mind of what I want to do. I can visualize the future of Uhuru. Oh, I know I won't see it all come true in my lifetime, but I get my satisfaction a few small successes at a time. They build to larger successes. I know we are on the right path, but I have deep concerns," said Dr. Tubojola.

"Concerns, about what?" asked Jim.

"My biggest concern is that we are mortgaging our future, by pledging our assets to secure loans to pay for our building projects. We are strapping future generations with the repayment obligations. We must make sound decisions that keep things in perspective as we go."

"Money matters are a big issue," said Jim.

"Yes. I am always concerned about money. Our sources are often political and thus subject to instability, but the offset is that I can see things happening. I take great pride in that."

"Well. You should be proud of this museum. It is impressive."

"Yes. Now, let's get back to Dr. Bronston. I think I left off discussing legal issues when we digressed. You must first have a visa, then a license, and then a permit to begin an archaeological excavation in Uhuru. All these things were in place for Dr. Bronston, shall we say, in spades. From a legal standpoint, I see no basis for suicide," said Dr. Tubojola. "He had no legal problems in Uhuru."

"That's good news. I'm writing all of this in my notes," said Jim.

"Dr. Bronston spent the majority of his time out at his archaeological site. I can only assume that he had no legal problems in the States. You might bring the matter up with his daughter. She would be a better source of information about that part of his life. I can't help you there."

"I'll be with her for the next couple of days," said Jim. "So far, she hasn't been able to provide me anything tangible to determine a cause for suicide."

"For the record, let me add I have known Dr. Bronston for many years. He has not always worked here in Uhuru, but I have maintained some level of contact with him even when he was working sites in other countries. Throughout this period of time, I have never noticed any personal problems that affected his behavior when I was with him. I know he lost his wife several years go. He took the loss hard, but he accepted life and went on. He told me he sold his house, and pocketed the proceeds. I believe there was no mortgage, but again I will defer to Nancy. He also had a life insurance policy on his wife so he recovered some financial gain there. I don't know about the costs incurred during his wife's last illness, but I think she was covered by health insurance. I didn't get the impression he was a wealthy man, but I don't believe he was in financial difficulties either. Again, I think Miss Bronston is the one to talk with about that. My impression is that he had no personal, professional, legal, or financial crises to deal with," said Dr. Tubojola.

"Well, Nancy is on her own financially. She did not depend on him."

"I suppose I could add that he was not known to have any vices. He did not drink, gamble, or chase women that I know of. I don't know what he did, except work. No one here at the museum has the slightest idea of what problem he may have faced that would drive such a highly educated, successful man to take his own life. The answer to the suicide question is in your hands," said Dr. Tubojola.

"I have the feeling I'm not getting anywhere. I mean, you have certainly been very helpful. I'm just not any closer to an answer to that question than I was when I arrived," said Jim.

"I suppose we could have warned you in advance about the real problem," said Dr. Tubojola. "None of us who knew him have a clue."

"I met his doctor this morning."

"Yes. Did that help?" asked Dr. Tubojola.

"Yes and no," said Jim. "Oh, again, I learned a great deal, but the only medical issue was high blood pressure which appears to have been under control. His health was good with no known problems. The doctor gave him a clean bill of health. There was no information that could help my investigation. Even the doctor could not believe he would do such a thing. I'm beginning to see why no one in Africa appeared helpful to the people back in Chicago."

Dr. Tubojola sat back in his chair and took two more puffs on his cigar, concentrating on the smoke as it rose above him.

"You didn't think your investigation would be an easy one, did you?"

"Frankly, I did not know what to expect. I didn't have any preconceived expectations. I was given very little other than suicide as cause of death. I was told that they expected me to find the motive behind it. Right or wrong, that was how I perceived my investigation," said Jim.

Dr. Tubojola sat forward in his chair, and then crushed his cigar in the ashtray on his desk. "Well now, Mr. Henderson, enough of our platitudes and generalities. Let's get down to details."

Jim was at a loss at Dr. Tubojola's sudden change in demeanor. He watched him turn in his chair to face his computer terminal again. Jim watched as Dr. Tubojola began to work at the keyboard as the monitor screen lit up in pale blue.

"There is something wrong at Bokuru, Mr. Henderson, and I want to know what it is. Perhaps this is what is relevant to your investigation, perhaps not." He tapped at his keyboard peering intently at the screen. From overhead a giant screen folded down in front of the bookcase on his credenza, blocking out most of the shelves. Suddenly the giant screen lit up in pale blue, matching the computer screen.

"Let's see," said Dr. Tubojola, as he continued tapping on his keyboard. "Sometimes I lose track of where I am. Hmm, let's see... A couple of minutes ago I was saying that Bokuru was different."

"Yes," said Jim. "You said most sites started by someone finding a bit of fossilized bone on the surface. I have been told that it was a cave site, but that is all I know."

"Yes. That's where I left off. Forgive me. I digressed. Bokuru was different, even from its inception, precisely because they did not find any bone fragments on the surface. The only thing they saw was a geological condition on the surface that indicated they had found a cave. The bluff had been worn down to the cave roof so what they saw was the cave walls and a collapsed ceiling. Our field geologist was the one who first spotted it. The cave was completely filled in with a semi-solid limestone matrix. Our geologists dated the matrix at 1.82 million years before present. We were really lucky."

"Lucky? How so?" asked Jim.

"The fill in the cave was made up of local river sand and fresh volcanic debris."

"That's what I've been told," said Jim. "What makes it lucky?"

"Volcanic debris is the most important tool we have in determining age. Radioactive isotopes released in volcanic eruptions are trapped in the debris. Because radioactive isotopes decay at ascertainable rates we can measure the amount of decay of one gas to another to determine how long ago the original eruption took place. Do you have any exposure to the use of potassium–argon dating in Chicago? It is the most common dating method we use in Africa today."

"No. Everything was recent. The archaeologists use Carbon–14 dating for all the sites I worked on," said Jim.

"I thought as much. A good Carbon-14 lab can date material back to a maximum of about seventy thousand years. We are talking about dating millions of years back in time here in Africa. Potassium-argon is the tool available to us, although there are some newer exotic tests coming on line. Bokuru is an ideal location to date because the volcanic debris washed into the cave," said Dr. Tubojola.

"I've read about the potassium-argon dating method," said Jim. "I've just never seen it in use. There is a carbon-14 lab in Chicago. I've been on a tour of their facility."

"Good. They also recently took potassium-argon measurements at the bottom of the fill and got the same results. Do you know what that means?"

"I was told that the uniform dates indicated the cave filled in all at one time," said Jim.

"That is correct. Our resident geologist verified this, and he seems to think that the cave was filled in by sediment washed in from a flood, filling the cave with mud and volcanic ash from a nearby eruption. Actually, he said the volcanic ash and dust was from the Alongo volcano about 40 kilometers north of the Bokuru site. Geologists have been able to pin down volcanic activity at the same time the cave filled."

"Is what makes the site so interesting just because it was a cave that filled with debris when it flooded? There must be a lot of caves like that," said Jim.

"The time of the event corresponds to a lot of changes in life forms in this part of Africa," explained Dr. Tubojola.

"It's amazing that modern dating techniques give us so much knowledge about the ancient past," said Jim.

"It wasn't always that way. Today geologists can tell a lot about climate, too. You would not believe it, but they know the Bokuru valley was wet, not dry at the time the cave filled in," said Dr. Tubojola.

"How can they tell that?"

"Because of the shape of the grains of sand in the cave. Dry, wind blown desert sand would have more flat edges, like cubes. What they found was round water worn grains from the river. It's amazing how much we know by looking at grains of sand."

"So the cave gave suggestions of a lot of promise?"

"Yes, and we encouraged Dr. Bronston to take a look at it."

"He did a lot more than look. He decided to excavate it," said Jim.

"Yes. As soon as he saw the site, Dr. Bronston decided to excavate it. His initial application indicated he hoped to find hominid bones, but personally I thought he would find evidence of hyenas or leopards, both of which used caves. There was other evidence of both animals near the valley, but no hominid bones had been found for hundreds of kilometers from the site."

"So you thought finding hominids was only a remote possibility?" asked Jim.

"Yes. Of course, carnivores preyed on our ancestors back then. A leopard or hyena lair would mean a good possibility of finding hominid bones, especially skulls, but only if there were any hominids living in the general area, which I thought was improbable. In any event Dr. Bronston thought a cave would be fruitful and justify the allocation of resources needed to excavate it. We had no objection because he was privately funded. In fact, we encouraged his efforts because hyena and leopard dens are rare and we had people interested in them."

"This is all very interesting," said Jim. "I'm learning a lot about African archaeology."

"About that time my relationship with Dr. Bronston was in one of its more difficult periods."

"How is that?"

"He took the position of not disclosing anything about a project until all the work was done and the reports made. He was concerned about early, unauthorized disclosure through the informal grapevine. I assured him of our ability to maintain confidentiality here in Elizabethtown, but to no avail. I should say we also have a "publish or perish" rule in Uhuru that addresses the situation where a site is excavated and the licensee sits on the discovery. To us, refusal to disclose properly is tantamount to a rape of our land. We have included criminal penalties to put some teeth into it. Some of the archaeologists in the past were more interested in advancing their own egos than they were science. So we enacted legislation to counteract that problem."

"We have some horrible examples of that in the U.S." said Jim.

"It has been a world wide problem. Our rule in Uhuru is that you must send in weekly status reports and make a full report within six months of closing a site, not to the press, just to us in this department. That way we know what is going on with our assets."

"It sounds like a good rule."

"Yes, but that rule kept my relationship with Dr. Bronston a bit frayed. He was a favored *prima donna* who refused to comply. But, I did reach an arrangement with him where he agreed to make weekly reports about Bokuru. In turn, I agreed to stay away from the site and respect his turf, so to speak," said Dr. Tubojola.

"Did it work out?"

"We both paid lip service to the agreement. He did send in weekly reports, and I stayed away from the site," said Dr. Tubojola.

"That seems fair," said Jim. "If he sent in reports, he must have told you what he found out there."

There was a moment of silence. Dr. Tubojola just stared at Jim.

"I should say that many early fossil discoveries from South Africa were from mining operations. Many hominid bones were found in old limestone caves."

"Like Bokuru," said Jim.

"Not exactly. The problem was that, over time, the South African caves had become distorted and twisted out of shape by geological events. The extraction process through mining operations further complicated any analysis. There were many fossils found in those caves, but because of the changes in the geology, the sites could not be dated with any degree of accuracy. Geologists can't date fossils, Mr. Henderson. They can only date the surrounding material in which the fossil is found. They could not determine the original cave structure or the original geological strata in the South Africa caves, making dating of the fossils next to impossible."

"I didn't know that," said Jim. "What about Bokuru?"

"Bokuru seems to be quite the opposite. We have a perfectly preserved cave, and we know the precise dimensions of it's interior. In addition, we can date the time it filled in with river mud and volcanic debris. The problem is that we know no more. We have no reports of finding anything inside the cave. The matrix is uniform throughout which tells us it remained undisturbed until now, but that is all we know."

"You expected Dr. Bronston to find something. How you do know that there just weren't any fossils in the cave? Maybe it was empty when it filled in. Maybe the resident animals fled before it flooded," said Jim.

"Dr. Bronston used the system of one meter grid squares," Dr. Tubojola continued, not answering Jim's question. The screen above showed the intersection of two lines, one vertical showing a north –south axis and one horizontal showing an east-west axis. "As you know all archaeological sites begin with the intersection of a base line and a meridian," said Dr. Tubojola.

"Yes, and their intersection is the datum point or reference point for all measurements," said Jim.

"Good. Your archaeological background is showing. The vertical line you see on the screen represents the meridian with north being located at the top of the screen. The intersection is clearly marked on the grid. In fact, when you go out to the site, you will find the datum point is memorialized by a concrete post with about twenty centimeters sticking out of the ground," said Dr. Tubojola.

A series of red squares appeared on the screen.

"Ah, the grid pattern for Bokuru, Mr. Henderson. As you will note, characteristically for Dr. Bronston's sites, the entire excavation is located in the southeast quadrant," Dr. Tubojola continued.

"That practice helps to avoid confusion when taking measurements," Jim commented.

"Yes, as long as you know that your datum point is north and west of the area you plan to dig," said Dr. Tubojola. "Well, in any case, what you see is the horizontal grid set by Dr. Bronston, in one meter increments. The first grid square is one south and one east, or 1S1E," he continued.

"Yes, I can see that, " said Jim, staring up at the large screen.

"Now, as I told you, Bokuru is a cave excavated from above so the site is shown in three dimensions with the third measurement being the depth below the datum plane."

"That's amazing," said Jim.

"When you go to Bokuru, Mr. Henderson, you will see a cap on the top of the datum post. That disc represents the horizontal plane known as the datum plane. All dimensions down into the cave are measured from that plane. They use lasers and mirrors for all measurements so they are very accurate."

The screen continued to flash changes until it showed a series of red lined cubes in three dimensions.

You put a lot of work into making this possible," said Jim.

"That's nothing. It's simple geometry. Now watch."

The screen changed again. The actual cave dimensions were superimposed over the grid in black until the whole three-dimensional outline of the interior of the cave was clearly shown within the red cubes. "The solid black lines mean we have at least ten actual measurements per meter. The dashed lines mean an element of estimation was used for the lines. When we receive the real dimensions in the weekly reports we upgrade our graphics," said Dr. Tubojola. "Let me also add that we use geophysical positioning and know exactly where the datum point is on the earth. We also know the distance of the datum plane above sea level. The cave, as you can see, is roughly forty feet wide, one hundred feet long, and about fifteen feet in height. Of course, the dimensions you see shown on the screen are metric," said Dr. Tubojola.

"You have the whole cave on the screen," said Jim. "I'm impressed."

"You are no doubt familiar with the computer concept of 'garbage in-garbage out' are you not?" asked Dr. Tubojola.

"All too well. It's a universal problem."

"Well, in the case of Bokuru, we seem to be suffering from nothing-in-nothing-out," said Dr. Tubojola.

"You're joking," said Jim. "Your graphics show the entire cave. I don't see anything missing."

"Well, I admit we seem to know a lot about the geology of the cave, but in reality we know nothing," said Dr. Tubojola. "As I said a moment ago, we got weekly reports from Dr. Bronston, but they simply added on a few more vertical or horizontal dimensions of the interior of the cave. What I am leading up to is that there is a total absence of any information about anything found inside the cave."

"Maybe they didn't find anything," Jim repeated.

"I don't believe that. Why would they keep digging? The advantages of a cave opening out just above a river would have made the cave desirable by all sorts of life forms from what we know about this earth two million years ago. The total absence of any information whatsoever leads me to believe that Dr Bronston was holding back, certainly as soon as they reached the bottom of the cave. To me, he was simply not telling us what he found. All I asked was that he let us know what was being excavated, but now I have an additional question."

"What is that?" asked Jim.

"I want to know why he was not telling us anything about what he found," said Dr. Tubojola.

"Maybe what he found was so insignificant he just didn't bother to say anything."

"You may be correct. It is possible, Mr. Henderson, but highly unlikely. When he died, I realized that he used to stop in to visit us periodically. He would stop into my office as frequently as three times a month. We usually had a lively chat right here in this office. Our conversations were always more social than on his work. We never resolved anything, but we both enjoyed our meetings immensely. Suddenly, after he died I realized, that for over the last two months, he hadn't come in at all."

"He must have been busy at the excavation," said Jim.

"Exactly. At the risk of appearing paranoid, I think it was part of his plan of secrecy, Mr. Henderson. He was protecting something. I have concluded that there is some deep dark secret at Bokuru. What did he know that he was unwilling to share?"

"Could it be related to why he would commit suicide?" asked Jim.

"I'll be all ears if you can show how events which occurred 1.82 million years ago could be related to a modern day suicide," said Dr. Tubojola. "Being realistic, I know you have little to work with, so, I, for one, will be anxious to hear the results of your investigation here."

"Right now, it looks like Bokuru is my only hope," said Jim, sounding as if it was more a matter of resignation than hope.

"If I am paranoid, and the site is truly sterile, nothing more than a hole in the ground, then I would ask that you tell us immediately. Use the radio out there. Mobutu will show you how to operate it. Let us know what Dr. Bronston found, no matter how trivial it may seem to you. I know I am asking a favor, but it is important to us."

"I'll do what I can. I'm happy to help," said Jim.

"Oh, if, on the other hand, I am right, and there is a meaningful discovery of some kind, let us know that as well. With your help, perhaps, we can induce Miss Bronston to step in and complete the excavation."

"If Nancy's father found something significant, I'm sure we can induce her to finish his work," said Jim.

"Good. Oh, of course, if she steps in, it will be her site. I don't want to step on her domain. If I go out there myself, it will appear that I am asserting dominion and control over the operation. I have learned to be sensitive about such things. I fear that such an act would scare her off, and I do not want to do that. That's why I'd like to ask for your informal input once you're out there and you have a day or so to sniff around. Just tell me what you see," said Dr. Tubojola.

"I'll be there tomorrow," said Jim. "I'll try to radio you before the end of the day."

"Take whatever time you need. Perhaps, you can understand now why I was so interested in your archaeological background. Somehow, fate has interwoven you into our lives here in Africa. If Bokuru is sterile, we can send Miss Bronston home and move Mobutu over to the giraffe bone site. That project would give him a real future and an excavation of his own. If, on the other hand, Bokuru is meaningful, then I need him where he is, working for Miss Bronston, assuming she will officially agree to stay."

"I see where you are coming from," said Jim. "Everything is interrelated."

"If I have to look for an outside archaeologist to come in for the giraffe site work, then time will be of the essence, which it always seems to be around here. Just setting the excavation boundaries for the giraffe site will free up the road equipment. Then they can be reassigned back to the road project before the International Bank makes an inspection."

"You can rely on my call," said Jim.

"Thank you. You see, your ability to assess what is going on at Bokuru is suddenly the key to my ability to make meaningful management decisions. Everything seems to come down to the question of what really is at Bokuru."

"And it's up to me to find the answer," said Jim.

"I realize that what is found in the excavation is probably not relevant to your investigation. This is something extra. Once you have resolved the issue of Dr. Bronston's death, you can pack up and go back home to Chicago. Your mission here will be over. For those of us locals who remain here, the question of what was found at Bokuru will still be important. Unfortunately, Mr. Henderson, everything hinges on you."

"You have been most helpful to me. The least I can do is to help out," said Jim, remembering his conversation with Mr. Kendall on the way to the airport back in Chicago. Jim did not believe in coincidences. Clearly, Dr. Bronston had not been communicating with anyone about his progress at Bokuru, and was apparently so busy he had no time for outsiders.

There was another long moment of silence.

"I notice that you were looking up at my collection of skulls on the credenza shelves," said Dr. Tubojola.

130

"I was looking for the screen. I didn't see it fold up out of sight," said Jim. "I didn't hear a thing. But yes, I did notice your skulls."

"The screen folds back into the ceiling automatically. What you see on the shelves now that the screen is out of the way is a collection of carvings of skulls running from the first small rodents up to modern man," said Dr. Tubojola, who stood up slowly. He stepped aside so he did not block Jim's view of the collection.

"It's quite interesting," said Jim.

"Well, thank you," said Dr. Tubojola. "I'm quite proud of it, actually."

"I don't see any missing steps. Everything seems to change slowly but inevitably to the next skull in the sequence, leading right up to man," said Jim.

"Yes. The whole collection was made to my specifications. Can you tell they are woodcarvings? None of them is real. They are all mahogany wood, painted white to look like bone."

"They look real. I would never have known they are wood if you hadn't told me," said Jim.

"As you can see they are not all to scale, particularly the smaller ones. In fact, many of them are pure conjecture. This whole collection is my idea of what we will find in the field in time, Mr. Henderson. However, now they are only a set of carvings. The exhibit is Art, Mr. Henderson, pure art, and nothing more," said Dr. Tubojola.

"Well, it's quite convincing."

"I'm glad you like it. I had a hard time getting this collection in here."

"Oh?" asked Jim, who thought, for a moment, he saw the lights dim. Suddenly, he realized, when he glanced out of the corner of his eye, it was raining outside. Through the drapes, he could see streaks of water running down the windows. There was a distant rumble of thunder.

"I hired a man from Tanzania who made wood carvings of human skulls for a living. He followed my sketches and notes. In my opinion, he did an excellent job. I had this collection made just for this office, but the Board of Trustees refused to allow me to bring it into the museum. They did not even want it displayed in this office."

"Why not?" asked Jim. "I think it's quite appropriate where it is."

"The trustees said it was not real, not an accurate representation. I said it was just art, and I was not putting it out on the museum floor as an exhibit. I told them it was just for my private office, but they said that was exactly the point. They thought that as curator, I should have plaster casts or accurate renditions or the real thing. The trustees offered plenty of material stored in our archives they felt would be more appropriate in my office," said Dr. Tubojola.

"But your collection is here on display. How did you manage to overcome their objections?"

"Well, I won when I threatened to take out my shelves and bring in some horrible piece of modern art that no one liked. That did it. They changed their position. There are a couple of trustees who still disapprove, but it is simply art, Mr. Henderson."

He walked over to the windows and pushed a button on the wall that controlled the motorized curtains. Silently, the drapes opened.

"I see we have an afternoon shower," he said, and then paused. "It will be gone within the hour. The history of the rise of man from an upright walking ape has been a difficult struggle to complete, but we have been preordained to climb this ladder to success. Sometimes I don't understand. Here we are at the top of the ladder, a single species with unlimited potential. We have paid a terrible price to get here. Now we stand on the threshold, but of what? That is the question that bothers me the most. I am concerned about all the rhetoric predicting our impending doom brought about by our own acts. To have worked so hard to reach this point of success only to disappear due to our own folly doesn't seem right," said Dr. Tubojola. "I cannot see the future. Our journey was too long and too hard. I ask myself for what, if we simply stumble at this point?" He pressed the button again, and the curtains closed. He turned, smiled weakly at Jim, and returned to his desk. "Well, enough of my idle ramblings and my skull collection. You have work to do. Dr. Bronston was our friend and colleague, Mr. Henderson. We are still numb with shock over his loss. I wish you well at Bokuru. Perhaps there is some clue for you out there. Frankly, I don't know where else to look. I'm afraid we are all going to be leaning on you to find the answers."

Jim could tell, from Dr. Tubojola's tone and the fact he had remained standing, the interview was over. Jim stood, ready to terminate the meeting and excuse himself.

"I wish I could tell you how an open excavation in the ground could point you to a motive for suicide, but your efforts are noble and deeply appreciated," said Dr. Tubojola. "A lot of people are depending on you to find the answers to this dilemma."

"I thank you for your time, and all the information you have provided. I feel a bit overwhelmed," said Jim

"Please remember that our museum and my department are at your service," said Dr. Tubojola. "If you need office space or secretarial help please call."

"Thank you for giving so much of your valuable time," said Jim.

They shook hands, and then Dr. Tubojola reached down and picked up a plastic card from his desk, and handed it to Jim.

"What I thought we could do is help facilitate the development of background information to assist your investigation. On a lighter side, this card will give you free access to our presentation '*Long Long Ago.*' It is showing in Theatre One down on the first floor. Take the elevator down to the lobby, then go back to the entrance to the exhibits. The theatre will be on your right. Just follow the signs. If you go now, you should just make the next show," said Dr. Tubojola.

"Thank you," said Jim.

"If you have a chance to see the exhibits later, remember that the larger dinosaurs are on the first floor and the minerals and geological exhibits are on the second," said Dr. Tubojola, smiling.

"Thank you for the pass," said Jim, examining the plastic card.

"Go quickly, Mr. Henderson. The theatre is interactive. No one is admitted once the presentation has begun."

CHAPTER SEVEN: *LONG LONG AGO*

When the elevator door opened, Jim stepped back into the museum lobby. To compensate for the lack of sunlight from the skylights in the ceiling high above, banks of spotlights bathed the central display of three duckbilled dinosaurs in bright, artificial light. They stood among tall, living, green plants and a cluster of live palms, which made the dinosaurs seem real.

Jim followed Dr. Tubojola's directions and walked past the information booth. He continued back along the rear wall of the lobby and followed the signs for Theatre One. Since he already had an entrance pass, he skipped the line at the ticket booth and went directly to the theatre entrance. A sign over the door read:

Theatre Docked
Boarding: Long Long Ago

There was a slot in the wall to insert his electronic pass. Once he inserted his laminated card into the slot, the door slid open for him to pass through. It closed quickly behind him. A sign in the wall ahead beside the passageway ramp to the inner dock entrance directed visitors to an open room on the right filled with banks of lockers. The room reminded Jim of a bus terminal or airport storage locker area. The lockers looked like the one he had seen at the airport customs terminal where items not allowed into the country could be stored until departure. Jim read the wall sign carefully. Once selected, the lockers were secured by use of the entrance card. All loose objects including coats, purses, portable cell phones, beepers, and cameras were to be stored in the lockers during the interactive presentation. A young, native attendant dressed in a standard, soft brown museum uniform stood at the entrance to the theater to assure compliance with the rules and to answer any questions.

Jim put his suit coat and briefcase into a locker, closed the door and rapidly inserted and withdrew his entrance card. The door on the repository locked electronically. After he had completed the procedure, he walked up the ramp to the bulkhead doorway and entered the interior of the theatre. A wall display at the entrance showed the seating arrangement. When he put his card in the slot under the display as directed, his assigned seat lit up, Seat 3 Row 4 L. The display screen showed one hundred sixty seats in the theatre split into two sections, one on each side of a central aisle. Above the display screen, a sign glowed:

Departure 10:00 minutes
Long Long Ago Seating

He stepped through the doorway into the theatre. It was very dark. He could not see any walls or the ceiling. The single aisle was lit by a row of red footlights running down to the front of the theatre. The seats seemed to be mounted on a platform that was suspended in a void. Jim carefully went down the aisle, following the group in front of him until he reached his row. He found his seat to the left of the aisle. The theatre was filling quickly.

The seats were unique. Each one was made of a single molded shape, contoured to hold the whole body. When Jim sat down on the soft seat cushion, a large restraining arm closed, locking him firmly in place. In addition, there was a seat belt, like those in an automobile. He felt as if he had been swallowed into the seat rather than sitting on it. There was a control panel on the armature in front of him attached to the restraining arm that locked him securely in place. The panel was made up of many colored lights that highlighted the few, simple controls. A small CRT screen immediately flashed "Fasten Seat Belt." The light went out as soon as he buckled the belt in place. A large, red master cutoff button labeled "Emergency" dominated the console. The label above it was designated "For Medical Emergency Use Only." Next to the emergency button was a smaller button labeled "Neutral."

Jim tightened his seat belt. The seat belt light on the panel blinked on then went out. Beside the neutral button was a smaller screen labeled "Time Meter" with glowing red LED lights. It was set at 000:00.

While he was examining the panel and the small CRT screen, a set of instructions appeared, floating in space in the middle of the theatre directly in front of the seats. There was still no evidence of walls or ceiling in the theatre. The instructions read:

Welcome to Theatre One. Please familiarize yourself with the seating schematic on the screen on your control panel. There is only one central aisle for entering and exiting the theatre. During the interactive presentation, the seating platform operates freely from its docked position.

In the event of a medical emergency, press the large red button on your console. For non-medical emergencies, press the

135

neutral button. In the event of a medical emergency the theatre will return to the docked position, and the presentation will stop. Only an attendant can restart the presentation when the emergency has been resolved.

The use of the neutral button will also put the theatre into the docked position. However, the presentation will continue while in a dormant mode. The interactive aspect of the program will resume when the neutral button is pressed again.

The release of any seatbelt will also put the theatre into a docked position where it will continue in a dormant mode. The interactive part of the presentation will restart when all seatbelts are refastened.

Please remain seated with seat belts fastened at all times. When the program is over wait until the words "Theatre Docked – Exit" appears on your console screen before leaving the theatre.

Theatre One has been designed for your protection as well as to maximize your enjoyment of the presentation. No food, drinks, cameras, phones, recorders or other loose items are allowed in the theatre at any time.

The presentation has been carefully structured to create a unique experience. While the display is multidimensional to enhance the dramatization, your cooperation is essential to assure the maximum effect for you and your fellow travelers.

Be prepared for the full presentation time of 1 hour.

All loose objects must be checked in the safety lockers located just inside the theatre entrance.

For safety reasons, children under 15 are not allowed in the interactive presentation.

For full family viewing, see the time schedule for dormant presentations of the program posted in the lobby.

Smoking is prohibited in all areas of the theatre.

After a few minutes, the floating instructions disappeared and the words *"Departure: Long Long Ago"* appeared where the instructions had been floating. Jim could feel the theatre platform begin to move as its shape and configuration changed beneath him. The seating platform slowly took the shape of part of a sphere, creating the sensation of floating in space. The seats behind Jim moved above and behind him. The seats in the rows in front of him slipped below, while the seats on either side of him partially drifted away, barely visible in the dark. Suddenly, he felt very alone, suspended in a black void.

After what seemed an eternity, he could see a small white speck in the distance glow, then pulse. With a giant flash and thundering roar, the tiny dot exploded into millions of spinning pinwheels of light, racing in all directions. Thousands of galaxies were born right before his eyes, spinning above and below him. Hot gasses lightly warmed his face as they streaked by. Expanding gas clouds and clusters of stars spun by.

Slowly, a single galaxy floated into the foreground, sweeping free floating stars into its spiral arms as it spun slowly like a giant pinwheel. Near the end of one of its spiral arms, a glowing mass of gas gently floated into the foreground. Gradually, the gas condensed as it, too, began spinning, drawing in solar debris growing ever hotter until the gas ignited into a young sun. The colliding debris slowly formed into orbiting rings that in turn condensed into the inner solid planets. The remaining gas settled into the larger, outer planets. Smaller clouds of dust and debris slowly settled into moons, orbiting around some of the planets. The solar system was born.

Jim found it difficult to concentrate on both the panorama unfolding before him, the small console screen, and the digital display showing the passage of time. The time meter read: "4,500,000,000 bp."

The entire seating platform tilted first up, down, back, then forward, and then from one side to the other, maximizing the view of the presentation as it unfolded in a giant panorama. The primordial earth moved into the foreground, identifiable only by its position as the third sphere from the young sun. All the inner planets were hot glowing spheres of molten rock, continually bombarded by cosmic debris as they swept out into orbits around the young sun. Volcanic activity erupted on the surface of each of the inner solid spheres. The volcanic matter spewed into space, hitting or being bombarded by meteors and hard rocks and occasional comets. One huge rock slammed into the glowing earth with such force that an immense cloud of debris spewed out into a ring orbiting around the earth. In time, the debris condensed into a hot, glowing moon.

Gradually, the intensity of the bombardment of the earth slowed, and the intense volcanic activity diminished as the earth began to cool. Steam and water vapor condensed, and an atmosphere of clouds blanketed the planet. The clouds condensed, producing the first rains that fell on the hot glowing surface, only to turn to steam and rise again creating new clouds. Lightning and thunder filled the ominous, glowing sky. The earth below, while cooling rapidly now, remained a hostile place. Steam and smoke from thousands of active volcanoes and fissures blocked the surface from view. Water condensed and the first seas began to fill the lower valleys. Gradually, the seas filled the foreground. Lightning, wave action, and the early tides stirred the primeval ooze, creating the first microbes out of the mixture of gases, water, and chemicals swirling in the early seas.

Microbes quickly changed to more complex life forms, and multi-cellular organisms soon dominated the seas. These early forms evolved, leading to a multitude of new, more complex species. The history of life on earth began to unfold before him.

The time meter on his console changed as the earth matured, becoming more hospitable. Life forms became larger than the microscopic multi-cellular organisms. More complex species evolved at an ever-quickening pace. The earth changed. The Ordovician and Silurian periods appeared and faded on the screen. Giant nautiloids raced through a pale green sea, chasing, or being chased in turn by a multitude of different kinds of sea scorpions. Soon they too faded. Strange plated fish filled the sea. The time meter on the console read: "350,0000,000 bp."

The rate of change on the meter quickened, and the scenes changed almost as a blur, fading from one into another. Then the meter slowed again as the first plants began to grow on the land. Life spread in a myriad of forms on land as it also flourished in the sea. The first amphibians appeared, while other creatures began to inhabit the land. The changing scenes sped up, then again, the rate of change slowed.

At the rocky edge of a pea green sea, two mouse-like creatures appeared from a den at the base of large, white, bleached rib bones of some long dead, giant creature. The shrews darted quickly over the rocky ground, finding an open, unprotected nest along the shore. They quickly broke open an egg, devoured the contents, and scrambled back to the protection of their burrow. Overhead, a shadow of a large airborne creature floated menacingly across the sea in their direction. Jim missed the name that appeared on his CRT console. The bleached bones faded, and disappeared.

The foreground filled with the fruit laden branches of a huge tree. Through the limbs, Jim could see distant waves lapping at the shore. Above the sea, the moon filled the night sky. A long-tailed, furry animal with large eyes leaped into the foreground with a loud screech and landed on a branch right in front of him. The animal was so close, he felt as if he could reach out and touch it. Momentarily surprised by the sudden appearance of the animal, he watched as it carefully selected, then carefully peeled one of the fruits. Jim missed all of the names on his CRT screen except the word lemur. The animal sat on the branch like a squirrel, eating the fruit and staring at him as if it knew it was being watched. The creature skillfully used its hands to manipulate the fruit to the best advantage. Suddenly, the lemur let out a loud yelp and bounded in a long, high leap off to another branch, disappearing in the dense foliage.

The tree faded and the sea retreated in the distance as the foreground slowly changed into a vast swamp, stretching out into the horizon. On the edge of the swamp was a shrinking forest where open savannah replaced the swamp and continued to expand as the climate became dryer. A group of four-legged, chimpanzee-like ground apes ran to the edge of the forest, hesitated, glanced around anxiously, then raced out onto the open plain to an isolated grove of fruit trees. They darted individually, each racing to reach the bright yellow fruit that hung heavily from the low hanging branches. Rising up on their hind legs, they ate quickly, grabbing at the fruit, calling out nervously to each other. Suddenly, a large wandering cat appeared on the screen, moving in toward the apes from far out on the grass. The cat moved stealthily in their direction, interrupting their raid. Uttering yelps and shrill calls, the apes ran from the open grassland back to the protection of the trees in the forest. The name "Proconsul" appeared briefly on the CRT screen, but again, Jim did not catch any of the other information. The time meter read: "18,000,000 bp."

The scene faded. A broad open savannah emerged. The heavy forest was gone. The foreground consisted totally of open grassland. A volcano smoked quietly in the distance. In the foreground, two saber-toothed cats were busy consuming the carcass of what appeared to have been an antelope they had killed. The carcass lay in an open area where the grass was thin. A few vultures landed near the kill, while others circled overhead waiting for the cats to leave. A group of a dozen upright, walking apes appeared brandishing sticks and branches. They tossed rocks at the cats, while they emitted shrills, screams and barks, filling the air with a loud terrifying cacophony of noise that induced the cats to confront this strange menace. They responded with roars designed to frighten the unwanted intruders away. The din continued for a few moments. Gradually the bedlam confused the cats, until they turned away, ultimately abandoning the kill altogether.

The cats disappeared into the tall grass away from the shouting clan. Once the apes perceived the kill was safe, they quickly fell upon the abandoned carcass. Jim caught the term *"Homo habilis"* on his screen. Three males moved to the perimeter, acting as sentries and watching for danger while the others quickly stripped meat from the bones. They used an assortment of crude bone tools. They ate some meat as they worked at the remains of the antelope, but most of the flesh was skewered on long thin poles. More vultures landed near the group of hominids. The sentinels wielded their sticks threateningly, keeping the vultures at bay. A pair of jackals appeared out of the brush in search of scraps from the kill. The unmistakable sound of hyenas could be heard in the distance.

Before a confrontation developed, the group of apes, consisting of males and females, young and old, rose together and moved silently away from the site, disappearing in the tall grass. After walking for some time, they crossed a meandering stream, and resumed their trek on the other side. Finally, they climbed a high rock outcropping that appeared like a ship in a sea of gently waving grass that stretched to the horizon in all directions. As the sun began to set and the shadows grew long, the group of apes made its way up through the rocks to the top of the outcropping where they huddled together for warmth under the protection of a large overhang. The apes settled down to share the raw meat they had scavenged from the abandoned kill. Sunset gave way to evening darkness as night fell across the plain, and the sky filled with stars.

Out of the heavens, just above the horizon to his left, Jim saw a white object grow steadily larger, burning brighter and brighter. Behind it, a long, glowing tail of whitish gas extended for miles as it moved silently across the night sky. It cast an eerie light on the plain below, illuminating a vast herd of animals feeding on the abundant grass. The feeding animals were oblivious to the presence of the galactic intruder. The meteor moved across from Jim's left to his right, until it disappeared from view below the horizon. After a moment, there was a giant flash and soft roar from the distant impact. Gradually, the glow from the impact faded and the full moon began to rise.

One by one, the hominids began to venture out from the protection of their overhang to stare up into the heavens above. Their forms were silhouetted in the moonlight. The distant volcano sputtered in a mild eruption of glowing ash and pumice that rose high into the cold, night air. Jim shivered. The sound of a woman's voice floated through the theatre:

Like your ancestors before you, staring into the heavens three million years ago, man today is also a transitional being between those on whose fossilized bones he stands and those beings not yet born who will someday replace him. Life's only constant is change, an imperative executed with cold precision by the never-ending rain of unseen radiation from the nearest volcano and from the most distant star. Each particle carries with it both the potential of the gift of new life and the threat of inevitable extinction.

As visitors, you have come from many lands to this place to find out who you are. This question, we hope, in part, to answer in this museum by showing you the road by which you came to be evolution's favored child with the unique ability to contemplate your own existence and that of the very universe that created you.

Take with you the knowledge that you are children of this earth and the broad African savannah. Someday you too will die so that others as different from you as you are from these early beings may in turn walk over your fossilized bones and marvel at the same universe that gave them the fleeting gift of life

The CRT screen read:

3,000,000 bp.
Last Scene
Long Long Ago

The scene faded into darkness as the aisle lights began to glow again, lighting the way back to the exit from the theatre. Jim's screen changed:

Theatre Docked
Exit Through Rear

141

CHAPTER EIGHT: *THE ILLUSION*

A short time later, Jim stood outside the front entrance of the museum looking at the hazy city of Elizabethtown basking in the late afternoon sun. It was still hot and humid, and a steamy mist hung in the air from the earlier thundershower. There was a strong, musky smell in the air that he now identified as the African earth. The stone steps were damp and spattered with occasional small pools of standing rainwater. In the west, just above the horizon, the sky was clear, but a blanket of dull gray clouds still hung heavily over the city. An occasional raindrop warned of the potential for more rain.

Jim's mind was filled with the images of the presentation he had just seen. For a brief moment, he thought he was on the steps of the museum in Chicago before reality set in and he remembered that he was half way around the world. He recalled the simple directions to the hotel. Nancy had written them down for him on a blank page in the notebook he carried in his briefcase. The instructions were to go down the steps, then walk to his right to the street corner. Once there, he was to cross the street to the north side, and continue walking two full blocks north. From there, he was to walk three blocks east. The hotel, she had said, would be on the corner, directly across the street.

The instructions were straightforward, and he was sure he would not miss the hotel. The old building would still stand out as an imposing structure here in Elizabethtown, since there were so few, large, old colonial, stone buildings in town. He looked again at the clouds and decided there was no need to take a cab. He was sure he could beat the rain. Just as he started down the steps, he caught a glimpse of a familiar looking white bus parked almost directly across the street. He stopped to pause a moment to take a closer look. He recognized it immediately as the one he had ridden in the day before on his trip from the airport. The bus belonged to the Temple of Tassan. The large black eye painted on the side seemed to be staring directly at him. He smiled when he noticed that the windows were all open. The bus was dry, so it must have arrived after the rain.

Two members of the temple stood on the bottom steps of the museum greeting the public. Both were dressed in long burgundy robes that looked identical to the one worn by the young man he met at the airport. He remembered the bus driver, David Johannson. The hoods on the robes of the two young men below were drawn up over their heads, so he could not see their faces clearly. He could not be sure if David was one of them. As he stood watching, looking for a familiar face, he noticed that they were handing out fliers. After pausing for a moment, he realized they were only passing leaflets to people leaving the museum. They carefully avoided handing any literature to those on the way in, a practice he thought was a bit unusual.

Jim started down the steps to see if he could identify David as one of the young men. By the time he reached the bottom steps, he could see the two faces under the hoods. Both appeared to be a few years older than David. Jim guessed they were both in their mid twenties. He was sure he had never seen either one before. Even though their hoods were pulled up, Jim could see that they both differed from David in that they were clean cut and had shaved their heads. In addition, neither one had a beard. The taller of the two approached him. Jim extended his hand in greeting, only to have a brochure thrust into his open palm.

The pamphlet was white like the bus, and it had the same black eye embossed on the cover. Below the eye was printed the words "The Illusion." Before Jim could open the brochure, the young man addressed him.

"Good afternoon, my friend. My name is Anthony. I'm from the Temple of Tassan."

"Hello," said Jim. "Thank you for the pamphlet. I was wondering why you only offer these circulars to those leaving the museum? I didn't see you giving any of them to people going into the museum."

The young man smiled. "You are very observant, my friend. The answer to your question is very simple."

"I am interested in hearing your answer."

"We refuse to give our fliers to new arrivals," Anthony replied in a pleasant voice. "You see, the new arrival is on a quest to find the key to their past. Those who come here are preconditioned, wearing the blinders of today's culture. They are not yet ready for us. They have come to this place responding to a desire to find their beginnings. They have accepted as fact that this place holds the answer. They would not be receptive to us, nor are they prepared for this brochure. Experience tells us they would drop it in the first wastebasket they find inside, without even looking at it. Brochures that go inside, my friend, do not come back out."

"I see. I think you are the one who is observant."

"When visitors leave this place, many of them will understand our message, for they will come away disappointed. They will finally be receptive to the truth," said Anthony.

"The truth?" asked Jim.

"This false temple is a cold and empty building. What the visitor finds is a fine interweaving of half truths in order to create the illusion."

"What is the illusion?" asked Jim.

"The illusion of evolution with the implication that the keys to its inner secrets are kept here in this building."

"That seems a bit over simplistic," replied Jim.

"This structure stands for the assumption that life can be explained from what is known here, within its walls. What is shown is mere speculation masquerading as science. The answers to the fundamental question about life are not here. This is a misleading place."

"So, to find the truth, you want me to come to your temple and make a donation?" asked Jim.

"No. No donation is required. You cannot buy your way to the truth. A trip to our temple may be of interest to you, but you will not see the truth because I can see that you are blind. You must open your eyes to see truth. Until you take off your blindfold, you will not be able to see clearly. A trip to our temple would not help you," said Anthony.

"How do I overcome my inability to see?"

"To find inner truth, you must find The Creator."

"Okay, so how do I find The Creator?"

"You can only find The Creator by praying and through meditation. There is no other way. Our humble temple can offer you only a place of solitude. The rest of your quest must be done within yourself. All we can offer is a place where you can undertake your search free from outside interruptions. If you are diligent, you will know when you are close to finding The Creator, for he is within you," said Anthony.

"You mean I will finally be able to see him?"

"You will not see him in a literal sense. If you are true in your search, you will feel his presence within you. It is then that you will know him. He is all seeing. He knows you and can see you, but you must work to be able to know him."

"If I can see him, what does he look like? How will I know when I have found him?"

"He is not a man. He is spirit. You must be diligent in your search to find him within yourself," repeated Anthony.

"I'm trying to understand your temple. Are you also saying that he is in all things around us as well as within us?" asked Jim.

"My friend, we both look at the natural world in wonder. We find our inspiration in it. We look at the bird and wonder how it came to be here. We have much in common, you and I. We ask the same question, but first let me apologize," said Anthony.

"Apologize for what?"

"We are taught at the temple to avoid using the old terminology."

"What old terminology?"

"The old words are out of date and too emotionally charged to be useful in any discussion."

"So how do we speak to each other?" asked Jim.

"Very simple. People can be placed into one of two categories. Those who believe that we were placed here on this earth by The Creator, as we are today, and will forever be, are called 'absolutists.' Those who believe we are here as the result of a perpetually changing world are called 'flexists.' Both accept that there was a time before man was here, and both require faith to reach their contrary positions about how we actually came to stand on this earth today."

"Using your terminology, flexists must take their position from science and the observation of nature, if I understand what you are saying?" asked Jim.

"Yes, and absolutists say that what they observe is the evidence of the hand of The Creator. All people make the same observation. The difference between them is their interpretation of the world they observe. Absolutists see The Creator, and flexists see natural selection. Absolutists see careful intelligent effort in the creation of nature, while flexists see careful intelligent effort in the examination of nature which they claim, but cannot show, is the result of random events," said Anthony.

"Now I see how you are using your terminology," said Jim.

"Flexists say absolutists have no proof of The Creator. Absolutists say flexists have no proof of change. Both staunchly believe in their positions and are unable to hear the arguments of the other. Absolutists say flexists are blind. Flexists say absolutists are deaf. We, at the temple, stand on these steps seeking an open mind."

"I wish you luck," said Jim. "An open mind is a rare commodity these days."

"What they both share is that it takes internal faith to reach their position. Neither can prove their case," said Anthony. "Both depend on faith."

"Maybe both are talking about the same thing?" Jim responded. "Maybe they are just using different labels for what they both see in nature. Maybe the universe is an inspiration to both."

"I wish life was that simple, my friend, but I think it is not. Flexists believe in a series of random events, pure chance, and absolutists are quite the opposite. They say nature and our own existence is the act of a kind and benevolent creator."

"I wish you were right. I really do, but you need to open your eyes and look around. When an airplane falls out of the sky, there are good people, and there are bad people on board. When they die, they all die together. I don't see that as the act of your kind and benevolent creator," said Jim. "I see a random event."

"The Creator works in mysterious ways, my friend. You must accept that as part of your faith."

"I'd like to say that's a cop out," said Jim, "but I can see we differ at a fundamental level. We will not be able to resolve our differences here on these steps today. All I can say is that in my heart, I wish you were right about The Creator."

"Look deep inside yourself. You did not come out of this building with a feeling of warmth, of connectedness. What you come out with is a feeling of emptiness. People come here to be reassured that man is the highest, most noble of all species on earth."

"Yes, I agree with you," said Jim. "Most people believe that, no matter how you label them."

"We, at the temple, rejoice with them, my friend. We also believe in the supremacy of man, but not because he is the result of change, but because he was placed here by his Creator. We differ from the high priests of science in this building in our view of how man came to rule supreme on this planet. We are ready to embrace those who leave here unsatisfied or unconvinced by its false presentation of the rise of man."

"Somehow I think you are trying to stand on a neutral ground. By using your terminology, your temple appears to be strictly absolutist," said Jim.

"That is true. To the absolutist, there is no mystery about our origins. We are here because The Creator put us here. It is that simple. To the flexist, there is a great mystery about the origin of man on this earth. They struggle to show the process of how man came to be here as the result of change. Flexists need proof. Absolutists do not."

"And you say Flexists have not been able to show change?"

"Certainly not. Would it surprise you, my friend, if I said our temple believes in Darwin?"

"You must be joking," said Jim.

"Darwin saw a struggle for the survival of the most fit taking place between the species on earth. He very carefully did not say where the species came from, only that they had to struggle to survive. We do not question that," said Anthony.

146

"But you must admit that some species die out and do not survive," said Jim.

"The Creator made the earth and all species on it. Unlike some, we at the temple do not believe he adjusts it. The Creator is not a tinkerer. The environment changes. We accept that. Creatures must strive to survive. Giraffes have long necks because they have learned to stretch to reach the highest trees for food. They are survivors. The Creator made the earth, but he does not manipulate it every day," said Anthony.

"What you are saying is that The Creator helps those who help themselves," said Jim.

"Yes. That is a fair observation, my friend."

"Not all absolutists would agree with your temple on that," said Jim.

"The point is that it all funnels down to the ultimate issue between absolutist and flexists. If you were to come back to earth a million years from now, who would greet you? As absolutists, we believe you would meet a man identical with man of today, and you could sit down on a park bench and carry on a conversation with him, just as we are now."

"Yes. I can see that as the ultimate absolutist position," said Jim.

"The flexists, who see nothing but constantly changing random events, would say that you would meet a creature standing here that you would not recognize and with whom you would not share a language," said Anthony.

"Personally, looking at the world today, I think in a million years from now there won't be anything here at all. If your example is correct about the great differences between both positions, then it is a question that will be solved in time," said Jim.

"Eventually, one or the other will be proven right."

"Yes, my friend, in time," said Anthony.

"I think there are different kinds of absolutist," said Jim. "I don't think everything is as black and white as you describe."

"You are intelligent, my friend. You can think. We should talk more. For now, take this pamphlet with you and read it at your leisure."

"I'll do that," said Jim.

"The pamphlet will repeat what I have told you, but it will tell you how to reach us. I think you would find a trip to our temple rewarding. The temple is just a few kilometers north of town," said Anthony. "The other followers would welcome the opportunity to tell you more about us."

"I may want to take you up on that invitation. I was hoping I would meet the young man from your temple who picked me up at the airport in Nairobi yesterday. His name was David Johannson," said Jim.

147

"Yes, I know him. He is with our temple. He is out there even as we speak. You will not find him here. He is a neophyte," said Anthony.

"What is a neophyte?" asked Jim, remembering how David had used the term, but unsure how Anthony would describe the classification.

"A neophyte is not a member of the temple. A neophyte is one who is sent here to absorb the cleansing environment of the desert. They are not here to seek something. They are sent here to escape the demons of the past. Neophytes are usually sent by their parents because they have serious personal problems at home," said Anthony.

"What kinds of problems?" asked Jim.

"Drugs, alcohol, and those kinds of things are the reasons they are sent here for rehabilitation. Neophytes do not come here because they have adopted our philosophy. Their parents read our advertisements in magazines and pay for them to stay here at the temple for a period of time away from home. Neophytes do not always adopt our message, even after staying with us for a number of months," said Anthony.

"They don't believe in your message?"

"They usually stay only for the period reserved by their parents. Neophytes go back home and take up where they left off. We don't anticipate that they will stay. Usually they forget this place as soon as they are gone. There are very few neophytes who stay with us once their time is up," said Anthony.

"Why is that?"

"They seldom reach the level of conscience required. The effort must come from within. They must find their own way. We cannot find it for them."

"But some do make it. You did," observed Jim.

"Yes. Should a neophyte qualify after two years, then only can he become a follower like the two of us here today, but only if he reaches the right state of mind. Only followers and priests are allowed to greet the public and solicit memberships and donations," said Anthony.

"So both of you are the next level above David?" asked Jim.

"It's more than that. As a neophyte, David is not a part of the temple. He is an outsider. As followers, we are a part of the temple. We adopt and live by its doctrines. There is a big difference between us."

"I see," said Jim.

"Everyone goes through the neophyte stage. For us, as part of the temple, we strive to reach a proper level of conscience so that eventually we can become priests. All followers stay because they want to become priests."

"David picked me up at the airport in Nairobi," said Jim. "He was out greeting the public."

"Yes. Neophytes do run errands into the city, mostly to pick up supplies for the temple. He was probably available to bring you here to Elizabethtown since he was on his way back from Nairobi," said Anthony, who turned away momentarily to hand brochures to two visitors leaving the museum.

"Let me tell you one more thing," said Anthony, addressing Jim again.

"Sure, I'm ready."

"Parents don't send their kids here to join the temple."

"They don't?" asked Jim.

"No, actually, they really want their kids to come home. Parents just want to dump some of the responsibility for bringing up their kids onto someone else because they cannot handle some problem the kid has back home."

"I see," said Jim.

"They want the kid back, problems solved of course, but they want the kid returned when the vacation is over. The last thing they want is for their kid to reject their home and decide to stay here," said Anthony, smiling at Jim.

"Oh," said Jim. "I think you may be right."

"Followers have to reject their parents and the world they represent," said Anthony, looking sternly at Jim.

For a moment neither spoke. Jim noticed two stacks of fliers near Anthony's feet and a metal pot on a tripod a few feet away set up to collect donations.

"Perhaps David will reach the level of conscience to become a follower," said Anthony, wistfully. "I do not know him that well. I think, however, it is more than likely he will be on the plane back home when his reservation time is up. I'm usually pretty good at guessing who will stay."

"Thank you again for this brochure," said Jim. "I was wondering what I need to do to arrange a meeting with David. I'm here in Africa to investigate the death of Dr. Edward Bronston, the archaeologist who just recently died. I understand David worked part time at Dr. Bronston's excavation site. I need to talk to everyone who worked out there," said Jim.

"Yes, of course,' said Anthony. "The temple is very familiar with Dr. Bronston. His camp was only a few kilometers from the temple. There is no problem. You will also need to meet with Eric Antonio. He is also a follower. I believe he also worked for Dr. Bronston. By the way, the Temple endorses Dr. Bronston's work."

"It does? That surprises me," Jim was amazed.

"Yes. He was a true scientist, not like the people of this museum. He simply reported what he found on or in the ground. He did not try to preach his own interpretations," said Anthony. "He was not on a crusade. He was a seeker of truth."

"I think I understand," said Jim. "In spite of his work, you saw him as an absolutist."

"We do not know his personal views, my friend. He simply never preached flexism. He is in a better place now."

"I hope so," said Jim.

"All you need to do is contact the temple to schedule some time there. You may just drive out if you want, but I would radio out first, just to be sure they will both be there when you arrive. Of course, our doors are always open to anyone who visits. The directions to the temple are on the back of the brochure," said Anthony.

"Thank you very much," said Jim.

"Dr. Bronston believed that what he found in his excavations were creatures that are now gone," Anthony continued. "He did not preach that one changed to another. We believe there were many creatures that are no longer with us. The more true scientists like Dr. Bronston learn about them, the more we will understand about The Creator," said Anthony.

"Well, thank you again," said Jim. "I appreciate your time. I have learned a lot from you today."

"May peace be with you always. Please do come out to our temple. We are open seven days a week. You will be most welcome," said Anthony as he turned to address new prospects who had stopped to pick up brochures.

"Jim noticed that the metal pot next to the two stacks of fliers contained some bills but mostly coins. Anthony had not asked for anything, so Jim reached into his coat pocket and retrieved his wallet. He took out a five-dollar bill and dropped it into the pot, realizing when he did so, that he had failed to exchange some money into the local currency. He would have to stop at the bank in the morning before they left for the camp. Hopefully, the bank would be open early.

He turned and walked down to the corner and crossed the street, where he paused and opened the brochure. It read:

The Illusion

Now that you have seen all that the high priests of this false temple have to offer, know that this place is an illusion. Portrayed here is a cold and uncaring universe of random accidents, a barren place. If you come away feeling empty, incomplete, uncertain or unfulfilled, it is because you know deep inside that this temple is false.

Know that God is the Creator of all that exists. You cannot hide. The all-seeing God knows your inner thoughts. He awaits you. This place is based on belief. There is no proof for what they preach. They say that God does not exist because they cannot see him.

They say we are believers, but cannot prove God exists. God is like the wind. You cannot see the wind, but you know it is there. You can feel it. Come to the temple. The all-seeing God lies within you. Come and rejoice with us in his presence.

Our temple never closes. We are open seven days a week. We are located on the east fork of the Outer Territories Road, 50 kilometers north of Elizabethtown. Follow the signs. Come for an hour, a day, a week, or a lifetime.

Jim slipped the brochure into his inner suit coat pocket and began walking briskly to the hotel. He never looked back. Dr. Umbawi, he remembered, would be waiting for him.

CHAPTER NINE: *DARWIN'S DEMISE*

When Jim arrived back at the hotel, Dr. Umbawi was not in the lobby. Jim went up to his room. As he unlocked the door, the telephone rang. The front desk attendant informed him that Dr. Umbawi had just arrived and would meet him in the restaurant. Jim took a couple of minutes to freshen up. He shaved quickly to get rid of his five o'clock stubble, changed his shirt, splashed on some aftershave, and then went downstairs to the restaurant.

Dr. Umbawi was seated at the same table they had occupied the previous evening, placidly reading the evening newspaper. When he looked up and saw Jim approach, he smiled and waved, motioning for Jim to join him. Jim saw him put the newspaper down on the serving table located immediately behind his chair, just as Jim reached the table.

"You look tired, Jim," said Dr. Umbawi, as they sat down. "I trust that your day was productive?"

"Productive? That, I'm not so sure of, but it certainly was interesting," said Jim.

"Tell me about it," said Dr. Umbawi.

Jim told him of his meeting with Dr. Bhatt.

"Wonderful," said Dr. Umbawi.

"Wonderful? How can it be wonderful? I went to his office convinced I would find a medical motivation for suicide, and I came away with nothing."

"To the contrary, Jim. You did just fine. Remember that your journey is one of elimination. If you can put medical motivation aside, you can go on from there. I see that as a real success."

"Well, I think I made some progress towards eliminating psychological causes as well as medical. Dr. Bhatt's impression was that Dr. Bronston was quite enthusiastic about his work," said Jim.

"I would say that was an accurate observation," said Dr. Umbawi nodding in agreement.

"Dr. Bhatt was very cooperative and gave me copies of all the documentation I could ever hope for."

"Even better," said Dr. Umbawi. "I do think you need more input to eliminate psychological causes. His opinion is useful, but you need more than that."

"I agree, but that was just the beginning."

"Please go on. Tell me about the rest of your day."

"Well, I stayed right on the schedule you and Nancy set for me."

"Good."

"I took a jitney over to the cemetery, and I met Nancy at the gravesite."

"How is she doing? I haven't seen her for a few days since she went to stay with a former schoolmate on the other side of Nairobi."

"She's doing fine. She appeared genuinely happy to see me. She's ready to take me out to Bokuru in the morning. I think our meeting was more social than anything else. It went well though." He proceeded to tell Dr. Umbawi the relevant parts of the meeting with Nancy.

"Good. She stayed at our house when she first came to Africa. She seemed to be taking things in stride, even though I knew she was very upset about losing her father. She basically told me the same things she told you."

"Her father didn't tell her much about what he was doing, especially the details of what he found there," said Jim.

"Perhaps not, but I think you have a good handle on several of the issues through her intimate knowledge of her father. I think we are getting close to eliminating personal, psychological and financial motivations for suicide as well. Wouldn't you agree?" asked Dr. Umbawi.

"Yes. I think so."

"So, was that it?" Dr. Umbawi asked. "Did she have anything else to say?"

"Well, no. I asked her about the possibility of an accident where the gun might have gone off in his hand by accident."

"Good question. What did she say about that theory?

"She told me he hated guns. She was emphatic that he prohibited guns from his excavation sites. She said everyone encouraged him to keep a gun just as protection against carnivores and snakes, but he stubbornly refused."

"I thought so," said Dr. Umbawi. "He told me the same thing on many occasions. Guns were out. I must confess that I was one of those who recommended that he keep a gun at his camp. I cringed when he told me that from time to time lions were known to be nearby and he thought one may have walked through the camp during the night."

"A lion walked through the camp?"

"They saw the foot prints the next morning. He shrugged the danger of the lions off. He said that the ones they knew about were not man eaters."

"How would he know that? Aren't they all carnivores?" asked Jim.

"Perhaps he interviewed them," said Dr. Umbawi, smiling. "I don't know, Jim. His cavalier attitude to danger always bothered me. The point is, if he decided to commit suicide, obtaining a gun for that purpose would not have been a problem here. He could have come here to Elizabethtown and bought one without anyone knowing."

"You're right. It would be that simple."

"If he had a gun and was playing around with it, there could have been an accidental discharge. That's possible. Still, he would not have had possession of a gun unless he planned to take his life with it," said Dr. Umbawi.

"Nancy told me that a friend of the family killed his wife with the family gun when investigating what he thought was a burglary many years ago. That was the primary reason for Dr. Bronston's strong position against guns," said Jim.

"I've heard the same story. The question remains, why would he even think about such an extreme act?"

"I agree, said Jim. "My search for his motive is the same, accident or not."

"I'm in the same boat with Dr. Bhatt and Nancy. I simply see no explanation for his action. From what we know about Dr. Bronston, the act of suicide does not make any sense to us. At the same time, I'm telling you that murder and suicide are similar. Both have a motive. As I told you, suicide is murder of the self. Your job is to find the motive." Dr. Umbawi paused a moment. "Look, we have talked long enough. Let's take a break and have a glass of wine. You have put in a long day."

"Fine," said Jim, smiling. "I could use a break." Dr. Umbawi had a way of putting things in perspective.

"I'll have my customary Chablis."

"And I'll have the same," said Jim.

"I figured you would order the same as last night," said Dr. Umbawi.

He raised his hand, and within moments a waiter arrived with a glass for Jim.

"Enjoy. A toast to your investigation, Jim. I think it is going well."

"A toast then," said Jim, as they touched glasses. "I'm not going to be happy until I have a lead on his motive."

"I believe you will find the cause of Dr. Bronston's death, no matter where the search leads. Just stay the course, Jim. Stay the course."

"I wish I had your confidence," said Jim. "Anyway, I did meet Dr. Tubojola after a brief lunch at the museum cafeteria with Nancy."

"Elizabethtown has a wonderful museum, doesn't it?"

"Yes. It is extraordinary," said Jim.

154

"My office at the university in Nairobi looks across the athletic fields and the river over to the museum there. The Nairobi museum is a good one, but this one in Uhuru is more modern. In time, the exhibits here will rival those in Nairobi. In the long run, this museum will begin to draw attendance away from its older sister."

"Well, this one is professionally set up, and I say that, even without seeing the main exhibits," said Jim, as he took a sip of wine.

"Tell me. What is your impression of Dr. Tubojola?" asked Dr. Umbawi.

"He is an extraordinary person. He knows who he is and what he's trying to do. He's very much a man in charge," Jim continued. "He has some heavy responsibilities."

"He is an important man here in Uhuru. Did he tell you anything useful about Dr. Bronston?"

"He told me Dr. Bronston had no legal problems here in Uhuru. He said all visas, licenses, and permits were in good order. He also said Dr. Bronston did not appear to have any financial problems. From his perspective, he was sure the excavation work was fully funded, and there were no impediments to a continued and successful excavation."

"Good," said Dr. Umbawi again.

"According to Dr. Tubojola, the entire museum staff was stunned at Dr. Bronston's sudden death. He said they all have the same problem with the suicide determination as everyone else has. Oh, he did agree with you."

"He agreed with me? That's a bit unusual. We tend to disagree more often than not. He likes my opinion as a consultant, but he usually makes a different decision than I would."

"Well, he said I would not find my answer to the motive question here. He agreed with you that the answer had to be out at the excavation site, at Bokuru."

"I see," said Dr. Umbawi. "Did he give you any clue about what he thought you should look for at Bokuru?"

"No, unfortunately not. He said he had no idea what Dr. Bronston had discovered. He was highly suspicious that Dr. Bronston was being evasive."

"How so?"

"He felt Dr. Bronston was not telling him everything. Dr. Tubojola strongly implied that Dr. Bronston had found something significant at the excavation site."

"Think nothing of that, Jim. Dr. Bronston and Dr. Tubojola have been at odds over the extent of the interim disclosure that is required.

155

Their debate has been going on for years. Dr. Tubojola believes that everything the field archaeologist does and finds should be disclosed in the weekly reports."

"Yes, he does. He told me about the law."

"He pushed that law through himself. That law has a criminal aspect to it, too. He is very obstinate when it comes to that issue. Maybe that colors his suspicions about Dr. Bronston."

"Yes. He certainly believes in weekly disclosure and written reports," said Jim.

"Their debate became somewhat emotional when Dr. Bronston started work at Bokuru because he had not been excavating in Uhuru for several years. The law was new, and he was not familiar with it. Dr. Bronston believed the law was wrong. He believed field workers must operate in total privacy, without pressure. He often said the archaeologist should not make any disclosure until all the fieldwork was done and there had been time to analyze the work and make a final report. Any other action would be premature."

"Dr. Tubojola said the weekly reports are supposed to be just preliminary."

"Dr. Bronston's fear, Jim, was that there are all too many leaks through the informal grapevine as soon as a discovery is made."

"Was that a realistic concern?"

"Yes, unfortunately, he wasn't paranoid. His concerns were justified by the history of archaeology all over the world."

"Dr. Tubojola has a different opinion," said Jim.

"Dr. Tubojola tried to put me in the middle."

"How did he do that?"

"He wanted me to impress Dr. Bronston with the need to comply with the law. You need to understand that their disagreement was not really serious, just superficially political. In fact, it was Dr. Tubojola who invited Dr. Bronston back to Uhuru specifically to investigate the cave site at Bokuru."

"Oh, really. You are the first to tell me that fact."

"Just remember, the weekly disclosure law was not passed because of Dr. Bronston."

"Then why was it passed?

"Dr. Tubojola's problems were with other archaeologists. However, he faced criticism from others that the law was being selectively applied against them, unless, of course, Dr. Tubojola could induce Dr. Bronston to also comply."

"Dr. Bronston was sending in cave dimensions on a weekly basis," said Jim.

"That's because they did reach an agreement."

"They did? Do you know what it was?"

"Dr. Tubojola agreed to stay away from Bokuru, and Dr. Bronston agreed to send in weekly disclosures. Then, Dr. Tubojola dropped the topic. In the early months, dimensions were acceptable since there was nothing else to submit and they reached the bottom of the cave."

"When I met with Dr. Tubojola, he was sure Dr. Bronston was holding back on something important at Bokuru."

"I remember the day when Dr. Tubojola called me," said Dr. Umbawi.

"About Bokuru?"

"Yes. He made a special call to tell me that he had received a report with the first "V" dimension," said Dr. Umbawi.

"What is a "V" dimension?" asked Jim. "I am not familiar with that term."

"That is a vertical distance down from the datum plane. They would not include that kind of dimension unless they knew the distance to the bottom of the cave. That measurement indicated they were confident that they had reached the occupation level. Dr. Tubojola's expectancy from that moment on was for more than mere dimensions. He was sure they would find something in the cave when they reached the floor."

"But Dr. Bronston kept sending nothing more than dimension numbers," said Jim.

"Yes, that is what Dr. Bronston would do."

"Maybe that's what made Dr. Tubojola suspicious," said Jim.

"I raised the issue with Dr. Bronston, but he stubbornly refused to discuss the matter. He said he was following the law. Frankly, I do not like being put in the middle of real world disputes. I am a teacher, and I would like my participation to be limited to that role," said Dr. Umbawi.

"Well, Dr. Tubojola made it clear to me that he felt Dr. Bronston knew more than just cave dimensions once they reached the bottom of the excavation," said Jim.

"I think the disclosures being made were simply Dr. Bronston's way of meeting the minimum requirements of the law," said Dr. Umbawi. "I would not read much into what he did."

"Dr. Tubojola showed me a three dimensional schematic of the interior of the cave on the museum computer. The projected schematic was quite impressive. The schematic was based on the updated information Dr. Bronston sent in weekly," said Jim.

"Uhuru has a public disclosure law that requires publication of results within six months of completion of an excavation," said Dr. Umbawi.

"That's a pretty short fuse."

"Yes, but in archaeology you can't refer to the work of another unless that work is already published. Thus, final reports make new discoveries available to other scientists as well as the public without unnecessary delay. The rule serves a valid public purpose."

"It sounds like a good rule," said Jim. "It just put a lot of pressure on final reports."

"Yes, but on the other hand, Dr. Bronston would say that you don't want to disclose prematurely or in part. Premature disclosure increases the chance for error. He was more concerned with accuracy and completeness than speed."

"I can understand his point," said Jim.

"Dr. Bronston's disagreement with the weekly disclosure rule was that not only did you increase the risk of the informal grapevine getting a hold of your information prematurely, but it was common knowledge that Dr. Tubojola violated his own rule by making preliminary information available to others. He would provide printouts and public displays to outsiders to enhance the stature of Uhuru and the museum. This was something Dr. Bronston considered to be publication," said Dr. Umbawi.

"Dr. Tubojola showed me what he currently had on Bokuru. He was quite proud of their ability to be up to date on a weekly basis. He showed the cave dimensions on a big screen."

"Precisely. That sort of demonstration was exactly what Dr. Bronston was complaining about."

"Okay. Now I understand why Dr. Bronston objected," said Jim.

"Dr. Bronston would call Dr. Tubojola's little display of data to you a legal publication under the law, such that third parties would now have legal access to the material. Dr. Bronston's point was that such preliminary information should not be disclosed until the final report was made and a full publication took place in the conventional sense, with all the checks and balances involved in the process. Publication puts the field results in the public domain," said Dr. Umbawi.

"Well, Dr. Tubojola is convinced there is something significant at Bokuru."

"Dr. Tubojola would always say that, no matter what was disclosed, Jim. He looks at archaeological artifacts as the personal possessions of Uhuru. He insists on knowing what the archaeologist is doing with his possessions at all times. That is just his mindset. You will understand him better if you understand his position. He is very predictable."

"So, who is right? Dr. Bronston or Dr. Tubojola?"

"They both have their points. There are simply different ways of looking at the same issue. Unfortunately, there is no easy answer. It depends on whose shoes you wear."

"Well, the museum computer installation is amazing," said Jim.

"The technology is state-of-the-art here in Uhuru," said Dr. Umbawi. "Tell me, did he show you his collection?"

"His collection?" Jim chuckled out loud. "Do you mean the skulls on the shelf?" asked Jim.

"Yes, his wonderful skull collection."

"Yes, he has it on the bookshelf behind his desk. It is very interesting and thought provoking," said Jim.

"Do you know I was one of those who objected to it?"

"No, he didn't tell me who specifically objected. Why did you object?" asked Jim.

"My vote does not count. I am just a consultant here in Uhuru. I am not a member of the board of trustees of the museum. I was nominated once to serve on the board for the museum in Nairobi."

"That would be an honor," said Jim.

"Yes, but I was rejected."

"Rejected, why?"

"They said I was eliminated due to a conflict of interest. The problem was that I was on retainer as a consultant to the museum here in Uhuru, and that automatically eliminated me. In any case, as I was saying, I thought the collection was most inappropriate in a museum. Something like that should never be anywhere in the museum. I believe his home would be a wonderful setting, but not in his office."

"Why not? It's just art."

"Exactly, Jim. It is not science."

"Dr. Tubojola said it was just art. He was very careful to emphasize that it was not a representation of anything real."

"You miss the point. He is the chief scientist in the country. Actually, that is not correct. More accurately, his is the highest representative for science in the country. In addition, he is a top administrator in the country. Still everything he does should be accurate and representative of true science. He is a role model," said Dr. Umbawi.

"So you don't buy the argument that the collection is just art."

"Certainly not," said Dr. Umbawi. "Those carvings consist of what he thinks we will find. They were made according to his specifications.

It is almost as if he is creating the human history by sheer will power. Archaeology can use all the help it can get, but it doesn't need that kind of help. Putting his carvings anywhere in the museum is fuzzy thinking, and that is what creates a lot of the criticism we face. He, of all people, should know better."

"I think I understand your point."

"His art exhibit suggests that our human history is a straight line beginning with lower forms of life culminating in modern man."

"Yes, I agree that's what it shows," said Jim

"That creates a false impression," said Dr. Umbawi, taking out a pen and drawing a multi-branched tree with many sub-branches on his dinner napkin. "This is the history of all life forms represented more accurately. Each life form has a history of continuous changes with the survivors being at the right place at the right time. They call it adaptive radiation. We are just one of several hominid species that have existed on earth. Mankind is a survivor by the luck of the draw, more than anything else. Our past is that of a multi-branched tree, just like all other life forms."

"I see," said Jim.

"I think Dr. Tubojola was also not being totally honest with you about his collection."

"How so?" asked Jim.

"You cannot, Jim, confront a true believer with science any more than you can confront a scientist about belief."

"I think you are right about that," said Jim.

"That is not to say that some scientists are not believers."

"What are you saying?" asked Jim.

"Take Dr. Tubojola, for example. Did he not tell you that humans got to the top of the proverbial mountain by hard work, by striving and diligent effort or something to that effect?"

"Yes. Come to think of it, that is exactly what he said."

"Hogwash, Jim. The puritan ethic."

"The puritan ethic? What has that have to do with this?"

"To those who believe in it, success only comes from hard work and keeping your nose to the grindstone. Only if you stay with your work will you be rewarded in the end."

"He did say that," said Jim.

"Then ask yourself, if hard work, striving, and goal seeking are to be rewarded, who will hand out the trophy?"

"Oh, I see what you are saying."

"Pure creationism, Jim. Pure creationism."

"I don't think Dr. Tubojola would consider himself a creationist," said Jim.

"You are right. If he were to look into a mirror, he would not see himself as he is, only as he perceives himself to be. I think his collection tells more about him than even he would be willing to admit."

"I see. That reminds me, I wanted to show you this," said Jim, as he reached into his suit coat pocket and pulled out the brochure from the temple. "I picked this up from one of the followers of the Temple of Tassan. They were handing out these fliers in front of the museum," he said, handing the brochure over to Dr. Umbawi.

"Yes," said Dr. Umbawi, looking over the brochure. "I am familiar with the Temple of Tassan. They have been demonstrating in front of the museum since it opened."

"Doesn't their presence bother you?" asked Jim.

"Not me. I'm just a consultant here in Uhuru. The question is whether their presence bothers Dr. Tubojola. This group does not promote violence. Their pitch predates modern civilization." He handed the brochure back to Jim. "Keep this one for yourself. I have a couple of these brochures in my office."

"Have you ever been out there to the temple?" Jim asked.

"To the temple? No, I have never been so honored. I do know two of their followers fairly well. Both attended one of my classes at the university in Nairobi some time back before they dropped out and joined the temple. Personally, I think you would be disappointed if you paid them a visit," said Dr. Umbawi. "I have a feeling there's not much to see."

"I spoke briefly with the follower who gave me the brochure," said Jim.

"Oh. What did he tell you? I'm not up to date on their philosophy."

Jim told Dr. Umbawi about his conversation with Anthony.

"Fuzzy thinking, Jim."

"What is?"

"Their whole position. They brainwash these kids so they can't think for themselves. Lumping Darwin in with their views is absurd."

"The guy sounded sincere in his beliefs," said Jim.

"That stuff about giraffes is old thinking. The last members of that school were back in the late 1800's. That is not how change works. They have muddled their fringe view with outdated science, creating a mishmash philosophy."

"Then, how would you classify them?"

"Confused, Jim. Confused. Did you notice that they are sexist?"

"No. I don't remember him ever mentioning women," said Jim.

"Precisely. You never will. There are no female priests in their temple. In fact, there are no female followers, nor are there any female neophytes either. They are extremists, Jim far more than just fundamentalists."

"You might be right,' said Jim. "I am trying to process everything that happened today, including my conversation with Anthony."

"They see The Almighty as male, and human males as created in his image. Females are just an afterthought."

"The story of Adam and Eve?" asked Jim.

"More than that, their credo is that only males can get close to the Almighty Creator. They are very biased. I think you will find they are out in the desert in a remote African country for a reason."

"You seem to know a lot about them," observed Jim.

"Look, the young man you met was playing games with you."

"He was?"

"He was trying to find a way to undermine your cultural foundation. He backed off when he saw you were too strong. Their whole approach is to snip away at your culture so they can prepare you for their own views. Did he prod you on religion?"

"He stuck to absolutists and flexists."

"I'm familiar with their terminology. He probably didn't see you strong on the religious front, so he attacked you as a flexist trying to show that absolutism was the better philosophy."

"Yes, and he used what you described as muddled thinking," said Jim.

"Of course. If you had appeared strongly religious, he would have tried such things as telling you the story of Adam and Eve was the story of the first love triangle."

"A triangle? I never heard of that one before," said Jim.

"That's what they would say. Then, when you would react as you just did, he would ask you if you really read the Bible carefully, and put you on the defensive."

"I see."

"You would respond that you hadn't read the Bible, at least not carefully."

"Which is true," said Jim.

"Don't worry about it. Very few have. It's the most unread book in history. Everyone has strong opinions about it, but only a rare few ever really read it. You would have given him the opening he was looking for."

"How so?"

"He would ask, how could you believe in it if you did not read it? He would then attack how the Bible painted The Creator as vindictive, demanding blind obedience. Then when you countered that you did not believe his summary, he would again ask if you had read it, and you would have to admit you had not," said Dr. Umbawi.

"All he would be doing was to induce me to question my beliefs," said Jim.

"Yes, now you understand. That's what I call an old 'Bennie Tassan mind game.'"

"Bennie Tassan, who is he?"

"As I said, I lost two good exchange students who were picked off from the campus in Nairobi by Mr. Tassan. They were both good students, so I decided to look into Mr. Tassan. It really shook me to have lost those two students to become followers of Mr. Tassan. I was worried that my teaching methods of trying to induce students to question their culture and come up with their own answers had gone too far."

"What did you find out?"

"Thankfully those two were the only ones I ever lost. I should say that they do still keep in touch with me, even today. It is just that I avoid discussions about their thinking or the basic concepts of the temple. My contact with them is purely social. If I were to press them, they would simply clam up." Said Dr. Umbawi. "I did not want to lose contact with them permanently."

"What about Mr. Tassan? Do you know much about their philosophy?"

"Only what I have learned from others. Benny, that's Bernard Tassan, was a carry over from the hippie generation in your country. He lived in California. He developed his own cult and preyed on freshmen at the big universities."

"Preyed on them, how?" asked Jim.

"He would use the same game to undermine their fundamental culture and values. Once he saw a weakness, he would exploit it and try to induce the students to drop out and join him. Much like other cults."

"Did it work?"

"Oh yes. He had a few cases of success. Students dropped out and rejected their school, parents, and society in general. He was successful in destroying a few good lives, but he drew media attention when some parents tried to pull their kids away form his influence."

"So he found himself in the spotlight. He should have loved that."

"To the contrary, Jim. He could not stand the heat. At that time, he had no agenda other than to fight the status quo. He had no program of his own, so he took a core group of followers and relocated here in the savannah of Uhuru to escape close scrutiny."

"It appears you have studied him carefully," mused Jim.

"As I said, I have maintained a casual relationship with my two former students. Actually, the last time I was able to try to discuss the cult, they had no positive replacement ideology that I could detect. I want students to learn to think on their own, but I don't want to destroy them."

"I only got a hint of what they believe," said Jim.

"Maybe you can push them in your interview process. I'd like to know where I went wrong. Those two students represent my biggest failure in life. I had great expectations for both of them. Now they are lost forever."

"I do have to meet with David, the guy who picked me up at the airport. I also need to talk with his friend who also worked for Dr. Bronston. I need to interview both of them as part of the investigation of Dr. Bronston's death," said Jim.

"Yes, you did mention them. That is a good idea to interview them. Remember, I am working on an appointment for you through my contacts. I will try to have them drive out to Bokuru while you are there and spare you a trip to the temple. Give me another day to work on that," said Dr. Umbawi.

"I appreciate your help," said Jim.

"I don't want to be completely critical of the temple, Jim. I'm sure they do some good along with the bad. Let's see. You said they used the terms 'absolutists' and what was the other?"

"Flexists," replied Jim.

"Yes. I forgot. Flexists, those who see the world as one of perpetual change."

"Yes," said Jim. "The follower I met said flexists see change as a natural process."

"There are some good books for you to read, Jim, that would document the clear observation of change in both plants and animals. The process has been documented in detail. Our friend Benny Tassan would, of course, avoid keeping up with current knowledge:"

"If there are good books, maybe we should take them out to the temple," said Jim with a grin.

"That would be a waste of time, Jim. You do not understand the concept of belief. You see, belief, any belief, is the adoption of a position as an ultimate truth without proof, and a total rejection of the rational side of your brain. No amount of reading or research will change a belief."

"So there are two sides to my brain," said Jim.

"Yes, and any challenge or threat to a belief position is met with a strong defense of the position that increases as the perceived threat increases. All they would do is burn the books, Jim. If you ever get another chance to talk philosophy with the follower you met, ask him about death."

"Death, why death?"

"Yes. Death. The concept of death is a mystery to the absolutists. Take the initiative, and put them on the spot," said Dr. Umbawi. "They create an afterlife so they can make life a mere transition in an attempt to jump over the concept of death. Put them to the task. For flexists, the concept of death has total meaning."

"Please explain. I am intrigued."

"Certainly. Without death, there can be no life. Of course, the flexist's concept of death does not have the touchy feely kind of explanation many would like to have. But death is totally reconcilable with their position. Give it a try. See if you can embarrass the temple at its own game," said Dr. Umbawi.

"Well, I'll first have to talk to the two fellows who worked at Dr. Bronston's site about their experience working for him. I'm afraid my encounter on the steps of the museum led me astray from my objective of finding a motive for Dr. Bronston's suicide."

"Don't be so sure, Jim. Your encounter could be quite relevant."

"How so?"

"Did I tell you that Dr. Bronston was a religious man?"

"No. I find that hard to believe, especially for an archaeologist."

"He told me on many an occasion that he believed in a creator," said Dr. Umbawi.

"That's hard for me to believe," said Jim.

"Generally, those who are believers are ones who also believe that The Creator put them here on earth for a specific purpose," said Dr. Umbawi.

"Yes, I agree with that."

"Then it reasonably follows that suicide would be a rejection of that purpose and an arbitrary return of the life that was given. I see that as a rejection of The Creator. To me, that is inconsistent with belief. Personally, I cannot see how a devout person can commit suicide," said Dr. Umbawi.

"But you just said you thought Dr. Bronston was a believer."

"The issue for you, Jim, is that you have to get into Dr. Bronston's head. You have to understand how he was thinking at the time the event took place. Religion is a volatile issue, but it is, unfortunately a part of the equation in his case, so I don't think we've wasted any time on the topic. As a believer, how could he do what he did?"

"The problem is that he's gone," said Jim. "Getting into his mindset at the time of his death is going to be a bit difficult."

"No one has said your job would be easy. Keep in mind that he kept detailed records. I think his field notes could act much like a diary. Dr. Tubojola could be right, and your trip to his camp may hold the lead you are looking for."

They ordered dinner and again, ate mostly in silence. As they were finishing a dessert of flan, Jim spoke. "Dr. Tubojola gave me a museum pass to the presentation, 'Long Long Ago'."

"Good for him. Did you enjoy it? I'm interested in your reaction because Dr. Tubojola and I wrote the original script several years ago."

"I didn't know that," said Jim. "The presentation was amazing. I've never attended such a modern presentation on the natural history of the earth. In fact, that was my first experience in an interactive theatre."

"Well, you could have seen that same presentation back in your country."

"I could?"

"Yes. This one in Uhuru is a duplicate."

"You said you wrote the script?" asked Jim.

"Yes. What we did was to try to find a studio in America to make the film for us. We were thinking, at that time, of a conventional two dimensional theatre presentation for the museum."

"What happened?"

"The script wound up in the hands of a studio in California that was looking into an interactive presentation for a big Las Vegas casino. They wanted to offer an evening attraction as an alternative activity after a day of gambling," said Dr. Umbawi.

"That's interesting. I would never have thought of Las Vegas for an archaeological film."

"The long and short of it was the studio liked our script. We worked out a very favorable deal for us. They could use the script for their casino, and we got a full duplicate interactive presentation for the Uhuru museum. That was the essence of the agreement."

"Well, the result is stunning," said Jim. "I would never have expected something so sophisticated and technologically advanced here in Elizabethtown."

"We were fortunate. The presentation has helped put Uhuru and the museum on the map. *Long Long Ago* has been one of Dr. Tubojola's favorite projects. So much has happened in the last few years to advance our knowledge, I'm afraid it is pretty dated now."

"Dated? It seemed current to me," said Jim.

"For one thing, the presentation is based on the Big Bang Theory. There is some challenge to that by those who say it's just another form of what you called absolutism."

"Really?"

"The big problem is that the whole script is straight Darwin. You know, survival of the fittest."

"What's wrong with Darwin?" asked Jim.

"He was brilliant for his time. He understood what was happening in the little picture, which was amazing because he did not know about genetics and the process of mutation that assures continual change. Still, he saw the evidence of what was actually happening."

"You called what he saw as the 'little picture'?" asked Jim.

"I call it Darwin's Demise, Jim. Today, we are reducing his significance, because he didn't see the big picture. Don't get me wrong, he didn't make a mistake. He just wasn't aware of the big picture."

"What did he miss?" asked Jim.

"You see, Jim, when you went to school you learned about the different geological periods, when life on earth changed dramatically."

"Yes, the end of the dinosaurs and all that," said Jim.

"Ah, yes, the Cretaceous-Tertiary boundary. The Iridium anomaly."

"What's the Iridium anomaly? I've never heard of that."

"Iridium is not a naturally occurring element on the earth. High concentrations in the strata at boundaries between geological periods were often cited as evidence of asteroid impacts. Such impacts were thought to be the sole determinative elements for the changes in the biology of the earth," said Dr. Umbawi.

"They aren't?"

"That's old thinking."

"Old thinking? I thought it was modern," said Jim.

"Asteroid impacts play a role in the natural history of the earth, Jim, but they are not determinative of mass extinction events," said Dr. Umbawi.

"I thought they were," said Jim, pausing to take a sip of his wine.

167

"If you want my opinion, when the dust settles over the debate, the Cretaceous-Tertiary boundary event will be shown to be not just limited to the impact of one large meteor in the Yucatan."

"It won't?"

"Oh, the event occurred, but the boundary event was a bit more complicated."

"How so? Can you explain further?"

"I think we will find that it was a multiple impact event, coupled with a significant increase in volcanic activity caused by the disruption of the earth's crust due to the main impact. However, my point is that the event was actually a process that took place over an extremely long period of time."

"I hadn't heard that before," said Jim.

"Don't depend on pop-culture television for your education, Jim. The so-called boundaries between periods shown in most text books as thin pencil lines were, in fact, much wider events covering thousands, if not tens of thousands of years."

"But I thought the sudden impact of a meteor wiped out the dinosaurs," said Jim.

"The dinosaurs were already in serious decline, but let me ask you a question, Jim. When you think of a sudden mass extinction event, what do you mean by sudden?"

"An impact is an instantaneous event," said Jim.

"You might be surprised. The professionals use sudden to mean any period of up to ten thousand years. Other mass extinction events stretch from ten thousand to a million years."

"That's not really very sudden," said Jim.

"Now, you see. You have to look at all the facts. Some dinosaur species appear to have existed after the so-called C-T event. In fact, the experts sometimes have trouble even defining what they mean by a mass extinction event. There are basic questions as to how many species have to become extinct in what time period to call it a mass extinction."

"So things are not as simple as they appear."

"There is confusion at the Cretaceous-Tertiary boundary, just as there is at the other boundaries. It is hard enough just to figure out if a fossil bed of small aquatic snails existed at a specific time period. That, in and of its self, can create monumental problems. The fossil record is crucial, but it is also rare. Look, impacts have some significance on the course of evolution of life on earth. They are the source of creation of the earth in the first place. It's just that we don't know to what extent," said Dr. Umbawi.

168

"I'm still struggling with the fact that one impact did not wipe out the dinosaurs and most other life forms in one catastrophic event."

"The concentration of iridium at what was thought to be the exact time of the event sparked the debate and many an imagination. The Cretaceous-Tertiary boundary was not an instantaneous event. The extinctions that took place were not due to a cataclysmic impact, but a slow gradual process, at least, that is the current thinking of the experts. The real key to mass extinction is climate."

"Climate? I don't think the general public is aware of that."

"Theories, Jim, theories. Too often the professional is rushed into print under a culture of publish or perish, before they are truly ready," said Dr. Umbawi, pausing to take another sip of wine.

"And the media jumps on the theory that is published without looking behind it," added Jim. "No one really cares about the facts."

"Precisely, Jim. Bad science can come out of poor sampling, poor collection of data, preconceptions, and simple bias. Along with poor analysis of the data, you have fuel for serious damage. Any or all of these flaws can lead to erroneous conclusions," said Dr. Umbawi, as he paused to take another sip of his wine.

"Well, you have succeeded in totally confusing me. I was not aware of all these factors. What else determines mass extinctions other than impacts?"

"Well, for example, sea level changes are a source of change. The sea level changes actually provide evidence of changes in temperature and climate. High sea level such as we have now is evidence of a warm period, whereas low levels are evidence that the earth was cool, with the water frozen at the poles in what we refer to as the ice ages."

"That's logical," said Jim.

"Other factors such as salinity and chemical make up of the seas are important too."

"If climate is so important, what triggers these changes in temperature? Where do the ice ages come from?" Jim asked, as he paused to take another sip of wine.

Dr. Umbawi reached around and grabbed another napkin from the serving table behind him, and began to sketch on it. He drew a crude sun and an elliptical orbit around it, with a dot for the earth on the ellipse. "The glacial and interglacial climate changes are the result of several factors, Jim. First, eccentricity of the earth's orbit around the sun is a factor. It has an approximate periodicity of one hundred thousand years. Another factor is the tilt of the earth's axis relative to the elliptic, which has a periodicity of about forty one thousand years."

"That's amazing," said Jim.

"Then you have to take into account when the earth is, in fact, closest to the sun, an event which occurs roughly every twenty three thousand years," said Dr. Umbawi, leaning back in his chair, smiling.

"Things are a lot more complicated than I thought," said Jim, staring at Dr. Umbawi's drawing on the napkin.

"The real issue is that each of these events is superimposed on the other. That's the real catch," said Dr. Umbawi, as he paused to watch Jim's reaction.

"When I was young, I think all my text books showed a circular orbit."

"Exactly. Our knowledge of the world has changed. The net affect of these things determines climate, and the climate directly determines the extent of life on the earth."

"This is becoming a lot more complicated than I ever thought," said Jim.

"You have to remember that everything is constantly changing. There are no constants except change."

"So, are all the headlines charging that man is causing the earth to warm just hype?"

"Not entirely. Man's increasing population has an affect, but the earth has been warming rapidly for thousands of years, while man's impact has not been significant until the beginning of the industrial revolution. The general process is something we have no control over," said Dr. Umbawi, who nodded for their waiter to refill their wine glasses.

"You have really opened my eyes to many things I was not aware of. You truly are a teacher," said Jim.

"We started this conversation on mass extinctions and the arrival of new species as evidenced by the changes in geological periods," said Dr. Umbawi, after taking a sip of his replenished wine glass. He turned over his napkin and sketched a large disk on it with a dot above and another below the disk.

"There is still more to the process. The entire solar system rises above and below the plane of the galaxy shown by this disk. Another theory is that the most intense cosmic radiation occurs when the whole solar system passes through this galactic plane, and the intensity and duration of the crossing could be the key to mass extinctions and new species due to increased radiation on the reproductive systems of all biological organisms," said Dr. Umbawi, sitting back in his chair, smiling again, as he stared over at Jim.

"I'm stunned," said Jim. "I never knew that so many factors were involved."

"A lot is just theory, Jim. As with a many things, you have to study what we know and draw you own conclusions. All too often scientists disagree widely among themselves."

"Well, they have me confused."

"I like the term 'punctuated evolution', Jim. The concept of punctuated evolution promotes the theory that events that destroy what was prevalent species that have survived for a long time coupled with the rising of new species that replace them, shows how Darwin's theory was only part of the picture," said Dr. Umbawi.

"I don't think I'm alone in saying that a lot of what you just said is new."

"You see, Jim, each species has a built in capacity to exist within a certain range of changes in the environment. Within that range, Darwin is right, but if the frequency or extent of environmental change exceeds the capacity for survival of a given species, it will become extinct. When even favorable natural changes do not have enough time to be passed on through the entire species before it encounters a new environment outside its built in range, it will disappear."

"Amazing," said Jim. "I'm learning more in one evening than I did in years of school."

"The success of a species for millions of years does not matter, Jim. No matter how successful a species was before the extinction event, it will be gone if the change is beyond its ability to cope. Of course, survival of any species also involves luck. A species has to be at the right place at the right time. Do I make any sense?"

"Yes. I'm just not up to date on all these new theories."

"The presentation you saw at the museum earlier today does show how the earth was formed to begin with, but it does not address the subsequent events properly. The presentation needs to show these events. An instantaneous event such as an asteroid impact, a comet like the Tungista event, or a super volcanic eruption like the one in ancient Yellowstone provide dramatic examples that would fit nicely in the program. However, the non-instantaneous mass extinctions need to be worked in if the presentation is to be accurate. Mass extinctions have, from time to time, wiped out from fifty to ninety percent of all living species on the earth. If the public is to understand who we are, and how we got here, we need to revise the presentation to bring it up to date."

"It should be easy to change your script," said Jim. "All you need is a pad and pen to write it then record what you have written."

"It's not the script. It's the money to rebuild the interactive theatre. I'm afraid it comes down to dollars and cents, Jim, just like everything else. Right now there is no money for that project."

"So, how do we die? What is the end for mankind?" asked Jim. "The presentation did not address the future. In fact, the one I saw stopped about four million years ago."

"The one you saw did not bring you up to date. You are right. It stopped at over four million years ago. To address your question, we are now in one of the largest mass extinctions in the history of the earth."

"We are? That's another thing I did no know."

"This one is different in that it is caused not by nature, but by man. Our own exploding population is the cause. Without some calamitous event, I think the story of Christmas Island in the Pacific may provide the example for our own story."

"Christmas Island, what happened there? I never heard of that story."

"Read up on it, when you are back in Chicago. Christmas Island is a small isolated island in the Pacific Ocean, like the earth floating in space. After it was discovered, the human population that lived there grew unchecked without regard to their limited resources or their fragile environment. They cut down all the trees, fished out the waters, and in the end, had to resort to living in caves in fear of being eaten by their own kind because there was no other food left."

"Oh, I will have to read up on that one."

"All the concern about the earth warming up may be incorrect," said Dr. Umbawi, looking intently at Jim.

"How is it incorrect? I thought the headlines were emphasizing the dangers to ourselves from doing things that were causing the earth to over heat too quickly," said Jim.

"On my desk at the university is a copy of an interesting thesis by a young graduate student working on his doctorate. He has been working on Baffin Island in the Canadian Arctic. His theory is that we are at the cusp of a significant change in the earth's climate, precisely because of the factors we discussed earlier."

"What is that theory?"

"He says that the temperature is as warm as it can get. His reading of the evidence is that the process of change has already started, and we are on the way to a new ice age."

"You are kidding," said Jim.

"No. He is quite serious. He is pegging his doctorate on it. He reminds the reader that there have been eight ice ages in the last one million years, with the last one ending one hundred ten thousand years ago."

"And the process takes place because of the factors you mentioned?" asked Jim.

"Yes. It's ice, not heat that has me concerned. His theory is a little disconcerting, even though we know the process takes place."

"It has happened before. Haven't we survived before?"

"Those who were here before us, yes, but we are the product of the melting of the last ice sheet. Our existence today is totally dependent on our complicated technology. Our civilization can not survive in a world that is considerably colder."

"But we could adapt as the temperature dropped?"

"The key to the theory in his dissertation is that the rate of climate change may be very rapid."

"Very rapid? How would that happen?"

"You might be right. We could adapt if the change took place over two or three thousand years. We might be able to keep up with that, but if the other theory is correct and the change takes place very quickly, such that we are well on our way, within two hundred years, civilization as we know it will be gone in the blink of a geological eye," said Dr. Umbawi sitting back in his chair to watch Jim's reaction. He paused and took another sip of wine.

"If that is true, we would not have the wooly mammoth and rhinoceros for food this time," said Jim.

"No. I'm afraid our success might depend on the evolution of the wooly cow. Currently, we are still depending on a food system that evolved with us ten thousand years ago. That's the factor of luck."

"I think I'm just an average person. I just take things for granted. Our whole conversation is a bit frightening," said Jim. "To be honest, I think the asteroid impact still scares me the most, probably because it is so easy to visualize."

"It doesn't have to be so frightening when it comes to our own extinction. Lots of people would argue that we have the brainpower to deal with the threats to ourselves. They say we have the ability to do things to anticipate such events, such as the threat of asteroid impacts. They are confident that we can use our brains to prevent such events."

"What can we do?" asked Jim.

"The question is not so much what can we do, as it is what are we willing to do. In a way, I suppose things are frightening because we are not taking any of the threats seriously, any more than we do the danger of our own population growth."

"I read somewhere that after the Jupiter impact, scientists in the U.S. started to do something about potential asteroid impacts," said Jim.

"I don't mean to be quite so pessimistic. It's just that your government allocated only a million dollars to the effort. They spend trillions on trying to find intelligent life in the universe. They even want to look for fossils on Mars, but they don't add to the equation that such life must have survived the same random process we have gone through. Alien intelligence would have to come to grips with how it evolved as well. Then it would also have to realize that it too had to deal with the potential sources of its own extinction in time to do something about those threats," said Dr. Umbawi.

"So you think all the efforts of looking for life in space are a waste of time?"

"Yes. We should be spending the money on saving the miracle that happened here. I think we are going to find that we are far more special than we give ourselves credit for being. What happened here is not likely to happen again, and I don't think we'll find the same miracle some place else."

"It's quite sobering, in spite of the wine," said Jim, pausing again to take another sip from his glass.

"Yes, " said Dr. Umbawi, doing the same. "I'd like to take a moment to thank you."

"Thank me for what?"

"For the memories. I have really enjoyed our conversation this evening," said Dr. Umbawi.

"For the memories? This is only our second meal together. We've never talked about thee things before."

"You don't understand. Didn't I tell you I was a regular customer here?"

"Yes, you did. You said this was your regular table. You said you came here all the time. In fact, you said the restaurant reserves this table for you."

"Good, Jim. Now isn't this a table for two?"

"Of course. Somehow, I pictured you here alone."

"Do not lock into your assumptions so quickly. It will impair your investigation."

"What do you mean?" asked Jim.

"Just this. You think our conversation to the edge of the universe has been a casual digression."

"It hasn't been?" asked Jim.

"You need to open your eyes or you will miss all the possibilities. Everything counts, Jim."

"You just lost me."

"This table has two chairs, Jim. This is my favorite place for dinner in all of Elizabethtown, but I shared my enthusiasm with another."

"Another?" Asked Jim.

"Yes, I dined here frequently, but I seldom ate alone."

"Dr. Tubojola? Was he the one who joined you?"

"Think again. Didn't I tell you how your room works here at the hotel?"

"Yes. You said it was paid for year 'round by the Chicago museum."

"Including meals for two," said Dr. Umbawi.

"Yes. You did say meals were covered. That's what we are doing tonight."

"When there were no formal guests from out of the country, would it surprise you that some one locally took advantage of the room, from time to time?"

"Local people would not need the room, the meals perhaps, but not the room," said Jim.

"Sometimes I think you are the perfect one for your investigation. Then, sometimes I'm not so sure," said Dr. Umbawi.

"You are trying to tell me something. Did you stay overnight from time to time?"

"At least you are thinking again. No, I always drove back home. The mysterious guest was Dr. Bronston."

"Dr. Bronston?"

"Yes. You see, he came into town about every ten days to two weeks. Oh, he would meet with Dr. Tubojola and there were always supplies to pick up and business to address, but he stayed overnight here at the hotel. When he was here, we always enjoyed a good evening meal, hearty conversation, and just as we have, a glass or two of wine."

"I'm still surprised. I didn't think of that."

"He had a good night's sleep on a soft bed and took a warm shower in the morning. After a quick breakfast, he was refreshed and ready for the dirt and dust of Bokuru for another two weeks."

"Amazing. I would never have thought of it," said Jim.

"I have allowed us the luxury of this diversion, Jim for two reasons. One is for you and one is for me."

"So this whole discussion was planned by you, and was not as spontaneous as it appeared?"

"Actually, it took off on its own, but you are right. I did not control our discussion. I let the conversation go wherever it led, intentionally. I suppose, in a way, I should apologize, but I would not use the term diversion to describe our conversation."

"No, you wouldn't?"

"There is a reason for everything. For me, our conversation has been nostalgic, a moment reminiscent of when Dr. Bronston and I sat here and discussed more than solved the great problems of the world, often, I might add, with great gusto and emotion, and perhaps, encouraged by an extra glass of wine or two."

"Just as we have," said Jim.

"Precisely, I thank you for that moment."

"You said there was a message for me?"

"Not so much a message, Jim. I don't expect you to solve the great problems of humankind. I would call it more of an observation. You see, I am mindful of your investigation. I thought it would be useful for you to know as much as possible about Dr. Bronston."

"I agree. I need to know as much as possible about Dr. Bronston," said Jim.

"You should know that we shared many of our views, and we shared the same fears."

"Fears of what?"

"Our greatest fear was that the human species may not be so dominant on the earth because of our assumed 'superior' brain. Our thinking was that perhaps we are here not so much because of our brain, but in spite of it. Our presence could be merely a fluke, a set of lucky, but otherwise random events," said Dr. Umbawi.

"So our intelligence may not be the key to our success as a species?"

"Dr. Bronston would not be so liberal in the use of the word success. He was concerned that the size of the hominid brain grew due to the use of the deliberate production of stone tools. We saw our brain as that of a craftsman. Unequalled, I might add, perhaps in the universe, but very limited in its potential."

"You don't think too highly of mankind."

"To the contrary. We have put men on the moon and cluttered the earth with great works, but these things do not show great intelligence other than as a clever craftsman. We have never been able to face our real social problems. We have armed ourselves to kill each other many times over with weapons of mass destruction that everyone chases with great vigor. In contrast, we have not been able to create the simplest form of life. Our society, the most advanced as craftsmen, is armed like none other, yet it avoids every social issue that appears before it. All human conflicts are solved by violence, not because we are violent, but because we do not know any other way than to resort to violence against our own kind to win. We resort to the use of our skill at making things. Weapons are like plows."

"How so?"

"Both are tools."

"That sounds a bit harsh," said Jim.

"We do absolutely nothing about our own population explosion because we do not have the ability to deal with the issue among ourselves. We know it may be our undoing, but we are powerless to do something about it. To do so would be to infringe on someone else's right to reproduce."

"You have some valid criticisms, but if our problem is genetic, we have no future."

"The true intellectual ability of man, other than the advanced capacity as a craftsman, is no more advanced than a troop of baboons, living a life of constantly changing alliances and a preoccupation with deceit against each other. In short, we were afraid we saw the imperfections of humans as a genetic, and possibly fatal flaw," said Dr. Umbawi.

"You are pessimistic about the future," said Jim.

"I didn't let us wander astray from your investigation, Jim. Your mission has been paramount on my mind. Dr. Bronston was my best friend. I will always remember the conversations we had right here at this table, but he did not warn me of his terrible decision to take his own life."

"Do you think he became depressed with the fact we do not address our world wide problems?"

"I have no answers, Jim. Yes, you might start there. Something triggered a senseless act. You have the unfortunate burden of finding out what that event was. Everything that helps you to understand how he thought could help. All I am trying to do is to help you in that endeavor."

"You have helped a lot," said Jim.'

"Unless you succeed, Jim, there are many of us here in East Africa who will never have closure."

"The difficulty of my investigation is sinking in," said Jim.

"At least you can understand why it is more than just the wine that we have to blame for our diversion here this evening," said Dr. Umbawi, sitting back in his chair. "I'm supposed to keep you on the straight and narrow in your search for a motive for Dr. Bronston's suicide. I hope

I haven't led you too far off course by looking into the far reaches of space."

"I think I'm beginning to understand how everything could relate to my investigation."

"Good. Perhaps we have discussed some international problems that you cannot solve by yourself, but it was not my intent to draw attention away from your investigation. However, you have to drop these diversions and come back to earth. You have an investigation to do," said Dr. Umbawi. "You need to remain focused."

"Both you and Dr. Tubojola are pointing me towards Bokuru, an archaeological excavation out in the middle of the savannah of Uhuru, as the place for me to look for his motive," said Jim.

"Basically, Bokuru is an open pit in the ground, Jim, but yes, that is where Dr. Bronston lived and died. He kept detailed field notes. If you can find and read them, I think you may find the key to your investigation. His notes may provide you with the only real lead into his mental state at the time, and perhaps the answer to why he would suddenly decide to take his own life. You must be able to see the world as he saw it."

"Well, I'm ready. Nancy is going to pick me up early in the morning," said Jim.

"Oh, don't forget this book on Dr. Bronston's life," said Dr Umbawi, reaching around behind his chair to retrieve two items from the service table. "Dr. Tubojola asked me to loan it to you. I also wanted you to have this manila envelope. It contains a copy of the complete police report, as I promised. You're going to be at the place of Dr. Bronston's death tomorrow. I can't think of a better place to review it carefully:"

"Great. Thank you," said Jim. "That file should help me a lot."

"Just one thing, Jim. Don't show the file to Nancy. I haven't looked at it, but I was told the pictures are pretty graphic. I don't think she should see them."

Just then their round of after dinner drinks arrived.

"Ah," said Dr. Umbawi. "Let's toast."

"A toast, then," said Jim, picking up his glass.

"Let's toast to your success at Bokuru."

"To Bokuru," said Jim.

They touched glasses with a light clink.

"To Bokuru," said Dr. Umbawi, smiling.

CHAPTER TEN: *A ROAD LESS TRAVELED*

The Safari Jeep lurched and swayed as Nancy drove across the desolate terrain following the dirt tract that served as a road. Jim looked at his watch. It was 9:45 AM local time. They had been traveling for over an hour. The open plain, with its tall termite mounds and scrub brush, stretched outward in front of them towards the horizon, as far as they could see. A long, swirling cloud of dust billowed along the road behind them.

Nancy was dressed in a safari suit consisting of long khaki pants, a matching long sleeve shirt, and a canvas safari hat. Jim, on the other hand, wore what he had brought from his apartment in Chicago: jeans, a faded, worn white, long sleeved dress shirt, tennis shoes, and a blue Chicago Cubs baseball cap. Nancy's fax had instructed him to wear long pants, long sleeve shirts, and hat, but he still felt out of place. The sun, she had warned in her fax, would be brutal and those not used to it needed to keep covered. He felt uneasy while she appeared to be totally comfortable, properly dressed for the environment.

She drove steadily at well over 50 miles per hour; confident of the road she was following. After all, he thought, she had been out to Bokuru many times before. The track took them generally in a northerly direction out of Elizabethtown. The mid morning sun was already high overhead and promised to live up to Nancy's description. The day was going to be a hot one. There were no clouds in the sky to hold out any hope of relief from rain. The scattered brush they had seen since leaving town was beginning to yield to an occasional acacia tree. Ahead of them, the trees were thicker, turning into a green forest in the distance. Jim had seen no wildlife other than a lone dik-dik and a few scattered impala that had quickly darted away at the noisy approach of the Jeep.

"I'm still amazed at your ability to induce the museum trustees to select me as the investigator," said Jim. "That was quite a feat."

"My father opened the door to the museum for me, but I had to make it on my own. They may listen to me today, but when I first started working at the museum I was alone and confused in a male dominated world. My father wasn't around to give me guidance. He was over here in Africa, so I had to learn how to deal with the realities of a single, workingwoman in the world of the museum. I didn't have any role models or even a mentor. The only females in the museum were secretaries and support staff."

"Well, they think the world of you now."

"It was not easy breaking through the male domination barrier. I had to develop a career strategy for myself. The biggest problem both in and out of the museum was sex discrimination. I had to control my emotions and learn to act like a professional. When I graduated from college, I moved into a career where all my predecessors had been men. There were no hard and fast guidelines. I had to develop my own personal rules as I went along."

"You obviously made the right decisions," said Jim.

"That's because I realized that the key for me was to develop my own self image. I realized that there was no future in acting meek and submissive and playing typical female supportive roles. I would go to a meeting and everyone expected me to pour the coffee. Don't get the wrong idea; I don't buy into strong feminist group objectives. I just had to find my own way. I had to create an image of who I wanted to be. I found that others would accept the image you paint of yourself regardless of color, gender, or anything else. Once others get the picture, they will actually help you achieve your goals," said Nancy.

"I don't think you're alone. Maybe you should write a guide book for women."

"I don't think so. My solutions were personal. I don't think in terms of other women. For example, my biggest secret is that I had the museum build a special, small, wood paneled private dining room out of part of the main restaurant off the lobby. I use this area to hold small, intimate dinners for special groups of potential donors. That's not just a feminist role, but it is my best solicitation device," said Nancy.

"It sounds like a unique approach," said Jim.

"Maybe, but I avoid kitchen work. The dinners are always catered. I avoid any direct serving responsibility. Both men and women perceive working in the kitchen or with food as a subservient career as opposed to management. That was one of the first things I learned. Any kind of service role is poison to a woman trying to create an executive image, Jim."

"I never paid much attention to that, but I think you're right," said Jim.

"I learned the hard way. I wanted to show my father that I could do it. He got me the job, and I was determined to succeed at it. Besides, working at the museum was a dream come true for me."

"Did you consciously decide to break away from your parents influence, rebelling and going into administration and management instead of becoming a field archaeologist? There's some concern in the museum that you might decide to change careers and go into the field just like your father did," asked Jim.

"I believed in what my father was doing. The past can help us find the key to our future. I just didn't think his work was relevant. I mean, so what if he made another big discovery? He may produce a headline or two, but new archaeological discoveries won't change anyone's immediate life. I wanted to make a difference. I think my job is far more relevant. All too often, discoveries are relegated to some minor treatise. Later, the true significance of the discovery is debated by a few learned scholars. In time, the discovery will always be replaced by another more spectacular find. I do more to make the past live when I arrange a special visitation day for an entire school class. Museums should not be dusty, old places. They should live, and they should be relevant to the lives of the public."

"I understand your thinking," said Jim. "I like your philosophy about making museums relevant."

"We have enough exhibits in our museums. We need to induce the public to come out and see them. We need that emphasis for a generation. Then we can go back to the field and look for new exhibits. We need a more educated public."

"Not to change the subject, but we are on our way to Bokuru, and I'm still not sure I understand what your father found out there. Dr. Tubojola didn't know. He was convinced that your father had found something really significant, and he was upset that your father wasn't reporting it. In addition, your people at the museum in Chicago didn't have a clue as to what your father found either," said Jim. "Did he find something or was he still just looking?"

"I don't have a clue as to what he found. Maybe he really didn't find anything significant yet. Remember, the work was still going on when he died. I know he was hoping to find hominid bones. That was always his goal. They can identify hominids from the skulls and teeth. He wouldn't dig in a given site unless he thought there was a good chance of finding hominids."

"Everyone keeps using the term 'hominid' but I'm not so sure I know exactly what they mean," said Jim.

"Hominids are bipeds, Jim. They were members of a family to which humans belong. The reference includes our ancestors and all related species that stood up on two legs just like we do. All the other species are extinct, except us. The first hominids were no more than upright walking apes."

"How far back do they go?"

"The prevailing scientific theory is that hominids first appeared in Africa about 4.5 million years ago. The early species had the ability to walk like we do, but they were far more limited intellectually. The early hominids had much smaller braincases. There were quite a few different species of them living a couple of million years ago," said Nancy.

"I thought that was what you meant, but I wasn't sure."

"Sometimes it's hard to determine if a particular species was part of the genetic stock that led to *Homo sapiens* or was just an offshoot. Those we identify as the species *gracile* included our ancestors. The more robust species are gone."

"*Gracile?*" Jim asked.

"Those that had more fine features, thinner bones, muscles, and teeth are described as *gracile*."

"So your father was looking for *gracile* hominids in the cave he was excavating?"

"Yes, but hominids did not live in caves, Jim. They had to stay in motion to keep hunting for food. At the same time, they had to avoid becoming food themselves."

"Who were their enemies?" Jim asked.

"Large birds, and carnivores including hyenas and leopards. Both predators took their prey into caves to eat after a kill to avoid other scavengers."

"If hominids did not live in caves why would your father be excavating a cave site to find fossils of their bones?"

"My father hoped the cave out here at Bokuru would be like the ones found in South Africa. He hoped to find some hominid bones in what he often called the kitchen midden or refuse dump from ancient kills left by leopards and hyenas. The post-cranial parts of the bodies of hominids were often consumed, but the skulls were usually too large to get their teeth over and were discarded. That's why many fossilized bits of craniums make up the contents of ancient caves. Carnivores concentrated on the smaller body parts with smaller bones that they could wrap their teeth around," said Nancy.

"Are there a lot of caves out here?" he asked.

"No, quite the contrary. This site is unique, precisely because it is a cave. In South Africa caves were a common geographical feature long ago, just as they are today. Caves have always been very rare up here. East Africa is a special place, Jim."

"That's what everyone keeps telling me," said Jim.

"East Africa was special two million years ago too, because it had many different kinds of environments. Different kinds of geographical areas are the key to speciation."

"Speciation?" Jim asked.

"The evolution of different species. Mutation is going on all the time, Jim. There is nothing you can do about it. Mutations occur at a regular rate. They just keep happening."

"So I understand."

"Just because some individual is born with a mutation does not mean that the entire species will pick it up. Mutations are genetic changes in the individual. Some have advantages in survival and some do not. They may be passed on to subsequent generations or they may be lost. Most changes are just lost in the population and have no selective advantage that will assure the change is adopted by an entire species," said Nancy.

"So what is the key?"

"Either there is a real advantage for the characteristic that results from the genetic mutation in the existing environment or the environment changes at the right time giving the change a selective advantage. The change must become significantly abundant in the population so that it gives the species a survival advantage."

"I'm not sure I understand how it works."

"There was a species of white moth in England. A mutation took place and some of the moths were born black instead of white," she said.

"Just a random mutation?"

"Right, but the mutation took place at the right time. Historically, it was at the beginning of the Industrial Revolution."

"What difference did that make?"

"The key to the beginning of the Industrial Revolution in England was coal. The burning of coal produced smoke and ash as by products, which coated the surrounding environment. This change in the environment meant that the black moth that stood out before the coating of soot on trees and plants now became camouflaged. Suddenly, the white moth stood out. Predation by birds, lizards, and others that lived off moths singled out the easily identified white moths and missed the black ones that rested on the soot. Over a few generations, the black ones thrived and the white ones almost disappeared," said Nancy. "Of course, since they no longer use so much coal the populations of moths have swung into a more balanced population of both colors."

"That is a good example. Now I understand," said Jim.

"My example is really oversimplified. There are many causes of mutation and examples of how the environment selects those that have a selective advantage for survival. Radiation continues to produce mutation, so everything is always changing."

"Even us?" asked Jim.

"Even us. In my example, man acted like climate," said Nancy. "Climate is the key."

"I'm learning a lot about natural history, but I don't see how it is going to help me with my investigation. What should I look for when we get to Bokuru?"

"The more you know about change, the better your scientific foundation will be. However, you raise a good question. I don't have an easy answer for you. What you need to know is that Mobutu Nyzeki is in charge of the excavation operation. This means he is the manager of the day to day digging. My father was responsible for the finish work. Specifically, he would separate the bits of fossilized bone that Mobutu finds in the matrix, that is, assuming they found something. If they found several pieces, he would try to assemble them into complete bones. His primary responsibility was to identify whatever Mobutu found. Just remember that Mobutu is the one who actually finds the fossils. He photographs every piece, measures it and records the *in situ* location in the site log. Mobutu's responsibility is to label where each piece of fossilized bone was found and then deliver it to my father for final identification. Actually, archaeologists look for much more than fossilized bone. They are interested in everything, plants, seeds, pieces of fossilized wood, leaves, you name it. To the trained eye, everything could be important."

"Just like we do on our field trips in Chicago," said Jim.

"Yes. The procedures are the same. That's why your background is good. Mobutu will be the most help to you. He worked closely with my father for over fourteen years."

"It sounds like he will be very helpful," said Jim.

"The geology out here is unique. Some people see geology simply as small incremental changes that take place over immense periods of time. Others see geology as a few violent events, like earthquakes and volcanic eruptions. In truth, what happened out here is both. Geology includes all the sand, ash, dirt, even the fossils which are now stone," said Nancy.

"It's pretty barren out here."

"This terrain may look permanent, but that is an illusion. The history of this area is that of violent events, followed by long periods of erosion by wind and rain. The Bokuru River runs along an ancient fault line. Due to tectonic activity, the north bank of the river dropped down below the river bed around one and a half million years ago. I think my father told me, the geologists determined that about two hundred thousand years ago, the north river bank tilted back up, becoming exposed to the elements as a long escarpment. That ridge has been eroding away ever since. The south bank, on the other hand, has never reemerged. All that exists today is the current riverbank and a few scattered rock outcroppings. The whole Bokuru River Valley is an extension of the Great Rift Valley. The top of the ridge on the north side is highest right at the camp, but further downstream by the excavation site, the top of the ridge has been lost due to erosion by wind and rain. In fact, the process of erosion is what has exposed the roof of the cave."

"So that's why the geologists were able to find evidence of the cave right on the surface?" asked Jim.

"Yes, only a thin layer of collapsed roof was left. Preliminary dating techniques using the potassium-argon test indicated the cave was very old. The geologists thought the cave formed around three million years ago."

"That's interesting," said Jim.

"Despite not finding any fossils on the surface, my father decided to excavate the cave from the top down. For the first couple of months, all they did was cut away what was left of the cave roof and start to remove the interior fill. They were only about three feet down when I was out here last," said Nancy. "A lot of what we see will be new to me, too."

"What did they find when you were out here before?"

"Nothing. They thought, originally, the cave might have filled in over a period of time. That meant they might find several occupation levels as it gradually filled in. But, my father told me, the age tests made periodically, as they dug deeper, revealed that all of the fill showed similar dates."

"What was the significance of almost identical dates?"

"That similarity in age convinced him the cave filled in all at one time. My father found the overburden which filled the cave was fairly uniform and made up of river washed sand with a heavy mixture of volcanic ash and pumice. The geologists concluded that the source of the volcanic debris was a large eruption that blanketed the area for some distance in every direction when the cave filled in. The eroded shell of the volcano is still out there. You can see it from the camp on a clear day."

"So when did this event take place?" asked Jim.

"The fill has been dated at 1.82 million years before present."

"That's a long time ago."

"To us, yes, perhaps, but in earth time it is only a very short interval. My father concluded that heavy rains and a river swollen with volcanic debris caused a flood that filled the cave in a single event."

"I see," said Jim. "That's really amazing."

"Today, the matrix is a very coarse sandstone which crumbles easily. Anyway, my father knew what he was looking for. He was convinced he would find the fossilized bones he was looking for on the floor of the cave as it existed just before it filled in."

"They can certainly tell a lot from the rocks," said Jim.

"It's amazing, Jim, what they learn from geology. To be a good archaeologist you have to be a good detective. Geology is one of the most important tools an archaeologist has. My father never lost faith in the excavation because the geology told him he was in the right place. He just didn't know how far down they would have to dig to find the cave floor. The geologists could not tell him that. I think my father found the bottom occupation level of the cave about four months ago," she said.

"Did he find anything when they finally got there?"

"From the time when they reached the occupation level of the cave, the information he provided just trickled away. He was very busy. You are right though. Assuming he discovered fossils, whatever he found, he did not share the find with anyone. So when you ask me what he discovered, all I can say is that he didn't find a thing before I left," said Nancy.

"Like you said, maybe he didn't find anything."

"I wouldn't be surprised since they didn't start out with anything to begin with. He didn't tell me anything about the excavation since my last trip."

"Maybe he was on a wild goose chase," said Jim.

"I'm sure he discovered something or they would have stopped by now. Of course, it was what he hoped to find that kept him going. He wouldn't stop until he had completely excavated the entire floor of the cave."

"But he added the additional staff. He must have found something to justify increasing the pace."

"Yes, that's true. Of course, maybe he was just trying to finish before the rainy season."

"Are they still digging now?" Jim asked.

"Yes, certainly. The work goes on. They never really stopped when my father died. Mobutu came for the funeral, but I told him not to let my father's death interfere with the work. If he stopped, he would lose his helpers. Everyone would move on to something else. As for what Mobutu or my father found exactly, your guess is as good as mine."

"Well, no one else seems to know either," said Jim. "Dr. Tubojola and Keith Kendall have both asked me to report back what I find out about your father's discovery as soon as I can."

"What does Dr. Umbawi say? They had a close relationship. If anyone would know if they found anything, it would be Dr. Umbawi. He told me how they met regularly and talked at length," she said.

"He said nothing to me except that they did meet and had long conversations. All we talked about is my mission to find out why your father would commit suicide. Motive was Dr. Umbawi's primary focus of attention. He has never raised the subject of what was found at the site. I don't think he knows anything," said Jim.

"Archaeological excavations in Africa are long, boring, tedious work, and all for only a few bits of scattered fossilized bone," she said. "Sometimes what they find just confirms prior discoveries. A site may be important, but it's often not very sexy stuff. Often it's just not newsworthy, so no one gets excited about it. Sometimes they find some small piece of fossilized bone on the surface. Then, after sifting the surrounding area they find nothing more."

"I see what you mean," said Jim. "The reality of archaeology is that it isn't very exciting."

"Field work can be very discouraging and down right boring."

"Do you think you'll make up your mind about your future while we are out here?" asked Jim. "You know, I think you should step in and finish your father's work, even if it's just a matter of writing the final reports."

"I've made no final decision yet, but, yes, I'll stay out here long enough to make up my mind. I know I have to make a decision in the next few days due to the impending rainy season. It's not fair to keep everyone waiting."

"That sounds fair," said Jim. "Your father would want you to finish his work."

"I know Dr. Tubojola and the museum are encouraging me to stay and finish the excavation field work. I understand why they want me to stay," she said.

"It's the Bronston name," said Jim. "It comes down to politics and economics."

"Always. I understand that, but I don't really want to change careers and become a field archaeologist, Jim. If Bokuru is a meaningful excavation, I'll stay and complete the excavation," she said. "I know Dr. Tubojola will back me up. But, I'm not a fool. I know they need the Bronston name to be responsible for the project if anything of value is found. I have an open mind, Jim. I know they want me to do it. On the other side of the question, you must realize that I don't want them to bring in an outsider to finish up any more then they want to bring one in," she said.

"The museum in Chicago, wants you to step in. They asked me to encourage you to do so," said Jim. "I talked with Keith Kendall about your role on the way to the airport."

"I know their interests, but I'm concerned with my qualifications. That's a big issue. I don't want to be a token female," she said.

"You know what your father would want. He would have been proud if you finished what he started," said Jim. "He believed in Bokuru. He would expect the same of you."

"I know it would help me with closure too," she said.

They drove on in silence for a few minutes.

"If you reach down behind my seat you'll find one of my father's old safari hats. It should fit you. Go ahead and put it on. You will feel more comfortable out here with a safari hat than the one you now have," she chided Jim. "That baseball cap is a bit out of place."

Jim retrieved the hat and replaced it for his baseball cap.

"Thanks," he said. "It fits."

"Did you get to see any of the presentations at the museum?" she asked.

"I saw the interactive presentation *Long Long Ago*."

"I've seen that one too. Did you get a chance to see *Rise of Man*?"

"No. Dr. Tubojola said that one is only in a standard film mode," said Jim. "He wanted me to see the one that is interactive, probably to impress me. Although I think *Rise of Man* would have been more appropriate for my investigation."

"I was just curious. Dad asked me how they addressed the chicken and the egg problem. That issue should have appeared in *Rise of Man*," said Nancy.

"The chicken and the egg problem?"

"The issue was whether the big brain came before upright walking or whether upright walking came first."

"That seems like a good question," said Jim.

"My father knew both presentations were written by Dr. Tubojola and Dr. Umbawi. He knew Dr. Tubojola was very opinionated, and from the old school."

"Which school is that?"

"Current scientific theory is based on the discoveries of the australopithecines from South Africa. They were upright walking apes with cranium capacities around 600 cc, whereas modern man has a capacity of around 1500 cc. The paleoanthropologists put the australopithecines in our direct ancestral lineage," said Nancy.

"I don't understand your reference to cubic centimeters."

"It's very simple. They take a skull, turn it upside down and fill it with sand. Then they measure the amount of sand it takes to fill the skull. Since the brain basically fills the skull, they use this sand test to determine brain size. It's crude, but it works."

"That's pretty simple. What you are saying is that they don't measure the size of the actual brain."

"Organic matter is not often fossilized. Most of the time they don't have anything that represents the actual brain tissue. Usually, only the remaining bones are fossilized. Organic matter, like brain tissue, decays too fast to be fossilized, unless highly unusual situations are there," she said.

"I understand. A minute ago, you said Dr. Tubojola was from the old school. You didn't explain what the old school was."

"Dr. Tubojola is behind the times, as far as theory goes. He believed the big brain developed first, and, while our ancestors were sitting around up in the trees thinking, they decided to come down and try life on the ground and take up walking upright. That school of thought believed the brain was the key factor for our evolutionary progress. It's an old idea, Jim. It's discounted today, but Dr. Tubojola is very opinionated. Dr. Umbawi would have insisted on being timely and correct. Dad wondered how they worked out the script for the film. Neither Dad nor I ever saw the final film," said Nancy.

"Well, I can't help you. I didn't see that presentation either. I only saw *Long Long Ago*. The hominids at the end were already walking upright," said Jim.

"So, maybe they just avoided focusing on the issue," she said.

"Maybe."

"Since we are talking about Dr. Tubojola, do you know about his plan for the park a few miles east of here?" she asked.

189

"Yes. Dr. Tubojola told me all about it at great length. He is very proud of it. It's more than a plan. It's a reality. He told me part of the park will open early next year," Jim added.

"I don't know all the details, but I think his plan is shortsighted and not well thought out."

"Shortsighted? I was impressed," said Jim.

"He is not taking into account the fact that the earth is rapidly warming."

"How would that affect his plans? They seem pretty carefully thought out to me."

"His source for water at the east end is the Bokuru River, which they are tapping upstream, as I understand it," said Nancy.

"Yes. He gave me a full account of how they plan to use the river."

"Well, the river begins at a shallow lake about 200 miles further upstream."

"Yes. I think he may have told me that."

"Well, if the lake isn't replenished, it will disappear from evaporation," she added.

"I asked him about evaporation for his artificial lake. That's when he responded that they would use the Bokuru River to offset evaporation," said Jim.

"So you see."

"See what?" he asked.

"His plan needs the river. That lake is fed year round by a couple of shallow streams from the East Mountains. The source of the water is the ice caps on the top of the mountains. They're melting so fast that they'll be gone within 20 years. When the ice caps are gone, so too will be the regular source of water for the lake that feeds the whole river system," said Nancy. "No Bokuru River, no lake for the park."

"Oh, I see what you mean," said Jim.

"Do you know the real main factor for human evolution?" she asked.

"If it's not the brain, I don't have a clue."

"Well, it's not the brain. It's the pelvis, or more accurately, the muscles that make upright walking possible. Form follows function. More frequent use of the muscles for more upright activity caused the mutations in the pelvis to allow the muscles to be used for upright walking to ultimately lead to the development of the modern pelvis structure," said Nancy.

"So then, why do we have a big brain?"

"Upright walking freed up the arms and hands," she said.

"So, a need to walk long distance for hunting and the ability to stand up to see greater distances for game were the factors that stimulated greater brain development."

"Old thinking, Jim."

"You mean that's not the way it happened?" he asked.

"No. That was the original theory, but it's discounted now. You see, that's a typical male archaeologist's chauvinistic view. Male hunting for meat played only a minor role in food collection and consumption. Current female archaeologists have pointed out that it was the females who gathered most of the food and carried infants at the same time. Females collected around eighty-five percent of the food while taking care of the young, all at the same time. The early females were most likely the deciding factor on the selective advantage of upright walking and free use of the hands, leading to the evolution of the big brain. The original theory was written by males and carried a male bias," she said.

"I would never have thought of that," said Jim.

"Nor did most male archaeologists. Many a bias has led true science in the wrong direction, Jim."

"Let me ask you a question."

"Sure," she said.

"Why would upright walking happen at all? I've read that upright walking is not as efficient as four-legged walking for most animals."

"That's simple. Our ancestors were not four-legged, Jim. They were apes, and bipedalism was far more efficient than knuckle walking on all fours, especially when changes in climate made their livable habitats smaller and further apart. That new, greater distance between habitats required walking to get from one location to the other. You can't compare our ancestors to four-legged animals. For us, bipedalism was a big advantage."

"Ever since I arrived in Africa, I think I've learned more than I did back in school," said Jim.

"Good. The main reason for our being who we are and not remaining just a bipedal ape is that we learned to use tools. As the climate changed, we learned to adapt to the changes. As a consequence, we began to bring about our own evolution. Forget what I just said. I was wrong."

"You lost me. What was wrong?" Jim asked.

"I think I just said that use of tools was the main reason for our evolution."

"Yes, you did."

"That's not correct."

"It's not?"

"No. Some time ago, the scientific community thought that the distinguishing characteristic that separated man from all other life forms was that *Homo sapiens* used tools."

"And that was wrong?"

"Of course. When a bird picks up a twig and makes a nest, it is using a tool. When a chimpanzee picks up a stick and uses it to prod for termites, that is using a tool. Man is no better than the sparrow if he picks up a heavy stick to use as a club. In fact, that shows a lot lower level of intellectual activity than the intricate nest built by the weaverbird. The use of items picked up in the natural world as tools does not help us understand who we are."

"So what is it if it is not upright walking or using tools?"

"What is significant is not the use of tools, but the manufacture of tools. Our evolution from an upright walking ape began when our ancestors first used one natural item such as a rock as a hammer and hit another rock or core to create an entirely new item. This was the creation of a tool as a hammer to create another tool such as a sharp stone flake used as an arrowhead or knife. The creation of new inventions not found in nature was the differentiating event that started us on our way."

"I think you may be right. If we keep evolving, what will we be like in the future?" asked Jim.

"That is hard to project. We are now a large factor in the evolution of the environment. We are contributing to the process of change, so we are no longer simply reacting to the environment. We are changing the environment as well. We may be locking ourselves into our present form. Our numbers are exploding because the world is in a warming cycle. When the world cools, who knows what will happen." she asked.

"You are a wealth of knowledge," he said. "You know, you drive like you travel this road every day."

"To be honest, I've never driven out here before. My father always picked me up. He jealously did all the driving. I think it was his male chauvinistic attitude," she said as she drove steadily along the dusty track. "Look around you. I can't possibly get lost. This is the only road out here in the middle of nowhere."

"Right. Since we left town, this is the only road I've seen."

"You may not have noticed, but there are small piles of rocks every so often along the side of the road."

"Yes. I've seen them. Why are they there?" said Jim.

"They're called cairns. They mark the road if wind or floods obscure it. It's hard to get lost."

"I didn't know what they were for. I guess I was more interested in looking out for wild life."

"Oh. I forgot," she said. "That's not entirely true."

"Forgot what?" he asked

"There," she said, pointing out in front of the Jeep down the road. "Can you see it?"

"See what?" asked Jim, peering through the windshield.

"Just ahead."

"Oh," said Jim. "I think I see a fork in the road. Yes, I can see it clearly up ahead. There's a cut off from the main road."

Nancy slowed the Jeep as they approached the split, where a side road turned off to the left. The main road curved to the right, while the less worn track branched towards the northwest. There was a weathered sign on a post in the middle where the road divided. The old weathered board nailed to the post read: "Temple of Tassan." Below the sign was a second board that had been roughly carved in the shape of an arrow, pointing to the right in the direction of the main road.

"I forgot, Jim. We do turn off onto on the road less traveled. The main road turns east and goes east past the temple. The cut off goes to Bokuru."

"A major intersection in the middle of nowhere," Jim observed lightly.

"It's misleading. The only others out here are wandering nomadic herdsmen and the temple."

"David mentioned the Temple of Tassan. They are also the ones who picket the museum. The temple's name is on the brochure they gave me. I kept one of their fliers and put it in my brief case."

"I've seen their brochure," said Nancy.

"Dr. Umbawi said they are anti-female."

"I don't know much about them. I think they came from either Los Angeles or San Francisco," she said.

"Dr. Umbawi told me the history of the temple and the founder," said Jim.

"All I know about them is that they have been out here for years, well before the museum opened in Elizabethtown. My father was working at a site up north when they first showed up out here."

She drove slowly past the sign, turning onto the side trail.

"So Bokuru is this way?" he asked.

"I did not remember this turn off because I wasn't driving. I'm sure it's the right way to Bokuru," she said. "It's the only road to get there."

"I may have to go to the temple while I am here," said Jim. "I have to interview all the people who worked for your father, including the two temple followers who worked part time."

"I know. Dr. Umbawi told me he was trying to arrange appointments with the part timers who worked for my father to meet with you at Bokuru while you are there. If that doesn't work out, I promise to take you over to the temple tomorrow so you can meet them there."

"Have you ever been there?" Jim asked.

"No," she said. "But it could be interesting to drive out there for a brief visit." They drove on in silence for about another half an hour in the mid morning heat.

"I think we have a welcoming committee, he said, pointing off to his right."

"Yes, I see them. There are two of them, an old man and a boy. They are Morani."

"Morani?" asked Jim.

"They are Masai and they are taking their cattle to the river. Masai herdsmen are a common sight out here. A hundred years ago they lived the life of warriors. Now they are simply herdsmen. They still call themselves Morani or warriors."

"It looks like they still carry their spears for ceremonial purposes," said Jim.

"They do carry spears, but not for ceremony."

"Then what are they for?" asked Jim.

"They have to look out for dangerous snakes and lions."

"Lions?"

"Lions stalk their cattle. They have to be prepared."

"Oh."

"See how the older one stands on one leg?" she asked.

"Yes, I see him," said Jim.

"They can do that for hours," she said.

"That's amazing. I could never do that."

"This land may seem uninhabited, but it is not. Herdsmen come up to the camp all the time for medicines and minor scrapes and bruises."

"Why didn't your father hire them instead of guys from the temple?"

"Because Masai will not do manual labor. They think any hard work with their hands is beneath their dignity. It is cultural."

"Not to change the subject, but I think I see it," said Jim, suddenly feeling a tinge of anticipation and excitement. He could only see a bright white reflection on a ridge some distance ahead.

"I see something white over there on that hill in the distance."

"You've got it," she said, as she drove intently through a stretch of very rutted but dry section of road. "That is not a hill. What you see is the north ridge escarpment. You're looking at the camp tents. I may not have told you, but Bokuru is divided into two parts. The camp, which you see, is where they eat and sleep. It's on the highest point on the ridge for miles around. It's on the opposite side of the river."

"What I see does look like a tent," said Jim.

"What you see is actually two big tents, right next to each other. They look like one big tent from this distance. The second part of Bokuru is the excavation site. It is about a kilometer to the left of the camp."

"I don't see anything."

"The site is also on the ridge on the north side of the river, so you can't see it from here. In fact, you can't see it from the camp either. The closest tent is the mess tent. The bunk tent is right behind it. The escarpment is actually the ancient riverbank, elevated in that tectonic uprising I told you about. The river still runs right below it along the fault line."

"How much farther away is it?" Jim asked.

"We're close. I'd guess about 10 kilometers. Years ago, everyone used old brown canvas surplus army tents. The problem with them was that they absorbed the heat and they smelled awful. The ones we use now are new light weight nylon which are much cooler and reflect back most of the heat from the sun," she said.

"If Bokuru is on the other side of the river, how do we get across?" asked Jim. "I can't picture a bridge out here."

"We have to drive across the river bed at a gravel crossing, just below the camp. We won't have any trouble today since we are near the end of the dry season. The water won't be over our wheels at this time of year. The site is landlocked during the wet season from January through April when the river rises. We are near the end of the best part of the excavating season. By mid January, this road will be a quagmire, and the river will be too deep and strong to cross at the ford. We really have to plan ahead if we want to work through the rainy season. The camp itself is on high ground and drains well. My father thought it was possible to stay in operation year round if they stocked up in the dry season. Bokuru is only accessible from this road. There is no other road in or out."

"I'll take your word for it," he said, as they approached the river with its thick forest of acacia trees and green scrub extending back from the south bank.

"As soon as we cross the river, we have to go through a hairpin turn and up a steep incline. The road was cut out of the slope by the ground team when they first selected the site. The camp is located right at the top of the slope."

"I can clearly see the tent now," said Jim.

"Remember, don't build up any great expectations," she said. "I know how everyone is depending on you to find the answer out here, but there really isn't much to see at Bokuru."

"The actual excavation and your father's notes are what will be important," said Jim.

"Yes. I think you're right."

"How many people work here?"

"Well, right now, there are only four full timers plus the two part time day laborers from the temple. M'Bee Omubo is the cook, and he's in charge of general maintenance of the camp and meals. Oh, I should tell you, no one uses full names out here. A simple common name is how I'll introduce them when we get there."

"That's fine," said Jim.

"Anyway, Mobutu Nyzeki is in charge for now. He has two years of college, and he's responsible for the general excavation. Both he and M'Bee have been with my father for many years. Some of the most famous discoveries attributed to my father were actually based on initial finds by Mobutu. Someday he will receive the recognition he deserves."

"How about the other two workers?" asked Jim.

"They are general laborers. There is Karimba Maru and Charga Malinki. That's amazing."

"What is?" Jim asked.

"The fact that I remembered their names. The laborers work directly for Mobutu. If my memory serves me right, they don't know a lot of English. Anyway, my father would not have confided in them, as he did Mobutu. Mobutu will be your most valuable interviewee."

"Great, I'll concentrate on Mobutu."

"Oh. There is another person you should know about," she added.

"Out at the camp?" he asked.

"Well, maybe."

"You mean maybe there is someone else?" he asked.

"Yes. They call him the Deacon, but I don't know his real name."

"The Deacon?" Jim asked.

"Yes. He's not a member of the staff or anything, but he might be out there. He's a weird duck, Jim. I don't mean to sound evasive, but he comes and goes on his own schedule. You never know if he's going to be there," she said.

"He sounds mysterious."

"I'd say odd would be a better way to describe him. He was out here the last time I was here, but he didn't stay because they were just starting the excavation and hadn't found anything."

"A fair weather archaeologist," said Jim.

"He is called the Deacon, but he is a leader from a church in the Salt Lake City area. He acts as a spokesman for a group that believes in a literal interpretation of the Bible. For years, they have been looking for proof in the American West that man coexisted with the dinosaurs."

"Is that before or after the flood?" Jim asked, joking.

"Don't laugh. This is serious stuff to them. The point is, mainstream science has ignored them. Look, I'm not being fair. The Deacon has a heart of gold. His church is like any other church. It does a lot of good. The Deacon is over here in Africa to run the church schools here in Uhuru. This is a poor country. They can use all the help they can get. The Deacon's church runs about a dozen schools for about two thousand kids who would have nothing if it wasn't for the church. They have clothes, shoes, food, and books all brought in by the church. People need religion and churches. They help provide clothing and education for the children. We have inner social needs that they fulfill. I don't mean to attack the Deacon or his church. It is just that when a member of a church tries to be a scientist armed only with the tools of his faith, he performs a disservice to his followers as well as to everyone else. Faith is faith, Jim. It requires no proof. Do you know what I think is the real problem with religion, or all religions?"

"No, but I'd like to hear your views."

"Ninety-five percent of man's knowledge of the natural world, the universe, and himself has been accumulated in the last 50 years. All the world's major religions are based on documents written a long time ago. We need to update them."

"I read somewhere that one of the Bibles was being rewritten to take out the heavy anti-female bias," said Jim. "I don't remember which one it was."

"See what I mean? That's a start Jim. Anyway, churches do a lot of good. The Deacon came to Africa with another objective, as well as running the schools."

"So what you are saying is that, in his spare time, he visits archaeological sites?" asked Jim.

"He spends his spare time traveling from one dig to another, thinking he is keeping the archeologists honest in their work. He thinks that scientists are either not looking for the biblical facts of our existence that would show that we have been here all along or there is a conspiracy of silence about what has been found. I think he's convinced that the true story of our past is being deliberately withheld. He's a self appointed watchdog."

"He sounds like a bit of a kook," said Jim.

"His personal views are a bit extreme, and his looks are a bit extreme, as well. He's about your height and about sixty-five years old. He has a full head of white hair and sports a full beard. He travels around in a characteristic black suit, white shirt and bow tie. What really sets him off, is his wide-brimmed, black hat, and the fact he wears tennis shoes," said Nancy.

"That's a rather unique outfit for out here in Uhuru," said Jim.

"Or anywhere else, for that matter. He'll stay up late at night in the light of the lantern reading the Bible and stroking his beard."

"If he interrupts the excavation operations, why didn't your father just throw him out? I'll bet he doesn't pay room and board when he's here."

"My father was smart. He just put up with the Deacon. He did his best to ignore him. I think that's what all the professionals do."

"It sounds like the Deacon would be pretty hard to ignore."

"My father told me that when the Deacon first came to Africa, he would bring a trowel and get right down in the dirt with the crews, digging away. But Dr. Tubojola had him arrested for excavating without the proper licenses and permits, so all he does now is travel around and make a nuisance of himself."

"He sounds like a pest," said Jim.

"My father knew that if he threw the Deacon out, he would run to the press and shout foul. He would claim there was a cover up of the ancient past and all sorts of things."

"He sounds dangerous," said Jim.

"Not totally, Jim. You see, one of his claims is that all the fancy classifications we have for different hominids are nothing more than an elaborate scheme to sell the public on the concept of evolution. He says all hominids are the same species," said Nancy.

"So the Neanderthals are not a separate species. I know there is a big debate about where they fit in," said Jim.

"Precisely the Deacon's point. The issue of which hominid is ancestral and what group one assigns a specific fossil is always a matter of scientific debate. He is right in that we are constantly changing our opinions of the significance and nomenclature for many of our famous fossils."

"I see," said Jim.

"The issue of identification of every new fossil hominid discovery stirs up great debate and controversy. There is no great conspiracy. Science isn't exact, but that is how science works."

"So, is he right?"

"The question always is whether the anatomy of a new find fits within the accepted range of variation for a given species."

"Who determines the range of variation?" asked Jim.

"That's the crux of the issue. Is the new discovery different enough to justify a new species with a new name? That is the real question."

"So how do you know?"

"That's the Deacon's point. The only general rule adopted by all archaeologists is that if a new find is identical to a specimen already named, the archaeologist with the new find must use the existing name."

"That makes sense," said Jim.

"Yes, but if there is any variation between the new find and the named species, the debate will be long and heated."

"But it's a public debate, isn't it? It's published in the papers. There's no secret about it, is there?" asked Jim.

"You're right. The Deacon is a little paranoid there, but when they are close to what most professionals see as a speciation event, where one species evolves into two or more, they are often dealing with nothing more than informed speculation, I'm afraid. The Deacon's point is that it is an opinion, and he believes that all such classifications are wrong."

"Maybe he's right."

"Not entirely. His idea is similar to going back to the study of skull shape to determine intelligence and personality, but because he has a grain of truth, and he has the ability to twist anything you say around. That means you have to be very careful when dealing with him."

"So you think he'll be at the camp?"

"I have no idea. I just wanted to warn you. We'll know if we see a vehicle we can't identify. Besides, he is very good at making his presence known. I wanted you to know about him in case he's there, or shows up unannounced."

"I've got the message," said Jim.

"I referred to the rainy season a minute ago."

"Yes, you did." said Jim.

"It's a misnomer. Actually, it doesn't really rain much here. The heavy rains are well east of here, up in the mountains. We only get a few inches, but the effects are the same as if they were here, but without warning. After a couple of inches of rain up in the mountains, everything turns to a quagmire down here from the increased water in the river."

"That's hard to imagine, right now," said Jim.

"Do you know what the real danger is in the rainy season?"

"No."

"Flash floods from the rains up stream. On a clear, sunny day suddenly, without any warning, a rush of water can raise the level of the river and inundate this whole area. That's the real problem. A few years ago, Dad told me they lost a geologist up river in a flash flood. All they ever found was his Jeep, buried up to the top in mud. He was at the wrong place at the wrong time."

"Oh."

"This area has a strange beauty to it, but don't be deceived. It can be extremely dangerous," she warned.

The road ended abruptly under the shade of thick acacia trees as they reached the bank of the river. The river was about 50 yards across, a dark, slow moving, muddy, brown stream. A flat-bottomed, wood rowboat was tied to a post driven in the riverbank. As they moved past the boat, Jim could see that it was full of water and resting on the bottom of the river. "Looks like the local yacht," said Jim, as Nancy eased the front wheels down into the water.

"The boys found it when it washed down the river. No one knows where it came from. They were going to calk it and use it for fishing the last time I was out here. It doesn't look like they've had time to start the project. I guess they're just too busy."

"How about crocodiles?" asked Jim.

"Oh, I'm glad you asked. Never go near the water's edge. The boys have been feeding garbage to an old rogue crocodile since they set up camp. They get some perverse pleasure out of watching it feed on the garbage."

"Maybe that's why no one has done anything with that old boat," said Jim.

"Personally, I'm concerned that old croc might see people as food because we feed it. The boys are just provoking an attack in my opinion," said Nancy.

"I see. I've got your message. I'll stay away from the water."

"If they didn't feed that crocodile, I think it would lose interest in this area and move on, instead of hanging around. There's really not much for it to eat around here, without the garbage. The great herds haven't crossed the river around here for a long time. Snakes, fish, and some turtles are all you will see," she said. "Just stay away from the river's edge. The water is so murky, you'd never see the crocodile until it's too late."

"So we shouldn't plan on an afternoon swim, " said Jim, in jest.

"Not unless you want to be dinner."

"So, what are those thousands of small birds all along the water's edge over there?" he asked, pointing upstream along the riverbank.

"Sand grouse," she said. "At least, that's what I think they're called. They come to drink at the river several times a day. The big numbers come here right at dawn and dusk. They breed down in the scrub brush on the northern plain. There are several species of them, but I don't know one from the other. I do know enough about African animals and plants to be dangerous."

"You'd fool me," said Jim.

"Hold on. We're starting across the river bed."

"I hope you know what you are doing," said Jim.

"You can see stakes on each bank that mark the ford."

"Ok, I see them."

"As long as we stay between the stakes, we're safe. I've seen my father do this many times before. Don't look so nervous. We'll be fine."

"I'm trusting you with my life," said Jim, grinning.

Slowly she eased the Jeep down the bank into the water, which was between one and two feet deep. She gingerly maneuvered the vehicle across the river and up the opposite bank.

"You did great," said Jim, grinning.

"The worst is yet to come," she answered.

Just as she had warned him, the road turned sharply up a steep incline that had been plowed into the steep escarpment, as she had described. Quickly they were up to the top of the ridge. She swung the Jeep around to their left, where they faced two large white tents.

"Here you are, Jim Henderson, safe and sound, 'zamani sana.'"

"You lost me."

"According to Mobutu, that's the name the Masai call Bokuru. I think a rough translation is 'the place of the ancient past'."

CHAPTER ELEVEN: *THE CAMP*

"M'Bee," Nancy called out as soon as she pulled up in front of the first tent and cut off the engine. M'Bee was waiting for them, standing in the entrance of the tent. He was a short native of little over five feet in height, and a bit portly, which Jim thought was appropriate for a cook. Jim guessed he was about sixty years old. He wore a cook's apron over a faded yellow tee shirt and khaki shorts. On his feet were unlaced tennis shoes and no socks, but most noticeable was his warm smile.

Nancy jumped down out of the Jeep and ran over and embraced him. Once Jim got out of the Jeep and slowly stretched out his cramped legs, he took a moment to look around his new surroundings. To the south, he could see back across the open savannah where they had just traveled that morning. The remnants of the dust cloud they had stirred up were now settling back to earth. The camp also had a commanding view of the open savannah to the north. The upturned crust of the earth that was now the ridge gradually sloped down to the northern plain. The top of the ridge and the slope were mostly barren, but along the crease where the plain had been fractured and buckled creating the escarpment, the terrain was a mass of jumbled boulders. Here, trees and brush extended through the rocks and out onto the open savannah where it yielded to tall, waving grass interrupted only by occasional clusters of acacia trees.

"Out that way you will see wildebeest, gazelles, and zebras. Those black dots you see way out there are herds of animals. The brush down at the bottom of the escarpment is wild sisal. That's where those little birds you saw down by the river have their nests," Nancy explained.

"How do you know so much about the plants and animals out here if you are just an occasional visitor?" asked Jim. "One minute you don't know them, the next you do."

"Even when I was little, I wanted to know the names of every tree and plant I saw. I drove my poor mother crazy back home. Out here, Mobutu is my source of information. My father had a one-track mind. He was focused on his work, and never bothered about his surroundings. I think that's why I liked the museum when I was young. They have thousands of collections carefully identified. I like to know everything about my environment," said Nancy.

"Yes, I can see that the museum is the perfect place for you."

"Actually, out here, I'm all thumbs. I only know a few names. I'm not sure I could even identify one antelope from another," she said.

"I can't get over how quiet it is," said Jim. "This place has a strange beauty, but the silence bothers me."

"Remember, it can also be dangerous. If you are like me, you will be tempted to walk down to the rocks at the base of the slope."

"I admit the idea had crossed my mind," said Jim.

"Don't do it. Scorpions, ants, wild animals are all local dangers, particularly down there."

"This place is misleading. It looks so peaceful and serene."

"My real concern, Jim, is snakes. Many of the poisonous ones are so well camouflaged that you are unlikely to see them until you step on them."

"I'll stay right up here where I'm safe," said Jim. "I have no love of snakes."

"I was going to point out earlier that the Masai are usually barefoot. I have this theory that the reason they're always walking right behind their cattle is not just to control strays, but to allow the cattle to either trample or chase off dangerous snakes so the herdsmen have a safe place to walk."

M'Bee passed by them on his way into the tent and returned with two cups of warm tea.

"Jim, I want to introduce you to M'Bee."

"Yes, suh," said M'Bee handing Jim one of the cups.

Jim noticed that M'Bee was losing his hair, but unlike Dr. Tubojola, only the very top of his head was bald. M'Bee still had a tuft of silver hair surrounding the sides and back of his head. "Glad to meet you M'Bee," he said accepting the cup of tea. M'Bee's smile seemed frozen in place.

"Yes, suh," said M'Bee, again.

Jim concluded his smile was probably more or less a permanent fixture.

"M'Bee," she said. "Jim is from Chicago, in America. He's going to be staying with us for a couple of nights. He's here to write up a report on my father's death."

"Yes, mum."

"I'm not sure how long I'll be here. I might leave when Mr. Henderson does, or I might stay," she continued. "One of you might have to drive him back to Elizabethtown."

"You stay," M'Bee said. "You new boss now."

"Maybe," said Nancy. "We'll see, M'Bee. You've been talking too much to Mobutu."

"Yes. Mum."

"I haven't decided what I'm going to do yet, M'Bee, but I'm here for a few days to help out until I make my decision. If I don't stay, I'm sure they will bring someone else out here to do the work. They'll keep going. You'll be fine."

"Yes, mum."

"Jim, you should know M'Bee sends his whole paycheck to his family. He's a Kikuyu from a village outside Nairobi. He's been with my father for over ten years."

"You've been very loyal," said Jim, addressing M'Bee.

"Yes, suh."

"Can you help M'Bee unload the Jeep, Jim? We need to bring all the perishable foods into the mess tent and take those two cans of gasoline out to the back of the other tent. You'll see a little shelter where they will be out of the direct sun," she said. "All gasoline is stored under a small cover. You can't miss it. We need to unload all the food. It goes right behind the prep table. The medicine is stored at the other end of the tent, and our clothes bags belong in the bunk tent. I'll take the special cot with the special mosquito netting where my father stayed."

"Fine," said Jim.

"You can take any fresh cot you want. There are quite a few that aren't being used. Don't take the ones with shoes on them. This camp was set up at the request of Dr. Tubojola to be able to handle visitors from the museum so they can come out for a day or two to see an actual archaeological excavation. When this camp first opened, there was a steady stream of other professionals, students, and tourists. After a while I think they drove my father up the wall. Anyway, there are plenty of bunks. Select any one you want. Just remember the ones with shoes on them are taken."

"Why would you put shoes on your bed?" he asked. "That's not how I was raised."

"You weren't raised in Africa. Scorpions and spiders like warm dark places, like shoes," she answered.

"Oh, no problem. Now I understand," said Jim, as he turned to take the jerry cans of gasoline out of the Jeep. Once the supplies were unloaded and Nancy showed him inside both tents, Jim realized that the camp consisted solely of the two tents, a water storage tank, a simple shower stall, a second Jeep, and a tractor with plow attached on the front and a drilling rig on the back. There was an area on the ground about fifty yards from the tents that had been cleared of rocks and debris, which Nancy described as the helicopter landing area. After they had unloaded everything, he sat down at one of the rough board tables in the mess tent and made a sketch of the camp in his notebook. He did not know what he was looking for, but it gave him a place to start. Nancy sat down opposite him. She shrugged her shoulders.

"This is all there is to the camp," she said. "This place is nothing but dust and sand. When the wind blows, the grit even gets into your food. You can already feel the heat this early in the morning. When the wind blows up the dust, everyone is pretty miserable around here. M'Bee says they had a brief dust storm blow in from the north this morning, but it didn't last."

"I don't see anywhere you could hide from that weather," said Jim. "You are in the worst place here, out in the open and right on top of the ridge."

"That's one of our vulnerabilities. A dust devil swirled right thru camp the last time I was here. It made a real mess of things," she said.

"I'll bet."

"There are a few things to remember. I already told you not to wander down by the river. Snakes as well as the crocodile are dangers down there. Oh, you better watch out for Siafu too."

"Siafu?" asked Jim.

"African biting ants. The last time I was here M'Bee and I were collecting firewood down along the river when we ran into them. They are horrible."

"What can you do?" asked Jim.

"I'm told, the only thing to do is to wipe them off with a gasoline covered rag, but I haven't seen them up here, just down along the other side of the river. They seem to like dead trees and logs," said Nancy.

"I'll stay away from firewood."

"Are you allergic to bees?" she asked.

"I don't think so."

"Good. They're everywhere. People from the States seem to be especially vulnerable to the African bee stings. If you have allergic reactions back home, the reactions are much worse if the African bees sting you here. I already told you about scorpions and spiders."

"Yes, at least once. How about lions and hyenas?" asked Jim.

"You will find them on the other side of those rocks, down below on the northern plain, but up here, no. They have never been a problem at Bokuru. You saw the Masai earlier?" she asked.

"Yes."

"If you look carefully out on the northern plain, you should see a few manyattas."

"What is a manyatta?" asked Jim.

"Masai villages. Masai live out on the northern plain for the most part because there is more grass and the grazing is much better than south towards Elizabethtown. If they come here for medical treatment or supplies, they will leave their animals down on the plain. Usually, they come up here, one at a time, so someone is always watching the cattle."

"You have no doctor here, " observed Jim.

"You're right, but we give out aspirin, iodine, eye drops, hydrogen peroxide, and denatured alcohol. We can treat bruises and scratches, or at least M'Bee does. He runs a little, informal clinic on the side. We do it to maintain good relations with our neighbors."

"That makes sense," said Jim.

"Oh, we don't carry tobacco products or alcohol. The natives are always asking for them, but my father thought they were harmful and would be abused, so this site has never carried them."

"That's a nice gesture to have medical supplies available for the natives," said Jim.

"It has a practical purpose. These herdsmen are our eyes and ears. Several years ago there was an archeological camp a few miles down stream. I don't remember the names of the staff involved, but the story my father told was that there were three men sent out to set up the camp and wait for the main group to arrive. When the rest of the party finally reached the camp, there were only the remains of the tents flapping in the breeze," said Nancy.

"No one was there?" asked Jim.

"It was empty. The camp was ransacked."

"Ransacked?" he asked.

"Yes. Everything was gone. They never found the equipment. The three people in the initial party were never heard from again, and remain missing to this day. That was almost 20 years ago. Things were pretty rough before Uhuru was established as a separate country. Even today, you still need everyone you can get on your side," said Nancy.

"This place is dangerous," said Jim. "I think I'll stay right here, in camp."

"Give me a few minutes to talk with M'Bee. Then I'll drive you down to the site."

Jim was mildly disappointed. He was convinced there was nothing at the camp that was going to help his suicide investigation. Somehow he had expected more, although he was really not sure what he had expected to find. He had been looking forward to seeing the camp. He had been told his answer as to Dr. Bronston's motive for suicide was here, yet there was nothing in the camp that gave him a hint, and beyond the camp was bleak open semi-arid savannah. The only thing left that he hadn't seen yet was the excavation pit. The excavation pit now remained as the only place left for possible leads.

The one thing he was sure of was, the people who stayed here had to be very motivated and dedicated to what they were doing. For that reason, he was anxious to meet them.

Jim's anxiety heightened when he tried to sit down with M'Bee for an initial interview. M'Bee, he quickly discovered, was limited in both his command of the English language and, in Jim's opinion, his true mental capacity. No matter what question Jim asked about Dr. Bronston, all M'Bee would say was, "So sad."

M'Bee obviously knew his job well. He was good at it, and he was obviously loyal. He had been with Dr. Bronston for many years. If Nancy were going to stay at the camp to complete the work, she would have to make up her mind quickly to be sure to keep him. As a result of his observations of M'Bee's behavior, Jim was convinced that M'Bee was clearly not a personal confidant of Dr. Bronston. In fact, Jim thought M'Bee's personal and mental limitations were precisely why he was here. He would certainly never leak information about any discoveries. He was a simple man and he lived a simple life. His needs were few. Nancy told Jim that M'Bee's job was to prepare all the meals, maintain all the equipment, and keep the camp clean and in good order. The one thing Jim was sure of was that M'Bee did not have any knowledge of what was going on at the site. M'Bee, he concluded, would be of no help in his investigation.

Jim was wrong both about M'Bee and the significance of the camp. Jim spent a few minutes stepping off the distances from one tent to the other, then he sat at the front table in the mess tent sketching a rough drawing of the camp for his notes. The physical dimensions of the camp were all that he had to work with. M'Bee was busy rearranging the stacks of supplies against the back wall of the tent, while Jim continued to work with his sketch of the camp.

After a few minutes, M'Bee paused for a moment. He bent over and picked up a small black book from one of the worktables and brought it over to Nancy. Jim, who was sitting opposite Nancy, was busy writing up an inventory of the supplies on hand.

"Here mum," said M'Bee, handing Nancy the book.

"Thank you, M'Bee," said Nancy, as she briefly thumbed through the notebook then handed it to Jim. "What do you make of this, Jim? It's my father's handwriting, but I don't know what it is. It's full of numbers and none of them make any sense to me."

Jim looked in the notebook. His heart skipped a beat. It was precisely what he had forgotten to ask about. He knew exactly what the numbers were. At the foot of his mother's bed in the nursing home in Carbonwood, Illinois, was a clipboard in a plastic folder hanging from the back rail. On the clipboard were pages of records of her daily temperature and pages of numbers just like the ones he was looking at. He smiled with recognition when he realized exactly what the numbers meant.

"I thought you told me you knew your father had high blood pressure?" Jim asked.

"Yes," said Nancy. "He told me he was taking medicine daily for it," she answered.

"When you were here last, how long did you stay?" Jim asked.

"It was about ten days, I think. I don't remember exactly, why?"

"Did you ever see him take his own blood pressure?" asked Jim.

"No," she said. "I didn't know he was doing that. Why do you ask?"

"These first two columns of numbers in this book are his entries for blood pressure readings. He was taking his blood pressure daily and writing down the numbers. The third number is a pulse reading. I think the next two columns are for the month and the day the readings were taken. Are you sure you never saw him do it?"

"No, but that's great he kept a record. What do the numbers show?" she asked.

"Well, I'm no doctor, so I can't tell you the significance of the specific numbers, but two things stand out. He had been taking readings daily for months. I haven't calculated it, but I'll bet this book goes back to the date of his last physical with Dr. Bhatt. Also, the numbers in each column are all close. I mean, there are no wild ones or any significant variation."

"So he was stable. The medicine was doing its job," Nancy observed.

"Exactly. Didn't you tell me there was no lantern in the bunk tent?" he asked.

"Yes, mosquitoes, flies and other unwanted insects are all drawn to the heat and light of a lantern, so we did not keep one in the bunk tent."

"Dr. Bhatt told me your father was taking daily blood pressure readings and keeping precise records since his first visit over two years ago. He gave me a copy of the readings for the whole year between his first visit and his second one, just four months ago," said Jim.

"That's good," she said. "So what's in this book?"

"This book is a continuation of those records since he came back out here."

"That's interesting," she said.

"The reason you did not see him taking his blood pressure readings when you were here was he took the readings late at night, right here in the mess tent where there was a lantern, and after you had gone to bed in the other tent. I'll bet he sat right here in the light of the lantern hanging right over my head. He kept the book in this tent because it was convenient for recording the readings right after he took them. No one thought to look here for his personal property after he died."

"That's an interesting observation. I'll bet you're right," she said.

"Let's look for the blood pressure kit. I'll bet it's right here someplace, too," said Jim.

It did not take long to find the blood pressure kit. M'Bee found an old open cigar box on top of the crates of food supplies, right next to the spot where he found the book. The box contained the battery-operated device, the armband and pressure cord, along with what Jim guessed were several months' supply of AA batteries for the device. The spare batteries were all vacuum-sealed in packets of four, just as they had been when purchased at a store. The device was similar to the one he had seen the orderlies use on his mother, half way around the world.

"You're right, Jim. My father always remained here in the mess tent when I went to bed," said Nancy.

Jim knew the significance of what he saw. For a moment, he felt goose bumps on the back of his neck. He reached into his briefcase, opened the folder labeled 'Bronston,' and slipped out the copy of the death certificate. The date of death recorded on the certificate was October 18. Carefully, he re-examined the notebook. He was right. There was an entry for every day of the month for the past four months. The last entry was October 17. He remembered what Dr. Umbawi had said about loose lips, and said nothing. He knew immediately what the numbers meant. With shaking hands, he slipped the death certificate back into the folder, then placed the folder along with the notebook into his briefcase and closed the lid.

Everyone he had spoken to had told him the truth. All of them had been right all along. Jim had either ignored what they said, or simply had not paid attention. He had been fixed with the original determination that Dr. Bronston's death was a suicide, and his job was to find Dr. Bronston's motive.

Suddenly, everything was upside down. Now, he was convinced Dr. Bronston had not committed suicide. If Dr. Bronston was intent on taking his own life, he would not continue to take daily records of his blood pressure, right up to the day he took his life. Why would he bother with monitoring life-sustaining functions if his intent was to commit suicide? Why continue to take blood pressure medicine if he intended to commit suicide? The only reason there was no entry for October 18, he realized, was that Dr. Bronston never came back to the camp that evening. He was already dead.

The records were out in plain sight, so Dr. Bronston could not have been trying to hide what he was doing. Jim had wasted his entire trip to Africa so far looking for something that did not exist. Now, he was focused. Now, he had two questions. First, who was guilty of murder? Second, why did they do it? He remembered Nancy's comment that she was sure her father did not commit suicide, but she could not answer why a smoking gun was found in his hand. She had also told Jim that he would be stymied, just as she was, by the smoking gun. She was right.

Jim decided to simply let the day play out as it was scheduled. He did not know where to begin. All he could do was keep his eyes and ears open. Now, he had to be on full alert for clues, not for suicide, but for murder.

He remembered that Dr. Umbawi and Dr. Tubojola told him he would find the answer to Dr. Bronston's death here at Bokuru, and the clues would be in Dr. Bronston's records. Within the first hour of his arrival at the camp, he already had his first significant lead, and it was in Dr. Bronston's records, just as predicted. What other surprise did Bokuru have in store for him? Jim wondered.

"Did you notice?" she asked.

"Notice what?" he answered, unsure if she was aware what the blood pressure readings meant.

"The Deacon isn't here."

"Oh."

"C'mon, Jim. It's time to take you down to the site to meet Mobutu and the crew." Jim followed her lead and climbed back into the passenger seat of the Jeep. He was content that she did not know that he was now on a murder investigation and that he was on his way to the one place that promised to help him find the answers to his questions. Mobutu was his primary murder suspect. The two laborers who worked for Mobutu had to be the next two suspects. Now, he was about to meet them all.

"A penny for your thoughts," she asked, as she started the engine. "You look a little lost."

"You could have told me about M'Bee," said Jim.

"Well, he is limited," she said. "I've noticed that before, but I knew you would interview him, no matter what I said. So, I just let you find out for yourself. I'm sorry I didn't warn you though. I guess I should have."

"No, you're right. It's better that I found out on my own," said Jim. "I'm the one who has to conduct the investigation and write the report."

"This afternoon, when we come back from a thorough examination of the site, we'll look through my father's personal trunk and his other personal things. I was going to do that myself, but the more I thought about it, I felt you should do it with me. There's nothing to hide. The police already looked for a note or letter. There should only be clothing in the trunk," she said.

"I've been looking forward to seeing the site. Everything has been pointing me to the excavation and his field notes for clues," said Jim.

"You're right. The site is the important thing, not the camp," she said. "I didn't expect you to find your answer up here. This is just the support operation for the site. I understand that the territorial police have already looked around, but I know you have to go through everything yourself as well. The camp is located a mile from the excavation, to take advantage of the better geography."

"So I noticed," said Jim. "Your father chose the high ground."

"This location has advantages and disadvantages. The camp is on the highest point for miles around. That means we don't have to worry about floods or heavy rains. We catch the breezes if there are any, and we have fewer mosquitoes than down by the river. Oh, while I remember, at night, leave the shoes you were wearing outside the mosquito netting. Mosquitoes hone in on warm damp shoes. Once they sit for a day or two, you can keep them on your bed."

"I'll remember that," said Jim.

"Each morning you have to fish around in your shoes with a stick to be sure there are no spiders or scorpions in them. Remember, at night you'll have to write down your notes in the mess tent. There's a lantern there we keep on as late as anyone needs it. Remember, there's no mosquito netting around that tent, unlike the bunk tent," she said.

"I'm sure the mosquito netting will help at night," said Jim.

"The two disadvantages of this location are that you have to cross the river to get here. In the rainy season, it is not always possible to cross the river, and the actual archaeological site is a mile further down the ridge. This camp does pose a real dilemma for me, though," Nancy admitted.

"What's that?" he asked.

"I know my father was intent on working year round."

"What's wrong with that?" asked Jim.

"He planned on working through the rainy season. Right now, we're getting near the end of the dry season. I'm not sure I agree with his plan. Things are tough when the river is impassible and the roads become a quagmire from all the rain. The work will become very hard too, even though we have good drainage. I think, keeping the excavation open may be the biggest decision I have to make," she said.

"If you stay," Jim added.

"I'll give you an hour with Mobutu. Then I'll pick you up and take you with me down to the river to help fill the water tank. We'll have lunch when we get back," she said.

"What about your crocodile?" Jim asked.

"We have an answer for that. I'll show you when we get there. When we come back, we'll load up lunch for everyone and take it down to the site. We'll spend the rest of the afternoon there. For now, let Mobutu show you around. I'll come back to camp and finish up the inventory with M'Bee. I need to know exactly what supplies we have on hand. If we stay open through the rainy season from January through April, we'll need to stock up well in advance," said Nancy. "We can't forget anything."

"I see your dilemma," said Jim.

"A trip down to the river before lunch will cool you off a bit," she added.

"Sounds good to me," said Jim. "I hope all my answers are at the site."

The Jeep lurched to life, and she headed down the narrow track along the top of the ridge.

"You've traveled half way around the world to inspect the excavation. I hope you're not disappointed when we get there," she said, looking over at him and smiling. "Just remember an archaeological excavation is only an open pit. Don't expect too much."

CHAPTER TWELVE: *THE SITE*

As the Jeep bounced along the narrow track, Jim knew something was wrong, terribly wrong. Nancy was concentrating on driving along the narrow ridge track that led down to the site leaving Jim alone with his thoughts. The visit to the site should be the most important event in his investigation. From the moment he left Chicago, his sights had been aimed at this event. Yet, somehow, the trip was no longer his primary focus. The camp had always been the back-up operation for the excavation, yet it was at the camp, and not the site, where everything had changed.

Jim had come to Africa to investigate a suicide. His intention had been to look for the motivation for that act. Everyone he met had told him not only that there was no motive for suicide, but they did not believe the suicide determination on the death certificate was correct. Even the coroner had hedged on his decision by entering "probable suicide" as the cause of death. Yet he himself had remained fixed with the suicide theory. He had rigidly not considered any other option, until now. Although he had retained the hope that he would find the key to a motive for suicide, he had not found a single shred of evidence that would provide the foundation for that conclusion. Still, all he had was the death certificate, which merely provided the conclusion of a third party. He was sure the certificate was supported only by the fact the gun was found in Dr. Bronston's hand.

After arriving at the camp, now everything was completely different. The others had been right all along. His heart had skipped a beat when he looked at the entries in Dr. Bronston's blood pressure notebook. For him, that small book of hand printed numbers was the turning point in his entire investigation. He knew suicide was no longer a viable option. A person about to commit suicide would not continue to take his or her blood pressure readings up to the evening before their death. It made no sense. Further, all the readings in the book were within the normal range for a normal blood pressure reading, so suicide was not likely motivated by an unusual medical condition. The entries in the book clearly indicated Dr. Bronston was interested in life maintenance, not termination.

On the other hand, he had no proof of foul play. If what everyone said could be trusted, an accident was improbable as well. He was left with the chilling prospect that his investigation had switched to one of murder, not suicide. The museum had sent him to Africa only because they also did not believe the conclusion stated on the death certificate. They were looking for confirmation, not an alternative theory of death. No one had mentioned murder as the cause of death. The museum wanted him to overturn the cause of death, if possible, but he was sure they were thinking of an accident as the cause, not murder.

Everything had changed, and his focus now had to be to find a killer and a motive for murder. The threshold question was, who would want Dr. Bronston dead and why? None of the people he had met so far demonstrated any detectable motive for murder. Everyone he had met admired and respected Dr. Bronston. All of them had strongly stood behind the position that Dr Bronston did not and would not commit suicide. But wouldn't a murderer also want to support the suicide determination to keep attention away from the facts? A murderer would not challenge the suicide on the death certificate. He or she would embrace it. No one had ever suggested murder, but they all challenged the suicide determination, so it made no sense that anyone of them was involved in Dr. Bronston's death. No one had taken that next big step in their thinking.

Jim felt disoriented, even lost. He did not know what to do. The only thing he could think of was to keep his opinions to himself, and let the others continue to think he was still focused on suicide. Because the death certificate had already been issued, the reality was that it created a presumption of it's own accuracy. It had the stamp of government approval behind it. To overturn the cause of death on the certificate, he would have to rebut that presumption by clear and convincing evidence. He could not go to the police at this time because all he had was conjecture. It was still his investigation. He simply did not know where to begin since murder was way outside his range of experience.

The one thing that had influenced, not only his investigation, but also the original government investigation, was the fact the gun was found in Dr. Bronston's hand. The official position and entire suicide hypothesis depended on that one piece of evidence. Thus, he thought, to overturn the conclusion, he would have to deal with that one pivotal fact. Obviously, the government authorities had jumped to a conclusion. The question, Jim realized, was, if he was dealing with murder, the gun had to have been placed in Dr. Bronston's hand after his death to make murder look like suicide. He was sure that the possibility of murder was not even considered by the government when issuing the death certificate. Assuming this possibility was correct, whoever the murderer was, he or she was in no hurry. The murderer had taken careful, deliberate time to alter the death scene to create the appearance of suicide. Who ever it was knew they would have the time to complete this alteration, even before they undertook the plan.

For Jim, that meant there was no witness at the site at the time of the murder to hear the shot or to surprise the assailant. Only the perpetrator and the victim could have been anywhere near the scene of the crime at the time of the act, and the perpetrator had to be totally confident that not a single witness was around. Jim, who had not been to the site, concluded that the perpetrator had to know that everyone else was a mile away up at the camp. To have that knowledge, the perpetrator must not have been a stranger to the site or the camp, and their presence at the site would not alarm any one.

For the moment, he had no idea who would profit by Dr. Bronston's death, so the motive for murder was a total unknown. He would have to concentrate on the element of opportunity to determine probable suspects. His list of suspects would be short and limited to those who were at the camp. He made a brief list in his head. Mobutu Nyzeki, interim manager, and the one who found the body was first on the list. M'Bee, the two site workers, and the two part timers from the temple followed. Then, he remembered that the Deacon was also a possibility. There was no one else.

At least initially, he decided he could eliminate M'Bee. His work was at the camp. An appearance at the site would have aroused suspicion. Besides, it was too far for him to walk down and back. Jim was pretty sure M'Bee could not drive. At least for the moment, Jim reduced his list to six suspects. That conclusion made him feel a bit better about his investigation. Besides, he was right on target. He was on his way to meet Mobutu and the two laborers. Since Mobutu was the one who reported the event, he was arguably the last to see Dr. Bronston alive. Mobutu also had to be the number one suspect because he would have had the opportunity. This fact put Mobutu well ahead of the two laborers who had to be next in line.

Jim knew he was out of his league attempting to conduct a murder investigation, but he was working on a mere conjecture at this point. No one would believe him, so he knew that in spite of his limited background, he was on his own. Admissible evidence was his background, and that was exactly what he needed. The blood pressure information had aroused his suspicion, but he needed hard evidence.

The excavation itself was no longer important except that he had promised both Dr. Tubojola and Keith Kendall he would let them know what he found there. Inspection of the excavation pit would not be crucial, but Jim now felt it would not be a waste of time. The interviews, on the other hand, would be crucial.

As Nancy reached the end of the track, he could see that the site provided very little to look at. She stopped next to an older, worn, dust-covered Jeep parked in front of a tent that was similar to the two at the camp. The only other significant thing Jim could see was the excavation pit itself, about 20 yards to their left. The pit was half hidden by a large white canvas tarp stretched over the opening of the pit. The back part of the pit had not been fully excavated and was exposed to the direct rays of the sun. Behind the pit was the overburden dump, consisting of a large heap of finely sifted sand. Beyond the excavation pit, the ridge dropped steeply down to the river below, and stretched beyond the river. He could see the open expanse of the savannah across which they had traveled that morning. In the opposite direction, the escarpment sloped gently down to a pile of jumbled rocks where the ridge met the northern plain. Thick brush grew around the rocks and extended out onto the open rangeland.

In the hazy, gray distance, he could see the cone-shaped silhouette of the dormant volcano. Between the ridge and the distant volcano, he could see several large herds of animals, appearing as dark specks in the distance. High out over the savannah, vultures circled in the clear blue sky.

As soon as Nancy cut off the engine, the silence seeped into his consciousness again. Compared to the noise of city life, Bokuru was a desolate place. How he could ever have thought African archaeology as romantic when he was back in Chicago, was beyond him now that he was here. The silence alone was unnerving. Then there was the heat. There was no drugstore or fast food franchise around the corner. Desolation was the only word that came to his mind to describe this part of Uhuru.

"Did I tell you, this tent is the supply tent?" Nancy asked breaking the silence and Jim's thoughts with a jolt.

"No," said Jim. "No one told me anything about it. I didn't even know it was here until just now."

"That's my fault. This tent is where the finish work would have been done before my father brought in the smaller finish tent. He wanted to work alone where he would have fewer distractions, away from the others."

"I didn't see any other tent," said Jim. "Where's the finish tent?"

"My understanding is that the small, finish tent is attached onto the back of this one. I'm sure that's why we couldn't see it on the way here."

"Is that the excavation under that tarp, over there?" asked Jim.

"Yes. Right now, the only ones here are Mobutu and his crew of two regular full time workers. I understand the two part timers from the temple have not been here since my father died."

"This is a small operation," said Jim. "We had more people on a weekend field excavation in Chicago."

"You're right, but it costs a lot of money to keep workers out here full time. Here, you only bring in the help you absolutely need and can afford. Remember, in Chicago, we were all volunteers."

"I forgot," said Jim.

"My father closed this site to outsiders about three months ago."

"Except for the Deacon," said Jim, smiling.

"The Deacon is a special case. My father claimed visitors caused too many distractions. He told me the operation was becoming a tourist trap and he couldn't get any work done with outsiders around," said Nancy.

"Was the Deacon around at the time your father died?"

"From what I've been told, the Deacon had been here a week or two before, but he wasn't at this camp at the time of my father's death."

"I was just curious," said Jim.

"Dr. Tubojola was very sensitive to my father's complaints. After my father demanded the camp be restricted, Dr. Tubojola steered people out to visit an abandoned site just east of Elizabethtown. His department has kept an old, abandoned excavation pit open and the tents up just for the tourists."

"I can't believe tourists would want to come out to a remote place like this. There's nothing here for them to see," remarked Jim.

"You have no idea how important it is for some people to be able to say they visited or slept over at an actual archaeological excavation," said Nancy. "Dr. Tubojola runs that abandoned site like a motel in the desert. Tourists don't mind the lack of amenities."

"That's incredible," said Jim. "When I think of tourists, I think of fancy, full-service hotels."

"You're missing the boom in eco-tourism where roughing it is in vogue. That type of tourist wants to experience the real flavor of being at an archaeological dig. They'll even pay extra to stay out at an actual site."

"I suppose no one tells them that old site is sterile," said Jim.

"I have no idea what they tell visitors out there. In any case, when Bokuru was open to outsiders, Mobutu gave the tours. My father could not be bothered. He was aware how important some of the visitors could be in making donations, but he did not like the intrusion. His first solution was to add the small private tent, but, in the end, he squashed the whole visitation concept. I know he would never show anyone any fossils they actually found. He was paranoid about possible leaks to the press."

"I see," said Jim. "Secrecy prevailed."

"My father always kept his discoveries under wraps. You are right. I think secrecy is the real reason he brought in the new tent. There's plenty of room right here in the supply tent, as you will see. He had to have a place down here at the site where visitors could find some shade and sit down out of the sun, so Dad just made a provision for any finish work to be done next door. He told me once they covered their detail excavation work with rags and towels when visitors showed up, so no one ever saw what was really going on. He said they would set up dummy finish work demonstrations using pieces of fossil from other sites you could not identify, just to impress the guests," said Nancy.

"Sounds pretty paranoid," said Jim. "Of course, they didn't do that here, because they cut off the tourists before they began finding fossils."

"Yes. That's my father. He never disclosed anything until all the fieldwork was done, and he was ready to publish his findings. I feel bad though."

"Why?" asked Jim.

"Because I sent a few big donors from the Chicago museum out here with their families. We always had requests from people who wanted to see a real archaeological excavation while they were on a vacation trip to Africa. I know visits helped bring in large donations. I was not in a position to refuse important donors the opportunity to come out here, even though I know I was irritating my father. Actually, I think he enjoyed the company when they first started this site."

"He enjoyed company? I thought he didn't want anyone around?" asked Jim.

"Before they found any fossils, visitors relieved the monotony. He saw no danger then."

"So when they started to find fossils, he threw out the guests," said Jim.

"Yes," said Nancy. "That's the way my father worked."

When they got out of the Jeep, no one came out to greet them. However, as soon as they started to walk toward the excavation pit, a tall thin native came up the ramp from under the tarpaulin. He was wearing a faded khaki shirt and matching shorts, heavy duty hiking boots, and a pith helmet. He easily strode up the ramp and over to meet them. He looked every bit the native archaeologist. His face broke into a warm grin as he approached them.

"Mobutu," Nancy called out in greeting, smiling broadly.

This was the man who had discovered Dr. Bronston's body, Jim reminded himself as he watched every movement that Mobutu made. At last he was to meet and interview his primary murder suspect.

A moment later, a second native came up the ramp behind Mobutu, pushing a wheelbarrow filled with finely sifted sand that he wheeled over to the refuse pile. Jim watched him as he dumped the contents onto the heap. The worker paused a moment to wave to them, then disappeared, pushing his empty wheelbarrow back down the ramp into the pit. For a moment, Mobutu embraced Nancy. Like M'Bee, his smile seemed frozen on his face. However, in contrast, he was tall, about the same height as Dr. Tubojola, differing from Dr. Tubojola in that he was unusually thin. Jim's best guess was that Mobutu was in his mid-forties.

"It's good to see you again, Mobutu," said Nancy. "I feel as though I have been away for years."

"Welcome back, Miss Nancy," said Mobutu. "I am so pleased to see you."

"I'd like you to meet Jim Henderson. He's here from Chicago to investigate my father's death, for the insurance company."

"Glad to meet you, Mobutu," said Jim, as they shook hands.

"How do you do?" asked Mobutu in clean, crisp English.

"I've heard a great deal about you," said Jim.

"I hope it's all good," said Mobutu, lightly.

"It is," said Jim.

"Come inside. Let's get in out from under the sun," said Mobutu, leading them back away from the pit and into the shelter of the supply tent. He motioned for them to sit down. Jim noted the wooden boxes that served as seats along a table made of old boards in the center of the tent.

"I want you to show Jim around, Mobutu. Put him to work if it will help. He has excavation experience in Chicago, and knows about field archaeology. I'm going to go back up and help M'Bee," said Nancy. "We have to complete an inventory of all the supplies on hand. If I can finish before lunch, I'll join you this afternoon."

"Yes, Ma'am," said Mobutu.

"I'll come back down and pick Jim up in about an hour. He can help fill the water tank. Your water supply is low. With more of us out here for a couple of days, you need to make a water run today."

"Yes, ma'am."

"We'll bring sandwiches and tea back down here for the crew when I come back."

"That's fine, Miss Nancy."

"By the way, M'Bee and I were looking for another big tin with a lid to store rice. You don't have one down here, do you? It seems I bought enough rice to fill seven tins but we only found six with lids."

"There are none down here, Miss Nancy. Six is fine, but seven is an unlucky number."

"Why is six so important?" she asked.

"Kikuyu are very superstitious, Miss Nancy. We have given up a lot of our ancient customs. Long ago the arrival of the white man destroyed most of the Kikuyu culture, but we have held onto one or two of the old superstitions. M'Bee is from the Narok district about 50 kilometers outside Nairobi. He is very superstitious. Seven is a bad number," said Mobutu.

"I'll remember that, Mobutu," said Nancy.

"That's why you have six, Miss Nancy. He would only keep six tins for rice," said Mobutu, smiling.

"I think I understand. What you say is interesting, Mobutu. For Mr. Henderson and myself, the number seven is lucky. Everything here seems backwards to us. Well, it looks like rice for all our meals the next few days. Without a sealed container, the rats and mice will get to that last bag of rice. We'll have to beat them to it," she said.

"I'll look carefully, Miss Nancy, but seven is bad luck."

"Thank you, Mobutu. I want to keep M'Bee working on the inventory this morning. How much rain have you had in the last two weeks?"

"Nothing," said Mobutu. "Everything is still very dry."

"My guess is we have enough time to bring out one big truckload of supplies before the rains start. I don't know what to do, Mobutu. I know my father had planned to keep the operation going during the rainy season, but personally I'm not so sure that would be a good idea. Once the rains start and the river rises, the crossing will be impassable, and the only road out of here will be a quagmire. There could be weeks between supply runs."

"Yes, ma'am."

"Whether or not to stay open may be a difficult decision." She paused for a moment.

"Yes Ma'am."

"Well, I'll face that later. All I want to do for now is introduce you to each other. It's important that you two chat without my interference," said Nancy.

"Yes Ma'am," said Mobutu.

"Mr. Henderson has to write up a full report on my father's death. He'll ask a lot of questions. Please help him any way you can. Tell him everything you know."

"Yes, ma'am."

Jim knew they had only been at the camp a couple of hours, yet Nancy's behavior appeared to indicate she had already made up her mind to stay.

"We'll see you when you get back," said Jim. "Don't worry about me, I'll be fine."

"I'll be back within the hour," said Nancy, as she stood to leave. Suddenly she was gone.

"Ituika," said Mobutu, nodding towards the Jeep as it pulled away.

"Ituika?" asked Jim.

"She has come to take over for her father. 'Ituika' is the ancient Kikuyu ceremony where the management of the tribe changes from one generation to the next. Of course, there can be no ceremony because her father is already gone, but it is the same. Our tribe has not had an actual ceremony for many years now, but she is right," said Mobutu.

"How is that?"

"It is best to stop and end the excavation season before January. It will be too dangerous if we stay open," said Mobutu.

"Why is that, Mobutu?" asked Jim.

"We could be landlocked for months, not just weeks. We would have to obtain all our supplies by helicopter."

"That might work," said Jim.

"Perhaps, Mr. Henderson, but that would be very expensive, and we would be restricted to doing finish work. We could not work in the excavation."

"Why not?" asked Jim.

"Because all the ground would be mud and we cannot sift mud. Everything has to be sifted for small pieces."

"Of course, that does make sense. I should have realized that." Jim changed the subject, anxious to address the questions he had for Mobutu. "I have seen resumes for everyone else I have met, but I don't know much about you, Mobutu," said Jim. "All I know is that you were with Dr. Bronston for many years, and you are an excellent fossil hunter."

"Thank you, Mr. Henderson. I was born in the eastern suburbs of Nairobi. I went to the church school when I was young. They helped me get into the university, and I went there for two years under the tradesman program. I have a two-year associate degree in field archaeology. I wanted to go on for the four-year degree, but I had no money. I was looking for a job when I saw a notice on the bulletin board at the university. Dr. Bronston was interviewing students for a summer expedition up north. I signed on, and I have stayed with him ever since. This is what I want to do."

"Well, you sound well educated, Mobutu."

"I read a lot, Mr. Henderson. Dr. Bronston helped me. I wanted to do this kind of work, and I wanted to escape our tribal past and the old superstitions. I wanted to learn as much as I could. I wanted to know the truth about the world."

"There are no classrooms out here, Mobutu."

"Dr. Bronston said that I had the best classroom in the world."

"How's that, Mobutu?" asked Jim.

"He said I had the real world. He said if I read many books while I obtained field experience, I would have the best education. I read everyday, Mr. Henderson. Dr. Bronston was my teacher, and he ordered books for me. I have many books at the camp that I read. Now that Dr. Bronston is gone, I don't know what will happen."

"I'm sure things will work out, Mobutu. Look, I have to be honest. I don't know where to begin to ask you the questions I have on my mind. I must start with the fact you were the one who found Dr. Bronston's body. Can you tell me about that?"

"What I tell you is true. I swear to it on the Githathi oath stone which is sacred to all Kikuyu."

"I will trust your word, Mobutu," said Jim.

"First, let me tell you how we work at Bokuru, so you will have a better understanding."

"Certainly," said Jim.

"Bokuru, Mr. Henderson, is difficult because everything is buried in compacted sandstone. We start out by breaking the sandstone into smaller pieces to work with, first by drilling. Then we open up the larger pieces by using a pneumatic expansion drill, which we run off the gas generator behind the finish tent. We have to use hammers, chisels, dental and carpenter's tools to break it down. If we find a bit of fossilized bone, we stop," said Mobutu.

"That's the material you gave to Dr. Bronston," Jim continued. "He took over from there."

"Yes. If we do not find any fossils, we break the rock down to rough sand, sift it, then dump the sifted sand out onto the overburden."

"Yes. I saw your sand pile. What happens if you see fossilized bone?"

"Usually, we can break the matrix down further right in the pit. The sandstone crumbles away easily. The fossils are all limestone, which is much harder. Fractures are usually found right along the fossil line. We break off about eighty percent of the matrix, photograph the fossil, and record the location where we found it. Then we label it and put it into a box and take the box up to the finish tent," said Mobutu, speaking slowly so Jim could take notes.

"I appreciate the details, Mobutu. Please, go on. What happens next?"

"Well, at first, Dr. Bronston did all the finish work, separating the fossils from what was left of the sandstone matrix. He would clean them, then reassemble complete bones from the pieces, if he could. That was his job. But, I'm getting ahead," said Mobutu.

"That's fine. Continue any way you feel comfortable," said Jim. "I need to know everything I can. But let me ask you a simple question."

"Yes."

"Bokuru is out in middle of nowhere. How in the world did you ever find this location? I mean, I can understand the location for the camp. You put it on the ridge at the highest point for miles in any direction. But this site is another matter. How did you ever find this place and decide to dig here?"

"We were very lucky with the camp. It is almost an ideal location. Thankfully, we are in Africa and not some place like China, Mr. Henderson."

"China?" Jim asked.

"Yes, the big problem in China is that you are never far from a large human population. You have to find your fossils before the local people do."

"Why is that?" asked Jim.

"Because a certain percentage of the people in China look at fossils as chicken or dragon bones which they search for diligently."

"Why?' asked Jim.

"They take them back to their villages and grind them up into a fine powder."

"Into a powder? What on earth for?"

"They market the powder for medicinal purposes," said Mobutu, smiling. "Like herbs."

223

"But fossils are just rock. Nature chemically replaces the actual bones with minerals that become hardened into rock in the shape of the bones. The original bone has long gone."

"Yes, Mr. Henderson. You are right. You do know archaeology. The problem in China is that the people are literally grinding up and consuming their ancestors. They will never know their past. By the time the archaeologist comes around to try to document it, they will have eaten it," said Mobutu, smiling broadly.

"Come on, Mobutu. You're pulling my leg. I can't write that down in my notes."

"You could. It is true. In China, the archaeologist first must find the fossil, and then secure it before it is lost to the apothecary. It is also true to a lesser degree here in Africa."

"I see," said Jim.

"There is also a large percentage of the people in China that sees the archaeologist as evil."

"Evil?"

"Yes. They see the archaeologist as one who disturbs graves, stirring up the final resting place of man and beast alike. These activities are seen as evil."

"Why do they think of archaeology as evil?"

"They are worried about ghosts, Mr. Henderson."

"Ghosts?" Jim asked.

"Yes, but we do not have these problems here at Bokuru," said Mobutu.

"How could you have these kinds of problems?" said Jim. "You are out in the middle of a barren land, far from anyone. How do you know so much about China? Have you ever been there?"

"No. You forgot. I read, Mr. Henderson. Right now I am reading about archaeology in China," said Mobutu, proudly.

Jim remembered his investigation. He might well be dealing with the primary suspect in a murder investigation. The concepts of murder and suicide seemed out of place here at Bokuru. Somehow they seemed like big city events that belonged back in Chicago or New York, not out in the savannah in Africa. His initial impression was that Mobutu seemed to be an unlikely suspect for a murderer.

"You are right about the camp, Mr. Henderson. The location was easy to determine. You must see we had no need for a camp until we had a site. Bokuru was not found by us."

"It wasn't? Who found it?"

"This site was originally discovered by geologists on the Uhuru Geological Survey."

"Somehow I thought it was discovered by you, personally," said Jim. "Come to think of it, maybe someone told me it was a geologist. I think maybe Dr. Tubojola told me a geologist made the discovery."

"Dr. Tubojola is a good man, Mr. Henderson. Sometimes I am given credit for things I did not do. The geologists saw the top of the cave exposed. It was partially collapsed. The cave walls also protruded out of the sand on the top of what was left of the ridge. The geologists knew that the ridge had been much higher in the past, and had worn down, exposing the cave. The cave was discovered while they were exploring for mineral deposits as part of the national geological survey," said Mobutu.

"I see," said Jim.

"Since they could tell that it was an ancient cave, they told Dr. Tubojola about it. No one knew this plain geological feature could be the possible location of an important discovery, but Dr. Tubojola thought it had promise. I think Dr. Tubojola simply thought it might be a good possibility for an ancient hyena or leopard den."

"So after Dr. Tubojola told Dr. Bronston about it, and Dr. Bronston undertook the responsibility of excavating it," said Jim, guessing the connection.

"Yes. Dr. Bronston had always been interested in the Bokuru River Valley. He was looking for an area to explore for hominid fossils. When he heard about the cave, Dr. Bronston thought it had a great deal of potential," said Mobutu.

"So, he decided to dig," said Jim.

"Yes. He was excited about the possibilities. Our geologists have a good understanding of the geological history of this area. They dated the fill in the top of the cave at 1.82 million years before present," said Mobutu.

"That's pretty precise," said Jim.

"Geology is not a problem at Bokuru, but it was still a risky decision for Dr. Bronston to come out here. It was even more of a gamble to decide to dig."

"Why? He knew it was a cave. Didn't the geologist tell him that?"

"Yes, but it is very unusual to begin an excavation with no evidence of fossils to start with. You have no idea what you might find, if anything. Dr. Bronston only had a hunch that the cave would be productive. He took a very big risk."

"So, he decided to dig, but he didn't find anything for a long time?"

"Yes, that is true, but Dr. Bronston did not expect to find anything until at least two meters below the datum plane."

"Why is that, Mobutu?"

"Because, not even hyenas or leopards will use a cave if it is too small."

"I see," said Jim.

"We found nothing at that level, and then again, nothing at four meters. There was no evidence of any occupation level at all. It seemed like a bottomless pit," said Mobutu. "It seemed to be an empty pit, filled with sandstone."

"But you kept going? You didn't stop? Why?" asked Jim.

"Dr. Bronston was committed to go to the floor of the cave, whatever the depth. They kept getting the same dates for the fill as they dug down deeper, which was very heartening."

"Why was that?" asked Jim.

"Uniform dates indicated that the cave filled in all at one time. We hadn't missed anything. There was going to be only one occupation level."

"I understand," said Jim.

"Even Dr. Bronston began to get discouraged when we passed four meters below the datum plane."

"You had sifted a lot of sand by then," Jim observed.

"Yes, but we kept going. Dr. Bronston said that this was a good potential australopithecine site. He kept saying that all we had to do was dig until we found the cave floor."

"Was he right?"

"He was right and he was wrong. He was right in that we were excavating at the right place, but he was wrong about what we would find," said Mobutu.

"How was he wrong? Do you know what he found?" Jim's heart began to pound. Was he about to discover his first lead as to why Dr. Bronston had stopped communicating with anyone about Bokuru?

"Yes," said Mobutu. "We found no australopithecines as far as I know. They are older and predated the *homo* line."

"So you didn't find anything," Jim concluded.

"No, Mr. Henderson. We did find something, but what we found was more advanced and much older than we expected. Our first find was in the human family."

"I thought Dr. Bronston didn't tell you what he found, and kept everything to himself?"

"I was the one who found it, Mr. Henderson," Mobutu stated simply.

"Found what?"

"A tooth. I know teeth, Mr. Henderson. I knew what I found."

"What kind of tooth?"

"It was a molar. We were just a few centimeters above the cave floor. We had just dug a trial trench to the bottom, and found the occupation level of the cave. I was sifting the overburden from the trench, and I found it right in the sifting tray. It was a molar, Mr. Henderson."

"A molar?"

"It was not just any molar. That one tooth was the first real indication that we were on the right track. The tooth was very human. It was an important find."

"I'll bet," said Jim, trying hard to keep his emotions in check. He did not want Mobutu to know that he was also committed to finding what was discovered at Bokuru.

"In my opinion, it was a tooth from *Homo erectus*, our direct ancestor. It was found right where Dr. Bronston guessed we would find hominid fossils. We knew we had reached the bottom of the cave two days before finding that tooth. The matrix was suddenly different. That's what told us we reached the bottom of the cave."

"How did you know it was the floor of the cave?" asked Jim.

"The matrix was very hard, gray limestone that had once been compressed mud on the cave floor. That tooth was just a few centimeters above the five grid level, the occupation level of the cave."

"I see. That must have been an exciting moment after digging so long and finding nothing," said Jim.

"The tooth was the first thing we found. Dr. Bronston was very pleased. He thought we had an advanced hominid when he first saw it. He stayed up all night checking it against photos we had of human, chimpanzee, baboon, australopithecine, and other types of teeth. Just before dawn, he agreed with me," said Mobutu.

"He agreed with you?"

"Yes, he concluded that it must be from an advanced *Homo erectus*. The next day I suggested we contact Elizabethtown and hold a press conference, but Dr. Bronston stayed with his old ways and decided no one should say anything, especially since all we had was that one tooth."

"That sounds rational."

"Yes, but no announcement was ever made about Bokuru. We have been in a secrecy mode ever since we found that first tooth," said Mobutu.

"Sounds a bit austere," said Jim.

"No, Dr. Bronston was right. All we had was one trial trench to the cave bottom and one tooth from that small trench. We had broken down and sifted a lot of sand and found absolutely nothing until that tooth appeared. I agreed with him, it was premature to say anything. That's when he brought in the finish tent and started working nights."

"I would think night time would be much cooler," said Jim.

"He would get up with us and we would start about 8:30 AM and work until around 1:00 PM, when the heat was unbearable. We would all stop for lunch and take a break until around 3:00 PM. That is when I would read, Mr. Henderson, as well as at the end of the day. The others would play games, or fish in the river, or feed the crocodile, but I would read. After our break, we would go back and work until 6:00 PM, the end of the workday for us. We are usually tired, and a bit discouraged at that time of day."

"Yes, I can imagine. Please go on," said Jim.

"We would go back up to the camp and have dinner. You need to understand that when we stopped, Dr. Bronston kept going. We left him down here. He said he did his best work in the evening hours. Once he had a plan, he would stay with it. He was very disciplined. He was willing to devote years to any one project."

"He had a one track mind," added Jim.

"Yes, he would stay at a site as long as it took. He did not get impatient for quick results. He often said that it took millions of years to make the past, so what was one life to unravel it's mysteries," said Mobutu.

"He really was truly dedicated," said Jim.

"Anyway, he would stay in his tent and remain working late into the evening, usually until 9:00 PM. He would turn off both lanterns, then take a walk around the site in the dark. He liked to do a little stargazing. I would drive down to the site to pick him up at 9:15 PM. He would have dinner when he got back to camp. He always ate late. He often told me that nature did not yield her secrets to the faint of heart. The one thing he taught me was patience."

"So, that was your regular routine. What happened on the night he died, on October 18?"

"First, you have to understand that Bokuru is very unusual."

"I keep hearing that. Was it because it was a cave site? I've been told that before," said Jim.

"Dr. Bronston called Bokuru 'the African Pompeii'."

"Pompeii?" asked Jim.

"Yes, he used that reference because Bokuru was so productive. There was no question in Dr. Bronston's mind that Bokuru was going to be one of the richest African sites for the discovery of hominid fossils. Within the first week after finding that first tooth, we found part of a jaw with teeth still in place, part of a skull, and bits of rib, two femurs and fossilized bones from over six other animals. Dr. Bronston was a very happy man. His hopes and dreams of a lifetime were being realized, Mr. Henderson."

"So you found a lot of pieces of fossilized bone."

"Many, Mr. Henderson, many. At first I needed help there was so much material. I was overworked, I was getting behind, so when David came around on his own, Dr. Bronston hired him on the spot."

"David Johannson?" asked Jim.

"Yes, David found us by just driving around. He was just curious about what was out here. I remember the first time he came to Bokuru because he parked down by the river. He didn't try to drive up the slope of the ridge. The steep incline scared him. He was just exploring on his own, but within a couple of days he became seriously interested in what we were doing. Since he was so interested, Dr. Bronston offered him a job to work in the excavation helping me."

"Doing what? He had no experience?"

"Sifting, mostly. But Dr. Bronston could not keep up with his work because, with extra help, we produced many more pieces of fossilized bone. Dr. Bronston became backlogged, so he moved David over to help him in the finish tent," said Mobutu, who for the first time was no longer smiling.

"Why not you? You are more experienced," asked Jim.

"Because my job is finding fossils. My experience is in the excavation work. I have good eyes for spotting fossilized bone, Mr. Henderson."

"I forgot that is your strength. That makes sense."

"About a week later, David brought a friend with him."

"Eric?" asked Jim.

"Yes, Eric. They would drive over here from the temple in different vehicles."

"Why two?"

"Because Eric would rise early to meditate at the temple with the other followers of his group, before coming here. David was not a real member, so he slept in and got up later. Eric would park his Jeep up at the camp, and ride down here to the site with us. He would leave with us when we went back to the camp when we quit for the day," said Mobutu. "He became a part of the team."

"Did he ever stay for dinner with you?"

"Neither of them ate dinner with us. Eric ate lunch with us and quit when we did. David would show up later and drive straight down here to the site. He never stopped at the camp. He worked late with Dr. Bronston, and he would leave around 7:00 PM in the evening. He always brought his own lunch and worked straight through. We would leave David and Dr. Bronston together in the finish tent at the end of the day."

"Is that what happened on October 18?"

"No. Eric missed the day before and he missed that day too. I think he has more responsibilities at the temple than David, so he did not come here on a regular basis. In the last month, I don't think David missed a single day except for Sundays. We work seven days a week, Mr. Henderson, but we have our long lunch break every day from 1:00 PM to 3:00 PM."

"So Eric didn't show up at all on the eighteenth?"

"No. David came at his usual time, and my guess is he left at his usual time too."

"But you don't know for sure?"

"To be honest, I wasn't paying any attention, no one was. All I know is that when I came down here to the camp at 9:15 PM to pick Dr. Bronston up, I knew something was wrong before I got here."

"Why was that?" asked Jim, realizing that if Mobutu was right, it was David who had the real opportunity. For the moment, Jim assumed Mobutu was telling him the truth. David would have been the last one to see Dr. Bronston alive. Now he had two primary suspects.

"The thing I noticed was the lanterns were still on in both tents"

"And that was unusual?" asked Jim.

"Yes. It was after 9:00 PM.," said Mobutu. "They should have been turned out by that time."

"So, when you got here, Dr. Bronston was not out looking at the stars, so you went in and found him lying in a pool of blood."

"Yes sir. He was sitting at his seat but his head was down on the table. I remember he had the gun in his hand. Everyone keeps asking me about that, but I remember the gun clearly."

"Was he dead?"

"Yes. When I realized he was gone, I immediately went up to the camp and we radioed for the territorial police. I didn't touch anything.

They asked me many questions. They recorded my whole story," said Mobutu.

"I have a copy of the complete police report with me. I'll bet there's a transcription of your interview in the file."

Jim tried to remain calm and show no emotions. He already knew Mobutu's story, up to what happened when he arrived at the site. The information could be verified by the other workers. For him, Mobutu was still a suspect because he still had the opportunity to shoot Dr. Bronston after David left, assuming Dr. Bronston was still alive when David left. Right now, Jim wanted to talk to David. His gut instinct was that Mobutu was not the killer, but perhaps David was.

"As I said, Dr. Bronston started working late when we reached the occupation level of the cave and started to find many fossils. But there is another issue, Mr. Henderson."

"What's that?" asked Jim.

"Archaeologists need to know whether a fossil was actually buried in the layer where it is found. That is a common problem in most sites, but not here at Bokuru. We are very sure of the geology. What we found was on the cave floor when the cave filled in."

"You knew what the tooth was. How about the other bones? Did you know what they were from?"

"No, not initially, Mr. Henderson. They had to be separated from the matrix of soft sandstone. That's what Dr. Bronston did. I did recognize that one tooth as hominid. Later, I could tell some of the larger pieces were part of specific bones, which I knew were also hominid. I can usually recognize hominid bones when I see them, but it was strange."

"How is that, Mobutu?"

"We expected to find only cranium pieces in a cave. Some of the fossils were of almost complete hominid leg and arm bones. I saw ribs, and pelvis pieces, even some pieces of back bone."

"Were they all from one individual?"

"No, Mr. Henderson. Many pieces, from many individuals."

"I see."

"Oh. There is one other thing that makes Bokuru special, Mr. Henderson."

"What is that?"

"The skulls."

"The skulls? You found skulls?"

"No, we found pieces of skulls, Mr. Henderson."

"Isn't that what you would expect to find?"

"Remember what we know about Bokuru. It is a cave that has been intact since the hominids died here. Remember, too, that it filled quickly with river silt and volcanic tefra, protecting the bones. There were no forces like cattle walking over them to break them. In my personal opinion, the skulls should have been mostly intact."

"But they weren't?" asked Jim.

"No. All the craniums were crushed. At first, I though the breaks were the result of our careless excavation work, but the breaks were not fresh and the edges of the skull pieces were worn," said Mobutu.

"What does that mean?"

"It means that the skulls were broken a long time ago."

"Why is that significant?" asked Jim.

"It made no sense to me, Mr. Henderson. When we find a piece of fossilized bone on the surface, the first question we have is to determine if it is a part of a skull. If it is a piece of skull, the second question is whether the edges are worn. You see if the edges are worn, showing that it is very old, the chances are the one piece is isolated, and we will not spend a lot of time looking for more pieces. If the edges are sharp it means the piece was broken off from others in recent times and there is a good chance we will find more pieces nearby. That is the site we schedule for extensive excavation."

"I see why pieces of skull are so important now, but what does the presence of worn pieces here at Bokuru mean?" asked Jim.

"That is just it, Mr. Henderson. I do not know. It is part of the mystery of Bokuru."

"The more I learn, the more mysterious this place becomes, Mobutu."

"Bokuru is very different, Mr. Henderson."

"I understand there were several different kinds of hominids that lived at the same time, around two million years ago. Have you been able to identify the one you found?"

"Only Dr. Bronston could do that. I can recognize hominid bone, but I don't know one hominid from the other. It takes a lot of training to do that."

"That probably does not matter. What is important is that David was the last one to see Dr. Bronston alive."

"Yes. It was a routine evening."

"How about the man Nancy calls the Deacon? Was he around at that time?"

"No, Mr. Henderson. He came here to Bokuru when the excavation was first started, but, since we found nothing at that time, he did not stay.

232

He came back briefly a couple of weeks before Dr. Bronston's death, but again he did not stay."

"You know I am here to make an investigation of Dr. Bronston's death. The death certificate was issued with suicide stated as the cause of death," said Jim.

"The gun was in his hand, Mr. Henderson. I saw it there when I found the body," said Mobutu.

"If that is true, and he did commit suicide, the big question is, why would he shoot himself? It just doesn't seem to make any sense to anyone I have talked to," said Jim.

"I have no reason, Mr. Henderson."

"Everyone thinks the answer why he did it, assuming he did, is here at Bokuru, and that means the one person who can help me find the answer is you," said Jim.

"It was a total surprise. It was very sudden," said Mobutu, sadly, hanging his head and looking down at the ground. "There was no warning. During the day, he was fine doing his work, then he was gone forever."

"I understand, but that forces me to ask if you think David shot him? He was the last one here when Dr. Bronston was alive. Do you think David could have done that?"

"They got along fine. I saw no problem between them, Mr. Henderson."

"No dispute over pay, working hours, or conditions in the tent?" asked Jim.

"Dr. Bronston brought David into the tent to work closely with him. Dr. Bronston was very comfortable with him. They got along very well. Remember, the gun was in Dr. Bronston's hand. I saw it."

"I don't know why Dr. Bronston killed himself. I have no reason for David to murder him either. I have nothing to work with," said Jim.

"I have no answers," said Mobutu.

"What else can you tell me? Think for a moment. You were the closest one to him. I don't think any of the others who work here had as close a relationship with Dr. Bronston, other than maybe David, during that last month, from what you tell me."

"You're right, but I have told you all I know," said Mobutu.

"Are you sure the Deacon wasn't around?"

"I am sure. We expected him to show up at any time, but he didn't."

"Let me ask you this, what if he showed up now? Would you show him the fossils you found?"

"The Deacon is a dangerous man. He will twist everything you say around in his favor. We avoided him, Mr. Henderson. In answer to your question, I would not show him anything. He did not follow the scientific procedures. He did not respect the detail work that is the key to what we do. He came here for his own purposes. He is looking for end results that support his ideas. He is not interested in details. If I showed him fossils, he would say that they were human and dated to the period of the dinosaurs. If I showed him the results of the dating, he would say the dates were wrong, that they had been misread, misinterpreted, or simply fraudulently reported as part of a conspiracy to hide the truth," said Mobutu. "The only way to handle him was to show him nothing and say nothing to him. There is no other way to deal with him."

"I see," said Jim. "But, you are saying that he was not here at Bokuru on the day Dr. Bronston died."

"Oh. I might have been wrong about the Deacon," said Mobutu.

"Wrong? How?"

"He was here just a couple of weeks ago. He stayed over one night and left the next day."

"That was when you were finding hominid fossils?" asked Jim.

"Yes, and he came into the pit, but it seems that as long as he was here we arranged to find only sand, Mr. Henderson. He has not been back since then."

"All you found was sand?"

"Nothing but sand," said Mobutu, smiling again. "For one day, Bokuru was a sterile site."

"What about the others? Wouldn't they have said something to the Deacon?"

"We sent the part timers home. Dr. Bronston went to Elizabethtown for supplies. We tied the flaps into the finish tent securely. I don't think the Deacon knows that tent is there. No one showed him anything. He left believing, at least for now, that Bokuru is just an open pit," said Mobutu, smiling proudly.

"I see," said Jim. "Are you saying that he has not been back since then?"

"We have not seen him again. Rest assured, we did not discover anything while he was here," said Mobutu.

"I understand how you handle the Deacon, but I'm lost Mobutu." Jim hesitated for a moment to let his words settle. "What I mean is, people just don't go around shooting themselves for no reason, and people don't shoot others without a reason, either."

"Dr. Bronston and I talked all the time. He was very excited about this site. We were all excited when we found that tooth. After that discovery, things just got better. We found more and more bits of fossilized bones. I was happy for Dr. Bronston. He had no reason to die."

"Well, I'm stumped," said Jim. "I really am."

"All the fossils we found are very rare," said Mobutu. "Dr. Bronston was very excited about our work. He said that the fossilized bones we found here were very clean, too."

"What do you mean they were 'very clean'?" asked Jim.

"The bones had no teeth marks. They were not chewed or ripped apart by predators."

"Is that significant?"

"It tells us the cave filled in right after the bones were deposited. There was no time for hyenas or leopards or other carnivores to reach them," said Mobutu.

"And that makes them very rare?" asked Jim.

"Very rare and many of them," said Mobutu.

"All dated at 1.82 million years ago?"

"Yes. We have several tests at the bottom of the cave with that result. The matrix is dated by the potassium-argon method, from the sediments. The surrounding matrix and not the fossils are what we use to determine age. All of the fossils were found at the same approximate level," said Mobutu.

"I've heard of the potassium-argon dating method."

"The geologists also did a paleo-magnetic study which showed that the site had normal north-south magnetic polarity at that time. That was what they expected, so it supported the potassium-argon dates," said Mobutu.

"I see."

"We also checked for comparative faunal dating," said Mobutu.

"Do you mean you looked for fossilized leaves of trees of the same period?"

"No, that would be flora. We found no plant, tree, or vegetative material in the cave. Nothing washed in. Dr. Bronston thought the silt-laden water just rose steadily and filled the cave quickly. We also look for 'fauna' or fossilized bones of animals in the matrix and sediment. If we know a species of animal existed during a certain period before it became extinct, we can use that knowledge to help date the cave."

"Did it work?" asked Jim.

"Yes, we found bones from twelve animals."

"What kinds?"

"We would put most of them in current families, like wildebeest and giraffes, but they were different. Over millions of years, species change. They all spread into new variations. Some variations live and some die out. Sometimes changes are dramatic. Sometimes they are subtle. But, over time, all species change. None of the species found in the cave was of a modern type and all of them are now extinct. The important thing, Mr. Henderson, is that all of the bones we found are known to have existed 1.82 million years ago. The 'fauna' test is not a precise test, but it provides a confirmation of the potassium-argon dates."

"This is all very interesting," said Jim.

"Come, follow me. I will show you the excavation," he said, as he stood to escort Jim to the pit.

"Before we go, let me ask you one more question," said Jim, as he stood up to follow Mobutu out into the sunlight.

"Certainly. You will have many questions. You must ask them when you first think of them, or you may forget them," said Mobutu.

"Yes. Did you ever see Dr. Bronston take his blood pressure?"

"Oh, yes. He took it each night, right after he ate dinner."

"Right up until the night before he died?"

"Yes. He took it every night, and he wrote down the numbers in a small black book."

"Thank you. How about a gun? Did he have a gun at the camp?"

"No guns, Mr. Henderson. He did not allow guns here at Bokuru. Dr. Bronston did not like guns."

"That's what everyone tells me. I'm right with you," said Jim, as he followed Mobutu out from the shade of the tent into the hot sun.

Mobutu stopped about half way to the excavation pit, and pointed to a cement post in the ground. "This is a datum stake," he said.

Jim remembered the discussion he had with Dr. Tubojola.

"Yes. I know what that is," said Jim, staring down at the cap on top of the post that evidenced the horizontal grid plane.

Jim followed Mobutu over to the ramp and down into the pit, beneath the sun canvas. This, at last, he thought, is Bokuru. The excavation pit was like a large room. The sun beating on the canvas gave the interior an odd yellow hue.

"That is Karimba," Mobutu said, waving to one of the laborers who was shoveling sand into the wheelbarrow. "And that is Charga, over there," he said, waving over to the second laborer who stood shirtless and sweating. Charga was shaking the screen mesh shaker back and forth on its spindly wooden legs. Jim noticed that Charga wore faded jeans and sandals with soles made of old tires. Jim waved back at both Charga and Karimba while they continued to work.

"You can see why we work here only until 1:00 PM. You can already feel the heat from the sun. It will be unbearable by 1:00 PM. That's when we quit for three hours."

"I don't blame you," said Jim as the perspiration was beginning to form on his forehead and back.

"Oh, I should tell you that we are all Kikuyu here, Mr. Henderson. We take off one day each week."

"Sundays?" asked Jim.

"No, it varies. We alternate. We cannot work seven days in a row. That is a bad omen and evil things will happen. For Dr. Bronston, and the followers from the temple it is different, but as Kikuyu it is important. Sometimes we would work part time on our day off, but we could not work for pay on our day off. That would be forbidden."

"Oh, I didn't know that," said Jim.

"Of course not. You are not Kikuyu. Over this way is the front of the cave," he said motioning ahead. "It still faces the river, just as it did two million years ago. At that time, this cave faced out over a lake."

"A lake? How do you know?"

"The cave floor was about three meters above the water level. We have excavated out through the cave mouth to the top of the talus slope just beyond what we believe to be the entrance to the cave, when it was last occupied."

"I understand." said Jim.

"We have not excavated the talus slope beyond the entrance because dates of talus slopes are not reliable, opposed to that flat rock you are standing near."

"Oh, yes, I see a round rock sticking up right by my feet," said Jim.

"Hearthstone," said Mobutu.

"You must be kidding. I've read enough to know our ancestors didn't have hearths back two million years ago."

"We have left it *in situ*," said Mobutu, smiling. "Dr. Bronston nicknamed it the hearthstone, but only because it is right outside the entrance where a hearth would have been located. It also appears it might have been subject to intense heat."

"I never heard of controlled use of fire that far back," said Jim. "Besides, wouldn't a hearth be back in the cave?" asked Jim.

"It is just a nickname for the rock, Mr. Henderson. But, in answer to your question, a hearth would have to be at the entrance because of carbon monoxide and smoke. Ventilation would have been necessary for a fire. We have left this rock *in situ* until we excavate more at the front entrance. We are not sure; the river could have swept it here. It could also have been in a lightning fire, who knows? We will look at it after all the fossils are removed. They are our priority now. It is just a nickname for the rock. We were lucky."

"Lucky? How so?" asked Jim.

"We could have had a reverse talus, where the cave was low and over time things were knocked down into the cave. In that case, the whole area inside the cave would not be reliable as to dates. We also do not have balk lines. We excavated to the cave walls and floor."

"I understand," said Jim.

"The actual cave was about five meters high, ten meters across and forty meters deep. Although it tapered into a pretty small space in the back, it is still hard to define a boundary. So, now over here, behind you, is the shaker area. We have two hand shakers and one mechanical sifter. After lunch, we'll bring down more fuel and a new belt for the mechanical one. It needs a little attention once it is started. This morning, we are working by hand. Why don't you give it a try yourself?" asked Mobutu.

"Me?"

"Sure. Just grab a shovel and put about three loads into the shaker and then sift it through. Charga will help you. You can tell your friends back home that you worked at Bokuru."

"This is amazing. We excavate the same way back in Chicago," said Jim.

"It is possible you might find some fossilized bone where they are working now."

"I'll give it a try," said Jim, picking up a shovel and loading up one of the screen trays. Charga grabbed the handles on the other end of the shaker as soon as Jim had loaded the loose debris into the tray. Together, they worked the shaker back and forth until all the fine material had worked itself through the screen mesh, reducing the material to beach sand.

Mobutu inspected the lumps of material that remained in the tray. He sorted through each one by working them with his fingers. They crushed easily into sand. "Nothing here," he said. "Try again. You are working just above the cave floor, so this is a good area," said Mobutu. "You should be lucky here."

Jim went through two more loads with the shaker, assisted by his new helper. Doing this type of work, day in and day out, for months would have been backbreaking, arduous labor, Jim thought.

"You do this work just like we do in Chicago," said Jim.

"Your experience shows," said Mobutu. "Do you use lasers for measuring in Chicago?"

"I haven't, but I know the professionals are using them. I was taught how to take measurements using steel carpenter tapes. Everything we did was done by hand."

"The basic concepts are the same. Lasers are more accurate and easier to work with. That is all," said Mobutu.

Neither of the next two loads produced anything. Jim realized that the entire contents of the cave had been sifted in the same manner. Jim was sweating from the strain of working the sifter. It was hot, even under the tarpaulin sun cover. Would someone who had been faithfully doing this type of work for Dr. Bronston for years suddenly decide to shoot him? If so, why? Jim thought it highly unlikely. If these people had a grudge against Dr. Bronston, it was likely they would have expressed it long ago. And it was doubtful that they would still be working here today as the three, plus M'Bee were.

Mobutu checked the few items that remained in the sifter from the last load. The results were the same, nothing but sand. "Nothing here, Mr. Henderson. Now you can see how we worked for months like this and found nothing."

"Yes, I see," said Jim.

"Look around you, Mr. Henderson. What is it that you think makes this site so special?"

"You already told me, it is a cave, and you found more than just skulls here."

"Good. You are learning. Bokuru is typical in that the hominid bones we are finding are all in sedimentary deposits near a body of water. The sandy shores of a river, stream, or lake are expected to contain a few fossilized bones of hominids. That is not special. Even the possibility that they could have washed into a cave during a catastrophic flood does not make it unusual."

"If that is what you expected, and that is what you are finding, what makes Bokuru so special?" Jim asked.

"It was the distribution of the bones, Mr. Henderson."

"The distribution?"

"Yes, the adult males were in the front of the cave, then the females followed in the rear of the cave by the juveniles, and young we are now finding near the back."

"That would be odd that they would be preserved in such an arrangement."

"Yes," said Mobutu. "Dr. Bronston thought that they all died at the same time, just before the cave was flooded."

"How could he be so sure?"

"Because they are found only on the bottom occupation level and their bones, as I said, were clean. In addition, the location of the bones was not random. The key, he felt, was that the distribution of the bones and, thus, the arrangement of the individuals indicated how they slept, with the young in back for protection. His hypothesis was that they lived here in this cave, and they died right here in their home, basically, as they slept," said Mobutu, looking intently at Jim.

"But I thought I was told that hominids lived out on the plains following their food sources and did not live in caves."

"That has always been the prevailing theory, Mr. Henderson. That is what makes Bokuru so very special. Bokuru is unique, in that respect."

"Oh." said Jim, listening intently.

"Dr. Bronston thought Bokuru would become the most important archaeological site in Africa."

"I see."

"Come with me. I have something I want to show you up in the supply tent. I need your advice, Mr. Henderson."

"My advice? Who am I to give you advice, Mobutu? I am just a visitor here. You are the expert."

"Perhaps the expert needs assistance. Come, I will show you," said Mobutu starting up the ramp. "I think you will find that I, too, need help from time to time."

CHAPTER THIRTEEN: *A MYSTERIOUS LETTER*

When they were back in the shade of the tent, Mobutu motioned for Jim to take a seat on one of the wooden box benches in front of the long, wooden table.

"So what do you want to show me, Mobutu?" asked Jim.

"It's right here, Mr. Henderson," said Mobutu as he went to the back of the tent. Mobutu retrieved an envelope that had been wedged between two cartons on the top of the stacks of old fish boxes that served as storage cabinets. Shortly, he returned to the table and handed the envelope to Jim. He resumed his seat at the table.

Jim read the address on the front of the envelope:

> Mrs. Elizabeth Bronston
> 1281 Broken Tree Road
> St. Louis, Missouri 09876

He noted the return address:

> Dr. Edward Bronston
> Box 10
> Uhuru Natural History Museum
> St. George Road 02
> Elizabethtown, Uhuru
> Africa

The end of the envelope had been torn off and there was no stamp or cancelled postmark.

"I don't get it," said Jim. "Nancy told me her mother died several years ago. I don't remember the exact date she died, but I think it was over four years ago."

"Yes, sir. It is almost five years now since her passing," said Mobutu. "Go ahead. Take the letter out of the envelope. As you can see, I have already broken the seal. I would like for you to read the letter and tell me what it means."

"That's a switch, Mobutu. You want me, a total stranger, to tell you what a letter means? A letter that is written between two persons I never met? You have known the Bronston family for years and I haven't. I only know Nancy. I never met her either one of her parents. Since I came here to Africa, I keep learning things about her that I never knew until now. I think you are asking the wrong person."

"Please. Read the letter first. Then you can comment on it."

Jim pulled the folded letter out of the envelope. The stationary was ordinary, light brown typing paper, matching the color of the envelope. He unfolded the stationary and read the hand-printed letter:

My Dearest Elizabeth:

You are the only person in whom I can confide. I have no one else to share my feelings with. My whole life has been one of care and deliberation, but I can no longer remain a man of restraint.

You have suggested many times in the past that I quit fieldwork and accept a comfortable teaching position at a university. In the past, I have begrudgingly acknowledged your rationale, but simply continued with my life of unbroken habit, ignoring your comments. Now I have my answer to your logic, and it is Bokuru. A field person can work for a lifetime and never encounter a discovery such as this one.

In many ways, this is the dream of my lifetime. Yet, I find myself writing with a shaking hand. I am deeply concerned about the implications of what we have found. I shudder at what may have taken place in this remote location so long ago.

Here is an event, frozen in stone, which occurred almost two million years ago. Yet, when I pick up the morning paper, like a ghost from the past, it haunts me. I hesitate to comment on its significance. My profound fear is that all God's children may be dead.

Nothing I have done in my entire career has prepared me for Bokuru. I will write you soon with the details. Please keep all I have said in strictest confidence.

Yours forever,

Edward

The letter was not dated. Jim put the letter down on the table and looked up at Mobutu who had a look of deep consternation on his face.

"I have no words, Mobutu. This is truly significant, but I have no idea what it means. There is only one person alive who could have any understanding of what he is saying, and that person is you."

"I have worked with Dr. Bronston for many years, Mr. Henderson, but I do not know the meaning of this letter. It makes no sense to me."

"I can't help you," said Jim. "I really can't. My only suggestion is that we must save this letter. It could even be important to my investigation, but at the moment I haven't a clue as to what he is talking about."

"When Dr. Bronston's wife was alive, Mr. Henderson, he wrote her regularly," said Mobutu. "When she died, he stopped writing the letters. Then, about two months later, he started to write to her again. At that time, he gave me a letter. I was instructed to mail it, which I did. I thought there was family to receive it. I was wrong. He had sold their home in St. Louis. There was no forwarding address."

"I see."

"Nancy was living in Chicago at that time, and, as you can see, he carefully did not address the letter to her. In time, the letter came back in the mail, and I intercepted it. At first, I did not know what to do. Everything at that camp was going well. We had no internal problems. I did not want to confront him and create an incident."

"So, what did you do?" asked Jim.

"I simply burned the letter, Mr. Henderson. I didn't send it to Miss Nancy because it was not addressed to her. I was sure he did not want her to see it."

"What did that letter say?" asked Jim.

"That's just it. The envelope was sealed. I never opened it. I just decided that Dr. Bronston knew his wife was dead, and he was just writing out of habit. I was convinced he didn't really mean for me to actually mail it, so I carefully burned it in the coals of our campfire, late one night when everyone else had gone to sleep."

"So, you burned it. But that was several years ago," said Jim.

"Yes, over four years ago. You have to understand, that was not the end."

"It wasn't?" asked Jim.

"No. It was the start of a pattern."

"How so?"

"He kept writing letters, and I kept burning them. That procedure continued even when we came here to Bokuru."

"So, the pattern started before you came to Bokuru, and this site had nothing to do with his habit of writing letters to his deceased wife?" asked Jim.

"That's right. Now, perhaps you understand."

"You're telling me, you don't know what any of the letters said, because you never opened them?" asked Jim. "You continued to burn them without reading them?"

"That's right," said Mobutu. "I never read any of them."

"But you still have this one. You didn't burn it," said Jim.

"I planned to, but he died before I had the chance. When Nancy arrived in Africa, I thought I should give it to her when she came out here to Bokuru. Then I realized I did not know what the letter said, and I was worried that it might mention the prior letters that I had burned, so I decided to open it."

"Well, you are in the clear. Dr. Bronston makes no reference to the prior letters," said Jim.

"But it's opened, Mr. Henderson. Miss Nancy will know that I looked at it."

"That's easy. Go ahead, destroy the envelope. I'll take responsibility for showing the letter to Nancy, when the time is right. Maybe she will know what it means. Let's not show her the envelope. I agree with you, the envelope should be destroyed."

"Then, I'll leave the letter in your hands," said Mobutu.

"Mobutu, there is something else. I need to know everything about Bokuru. This letter tells me there is something here that I don't know about, Mobutu?"

"I will burn the envelope. I know nothing about what he may have said in the prior letters. I can't help you about the meaning of this letter." Mobutu hesitated, "But, yes, there is something more in this tent I can show you. Maybe it will help your investigation. Maybe it will help you interpret this letter. I don't know," said Mobutu.

"Right now, anything may help," said Jim. "I hope it's not as shocking as this letter. I'm not sure how much more excitement I can take in one day."

"Perhaps, Mr. Henderson, you should be prepared."

Mobutu got up from his seat and went back to the storage boxes in the back of tent. After rummaging around a minute or so, he retrieved one of the wooden boxes and brought it back to the long table and placed it in front of Jim. He then took a seat on the opposite side of the table, watching Jim's face carefully. Once he felt comfortable with the moment, he reached into the box and took out a large flat gray rock and put it on the table.

"Is this from the cave?" Jim asked.

"This rock is special."

"Special? I've heard that word before," said Jim.

"Yes. What you see is part of the cave floor. It is a piece of rock, broken out of the cave, that we keep here for security."

"Security? Is this another mystery?"

"Perhaps. This is not fossilized bone, so it is not kept in the finish tent, but right out here with the non-hominid fossils of animal bones we found in the cave."

"Well, it doesn't look like much," said Jim.

"Dr. Bronston thought it might be more important than the fossils," said Mobutu.

"It's just a rock," said Jim. "It doesn't look very special to me."

"I saw it about four weeks ago. No one else saw it because it was part of the cave floor. I covered it with sand when I saw it, so no one else would see it. Later that evening, when I came down to pick up Dr. Bronston, I told him what I had seen. We both went down into the pit with a lantern and a couple of picks and dug out this piece when no one else was around. We brought it here and put it in this box. Dr. Bronston swore me to secrecy. You are the first to see it and know anything about its existence."

"How about the Deacon?"

"No, he has never seen it."

"You are playing games with me. The letter, I can understand, is important, but this is just a plain gray rock. It may be a piece of the cave floor, but it is still just a rock," said Jim.

"That is where you are wrong, Mr. Henderson. Please, pick it up and turn it over. The other side is important. You will see, it is a very special rock," said Mobutu. "Look at the other side carefully. Right now, you are holding it upside down."

Jim turned the rock over. He held his breath.

"I don't believe it," Jim exclaimed. "There is a foot print, right in the rock. The print is very clear. It looks like the footprint of modern man."

"No, it is not modern. This is a very unusual print. The rock was compacted river silt from 1.82 million years ago. The rock is composed of mud from the bottom of the cave, Mr. Henderson. What you see is a the result of a foot pressed down into the bottom of the cave floor, before it was covered by the debris washed into the cave when it flooded."

"Is this the footprint of the hominid whose fossilized bones you found?"

"That's just it. Dr. Bronston said this footprint is too large for the individuals whose bones and skeletons we were finding."

"Too large?" asked Jim.

"The body of the individual who would have for this footprint was too heavy for the hominids skeletal remains we found here," said Mobutu. "Dr. Bronston said this footprint is more important than even the bones and skeletons we were finding."

"More important?" asked Jim. "How so?"

"He said this is the footprint of the 'other fellow'."

"The 'Other fellow'? What other fellow?"

"Dr. Bronston said the cave floor was trampled by the Bokuru fellow. If you look carefully, you can see many imprints where Bokuru fellow stepped on the cave floor and left his own prints. Then if you look more closely, Other fellow's print is on top of them."

"Well, whoever this footprint belongs to, it's unbelievable. You have a footprint from almost two million years ago."

"Archaeologists have found other fossil footprints in Africa," said Mobutu. "Ancient footprints are fairly rare, but what makes this one so special is where it was found."

"In this cave, on top of the other footprints?"

"Yes, Mr. Henderson, now you've got it. That is what Dr. Bronston said was so very important. He said this footprint is the most significant footprint ever found in Africa."

"Well, you lost me. What does that mean? All I see is one footprint. If there are others, they are not distinct here. I don't see them," said Jim.

"Dr. Bronston said the Bokuru fellow was smaller and his footprints were not so deep," said Mobutu.

Jim could hear the Jeep coming down the narrow roadway from the camp. Nancy was on her way back to pick him up.

"Are you sure no one else knows about this footprint?" Jim asked.

"Yes, only Dr. Bronston knew about it. He was insistent and instructed me to tell no one about it. No one else has even seen it because we collected it at night and hid it here right away. I covered the hole where we extracted it so no one would know this piece was gone. No one else knows that part of the cave floor has been removed."

"What about David? You told me David worked in the finish tent with Dr. Bronston. If they worked closely together, he must have known."

"You have to understand how Dr. Bronston worked, Mr. Henderson. He believed in compartmentalizing all of the work. Two months ago, when the finish work was backing up, and we had already brought in the two part timers from the temple, Dr. Bronston moved David from general labor into the finish tent to help separate the matrix from the fossils. The boxes I brought up to the finish tent had the lids nailed on loosely. Dr. Bronston would then take out the fossils he wanted David to work on. They worked in the finish tent at the same time, but Dr. Bronston deliberately would not show everything to David. He always kept each one of us working in his separate job. No one knew how his work related to the final cleaning and bone assembly. He always worked that way."

"So, he was very secretive," said Jim.

"Yes, he was the only one who would see the results of the assembly of pieces into complete bones and skeleton fragments. Remember, this rock was removed at night and brought directly into this tent and sealed in its wooden box. The two of us were the only ones who saw it. I have kept it in this box, out of the way. It has never been moved since I placed it here. I am sure no one else has seen it. David was too busy with his work to explore any of the sealed wooden boxes out here."

"My head is spinning, Mobutu. First you show me the letter. Then you show me this footprint from the floor of the cave. I don't know how either of these items is related to the other, or if they are related to my investigation of Dr. Bronston's death. My suggestion, for the moment, is that you put this rock back where you have been keeping it. Let's agree to tell no one else about it yet, not even Nancy. I want to discuss what you have shown me here in more detail later, after lunch."

"Yes, sir."

"Look. Why don't you put the letter back where you found it, too? We'll show it to Nancy when the time is right, later this afternoon."

"Yes, Mr. Henderson. I agree."

"What you have shown me this morning must be our secret for now. For now, do not say anything to anyone," said Jim. "I'm overwhelmed. I need to think about what we should do next."

"Yes, sir. You are the first person I have shared these finds with," said Mobutu, as he took the rock off the table and carefully placed it in the wooden box. Mobutu put the crate back in its original location and slipped the letter back between two boxes just as Nancy pulled up in the Jeep. Nancy had the water trailer in tow behind the Jeep. Jim needed time for a break, time to think.

CHAPTER FOURTEEN: *THE SERPENT*

The day was perfect. The morning sun was high over the African savannah. There were only a few wisps of clouds in a clear, blue sky. Gone was the choking dust stirred by the wind of the day before. He was here to face the serpent, and everything was ready. He wriggled, prone on his belly, crawling the last few feet to the highest point on the rock outcropping. He nestled down behind a large rock that kept him hidden from the camp across the river. Comfortable that this position was sufficient for the task at hand, he glanced up in the sky.

He did not want to do this, but he did not know how else to stop the serpent. He wished there was some other way, but he had carefully eliminated all other options. Besides, looking up, there was the sign. A vulture floated high overhead. The magnificent bird glided, circling in a lazy loop, floating silently watching the earth below.

This was not an ideal location for the encounter, but it was the best spot he could find on this side of the river. His view of the camp was unrestricted. His vision of the tents was clear on the opposite ridge.

He eased himself into position, and tried to line up the rifle for a shot at the tent, but he could not see anyone there. He put the rifle down and peered through the wider field of his binoculars. After a minute, he could see M'Bee alone in the tent. Panning the glasses along the ridge, he finally spotted the target further along the escarpment at the excavation. He knew a shot would be too difficult at this distance. The supply tent was too far away from where he lay hidden. He dared not move from this spot. He decided the target would have to come to him. Patience was the key to his success.

As he watched, two people come out of the tent and climbed into the Jeep. Hitched behind the Jeep was the small trailer used to transport the cylindrical tank used to collect water from the river to supply the needs of the camp. The trailer was another good sign. They only used it when they were about to make a run down to the river to fill the water supply tank. If the target were going to the river now, he would have a much better shot at a closer range.

It was a hot day. There were no mosquitoes and no flies to annoy him. Today was a second chance. He never wanted to hurt anyone, but there was no other way to stop the serpent. The first time he thought the job was done, only to learn later that the serpent now had a second head to replace the one that was gone. Erroneously, he had assumed that the serpent was dead. Thankfully, he had been warned. This time he would make no mistakes. He twisted his body so he could focus on a river shot. As he predicted, the Jeep passed the camp without stopping. When he saw it start down the incline to the river below, he adjusted the scope for what should be an ideal shot, knowing exactly where they were headed to fill the water tank. There was a great deal of responsibility on his shoulders in undertaking this mission. No one else could do it. He alone knew the terrible danger the serpent posed.

The first time had not been a failure, only a partial success. There was simply more to the mission than he originally thought. He had been naïve. This time would be the final act to complete it. There was no turning back and no escape for him. His own life meant little in light of the risk of the serpent.

This morning, he had risen with the first rays of sun. Alone, he left while the others slept. They would not be up for meditation for at least another hour. He left without being seen. Experience told him no one would notice that he was gone for several hours, and by then it would be too late for anyone to interfere. The approach to the river was his initial concern, for it involved traveling across the broad open plain to reach it. He had to avoid being seen at all costs. Thankfully, at that early hour, those at the camp had also been sleeping, and he safely made it to the shelter of the thick acacia trees further upstream. The trees continued to give him protection as he had driven down behind the outcropping.

As the sun came up, all that remained for him to do was to wait. Once the most dangerous part of the mission was successfully accomplished, and everyone at the camp had risen, only the task at hand remained. He had no help, no back up. What he did now was the only way. He did not choose this mission. It was chosen for him. At this point, success now depended only on his ability to see it through. The stakes were high, but he was ready.

Fame was not his goal, but someday others would know that what he did was right. His bravery would be admired, and his actions understood. The serpent had to be contained. Timing was critical. Another day would be too late, and all would be lost.

The Jeep was closer now. He watched as it steadily reached the bottom of the ridge, crossed the ford in the shallow river, and then turned along the sand bar to what he knew was the customary site the camp used to fill the water tank. He had seen them perform the operation many times before. He knew it would take a few minutes to set up the equipment before they would start the pump. Their activities would give him ample time. There was no need to rush.

Sweat ran down his forehead from being in the direct rays of the sun. He had forgotten to bring a hat to protect him from the heat of the direct rays. He put down the rifle for a moment to wipe his brow with his sleeve. The Jeep stopped near the pool in the river with the driver's side facing him. He picked the rifle up again and adjusted it in his arms until he was comfortable. Then he opened the chamber, put in the first shell, and slid the bolt into position. The rifle was ready for firing. Keeping the gun cradled in his arms, again he used the binoculars. The driver's door did not open. Instead, the passenger got out, went back to the trailer, and tested the gasoline engine that was mounted on the front of the trailer.

He put the binoculars down and aimed the rifle through the cross hairs on the gun sight, lining up on the door. The passenger stepped across the tongue of the trailer hitch and started towards the driver's door. Suddenly, a bright flash of sunlight blinded him as it reflected off the rear view mirror that dangled loose from its mount on the driver's side of the Jeep. He squinted and blinked his eyes. The sunlight from the mirror was annoying. The driver's door was opening. His opportunity had arrived. He looked through the gun sight again, and slowly took up the tension on the trigger. Just as he pulled it, the sunlight flashed again, causing him to flinch at the instant he squeezed the trigger. There was a loud clap of thunder.

The cluster of sand grouse, gathered along the riverbank, rose in response to the sudden crack of the rifle as one and flew off in startled flight. For a moment, he could not see anything. He automatically pulled back the bolt and expelled the spent cartridge. Calmly, he placed another shell into the chamber and slid the bolt into place, aimed quickly, moving the barrel slightly to the right, lined up the passenger in the sight glass, and pulled the trigger again. Another deafening explosion resounded from the rifle. Up river, the sunning crocodile, aroused by the first shot, slithered quickly into the water at the sound of the second.

He carefully put the rifle down and picked up the binoculars. There was another blinding flash from the mirror. He looked again. The windshield and the passenger window were blown out. Shards of glass were scattered everywhere around the Jeep and glistened the reflection of the sun back into his binoculars. A large boulder partially blocked his view of the ground, so he could not see the bodies clearly, but they were on the ground. There was no motion, no sound, no sign of life. His heart skipped a beat. He took a deep breath and watched closely for a minute.

He looked up into the sky. The vulture was gone. Satisfied that the job was done, he slid back down behind the ridge and reached for the pistol strapped to his belt. It was over. He had saved the world from evil.

****

After driving down the steep ridge incline, across the river, then out along the sand bar, Nancy parked in front of the water hole where they always filled the water supply tank.

"It's funny. When I'm out here, I revert to my tomboy childhood. I could have just let M'Bee do this job, but it needs to be done, so I thought I'll do it. Maybe that's why it has been relatively easy for me to work in a predominantly male world."

"I thought the museum would be open to females," said Jim.

"Don't be so naïve. Anyway, my father had this trailer modified for the camp. It's actually a small boat trailer. My father bought it on the coast north of Mobassa."

"It looks very practical, but let me ask you a question. They don't give you a hard time at the museum, do they?" Jim asked.

"No, not really. Male chauvinism is buried deep in the human psyche. It has roots into the very fabric of our society. It's not a big thing at the museum. It's the little things that add up. I just have to be very careful how I act," she said.

"How so? I'm not prying. I just had the feeling that the museum was an easy place to work. You're shattering my image."

"I told you on the way out here, I don't do dishes."

"Yes. You also said you don't get coffee," said Jim.

"That's exactly what I meant. It's the little things. Coffee is one of them. If a female wants to be accepted as a manager, she must shake off all vestiges of the domestic, subservient female image. Getting coffee is one of the things a female manager must not do. I don't type my own letters. I don't clean up messes or do anything that has a hint of being domestic or subservient," said Nancy.

"I see."

"It's hard, because I think I'm the kind of female who is very domestic. I have an inner desire to automatically clean things up. If the table is dusty, I want to get a cloth and wipe it up. But if I do, I've blown my image. Even when we use caterers, I have this urge to help put out the glasses. I have learned that if I do those things, they are lethal. It's not just males who you have to worry about. Females will quickly stereotype a woman into a subservient female role if she does certain things. I stay away from dishes in a public situation, no matter how hard it is, Jim. If I want people to accept me as a professional in upper management, I must play the role. I must create the image of how I want others to perceive me. Do you understand what I'm saying?" she asked.

"Yes, I just never thought about your comment about dishes. When I think about it, you're right," said Jim. "You are very astute about human behavior."

"The biggest problem that most archaeological sites in Africa face is lack of water. Potable water is heavy and awkward to move around. The biggest problem is that water is almost always polluted. As you can see, we are extremely lucky here at Bokuru. The river is right below the ridge. It's not terribly polluted, and it flows year round," said Nancy, changing the subject.

"You're lucky."

"Let me warn you, though. Use the water sparingly if you take a shower, and don't swallow it. That water is not treated. For our drinking water, we first run it through a filter system and then we boil it, and add anti-bacterial chemical agents. M'Bee will show you which water to use if you get thirsty," she said.

"I promise."

"All of our water comes from this small pond. Mobutu dug it out for us."

"Why not just pump it out of the river?" asked Jim.

"Two reasons. First, our resident crocodile is always a risk. Second, animals upstream usually pollute the water. Cattle are especially a problem. By using this pond, we have some natural filtration through the sand. The selection of excavation sites is always dictated by where the fossils are located, not by the best campsites. We are just lucky that we have a good water source nearby," said Nancy.

"You really are fortunate. Your water source is right below the camp," said Jim.

"There are two pieces of pipe out on the trailer. The short one hooks the pump to the water tank. Both ends and fittings are identical so it doesn't matter which end you attach first. The pipes are easy to set up."

"Great," said Jim.

"The longer pipe has a fitting only at one end which is attached onto the pump intake. The other end has a double screen over it. You will have to prime the intake pipe first. M'Bee told me to submerge the whole pipe in the pond and let it fill up before lifting up both ends. That way, you keep the pipe full of water when you attach the fitting to the pump. The second step is to start the engine and immediately put the open end into the pool. There may be another way to do it, but that's the one I remember," said Nancy.

"That should be easy."

"Good. I'll leave you to carry it out. Several months ago, I was visiting a wealthy industrialist from Ohio. As so often is the case, he tried to flirt with me, with the not so subtle promise of an exchange of affections for a big donation. I had to diplomatically steer him away, while at the same time, not bruise his fragile ego. I managed in time to induce him to make a sizable donation to the museum in his will," said Nancy.

"So you won out in the end," said Jim.

"I may have rejected his advances, but he didn't stop. He just switched to some young woman he met in a bar. He immediately wrote a new will and cut out both his family and all his charitable donations," said Nancy.

"So, you were back where you started," Jim observed.

"I didn't quit. When he died, I approached both the new girl friend and his ex wife. I obtained small donations from both. I will follow up with them next year. The saddest part is that I believe he went after the girlfriend to get back at me. I think he went to the grave convinced that I was in love with him and that he had hurt me by taking up with the girlfriend. That's how deep chauvinism is, Jim."

"I guess I really didn't have a very good handle on the liabilities of your job. I can see now it is a lot more difficult than I thought," said Jim.

"There are two sexes, Jim, and they are not alike. Men are good at the modern equivalent of throwing spears and women have babies. They are both human beings, but a woman who wants to succeed in the business world has to learn to survive in a male dominated world. It's just a fact of life."

"You're right," said Jim. "It's unfortunate, but true."

"Men's attitudes drive women paranoid, Jim. Look at me."

"You are dealing with it," Jim observed.

"That's not exactly true. The real reason I have not made a commitment to step in and replace my father is that I'm scared."

"You? Scared? Of what?" asked Jim.

"Yes. You have to understand that my father got me into the museum."

"Yes. I know," said Jim.

"He opened the door, and his reputation protected me at first, but we are way past that stage now. He's gone, so my concerns are stronger."

"Do you feel he is no longer here to protect you against male bias in the administration?"

"Yes. I'm afraid that I may lose my power, that taking an assignment at a remote archaeological site here in Africa would be tantamount to political suicide at the museum, and I would lose my security. My power base would be gone."

"Your power base?" Jim asked.

"Yes. I have worked hard, Jim. I am the primary contact with the big donors right now. The increase in attendance at the museum is a direct result of the program I built, going to the schools instead of waiting for them to come on their own. The Bronston family name is no longer a security blanket at the museum. My contact with the attendees and the donors protects me."

"I see what you're saying."

"If I'm away from the museum for an extended period of time, I could lose my influence there. As a female, I am extremely vulnerable. My father knew the politics of the museum. He knew how to advise me. Now, I don't know what to do," she said.

"I suggest you discuss your concerns about maintaining contact with your donors with your boss, and work out some procedures so you are still in control."

"You obviously think they will listen," she said.

"Personally, I think you are overreacting. I had a discussion with Mr. Kendall on the way to the airport. From what I could tell, they are genuinely concerned about you and they know your value to the museum. They want you back there as soon as possible. They're just using the Bronston name here in Africa. They see Bokuru as a necessary but temporary assignment for you," said Jim. "That is, if it is significant enough for you to justify staying," said Jim.

"Thank you, Jim. I keep forgetting that we don't know what my father found out here."

"If you want my advice, don't worry about your future," said Jim.

"I'm sure you're right as usual. When I decided to come down to the river, I didn't ask M'Bee if everything was working on this rig before I took off to meet you. Before you set everything up, see if the engine has gas in it. Then check whether it'll start. There's no sense in wasting time. If we have any trouble, we'll forget the whole operation and let M'Bee do it later this afternoon," she said.

"Okay."

"I'll be honest. I had trouble starting the engine the last time I was out here. I don't know what I did wrong. I'm all thumbs around mechanical equipment. Maybe it was something I did," she said.

"Not a problem," said Jim.

"Did I ever tell you how I solicit my big donors?" she asked.

"You told me about the special dining room you had them carve out of the restaurant."

"When they built the special dining room, I had them add a master control switch," she said.

"A control switch for what?" Jim asked.

"I had them install a switch so I could control the motors for the big curtains that hang over the east windows in the Hall of Bones."

"Oh, I know the Hall of Bones. That is the big room where the big dinosaurs are displayed," said Jim.

"The side door of the special executive dining room leads directly into the hall. I take our guests out that door and down the hall to the executive lounge, which is furnished with soft chairs and couches. That is where I make my pitch."

"I am familiar with the lounge. We met there once, after a fund raiser."

"If I set my schedule right, when I open those blinds, the moon is just coming up and reflects off Lake Michigan. The moonlight streaks in, casting the Hall of Bones in a soft, eerie light. It creates quite an impression. By the time I'm ready to make my presentation, the donors are ready to make a contribution larger than they anticipated before dinner. I ask them to donate twice what they were contemplating."

"That would be an impressive sight with the dinosaur skeletons in the moonlight," said Jim.

"I don't have to sell the museum, Jim. It sells itself, and no one pays attention to me. I'm just the messenger. Gender is never a factor."

"You are amazing, Nancy. You really do know what you're doing," said Jim.

"I think the most satisfying moment I ever had was when I got a letter."

"A letter?" he asked.

"Yes, the letter came with a donation from an executive who missed the dinner. The others who were there told him about the experience."

"And he sent you a letter with his donation?" Jim asked.

"He said he had never been to the museum, but it was important to him just to know it was there."

"That was nice," said Jim.

"Yes, it was. He said it was deeply comforting to know that humanity cared enough about the past to preserve its history in a place free of the dogma and politics of the day, a place where being politically correct did not apply."

"That was an exceptional comment," said Jim.

"Do you know what he called the museum?"

"No. What?" he asked.

"He said that, in the ultimate sense, a museum is a place of true courage where you could see truth for what it really is," she said.

"Yes, but I remember being there for one of the archaeological meetings. I was walking down the Hall of Bones to get to the small auditorium, when I overheard a small boy and his father talking. The small boy, I think he was about six or seven, asked his father if the dinosaurs were real," said Jim.

"And what did the father say?" she asked.

"He said they were made from cow bones by those who were against religion," said Jim.

"There are some people who still think the earth is flat, Jim. We cannot reach everyone. We use metal detectors and we check packages at the front door, but we cannot force people to leave their culture and biases at the door. Someday, that boy will grow up. Maybe, he will question his father's narrow views. I'd like to think his trip to the museum will play a significant part in his educational growth. We cannot reach the father. Maybe we can reach the boy."

"I like your perspective," said Jim.

"We need more museums, Jim, and we need more people to visit the ones we have."

"I think I finally understand why you have been promoted to the position you have. I'm going out and check the pump engine," he said, stepping out of the Jeep.

Jim went back to the trailer and picked up a small stick from the ground to check the fuel level in the gas tank. The stick was wet. "There is plenty of gas. I think it's full," he said.

"Good. Try it. If it starts, turn it off right away, then hook up the pipes," she said, leaning her head out of the open window.

Jim adjusted the choke then pulled the cord. The engine leaped into life so he quickly shut it off, following her instructions.

"It's fine," he said, climbing over the tongue of the trailer to come around and open the door for her. As he approached the driver's side of the Jeep, she opened the door on her own and started to climb out. At that moment, he tripped over a piece of dried wood lying at his feet, and stumbled forward falling into her. Since she was not yet standing with both feet firmly on the ground, he caught her off guard, and she lost her balance and fell with him.

It was at that instant the first shot hit. There was a loud explosion. The bullet passed between them, through the open window of her door, smashing through the windshield and turning it into a white froth of shattering glass. On its track, the bullet then passed through the edge of the front fender before burying itself harmlessly in the dirt. As they fell to the ground, the second shot missed them by mere inches, passing through the spot where Jim had been standing. It missed him only because he had moved at the exact moment the marksman winced, pulling the shot slightly to the left.

The second bullet also passed through the driver's open window and slammed through the glass in the passenger's window, shattering it. The second shot produced more shards of glass that exploded in the air. All they heard as they fell to the ground was the loud explosions of the gunshots, followed by the sounds of shattering glass. They were lucky. Both shots had missed their intended marks.

"Someone is trying to kill us. I don't want to die," she said in a harsh whisper.

"If we lie still and play dead, we may luck out. He was so close; he may not realize he missed. Stay flat and still," Jim whispered nervously, his voice tense. "Don't move, " he repeated sternly.

The events happened so fast; there was nothing they could do because they had already fallen when the shots were fired. Every instinct inside Jim told him to get up and run behind the Jeep and hide. But, he knew they had to remain still, as if they had been killed and hope the assailant would leave. For what seemed an eternity, they lay on the ground, motionless.

Finally, Jim glanced over at Nancy. She seemed to be in shock. Her face was pale, frozen in fear. He knew he was also panic-stricken, but he forced himself to remain calm. "Are you all right, Nancy?" he whispered after a couple of minutes.

"I'm fine," she answered also in a whisper. "No, I'm not. I'm petrified."

Jim hesitated for a few minutes, then he whispered, "There haven't been any more shots. I think it's safe to crawl around to the other side of the Jeep. Don't get up. Stay down on your belly. Let's get out of the line of fire. Don't look back. I'll be right behind you," said Jim.

She moved instinctively, crawling over the river stones around to the front of the Jeep. She did not stop until she was directly behind the right front tire. As soon as he also reached the protection of the wheel, he knew they were safe, at least for the moment. The engine block and wheel assembly would stop any more bullets.

"Are you alright?" she asked in a whisper, trying to keep the fear out of her voice.

"Under the circumstances, I'm fine," said Jim.

"What's happening?" she asked. "Why is someone shooting at us?"

"I don't know, but stay down. Don't try to stick your head out to look around. We have to stay right here. Whoever it is may have missed the first time, but he will have adjusted. We won't be so lucky again."

They both winced as they heard another shot, but this one was muffled, more distant and less high-powered. It seemed far away by comparison.

"What was that?" she asked.

"Another shot, but not aimed at us. Maybe he's shooting at the camp, or a wild animal."

For some time, they remained crouched behind the Jeep. Neither spoke.

Beyond the Jeep, in the direction from where the shots were fired, there was no sound, only silence.

"You saved my life. I don't know how you did it. I didn't know you were in the military service," she whispered.

He held out his hand in front of them. It was shaking.

"See my hand? I've never been in the service," Jim said. "I didn't save your life. I tripped, just a second before the first shot. I fell into you and knocked you down. It was the luckiest thing I ever did. I was at the right place at the right time, that's all. We were incredibly lucky," said Jim.

"I still think you're my guardian angel. What can we do now?"

"Do you have a radio or CB in the Jeep?" Jim asked.

"Are you kidding? Even the original radio receiver has been taken out. In the territories, they only repair the parts that are essential."

"Then there's nothing we can do, except wait and stay out of sight. We're sitting ducks. Whoever it is, has us in range," said Jim.

"What if he comes down to finish us off?" she asked.

"There's little we can do. If that happens, I suggest we make a dash for the river. Maybe we can make it to those rocks on the other side," said Jim. "Can you swim?"

"Of course," she said. "But your plan doesn't sound very reassuring to me. Besides, I think you are forgetting one thing."

"What's that?" he asked.

"Our resident crocodile. I'll bet it's around here somewhere."

"Oh. Well, that's all I could think of."

There were no more shots and no further sounds. Their only hope was that someone at the camp heard the shots and would call for help, but that, he knew, would be a long time in coming, even by helicopter. He remembered they did not keep guns at the camp.

"Someone wanted to kill us, Jim."

"I'm a stranger here," he said. "No one knows me. The question has to be who is after you."

He was just talking. He knew he had not shared his thoughts about the blood pressure readings, nor had he told her about what Mobutu had shown him at the site. Could the letter or the footprint have anything to do with someone shooting at them? He wondered. He doubted it. This was serious. He didn't see how an archaeological excavation had anything to do with their present situation. This was something different.

"Don't point the finger at me," she said. "I'm also a stranger in Uhuru. I don't have any enemies in Africa. I d like to think it was a drunken hunter with a no experience, but those shots were clearly aimed at us, and they were too close to be random."

"That's for sure," he said. "Whoever it is, they know exactly what they are doing," said Jim.

They remained hidden behind the Jeep for what seemed like an hour.

"Wait. Can you hear it?" Nancy asked. "It's the Safari Jeep. I recognize the sound of the engine."

"I hear it, too. Don't look up," said Jim. "We can't move. I hope Mobutu has more sense than driving down here to rescue us before the police get here. He's not armed. He'll be an easy target."

It was the Safari Jeep. Slowly, it came down the bluff, across the ford, then back along the road to Elizabethtown, through the acacia trees and out of sight. Jim was sure the driver had not seen them parked out along the riverbed at the watering hole.

At least there were no more rifle shots, Jim thought to himself.

Again there was a long period of silence. Jim was convinced no one else knew where they were or that they were trapped behind the Jeep. They would have to continue to stay hidden where they were.

After what seemed like an eternity, but in reality was probably no more than half an hour, they heard the Safari Jeep come back. This time the driver sounded the horn three times. The Jeep turned off the road and slowly headed along the sand bar in their direction. The driver again pressed the horn three times. This time, the sound was much closer. Someone had seen them after all.

"It's an all clear signal, Nancy."

Within a few minutes, the Safari Jeep was parked next to their Jeep. Mobutu, M'Bee, and both laborers climbed out. Nancy jumped up quickly to show they were uninjured, and within moments they were all grabbing and hugging each other in relief. They were finally safe.

"Are you all right?" Mobutu and M'Bee seemed to ask at the same time.

"Yes," said Nancy, "We are both fine."

"Someone tried to kill us," said Jim. "I think the shots came from the rocks by the river crossing."

"Yes. We know. It's safe now," said Mobutu. "He's dead."

"Who?" asked Nancy. "What do you mean he's dead?"

"The sniper," said Mobutu. "David, the part timer from the temple who used to work here. His body is up on the rocks on this side of the river. He shot at you then killed himself. He must have thought he had succeeded. He committed suicide."

"You're kidding," said Jim, stunned. "David is the one who picked me up at the airport. He was just a mild-mannered kid. I don't believe it."

"Believe it, Mr. Henderson," said Mobutu. "There was no question of identification. We did not touch the body. Everything is just the way we found it. As soon as we saw that he was dead, we backed off and came down here to find you. Frankly, from back up on the road, it looked like you were both gone. Your Jeep is a mess. You have no idea how relieved we are to see you."

"Probably as happy as we are to see you," said Nancy.

"When we crossed the river, we went along the road to try to scare off whoever it was. That was when we saw the old temple bus hidden in the bushes behind the rocks. We stopped to look around and found David's body up near the top. If we hadn't seen the bus, we would never have found him. We had no idea where the shots came from," said Mobutu.

"Neither did we," said Nancy.

"We could see your Jeep, of course, and it looked bad," said Mobutu. "We just hoped to scare him away. We had no guns."

"You were very brave," said Jim. "Actually, I'd say you were foolish to come down here unarmed. You should have waited for the police."

"We need to call them right away," said Nancy.

"I already radioed them. They are on the way," said Mobutu. "They should be here soon."

"Our Jeep is part of the crime scene. We'll have to leave it here while they make their investigation," said Jim.

"How did he commit suicide?" asked Nancy.

"He used a pistol," said Mobutu. "It's still up there next to the body."

"That must have been the third shot we heard," said Jim.

"We heard it, too. Right now, we need to get you both up to the camp. You may not know it, but you're both shaking. You are in shock. You need some hot fluids and a blanket," said Mobutu, looking over at M'Bee.

Mobutu was right. Jim could feel the weakness in his knees. He needed to sit down.

"Lunch is ready. Lamb stew and hot tea," said M'Bee, smiling as he always did.

CHAPTER FIFTEEN: *THE FOLLOWER*

The police commissioner and a lieutenant, who also acted as pilot, arrived by helicopter at 3:00 PM. Mobutu told Jim the commissioner had a reputation in Uhuru for solving difficult murder cases. He was, Mobutu said, a stickler for details. The lieutenant was along primarily to act as pilot. Mobutu thought the commissioner came in person because the police department had received so much criticism in the handling of Dr. Bronston's death. This time, the commissioner was unwilling to delegate any responsibility in the investigation of a second, violent death at Bokuru in such a short period of time. This time, in contrast to when Dr. Bronston's body was found, the commissioner arrived on the scene in person.

When they arrived, they interviewed everyone at length. The commissioner also expressed an interest in interviewing Eric, David's roommate. The commissioner carefully took notes and taped each interview. Jim could not fault his procedures.

After the interviews were completed, Mobutu drove them down to the river to inspect the crime scene. A supply of bed sheets was taken by Mobutu to collect David's body and bring it back to the camp for the flight to Elizabethtown.

After they left, Jim sat at a table in the mess tent. He removed the copy of the police file from his briefcase, spread it out on the table, and began examining the materials. He read a notation in the file that that the gun had been placed in an evidence vault at the police station. The only fingerprints found on the gun handle were those of Dr. Bronston. At the request of the commissioner, Nancy had seated herself at the radio table in the back of the tent, trying to reach Eric at the temple.

"You know, when you get right down to it, if they didn't find the gun in your father's hand, they would not have a shred of evidence to support their suicide determination," said Jim. "I think the gun is what threw everyone off."

"Isn't that what I told you all along?" she asked.

"There is nothing in this file to indicate they made any effort to look for signs of gun powder residue around the entry wound or on your father's hand. I'm certainly not an expert on violent death, but I know powder burns around the entry point would tell a lot," said Jim.

"Why is that so important?" asked Nancy.

"They could tell the distance of the gun from the head when it was fired. There would also be blood, too. There would be a spattering, maybe not much, but it would be present around the wound and on his hand and the gun, if he had held it to his head when he pulled the trigger. The report does not say anything about either issue of blood on the gun, his hand or his head," said Jim, as he thumbed through the file.

"I thought you didn't know anything about violent death cases?" she asked.

"I'm no expert. All I have to work with is common sense. All I find in the file is the statement that the cause of death was a self-inflicted gunshot wound to the head. If that's true, I'm stuck with the big 'why?' question, again." He paused. "Wait a minute. There's a note here, just above the signature of the officer who signed the death certificate."

"What does it say?" she asked.

"It says, if the gun had been missing or had been found far away such as in the other tent, they would have had a suspicious death. In suspicious death cases, they would have conducted an autopsy. Since the cause of death was not suspicious, they ruled out the autopsy. The term 'probable' was added in front of suicide because it was their practice to add that term to protect the person who signed the death certificate. The signatory was simply following that procedure."

"See!" she said.

"See what?" Jim responded.

"Can you read the name of the person who signed the report or the death certificate?"

"No," said Jim. "It's not legible. It's printed above the signature. I just can't read it."

"Just as I said before, it's a cop out, Jim. My father didn't do it. Does your file show anything about a suicide note being found at the scene?" she asked.

"No."

"I think that's important. Certainly, the absence of a written note is evidence he didn't commit suicide," she said.

"I read somewhere back home that the absence of a note in a suicide case is not a surprising event. If my memory is correct, I think the article I read stated that it was actually quite rare to find a note in this day and age. Maybe back in the 1800's notes were common, but these days, notes are actually quite rare. Wait a minute, there is a memo page here in the file. It says a lieutenant in the police station in Elizabethtown placed a call to Dwayne County, Minnesota, where David lived, to check on his past records. Apparently, they checked everybody out anyway."

"That should be interesting," said Nancy.

"The memo says he talked to a detective Billings who answered the phone in the sheriff's office in Minnesota."

"What did the detective have to say?" asked Nancy.

"Detective Billings said there were no open investigation cases on David and no outstanding arrest warrants."

"It sounds like David was the all-American boy next door," she added.

"Hold on. He went on to say that David did have three convictions for theft and burglary, but David served no time since he was a minor. The sentences were all suspended."

"So, he does have a bit of a checkered past after all," she added.

"Yes, but there is more. Listen to this. It says the detective was the chief investigator at the scene of the death of David's parents. The detective's personal feeling was that both deaths were suspicious, but he was overruled by the local coroner and state's attorney due to lack of evidence. The case was closed. The deaths were ruled a murder-suicide," said Jim.

"That's very interesting."

"The cause of the deaths was listed as murder of the wife by the husband and then suicide by the husband," Jim concluded.

"That's tragic, if it's true," she said. "It could have had a severe emotional affect on David."

"Yes, but the memo also says the detective remembered that the only evidence they really had was the gun found in Mr. Johannson's hand."

"Oh," was all that Nancy could say because she was interrupted by a voice on the radio. Jim continued to go through the file while Nancy made contact with the temple. Jim had just written down the words 'murder - motive' on the open page of his notebook when Nancy turned to address him.

"Jim, I have finally reached Eric Antonio. He's on the way over here to Bokuru. He says he'll be here within the hour."

"That's great," said Jim. "The commissioner will be glad to know that."

"I told him what happened today. It was a funny conversation. He kept saying it was 'all his fault.' He repeated that statement several times."

"His fault?" asked Jim.

"Yes. He was very clear in taking the blame for everything. He was especially clear that he was to blame for what happened to my father," said Nancy.

"I don't understand how David shooting at us could be his fault. If he's saying that your father's death was also his fault, he's got some explaining to do. I don't understand what he's talking about," said Jim.

"Well, I don't know, either," said Nancy. "We'll find out soon enough. He's on his way here."

Eric was late. Over an hour and a half later, he drove up in a rusty, faded yellow Jeep that had no top and no headlights. He parked just outside the open mess tent just a few feet from where they were sitting. Eric was a tall, lanky young man in his mid-twenties, dressed in blue jeans, a faded long sleeved red shirt, and boots. He was just a couple of inches shorter than Mobutu. His face was clean-shaven and his head was bald, clean-shaven like the temple followers Jim met at the museum. His skin had an olive complexion characteristic of those living along the Mediterranean. He left a faded old safari-type hat on the dashboard. The expression on his face was drawn and tense.

"Hello. I'm Eric Antonio," he said, as soon as he jumped out of the Jeep.

"I'm Nancy, Dr. Bronston's daughter. I'm the one who spoke to you on the radio," she said, as she came over to greet him. "This is Jim Henderson. He's an attorney from Chicago, here to investigate my father's death for the insurance company. He was with me this morning," said Nancy.

"Glad to meet you both," he said as he shook hands with each of them. "I wish we were meeting under better circumstances."

"Thanks for coming on such short notice," said Nancy. "Let's go into the tent where we are out of the sun."

They took seats at the first table where Jim had left the open police file. Jim closed the folder so Nancy would not see the photos. Jim and Nancy sat facing the open front of the tent, and Eric sat opposite them.

"First, before we start," said Eric, "Please. I must know that you are both all right."

"Thank you for asking," said Nancy. "We're both fine. Thanks to quick action by Mr. Henderson, we have no injuries other than being in a bit of shock."

"I take no credit, Eric. We were both very lucky, that's all," said Jim.

"I'm relieved that you are both safe," said Eric. "That's what is important."

"You can see the helicopter out back," said Nancy. "The police commissioner is here. He and an assistant are down at the river with Mobutu right now."

"I know," said Eric. "That's why I was late. I met them on the way here. They asked me to identify the body. They want to interview me again at length when they come back from the river. They were going through the temple bus when I arrived. Mobutu had already identified the body, but they were interested in having me confirm it. I think they are about ready to bring the body up here and fly it out this afternoon. They have to be back in Elizabethtown before dark. From what I understand, the lieutenant, who is the pilot, is not qualified to fly at night."

"Eric, when we were talking on the radio, you told me it was 'your fault' when I told you what happened," said Nancy. "What did you mean by that? We thought David acted alone."

"Oh, yes, ma'am. He did act alone. I just hope you will forgive me. I didn't know about the incident today until you called. That was a total surprise. I knew about your father's death, but I thought it was a suicide. When you called on the radio, everything fell into place. I knew then that your father's death was not a suicide. I realized I should have anticipated that the events of today would happen, too," said Eric.

"You'll have to explain," said Jim. "You lost me."

"I didn't know the site was open and the excavation work was still going forward until you radioed today, Ms. Bronston. Somehow, both David and I thought the site was permanently closed after your father's death. That's why we didn't come back here to work since his death," said Eric.

"Well, apparently no one called to tell you anything, either," said Nancy.

"If David pulled the trigger, not you, how can you be responsible?" asked Jim.

"You also said you were responsible for my father's death," said Nancy. "How could you have had anything to do with it?"

"Don't you see? Dr. Bronston didn't commit suicide," said Eric.

"How can you be so sure?" asked Jim.

"David murdered him. I'm sorry, Ms. Bronston. I'm sorry for everything," said Eric.

"Up until this morning my entire investigation has been an attempt to find a motive for Dr. Bronston's suicide," said Jim.

"But you never found one, did you?" asked Eric.

"No. Frankly, everyone I talked to said they didn't believe Dr. Bronston could ever commit suicide," said Jim. "I only started to believe them this morning. That's when I first became suspicious. Since then, things have happened so fast; I haven't had time to think. My primary murder suspect was Mobutu, until he told me David was the last one who saw Dr. Bronston alive. Of course, I'm assuming that Mobutu was telling me the truth. Assuming he was, that put David at the top of my suspect list. That was my thinking when we left to go down to the river. Mobutu, and the two laborers were also on my list, but David was the primary focus of my attention," said Jim.

"What Jim is really trying to say is that everyone has been trying to live with the fact that my father committed suicide, because the gun was found in his hand. We weren't giving Jim much help," said Nancy.

"To understand why these events are my fault, you must first realize that your father's death was murder, and not suicide, Miss Bronston. Please. I know I'm not handling this right for you. I know I must sound pretty inconsiderate," said Eric.

"That's not a problem, Eric. I'm beyond that. Please proceed. You have my attention."

"Yes, ma'am. Thank you."

"I have always believed that my father didn't take his own life. Suicide was totally out of character for him. I never believed that he could or would commit suicide. Please tell us how you deal with the fact the gun was found grasped in my father's hand? That is the one fact that has hung everyone up," she said.

"That's just it," said Eric. "The gun is the key to murder and not suicide."

"You lost me," said Jim. "It seemed the reverse was true."

"Before I came to Uhuru, I was at the university in London, England. That was about three years ago. I was watching a television show one evening after class."

"What show?" asked Jim.

"I don't remember exactly, but it was one of those detective programs about true crime stories. The producers showed how law enforcement scientists catch the bad guys using modern technology. On that show, the crime scene looked like suicide. The gun was grasped tightly in the hand of the victim, and that was it," said Eric.

"Was what?" asked Nancy. "You are not making any sense."

"That was the key, don't you see?" asked Eric. "They brought in all sorts of forensic and firearms specialists as witnesses who testified that if you commit suicide with a gun, the muscles in the body go limp at the moment of death. Oh, the gun will be there, of course, but somewhere nearby. When the muscles relax at death, the victim drops the gun. The fact that the gun was found in the victim's hand was itself evidence of murder and not suicide," said Eric.

"This is all new to me," said Nancy, astonished. "I never heard that before."

"The gun had to be placed into the victim's hand after death by the murderer, Ms. Bronston. That was the key to solving the case on television, and it's the key to your father's death," said Eric.

"You have confirmed my suspicions from this morning," said Jim.

"I have not been privy to your search for a cause of death, but you must understand you have been accumulating evidence that backs up murder and not suicide," said Eric.

"You're right. I have a copy of the police report right here with me. You must know that what you say totally conflicts with the conclusions in the report," said Jim.

"Well, the report is wrong, Mr. Henderson. If they saw the same television show I did, they would have come to a different conclusion," said Eric.

"I'm sure they would have," said Nancy. "The gun in my father's hand was all they ever had."

"I'm having trouble shifting gears," said Jim. "Until this morning, I was looking for a motive for suicide. Now, suddenly, I'm looking for a motive for murder? Can you find out exactly which show you saw so we can find out who the experts were? I think we are going to need them, Eric."

"I'm sure we can trace the program. If you need more proof, ask yourself, Miss Bronston, where did your father get the gun he supposedly used? Your father prohibited guns out here. He gave everybody a real lecture on that. If he didn't have a gun, how could he use one to commit suicide?" asked Eric.

"So, where did the gun come from?" asked Jim.

"The gun came from David," said Eric. "David was a gun fanatic. He had a whole collection, a small arsenal. He told me he was a member of a gun club back in the States. He kept his collection hidden at the temple. I think the priests were afraid of him. When they found his arsenal, they told him the guns had to go."

"What did he do with them?" Jim asked.

"Simple. He brought them here, to this camp, Mr. Henderson."

"How do you know?" asked Jim.

"I was actually an accomplice in the move. I helped him bring a long metal trunk here. He stored it in the bunk tent under the cot that was assigned to him so he had a place to sleep if he wanted to stay overnight."

"I don't think he ever stayed over," she said.

"You're right. He never did, so no one interfered with his cot or what was underneath it. No one knew the trunk was right under the cot. If they did see it, I'm sure they just assumed it was full of clothes. Certainly, your father did not know it contained David's arsenal," said Eric.

"I think you may be right," she added.

"One other thing to keep in mind, Ms. Bronston, is that the trunk was always locked."

"Locked?" asked Jim.

"David didn't want anyone messing around with his guns. He was very protective about them. Besides, he didn't want your father to find out he had guns here at the camp, Ms. Bronston."

"Wasn't there another key?" asked Jim.

"As far as I know, there was only one key, and David kept it on a lanyard around his neck at all times, even when he slept," said Eric.

"How did you know that trunk had his gun collection in it?" asked Nancy.

"I saw him pack it at the temple. I'm willing to guess the trunk is still under his cot. I'll even bet the rest of the collection is still in it," said Eric.

"You sound pretty sure of yourself," said Jim.

"The police only found the rifle and the pistol he used with him. While I was down there, all they found in the bus was some additional ammunition for the rifle. There are a lot more guns and ammunition in his collection," said Eric.

"I'm sure my father never owned a gun. I don't think he ever shot one for that matter, either," said Nancy.

"Even if your father wanted to commit suicide, he didn't have a gun, Ms. Bronston. Your father didn't know David had that arsenal in the bunk tent. Even if your father discovered the trunk, he did not have a key to open it," said Eric.

"This is unbelievable," said Jim. "Everything you say makes sense. I guess I haven't done my job as an investigator. You're telling me things I should have found on my own."

"You've been doing just fine," said Nancy. "You didn't know about the trunk."

"Look," said Eric, "I just saw David's body. The lanyard was around his neck. I could see it, but I couldn't see the key because the end of the lanyard was down inside his shirt, but I'm sure the key is there. We can check when they bring his body up here."

"This is shocking," said Nancy. "I don't know what to say."

"You both look lost," said Eric. "We can take a walk over to the bunk tent and check out the trunk if you want. Maybe it's unlocked."

"I believe you," said Nancy. "I'm sure the trunk is there, just as you say it is."

"Well, that does explain the gun. We had no idea where it came from," said Jim. "That was one of the problems I had in finding the solution. When did David get the rifle and pistol he had with him today? He hasn't been back to the camp since Dr. Bronston died."

"I think he always kept a gun hidden in the bus. That would be my guess. Guns were like a security blanket for him."

"That makes sense," said Jim.

"There's one other thing, Miss Bronston. "You told me Mobutu discovered your father's body," said Eric.

"Yes," said Nancy. "He has always said that he was the first one there."

"You are presuming that he was also the last one to see your father alive in your suicide hypothesis," said Eric.

"Wasn't he?" she asked

"No. You said it, Mr. Henderson. I'd be willing to bet it was David. You see, David was working for Dr. Bronston on the day he died."

"Go on," said Jim.

"We traveled in separate vehicles when we came here the last month, because David stayed late and worked with Dr. Bronston, late into the evening after the rest of the crew had quit for the day. I know because most of the time David drove the bus, and I drove the Jeep out front. The two of them would still be working when the rest of us came back up here to the camp. As you can see, my Jeep has no headlights," said Eric, turning and nodding in the direction of the yellow Jeep parked outside.

"It has no roof, either," said Nancy.

"Exactly, I did not work at the site on the day your father died, but I always had to leave before dark, so you see David was left alone working with your father late into the evenings. He had the opportunity that evening," said Eric. "Mobutu and the staff left each day at dinner time. They followed a regular pattern."

"Mobutu told me the same story," said Jim.

"This is hard to deal with," said Nancy. "I didn't think about David being down at the site, because I was focused on suicide, like everyone else, but I believe you, Eric. I'm ready to accept the fact that David killed my father. Everything you have told us fits together, although I never heard of the muscle relaxing theory before."

"I think you will find I'm right," said Eric.

"Then, the one thing that still bothers me is that you said it was your fault. If David killed my father how can it be your fault?" asked Nancy. "You still haven't answered that."

"I could have warned your father. You see, David told me he was going to do it," said Eric.

"What! Do you mean David came up to you and said he was going to kill Dr. Bronston, and you didn't do anything about it?" asked Jim.

"Well, no, not exactly. What he did say was that this site was evil."

"What does that mean?" asked Jim.

"He said it was an evil serpent. You have to understand, David was a hothead."

"Irrational, or just highly emotional?" asked Nancy.

"In the last three weeks, he became very agitated and acted strange in a lot of ways, so I didn't pay much attention to what he was saying," said Eric.

"How was he irrational?" asked Jim.

"For example, he asked me once how I would kill an evil serpent."

"What did you say?" asked Jim.

"I didn't answer his question. I didn't know what he was talking about, and his behavior scared me, so I didn't respond. Anyway, he answered his own question," said Eric.

"What did he say?" asked Nancy.

"He said, and I remember this clearly, he said you had to cut off its head. Later he said the serpent had to die. Then he said he and he alone was chosen to do it. He sounded pretty bizarre, but that's what he said. I just didn't do anything about it. I didn't have any idea what he was talking about. If I had just figured it out and warned your father Miss Bronston, he might still be alive today. I just didn't think David was capable of murder."

"That's not your fault," said Jim. "How could you possibly know that this site was the 'evil serpent' and Dr. Bronston was the 'head' of the serpent? In addition, you would have had to understand that his reference to 'cutting off its head' meant David was going to kill Dr. Bronston. As hindsight, it seem pretty obvious to you, but there's no way you could have known exactly what he meant and what was going to happen. You're being too hard on yourself. No one could have predicted what happened," said Jim.

"I'm the only one at the temple David confided in," said Eric. "There was no one else."

"You mean he never talked to anyone else?" Nancy asked.

"You have to understand the culture of the temple. The priests think of themselves as being the ancient Essenes, Ms. Bronston."

"The Essenes?" she asked. "I'm not familiar with who they are."

"They were the 'Sons of Light' who lived in the desert of ancient Palestine in biblical times. They were an ascetic Jewish cult that existed from 2 centuries B.C. up to 3 centuries A.D.," said Eric.

"Oh," said Nancy.

"The priests at the temple are strict disciplinarians. One whisper that does not line up with their strict regimen, and you are expelled. I was not only the one who shared a sleeping hut with David, but I was his mentor. It was my obligation to keep an eye on him. Every neophyte is assigned to a follower. I was given the responsibility to look out for his welfare. I was also the only other person from the temple who worked here," said Eric.

"So, you knew him pretty well," she observed.

"Yes, and the problem was that when his behavior became more bizarre, I just looked the other way. That was my mistake. I didn't know what to do. I never had to deal with anyone like that."

"You don't think the priests could add anything to help?" asked Nancy.

"No ma'am. You could come out to the temple tomorrow if you want, but the only ones you will be able to talk to are the followers. The priests speak to no one but each other. If you come out, I think it would be a waste of your time. The priests are into their own world. They just put up with neophytes like David. They run the place like a camp for delinquent minors, but the daily management is delegated to the followers. Anyway, this excavation site was evil to David. He was very clear in what he said. You don't have to be a genius to realize that your father was the head of the site."

"Yes. That's true," said Nancy.

"Your father was the one in charge. Look, David was shooting at you, Miss Bronston, not Mr. Henderson. You became the new leader. To David, you were the one keeping this site going. I think David saw you as the new head of the serpent," said Eric.

"Did he give you any hint of why he thought this site was an evil serpent?" asked Jim.

"No. I didn't know what he was talking about. Oh, I guess I should be more accurate and say that I was not paying attention. If he told me anything about what made this place an evil serpent, I didn't pay any attention, so I missed it. That's why I have no idea what he is talking about," said Eric.

"I'm going to disagree with you, in part, Eric. I think that second shot had my name on it. I agree that I was only a witness, but he wanted to take me out, too. You said something that may be important, though," said Jim.

"I did?" questioned Eric.

"Yes. You said that Nancy was keeping this site going. But, you also said earlier that both you and David thought this site was shut down," said Jim.

"Yes, that's true. I was surprised when Miss Bronston radioed me today and told me the site was still open. David and I both thought this site was closed forever," said Eric. "I'm not sure why we were so convinced, but we were."

"That may be it," said Jim. "David didn't shoot at us until after he learned from me that Nancy was replacing her father. You see, Eric, what happened today could, in a way, be more my fault, not yours," said Jim. "I'm the person who told him Nancy was taking over."

"You told him?" asked Eric.

"Yes, on the bus ride to Elizabethtown, after he picked me up at the airport," said Jim.

"I didn't know about that," said Eric.

"Let's assume you are right, and David thought Dr. Bronston was the head of the evil serpent, and, let's agree that David killed Dr. Bronston. Up to the time he picked me up at the airport in Nairobi, he was sure he had accomplished his goal, to kill the evil serpent. He was becoming complacent. He must have known from all the talk that the death was determined to be suicide, so he was not under suspicion. Then, simply by accident, David was the one who picked me up on the way to Elizabethtown. On the trip I told him that the site was still in operation, and Nancy had stepped in to replace her father. That must have been when David realized that his mission was not over. He decided he had to deal with a new head of the serpent, and he concluded that he had to kill her, too," said Jim.

"You forgot I still haven't accepted the job yet," said Nancy.

"No, but David didn't know that. I don't know exactly what I said to David on the bus," said Jim. "But, I do remember David reacted strangely when I mentioned that you were coming out here to take over. He had an odd expression on his face, but it did not mean anything to me at the time."

"That fits," said Eric. "Actually, David convinced me the site was closed. I never checked it out on my own."

"So you see, I could even blame myself for what happened today, but that's absurd," said Jim. "We cannot blame ourselves, Eric. Let's assume you are right. Let's assume David killed Dr. Bronston and made an attempt on Nancy today."

"I think that's what happened," said Eric.

"That means we have murder and attempted murder. The issue is not who did it. We know that. We just don't know why he did it. No one has shown me David had a motive for a personal vendetta against Dr. Bronston. Remember, he never even met Nancy," said Jim, decisively.

"That's true," said Nancy. "I never met David."

"David's motive has nothing to do with his victims personally, except that their deaths would, at least in his mind, have the effect of stopping this excavation," said Jim.

"Keep going," said Nancy. "I think you are on to something."

"I think David's direct and immediate objective was to shut down this operation," said Jim. "It's that simple."

"Yes, but that begs the real issue," said Nancy. "The question is why did he want to shut down the site? If everything we have said here is true, shutting down Bokuru is the real key to finding his motive."

"Yes, and if we are to make a good case with the authorities to convince them to change the cause of death for your father, Nancy. We have to answer that question. You're right. The issue is, why was he so obsessed with closing this site?" asked Jim.

"We're not solving anything. I worked here, too. I saw nothing unusual," said Eric.

"There is much more to David than we have discussed. I should have acted long before today. The more I think about it, the more his behavior was increasingly irrational. There were signs something was bothering him."

"Can you give us an example?" asked Nancy.

"He drove the Jeep I'm using today out into the desert in the evenings by himself."

"Is that really so odd?" asked Nancy.

"Remember, this Jeep does not have any headlights," said Eric.

"I think we all act in strange ways sometimes," said Nancy.

"It's odd if there's nowhere to go. I checked. He never drove over to this camp on his late night escapades, and there was nowhere else to go. I never knew where he went. He just drove out onto the savannah. I guess he just sat out there looking at the stars."

"I'm still not so sure that makes him a murderer," said Nancy.

"Perhaps not," said Eric. "His behavior was bizarre. He couldn't even see where he was going when he took off in the dark of night. He drove off without headlights. No, his behavior was a warning sign. I was his mentor. I should have done something, but I didn't know what to do or who to talk to, so I just ignored his actions and did nothing. There is so much I could have done. I must bear the responsibility for what has happened," said Eric.

"Don't be so harsh on yourself," said Nancy.

"We still don't know why he wanted to shut down the site," said Jim.

"I'm not so sure you should spend a lot of time looking for a rational basis for his actions," said Eric.

"I remember reading about a murder case back home," said Jim. "The kid involved killed his own mother. He had exhibited a lot of psychotic behavior, like you have referred to, Eric, but the kid was convicted of murder. The court found that underneath all the strange behavior, he knew what he was doing and had the mental state conducive for murder. There was deep rational thought that made him culpable. I think David knew exactly what he was doing. He knew the difference between right and wrong. Murder is murder, as long as you know the consequences of your actions, no matter what the reason. I think our question is valid. We shouldn't just dismiss his actions as the acts of a psychotic," said Jim. "There was more to him than simple paranoia. He knew what he was doing. There's a reason he wanted to shut down the site."

"Our Temple is strictly non-violent in its teachings. They emphasize prayer and meditation to find the Creator within," said Eric. "David's actions did not come from the temple. He wasn't here long enough to absorb the teachings of the Temple. We have had bad cases before. Sometimes, love, understanding, compassion, the normal, expected human emotions are missing in the neophyte. There are people who seem normal on the surface, but deep inside they are true aliens," said Eric.

"Aliens?" asked Nancy.

"Yes, aliens. Their brains do not work the same as the rest of us," said Eric. "What David did is my fault and my responsibility. I know he acted irrationally, but I alone could have done something about it."

"You should have been able to turn to the priests for help," said Nancy.

"Well, I don't think anyone could have done much," said Jim. "We can't blame you, Eric, any more than myself. I don't want to change the subject, but where is your robe? When I met David, he was wearing a robe. I thought you wore them all the time?"

"I don't wear one when I come out here. I just wear it at the temple and in town when we meet the public outside the temple. They're not strict about it, until you are a priest. The temple is not a cult. We have no pulpit, no zealot pitching anyone to join him and be saved. We do not believe in a strict interpretation of the Bible," said Eric.

"The issue of creation versus science and evolution could have been a touchy issue for David. He had a strong, fundamental Bible background," said Jim. "I know you say that working here is acceptable to the temple because finding the past is not a problem. I understand it is only when someone claims one creature evolved into another that there is a conflict with your beliefs. I find most people have very deep beliefs, which they do not always express to others. Instead, people often hide their true feelings until they reach a boiling point. If you ask me, David's feelings should not be discounted lightly. To what extent David's beliefs could have influenced his conduct, we will never know. Unfortunately, he took his convictions with him. I just have concerns that make me want to keep an open mind when we look for a motivation for his extreme actions," said Jim.

"Remember," said Eric, "David was just a neophyte at the temple. He brought his inner thoughts with him when he came here. Neophytes are not here because they are true believers in the temple philosophy. They are here because someone sends them here and pays for them to stay for a set period of time. Someone has to buy into the temple's concepts and believe that the temple experience will change the neophyte. They must believe that the purity of staying out here in the desert will change them for the better," said Eric.

"Does it work?" asked Nancy.

"Does prison change the prisoner?" asked Eric. "Actually, I don't know. I don't think anyone has made a real a study of what a short stay out here does for the neophyte."

"What does the name 'Tassan' stand for? " asked Nancy.

"Our leader was once known as Benjamin Tassan," said Eric. "To us, he is our supreme holiness."

"Well, I, for one, want to thank you, Eric, for what you have done. Coming here has lifted a great weight off my shoulders," said Jim.

"Maybe, now I can find closure. I'd like to go over and see the trunk you mentioned that David kept under his cot. You know, you're going to have to go through this whole dialogue all over again with the police commissioner," said Nancy.

"Yes. I know, but there is one thing that might help," said Eric.

"What's that?" asked Jim.

"Whether they traced the gun found in Dr. Bronston's hand. If it belongs to David, that will really wrap things up."

"The file says it's in the police vault. I have a copy of the report here. I have just started to go through the file. Would you like to take a look, Eric?" asked Jim.

"Sure. I mean, if you think my looking at it might help," said Eric.

"You might see something that triggers something else in your memory," said Jim. "I didn't get a chance to look at the pictures, but I understand they are pretty gruesome. I don't think Nancy should see them."

"I agree," said Eric, looking at Nancy.

Jim slid the folder across the table to Eric.

There were a few moments of silence while Eric thumbed through the file folder. His face was hard and serious. Finally, his lips parted in a small smile. "It's right here," said Eric, looking over at Jim.

"What is?" asked Jim.

"Excuse me, Miss Bronston. Please, Mr. Henderson, look at this picture. The whole story is right here," said Eric, handing the single photo over to Jim.

"I'm not going to look," said Nancy. "I have a picture of my father alive in my mind. I want to keep his memory that way."

Jim picked up the photo.

"You can see his head down on the table," said Eric.

"Yes," said Jim. "It's very clear."

"It's down on his right side. His left side is up," said Eric.

"Yes, it is," said Jim, as he examined the photo.

"You can see the entry wound right above his left ear. It is just a small dark spot," said Eric.

"Yes. I see it," said Jim.

"Dr. Bronston was right handed. A right-handed person cannot reach around and shoot himself in the left temple. It is virtually impossible," said Eric.

"Eric, you're right," gasped Jim, astonished. "There is no way he could have shot himself. I've been carrying the proof of murder with me since last night. I've had it with me all this time."

CHAPTER SIXTEEN: *CAMPFIRE*

That evening, they ate outside. They sat on two long boards propped up on river stones, facing an open fire set in a rock-lined pit behind the mess tent. M'Bee used the burning coals to cook the evening meal of goat, a baked sweet potato, rice, and corn bread. After the main meal, he served a special treat of strawberries and melon from the fresh supplies that Nancy had purchased in Nairobi. Mobutu, Jim, and Nancy sat on the first bench while M'Bee and the two laborers sat on the second. M'Bee stirred the dying embers of the fire with the long stick he had used to tend the fire. Sparks swirled up into the evening sky flickering out as they floated up into the heavens.

After interviewing Eric for about an hour, the territorial police left in the helicopter with David Johannson's body. They left around 5:30 PM, leaving enough daylight to be back in Elizabethtown before dusk descended. Eric, too, left right after the helicopter disappeared on its way back to town. Nancy tried to coax Eric into staying for dinner, but he offered the excuse of the weather. He claimed he had to be back at the temple before dark since he had no headlights. He also claimed he wanted to avoid the threatening thunderhead that loomed out over the savannah in the north. He mentioned that his Jeep had no roof. According to Eric, the canvas tarp used to protect the Jeep from rain in emergencies had been left back at the temple. Although the sun sets quickly near the equator, the sunset was late at this time of year. Jim suspected the real reason for Eric's refusal to stay, was the fact the temple was strictly vegetarian. Whatever his reasons were, Eric left before dinner was served.

Now that dinner was over, the six of them remained at the camp alone with their thoughts in the quiet of the early evening. The atmosphere was a stark contrast to the turmoil of the day. All were quietly subdued by the shock of the events of the day.

"You are an amazing cook, M'Bee," said Jim. "You should go to work in a five star restaurant in Nairobi. Your talents are being wasted out here in the bad lands of East Africa."

"Yes, suh," said M'Bee, stirring the coals again.

"Strawberries," said Jim. "Nancy, I can't buy fresh strawberries in Chicago at this time of year."

"You can if you shop in the right places. They come in from California and Florida. Melons and strawberries are grown year round in Kenya," she said. "Kenya is a lot like Florida."

They watched the sun set gracefully in the west. For a long time they sat in silence. The sunset was truly spectacular. For Jim, African sunsets on television did not give justice to the sheer beauty of what he was experiencing now. As the sun disappeared and darkness fell, the stars slowly appeared until the effect was almost claustrophobic. Jim had never seen so many stars, except in the artificial presentation of *Long Long Ago* in the museum. The brilliance of big city lights washed out most of the stars back home. Only on a sailboat, far out from land on Lake Michigan, had he observed a night sky that approached the magnificence of this evening.

"This would be a great place to have a telescope," said Jim, addressing no one in particular. Only in remote places like this camp, far from the blinding lights of civilization, could the night sky be seen with such clarity. It was easy to understand how ancient civilizations had been so fascinated by the heavens, particularly those close to the equator.

The impending thunderhead was quickly moving in their direction, blocking out the stars like a giant ink stain stretching across the evening sky. Lightning flashed ever closer, followed by the distant roll of thunder.

"Rain soon," said Mobutu, breaking the silence.

"Yes," said Nancy. "The rains are early this year."

Her voice suddenly reminded Jim of their meeting in the supply tent earlier that day with Mobutu, and their agreement not to tell Nancy about the mysterious letter. He remembered the obligation to Mobutu to tell her was his. He and Mobutu had both kept their commitment not to mention the letter to the territorial police. As the first raindrops spattered on the dry soil, a soft, damp breeze blew in from the north bringing with it the refreshing smell of cool rain.

"It's amazing," said Nancy.

"What?" asked Jim.

"Right now, I think I should be in shock or something. I should be terrified. I mean, David Johannson tried to kill us just a few hours ago. Somehow everything seems so unreal."

"We are lucky to still be here," said Jim.

"Yes, and I'm totally calm. I don't remember being so at peace in my life."

"An individual's reaction to traumatic events can vary widely," said Jim.

"It's just strange, that's all. I think, finally knowing how my father died helps a lot."

"Now you can let him go," said Mobutu.

"Yes. I think you are right, Mobutu," said Nancy.

"Not completely," said Jim. "We still haven't solved the puzzle."

"Thanks to you, we know that my father was killed by David Johannson, and we are safe because David is also dead," she said. "Finally, we know my father did not commit suicide. What is left to solve?"

"We haven't figured out the motive. We still don't know why David did it. I came here to Africa looking for a motive for suicide. Now we need to find a motive for murder. The motive is still a mystery. I believe David's motive is important if we want to understand your father's murder. I also think David's motive may have something to do with what your father found here at the site."

"Why do you say that?" asked Nancy.

"We still haven't been able to identify the evil serpent," said Jim.

"There is an old Kikuyu story, Mr. Henderson," interjected Mobutu. "It tells of an evil serpent."

"Tell us about it," said Nancy. "Maybe it will help."

"Way back when Nairobi was just a railroad yard and the first trains came to Kenya, some of the Kikuyu warriors organized raids against the railroad."

"They attacked the trains?" asked Jim

"Yes. They attacked the iron horses with spears," said Mobutu.

"That's incredible," said Nancy. "It doesn't sound very effective though."

"Yes, ma'am. You may be right, but to the Kikuyu, they were attacking the evil serpent."

"They saw the train as an evil serpent?" she asked.

"They saw the arrival of the white man as the evil serpent. They feared his culture. The white man made the natives second-class citizens in their own land. They watched the white man steal their land and bring diseases for which there was no native resistance. That was the evil they wanted to stop. They saw what was happening to them as the evil serpent, Miss Nancy. They threw spears at the engines because they wanted to cut off the head of the serpent," said Mobutu, smiling.

"Well, I don't know what David's evil serpent was, but I know where it is," said Jim.

"Where is that?" asked Nancy.

"In the finish tent," Jim answered.

"What makes you say that?" she asked.

"Several things. First, there is nowhere else to look. The finish tent is the one place I haven't seen yet, and I don't think you have either. That is where David and your father worked together closely."

"Yes," she said. "We were going to go there after lunch, remember? That was the plan until David shot at us. That tent was added after my last visit, so you are correct. I have never been in it. Of course, that's where my father died, and I've been avoiding going in there as long as possible," she said, looking over at Jim.

"That's understandable. Second, only Mobutu, who found your father, and the territorial police have been in that tent. The police were only there because your father's body was found there. Their vision was narrow and their visit was brief. Outside of their brief intrusion, no one has been in that tent. No one has made any investigation into what your father discovered," said Jim.

"That's true," she said.

"In reality, only two people worked there, David Johannson and your father. Now, Nancy, they are both gone. I don't want to sound melodramatic, but that does mean as far as what was discovered at the site, the only two people who knew the secrets of Bokuru are gone. No other living person has any idea of what was found down in the pit," said Jim.

"Well, that is a dramatic way to say it," she said. "You have caught my attention."

It was starting to rain lightly. Everyone moved into the shelter of the mess tent where M'Bee busied himself making tea and handing out sweet cakes. Mobutu lit the lantern.

"I'm all ears, Jim," said Nancy, as soon as they had settled down at a table. "Tell me what else you have been thinking."

"Well, everyone told me that the answer for your father's motive for suicide was here at Bokuru. Now the question is, what motivated David to kill? I think the answer to this question is also here at the site," said Jim.

"So?" she asked. "What do you think is at the site that could trigger David to kill?"

"I don't know. I have seen the excavation pit and the supply tent. The one place I have not seen is the finish tent. I think the secret for why David killed your father is in that tent," said Jim. "In fact, I'm sure of that much."

"That makes sense," she said. "There is no where else to look."

"Everything that is found at the site, every bit of fossilized bone, was found by Mobutu," said Jim.

"Yes," she said

"So why is it that Mobutu doesn't know anything?" asked Jim.

"That's what confuses me," said Nancy.

"That's because all he found was bits and pieces. Your father put the pieces together into complete bones in the finish tent. Only he saw the big picture. Those bones were assembled and retained in the finish tent. They are still there, Nancy, in the finish tent."

"So, a reassembled fossilized bone drove David to kill my father?" she asked.

"Something like that. Look, I'm not being totally honest with you. I haven't told you everything."

"You haven't?"

"There's a letter written by your father in Mobutu's possession," said Jim.

"A letter? " she asked.

"Yes, a very interesting letter. It's addressed from your father to your deceased mother. What is really weird is that your father gave it to Mobutu with instructions to mail it, just a few days before your father's death," said Jim.

"That is odd," she said. "My mother died over four years ago."

"Mobutu and I thought it was odd, too. The point is that it was never mailed. Your father gave it to Mobutu, who had forgotten all about it when your father died. He didn't remember it until today when I was with him at the site. Since I was here to investigate your father's death, he gave it to me to read. I was going to give it to you right after lunch when we were scheduled to go through the finish tent, but we were interrupted. We weren't going to give it to anyone else until you had a chance to see it," said Jim.

"That was considerate of you," said Nancy. "Since you read it, you can tell us what it said."

"Frankly, it's strange. We can discuss what we should do with it after you look at it. I really believe the answer to why David killed your father is in that tent, especially after I read that letter," said Jim.

"Maybe that letter has some clue as to David's motive," she said.

"You'll have to read the letter. It tells you he found something, but it does not give you any hint of what it was," said Jim.

"Of course, I would really like to know why David Johannson killed my father. The answer to your question, if I would like to go down to the tent and see the letter is, yes. Just remember, Jim. I brought you here to Africa to prove that my father did not commit suicide. You have done that. You have not only shown that he did not commit suicide, you've shown he was murdered. Now we know the perpetrator was David. You have done all that I wanted," she said.

"I only helped. Actually, Eric was the one who found the answers," said Jim. "David gave himself away."

"Without your presence here, I don't know where I would be, maybe dead. Anyway, you are not satisfied. You keep going. You asked if I want to know why David killed my father."

"Yes," said Jim. "Just knowing he did it is not enough. We need to know why."

"All I can say is, you can't bring my father back. You can't walk on water, Jim, but the answer is yes, I'm curious. I do want to see that mysterious letter."

"Good. The answer must be in the finish tent, just waiting for us," said Jim.

"I have to confess that I have another reason to go with you to the site."

"Another reason?" asked Jim.

"Yes, I need to know what my father discovered. I still haven't decided whether I should stay and finish the work here. My decision hinges on what he found on the bottom of the excavation pit. I still need that answer."

"You're right, I forgot. Just remember, I think both answers are related," said Jim.

"Maybe, but what really intrigues me is that you found a letter that doesn't give you any answers," said Nancy.

"I'm sorry. I can't help," said Mobutu. "I don't know what the letter means."

"The answer is in the finish tent," said Jim. "I think something that happened 1.82 million years ago is related to the reason why David killed your father and tried to kill you," said Jim. "As strange as that may seem, that's what I think. That's all I have to work with until we check out the finish tent."

"You are being very mysterious, but I know what's coming next," she said.

"What's that?" asked Jim.

"You want to go down there tonight so we can see for ourselves," said Nancy. "Right now."

"Yes," said Jim.

"Even in the rain?" she said.

"Yes, even in the rain." said Jim. "If you stop and think about it, you'd stay awake all night wondering what is down there. If we don't go now, I know I won't be able to sleep."

"I'm curious about that letter. Why wouldn't my father write a letter to me instead of addressing it to my deceased mother? That still makes no sense," she said.

"The letter is vague, Nancy. I think it is intentionally evasive. I think whatever your father found here at Bokuru is tied to David's actions, and I am convinced it is still in that tent. Whatever it is it may be the reason for murder," said Jim. The rain was coming down hard drumming loudly on the canvas roof of the tent.

"The whole thing bothers me," said Jim. "I don't want to stay up all night, wondering."

"The rain will be gone in the morning. We will have daylight then," she said.

"True, but do you really want to stay up all night wondering?"

"So, you want us to go now, in spite of the miserable weather?" she asked.

"Yes. The rain won't last long. This is just an evening shower. I don't want to lie awake tonight just to wait for dawn," said Jim.

"Okay. I'm curious too," she said. "Let's go. I'll sleep better knowing what's in that letter and in the tent. You're right; a little rain won't hurt us. Besides, the site is only a mile away."

"Good," said Jim.

"Do you have flashlights and rain gear Mobutu? It could be a little messy," Nancy added.

"Yes, ma'am," said Mobutu, smiling in a manner that Jim knew meant he was relieved that the issue of the letter had been discussed and there was no mention of his burning the prior letters. "I'll get ponchos and some flashlights. They're stored right in the back of this tent," he said, as he rose to go back to retrieve them.

"Then it's decided, the three of us will go," said Nancy. "We don't need to take everybody. M'Bee and the others can stay here and keep any eye on the camp while we are gone."

M'Bee nodded in agreement.

"We'll need some hot tea, towels, and blankets when we get back," said Mobutu, looking over at M'Bee, who nodded again in response. "I think we're going to be wet when we get back."

"The Safari Jeep is right outside," said Jim. "A couple of steps, and we'll be safely out of the rain and on our way. The secret of Bokuru awaits our arrival. I think we're about to find out what that secret is."

CHAPTER SEVENTEEN: *HO-011*

Mobutu drove the Safari Jeep slowly along the track from the camp to the site while the rain continued unabated. Nancy sat up front with Mobutu while Jim sat in back. They all were leaning forward in their seats trying to see through the gloom ahead. Mobutu cautiously drove the Jeep along the narrow strip that served as a road, skillfully avoiding the edge where the Jeep could slide off the ridge and plunge down to the river below. The two beams of the headlights were immediately absorbed in the fog and rain, restricting visibility to just a few feet. By staying in low gear, he was able to maintain traction.

"Keep reminding me, Jim Henderson, that the reason we are out in this absolutely dreadful weather is that there is some unknown discovery in the finish tent that no living person has ever seen," said Nancy. "I need some reassurance that this uncomfortable trip in the dark isn't crazy. I am beginning to think I was insane to agree to it."

"That's it," said Jim. "We're on our way to see something significant, what ever it is. Remember, whatever we find, it cost your father his life. There has to be something significant down there."

"How do I know that you and Mobutu aren't playing a joke on me?" she asked. "How do I know you haven't been in that tent already? Maybe you just want to get me out into the rain?"

"I helped put up that tent months ago, but once it was set up, I never went inside," said Mobutu. "No one thought to look around when we removed your father's body."

"I'm just trying to put everything together," said Jim. "Bokuru is like a puzzle without all the pieces. I am convinced the finish tent is significant. We just don't know why."

"I am puzzled why David would want to force the closure of the site. It is interesting that he thought that killing my father was a means to that end," she said.

"I think something in the finish tent triggered his actions," said Jim.

Occasional flashes of lightning relieved the claustrophobic effect caused by the darkness of the evening and the gloom of the rain. Carefully, Mobutu drove closer to their destination, his eyes fixed straight ahead on the road.

"The tires on this Jeep do not help, Miss Nancy," he said.

"What's wrong with the tires?" she asked.

"They are open road tires for traveling long distances in dry weather. They're not designed for mud and wet slippery ground. We have the wrong tires, Miss Nancy," said Mobutu.

"Well, you have to do the best you can with what you have, Mobutu. We can't change the tires now," she said.

"No, Ma'am. I was just complaining. We'll be all right if I go slow," said Mobutu, defensively.

After what seemed an eternity, the shape of the supply tent emerged in the light of occasional flashes of lightning through the stark darkness of the African night.

"There it is, " said Jim, pointing out ahead. He pulled the hood of his poncho up over his head and tied the chinstrap.

"We're almost there," said Nancy. "You're right, I see the tent."

The only sound other than occasional rumbles of thunder and the steady drumming of the raindrops on the canvas roof was the monotonous squeak of the timeworn wipers as they flopped back and forth in the rain. The wipers barely cleared the windshield. Carefully, Mobutu eased the Jeep as close to the tent as possible, avoiding the guy ropes and support stakes. Skillfully, he maneuvered the Jeep within a few feet of the front entrance. All they had to do was jump out and cover the few feet to the shelter of the tent.

"It will be extremely dark when I turn off the headlights," said Mobutu. "We'll need both flashlights, Miss Nancy. Stay together until we get inside the tent. As soon as we are inside, take off your ponchos; otherwise you will be wet from the humidity. To stay dry, you must take them off as soon as you can."

"We'll be right behind you," said Nancy.

"There's a lantern hanging from the ridge pole in the middle of the tent. I will try to reach it as quickly as I can. Once I light it, the lantern will give us plenty of light. There is a second lantern in the finish tent as well. Just stand inside the entrance of the tent until there is light from the lantern. That way, you won't trip over the boxes on the floor," said Mobutu.

"We'll follow your lead," said Nancy. "You have the better flashlight. The batteries are almost dead in this one."

"Since you do not have a flashlight, Mr. Henderson, stay close to us," said Mobutu. "Are you both ready?"

"Ready," said Jim.

"Ready," echoed Nancy.

Mobutu turned off the headlights, and they were plunged into darkness. Then he turned off the engine. Now, the only sound was the din of the rain beating on the roof of the Jeep. Nancy's flashlight did not work. "Damn," she muttered, shaking it against the dashboard. It flickered then came on, but its beam was a dim yellow halo. Mobutu turned on the one he retrieved from the dashboard, and the interior of the Jeep was instantly filled with light.

"Just remember one thing before I step out and get drenched, Jim Henderson," Nancy warned.

'"What's that?" he asked.

"We could have done this in the warm, dry sunshine in the morning."

"We all agreed to do this together," said Jim. "I don't think we'll regret it."

"We're all set," said Mobutu.

"You go first, Mobutu. You know the way and your flashlight is better. Mine won't help much," said Nancy. "Go ahead now, we'll follow you."

"Ready," said Mobutu. "Stay close behind me."

Simultaneously, all three opened the doors of the Jeep and stepped out into the drizzling rain. Jim scrambled to keep up with Mobutu and Nancy in the semi-darkness. He slid on the muddy ground, struggling to keep his balance as he followed them towards the tent. There was just enough light for him to see where he was going. The rain was heavy and the ground was soggy. When he reached the protection of the tent, Mobutu held the front flap open for Nancy and Jim, shining his light so they could see inside the tent.

"Stay right here," Mobutu said, as soon as Jim was inside the tent. "I'll turn on the lantern now."

For a minute, the beams of light from the flashlights were all that pierced the darkness. Jim remembered to remove his poncho. Mobutu was right. The fabric did not breathe, and it was already becoming damp on the inside. The poncho was uncomfortable just as Mobutu had warned. Suddenly, the warm glow of the lantern flooded the interior of the tent.

Mobutu motioned for them to sit on the boxes in front of the long board table. Jim remembered their visit earlier in the day. It seemed like a long time ago that he had read Dr. Bronston's mysterious letter to his wife. As soon as they were comfortable, Mobutu retrieved the letter from its hiding place between the two crates and brought it over to Nancy. Sitting beneath the lantern, she read the letter in silence. Only the dull drumming of the rain on the tent and the hissing of the lantern broke the stillness.

Jim watched her face for any sign of emotion as she read the letter. She frowned, then read it a second time. After pausing a minute, she looked up. "I give up. I don't understand," she said. "I see what you mean. This is an unusual letter. Clearly my father wrote it, I recognize his handwriting and his signature. The first thing that bothers me is why he addressed it to my deceased mother and not to me?" she said, frowning again. "I have no idea what the letter means."

"I agree, it makes no sense," said Jim. "My best guess is that he found something here at Bokuru that shook him up, something really significant. Whatever it is, he needed to talk to someone about it. At the same time, he knew, at least for now, he had to keep whatever he found a secret, so he wrote to the one person who he knew could keep a secret, his dead wife."

"I agree," said Nancy.

"In the end, your father decided not to say anything at all, even to your deceased mother. I think he wanted to say something, but held back at the last," said Jim.

"But she died four years ago," said Nancy. "Writing to her doesn't make any sense. I see your point. I understand the way he thinks. I know he wouldn't write me, probably because I work for the museum that is supporting his excavations. He wouldn't want me to feel any pressure to hide anything from my employer. To that extent, this letter is true to his character. I understand that now, but writing to my deceased mother is a bit bizarre."

Mobutu looked over at Jim for a brief moment. Jim knew not to say anything about the prior letters. "He couldn't take a chance in writing to anyone who could have the potential of leaking the secret of his discovery," said Jim. "Even when he finally drafted the letter to your mother, he didn't say anything concrete. He remained cryptic. That's the most important point about this letter. It doesn't say anything. It confirms that Dr. Tubojola was right all along."

"Dr. Tubojola? Right about what?" asked Nancy.

"He sensed your father was holding back, hiding something about this site."

"My father would never disclose anything until he had all the facts," she said. "That's just the way he was."

"Yes, but before he completed his work, he needed to share his work with someone so he picked your deceased mother, probably just to release some of his pent up frustration," said Jim.

"You're probably right," she said.

"Mobutu doesn't think your father intended for the letter to actually be mailed. Anyway, when your father died, Mobutu was stuck holding the letter. He could either burn it or give it to you. He decided to give it to you when you came out here. He just thought it might help my investigation. That's why he showed it to me first," said Jim.

"Thank you for saving the letter, Mobutu," said Nancy. "Unfortunately none of us has any idea what it means. Frankly, I look to you as the foreman of the site for a possible answer to what is here. What disturbs me is that you don't know what it means either."

"Mobutu knew the address for your mother was not good. He knew the house in St. Louis had been sold many years ago and there was no forwarding address," said Jim.

"You did the right thing, Mobutu," said Nancy.

"I wasn't sure what to do, Miss Nancy," said Mobutu. "I forgot about the letter until this morning."

"You should keep the letter, Nancy," said Jim. "It does show what his mental state was close to the time of his death."

"You think the explanation for this letter is right next door, Jim?" asked Nancy.

"I do. I just can't imagine what the explanation may be. I have the feeling I should know, but for some reason the answer evades me. I'm at a total loss," said Jim.

"Well, let's go take a look," said Nancy, as she started to stand up. "Since Mobutu doesn't know either, we're not going to figure it out on our own just sitting here. We have to look in the tent."

"I dug up the pieces, one at a time. I don't put them together. I just don't know what that letter means," said Mobutu. "We found many parts of hominid bones. That's all I know."

"You may have just told us the answer," said Jim. "It's not what you found, but what Dr. Bronston did with the pieces that will give us the answer. Right now, it's time to go into the finish tent and look for ourselves."

"Do we need our ponchos, Mobutu?" asked Nancy.

"No," said Mobutu. "Leave them here. The two tents are bound closely together. Just go through the back of this tent," he said, pointing to the back exit. "All we have to do is pull back the flap, and we can enter the finish tent." Mobutu reached up and removed the lantern from its hook. "Follow me," he said, as he pulled the flap back for them to pass through.

Once inside the finish tent, they found that it was much smaller than the supply tent. Wooden crates were piled high against the sides of the tent and others were jumbled in a disorganized manner, crowding the interior. Along the back wall, was a rough table made of wood boards placed over a base of the same type of boxes. On the workspace on the table, Jim saw a variety of dental tools, an electric drill, overhead lamp and other variously shaped picking tools used to separate the fossils from the sandstone matrix. A larger table filled the space in the center of the tent. Again, the table was also made of rough boards resting on a foundation of wooden crates. Additional equipment, two large open bound books, and a number of bits of fossilized bones cluttered the larger table.

Jim was horrified as he took in the workspace in front of them. No one had cleaned up the crime scene. Dark red, dried bloodstains on the books and boards in the middle of the table where Dr. Bronston's head must have rested were still there. He quickly glanced over at Nancy.

From the expression on her face, she did not indicate that she was affected by the sight of the bloodstains. Instead, she quietly stated, "This is my father's place. I can feel his presence here as if he were still alive. It's uncanny. I didn't know what to expect or how I would react when I got here, but I feel as if he is here in this tent right now. From the way the boxes are stacked, the handwritten notebooks carefully inked in, everything is just as he would arrange it."

"I am worried," said Jim. "This is where your father died. The bloodstains are still here. Are you sure you are okay? You don't have to stay here if you don't want to. You can wait in the supply tent."

"I'm fine. I'm comfortable. I feel as if his spirit is here. I think he will help us find what we need to know."

Mobutu lit the second lantern and the tent was flooded in the bright light of both lanterns. Outside, the thunder rumbled and the rain increased its pounding on the top of the tent. Nancy moved around the large table and sat down at what had to have been her father's workbench. She started thumbing through the books and papers on the desk, ignoring the bloodstains. Mobutu began searching among the boxes stacked along the sides of the tent. The worktables took up so much space, and the tent was so small there was little space for them to move around. Jim could not visualize how two people could work here in the heat of the day.

Jim inspected the smaller workspace where he assumed David Johannson had been assigned to clean fossils from their matrix of sandstone. On top of the workspace was a piece of rock Jim was sure David had been working with on his last day at the site. Jim could see what appeared to be part of a fractured leg or arm bone imbedded in the soft sandstone. All of a sudden, he remembered the 1.82 million year old footprint in the box back in the supply tent. If these were the bones of the Bokuru hominid, who was the "other?"

"This is just like my father." Nancy said, looking up from where she had been reading in the open record book. "Everything here is handwritten in indelible ink. The bottle and pen are still here. My father was right out of the Benjamin Franklin era. Why he never switched over to a computer I never understood. He had electrical power from a generator out back. I can barely read his handwriting."

"Look," said Mobutu, "This box is open." He carried an extra large wooden crate from the stack and put it on the table in front of Nancy. The crate was larger than the others in the tent, roughly assembled from two fish crates. Unlike the others, there was no lid on the crate. Nancy moved the record books aside to make room for Mobutu to place the crate down. On the end of the box was a painted label "**HO-011**." Beneath the heading was the designation "**Box 01**." Mobutu lifted an object out of the crate and gently placed it on the table. To Jim, it looked like a covered high lamp base without its shade. Nancy picked up the empty crate, and put it on the ground, out of their way.

"What is it Mobutu?" she asked.

Slowly Mobutu lifted the cloth cover from the object. For the moment, time seemed to stand still. The three of them were too shocked to speak.

"What is it?" gasped Nancy breathlessly.

"Unbelievable," Jim exhaled slowly.

Mobutu, who was still holding the cloth cover, sat down. Stunned, he said nothing. "Not human," he finally muttered.

"Obviously, the skull was reconstructed by gluing together many pieces of a broken, fossilized skull," said Jim. "The question is, what is it?"

"It is human-like, but it's clearly not human," said Nancy.

"Right. It's not human," echoed Jim. "Whatever it is."

Trying to remain objective and scientific, Nancy categorized what she was seeing, "First, the head is too big," she said. "It's also too round. The eye sockets are too oblong, and way too large. The sockets are more widely spaced apart than *Homo sapiens*. The body is missing, but the head would be too large even if the body were that of a large man. The cranium is disproportionate for anything I've ever seen or heard of. "

Jim had never seen anything like it. The upper and lower jaws and the teeth looked remarkably human, but the comparison ended there. Nancy was right. The cranium was oversized, more than twice that of a

Homo sapiens skull. Yet, it was the eye sockets that caught his attention. They were unlike any Jim had ever seen. Clearly, what they saw before them was a new and unknown super-intelligent species, judging by the size of the skull alone. This unique skull had to be the secret that Dr. Bronston had so carefully protected.

"So, is this what your father was hiding from the Chicago museum and from Dr. Tubojola?" asked Jim.

"I think he was hiding it from the world," said Nancy. "This is not something he would announce, except on a very special occasion. They haven't even finished the excavation work. If this creature wasn't extinct for two million years, I'd say you would have to worry about a public panic."

"It's 1.82 million years old," said Jim. "I think we're looking at what caused David to panic and commit murder. It's not the skull itself, but what it represents that I think David saw as the serpent."

"I think you're right about the serpent," said Nancy. "My father was probably not just struggling with the problem of when to announce the discovery, but whether to disclose it at all. The bigger question had to be whether the public was ready to accept it. I have seen a lot of things, but in my opinion, this is the most astounding archaeological discovery ever made. That includes King Tut and all of his golden treasures," said Nancy.

"Yes, but King Tut was human," said Jim. "I'm no expert, but this isn't our species or anything closely related to it. Now that letter begins to make sense."

"I agree this isn't human. The answer, as you said, is that it lived here almost two million years ago. My father was right in keeping it secret. Right now, the three of us are the only living beings in the world who know about it. We're going to have to swear ourselves to secrecy, and call Dr. Umbawi right away," said Nancy.

"You mean, Dr. Tubojola," Jim corrected her. "He's the curator of the museum here in Uhuru. More importantly, he's the Minister of the Department of the Interior, which has jurisdiction over all archaeological excavations and their findings. Remember, Dr. Umbawi is just a consultant to the museum from Kenya."

"Of course. You're right," said Nancy. "We must call him as soon as we can. Right now, I think you should cover it back up, Mobutu. It gives me the creeps."

"Yes, Miss Nancy," he said, as he put the cloth carefully over the skull.

"Dr. Tubojola is the one person who will know what to do," said Jim.

CHAPTER EIGHTEEN: *A FABLE*

"Wait," said Nancy, "Here it is."

"What is?" asked Jim.

"It's right here," she continued. "A second letter."

"A second letter?" asked Jim.

"Yes, Jim. There's a second letter here from my father, addressed to my mother."

"You're joking," said Jim. "We're ready to go. I think the rains have almost stopped."

"No. Wait," said Nancy. "Sit down. This letter was between two pages in the record logbook. Listen while I read it out loud."

"Are you sure you want to read it to us? It could be personal. Maybe you should read it alone by yourself first."

"There are no secrets here among the three of us," she said.

Jim and Mobutu sat down on the nearest boxes they could find.

"Go ahead," said Jim.

"Well, the letter is addressed just like the first one. The return address is the museum in Elizabethtown."

"Are you sure you don't want to read it to yourself first?" Jim asked.

"Yes. I'm ready," she said.

"Then go ahead. We're listening," said Jim, looking over at Mobutu.

Nancy took a deep breath and began to read the letter.

Dear Elizabeth,

What we have found here at Bokuru is extraordinary. For me, the right words to describe it are hard to find, but I will try. I know you are going to tell me that it is my professional responsibility to collect data, report what I find, and let others speculate on it's meaning and make any required identification. I have restricted myself to the role of a field archaeologist all my life. This one time, I feel compelled to express my inner feelings and indulge in pure speculation on what we have found here at Bokuru. I decided to bend the rules a bit at the expense of being labeled a splitter and openly declare that we have found a new species. I'll still let others classify what we have found and assign the name. That is not my concern at this time.

In spite of the fact there is much more work to do, and everything I have is of a preliminary nature, I have taken the liberty of putting together a theoretical story of what might have taken place here 1.82 million years ago. I admit it is pure conjecture on my part, so I have simply called it 'A Fable.' In time, perhaps, more facts may lend credence to my tale.

Once upon a time, perhaps 2.5 million years before present, a tribe of *Homo erectus*, our true ancestor, traveled out onto the open savannah of what is now Uhuru. The tribe followed a herd of antelope as it moved in their seasonal route to greener pastures further north. Year after year, the migration took place. In time, the tribe realized that water, while available year round in the small valley, was virtually non-existent out on the open plain.

Eventually, the tribe became aware that it was easier to remain in the valley and wait for the herds than it was to chase them over parched ground for hundreds of miles. For thousands of years, they remained in the valley and the game came to them.

Climate determines life on earth. As the earth cooled, water became scarce, locked in the expanding polar ice caps. As the deserts spread and the land on the plains became hostile, there was still plenty for the tribe to eat in their valley, even when the herds ceased passing through the valley. Life in a cave provided protection from the heat of the sun and from seasonal rains. The hominids had to adapt to a changing climate. The selective advantage of increased intelligence became the key to their survival. Advanced technology offset a diminished natural bounty.

Along with technology, the close cooperation between individuals to a degree not understandable by man today became essential. Because the small valley provided a limited source of food, the hominids remained small in stature. Their arms and legs gave up strength to support an expanded cranium, housing an even larger brain. This larger brain became more important than brawn in their ability to remain in the small valley. The group learned to control fire, develop advanced tools, domesticate animals, begin true farming, cultivate crops, and most importantly to undertake the first true public works project. They dammed the Bokuru River, flooded the valley, thereby creating a large lake that provided water that turned the valley into a green oasis.

As intelligence evolved to handle their advanced technology, greater social cohesion became crucial for their small population. The need to control the size of their population and avoid any strain on their resources assured the advantage of superior intelligence.

As the brain increased in size to twice that of a modern human, nature sacrificed the thickness of other bones to provide for the increased size of the skull. The cranium became thinner as it became larger. The thinner skull left the hominids susceptible to sunstroke. The protection of the cave became a survival necessity offering protection against the midday sun. True night vision evolved to allow the hominids to handle their chores at night and avoid the midday sun. The human eye, so useful in communication in other hominids, yielded to the larger, dark impenetrable eye, like that of a leopard. The little hominids became true creatures of the dark.

While they advanced through evolutionary change, they also became trapped in this small valley. They could not travel beyond the minimal distance that allowed them to return to the shelter of the cave before sunrise. While superior in many ways, they were truly a fragile species, specialists in survival only in their small valley. Positive random genetic mutations moved through the small population quickly and these changes took place in a geologically short period. The hominid evolved from a crude, early *Homo erectus* to an entirely new species, one more advanced than any other that the earth had ever seen. The Bokuru hominid became nature's true experiment with advanced intelligence and an extremely large brain.

The event that determined the course of the history of life on this earth occurred approximately 1.82 million years ago. This event occurred at the beginning of the

rainy season, probably early in December since the
sluice at the dam had been set at maximum height to
allow the lake to fill. When their evening's work was
done, the Bokuru hominids went to sleep in the early
dawn in anticipation of the darkness of the next night, a
night that, for them, never came. On that day, the Ikanga
Volcano, just north of the valley, began a giant eruption
that filled the sky with dust and pumice. The particulate
matter that gathered in the atmosphere gradually blocked
the sun for many miles in all directions. While the
Bokuru hominids slept, the volcanic debris accumulated
on the earth and choked the river as it fed the lake.

The ash fall caught a small hunting party of *Homo
erectus* north of the valley unprotected on the open plain.
As the day turned to night, the hunting party found itself
caught in the heavy downfall of volcanic debris. In
panic and fear they turned back towards the south to
escape. At first, they chased the distant sunlight on the
horizon. But, when all light disappeared, they stopped
when they reached the river. In hope of finding shelter,
they traveled along its bank, following it downstream.
Finally, they saw the distant glimmer of the fire in the
mouth of the cave, a bright beacon in a world strangely
plunged into darkness.

There they stood, covered with soot, frightened,
hungry, and exhausted at the mouth of the cave. Staring
beyond the flames at the startled group of Bokuru
hominids roused from their slumber by the appearance
of intruders, species faced species. For a brief moment,
fate hung in the balance. Perhaps, just perhaps, had the
hunting party seen a familiar human eye showing a bit of
warmth, compassion, or understanding with the slightest
indication of a welcome expression, history would have
taken a different direction. However, when they looked
for that inviting sympathetic glance, all they saw was the
deep, dark, unfathomable, expressionless eye so keenly
adapted for night vision, but no longer capable of the
expression of emotion.

The hunters reacted instinctively, perhaps out of fear,
perhaps out of frustration. They struck out physically,
effectively wielding the clubs with which they were

so comfortable. They struck head blows against which there was no defense by the fragile Bokuru hominids who could offer no resistance. Violence was incomprehensible to the little hominids. Their frail little bodies had no strength for conflict. Within moments, the cave belonged to the hunting party and the Bokuru hominids lay dying on the floor of the only home they had ever known, their fragile skulls crushed by the blows of the hunter.

The next day, when the morning sun rose bright and the sky was clear, the rising water from the Bokuru River reached the entrance to the cave. The hunting party, threatened by the impending flood and encouraged by the promise of fair weather, left the protection of the cave, and moved out into the open savannah, and began the long journey home.

Nature's experiment with true, superior intelligence was over. The Bokuru hominid was extinct. Without the little Bokuru hominid to adjust the sluice on the dam, the lake continued to flood, filling the cave with river sand and volcanic debris and entombing the terrible secret of this place.

Over eons of time, the interior of the cave became stone and the broken bones of the hominids fossilized, freezing the event of that day until modern man came here 1.82 million years later to gaze into the past.

End of fable

I humbly apologize for my uncharacteristic ramblings, but I felt I needed to express myself to someone and tell my rendition of what might have happened here at Bokuru so long ago. I will leave the burden of naming this species to others, as well as the obligation to ponder the implications of this find. Personally, I feel honored that I am the one who was privileged to make this extraordinary discovery.

Eternally yours,

Edward

"Incredible," said Jim. "Just think, murder today is woven into murder 1.82 million years ago."

"Hold on," said Nancy. "This story is fiction, a fable. He carefully labeled this letter that way. He said it was just a story. There is nothing scientific about it. It is not fact. It is a bit of fanciful imagination created by my father. Of course, the skull is real. We see it is right before us. We have to report that to Dr. Tubojola right away, but, Jim, this letter is not the expression of my father as a scientist. He has indulged in wild speculation, something he normally did not do. His reputation would be ruined if this letter were made public. His contemporaries would destroy him. He was so careful throughout his life to protect himself from scientific attacks by his contemporaries. I cannot let one letter destroy all that he worked for."

"I know," said Jim. "I think he knew that. Why do you think he wrote to your mother? He never intended for any one to ever see this letter, or even the first letter."

"I agree the hominid and all the records and artifacts here must be turned over to Dr. Tubojola. However, I'm going to destroy these two letters. I cannot have my father's name and reputation damaged by them. He spent his life taking great pains to be scientific, following only what the facts told him. These letters could destroy all that he ever stood for, all that he ever did. If this is the most important discovery of all time, these letters would only taint it. I can only ask that both of you say nothing about the existence of these letters. We must agree they never existed, whatever happens. Do you agree?" Nancy pleaded.

"Yes, Miss Nancy," said Mobutu.

"I agree," said Jim. "These letters were never intended to be seen by anyone. They belong to you. The decision of what to do with them is yours."

"Then, enough said, I think we need to go back to the camp and call Dr. Tubojola. We need his advice," said Nancy.

"Dr. Tubojola will know what to do," said Jim.

CHAPTER NINETEEN: *SMYTHE'S DISCOVERY*

The next morning, when Jim awoke, he immediately sensed that something was wrong. Normally, he woke early, but he could tell from the way the sun streaked between the tent flaps he had overslept. After a quick look around the interior of the tent, he could see he was alone in the tent. He grabbed his shirt, slipped on his pants and shoes, and then stuck his head outside. His fears were correct. The sun was high overhead. He guessed it was at least midmorning, and probably closer to noon. The second thing he noticed was the helicopter resting on the rough landing area. A stranger, who, Jim assumed, was the pilot, was seated on a large boulder beyond the perimeter, casually reading a newspaper.

Dr. Tubojola was already here, he thought. Jim walked across the tent and out over to the adjoining mess tent. When he entered the tent, he saw that the whole camp crew was there.

"Ah," said Dr. Tubojola. "You're just in time, Mr. Henderson. You have saved us the burden of waking you. We did want you to get your rest. You have been quite busy, I see, since your arrival in Africa. It appears that jet lag has finally caught up with you."

"I'm up," said Jim, as he started to button his shirt.

"Now that you are here, please feel free to stay. I have just finished with everyone else so your timing is perfect. We are ready for you."

Jim stood just inside the tent, half awake, struggling with the buttons on his shirt. Dr. Tubojola stood behind the food preparation table. Dr. Umbawi was seated on Dr. Tubojola's right, and another man, who Jim did not recognize, was seated on his left.

On the table directly in front of Dr. Tubojola, was the skull of H0-011. Beside the skull in front of the stranger, was the open site logbook that Nancy had examined at the table in the finish tent the evening before. Jim noted mentally that the stranger was clearly not a native of Uhuru. He looked English. He had black, wavy hair, a black moustache, and black plastic, rimmed glasses. He appeared to be about fifty years old. Nancy sat on the front bench of the first table just to the right of Dr. Tubojola, while Mobutu sat on the front of the table on Dr. Tubojola's left. M'Bee and the two laborers sat on the back seat of the table behind Mobutu.

Nancy did not look up or acknowledge Jim's arrival, but Mobutu turned and nodded, smiling in Jim's direction.

"I'd like you to meet Raymond Smythe," said Dr. Tubojola addressing Jim.

"Good Morning," said Jim, addressing the stranger.

Mr. Smythe nodded acknowledging Jim's greeting, but said nothing.

"Mr. Smythe is here in Uhuru working with our department as part of his field training program for the coroner's office in London, England," said Dr. Tubojola.

Mr. Smythe smiled briefly, and nodded again toward Jim.

"Mr. Smythe is a graduate accountant, but his true love is forensic pathology. He is with us for six months as part of his training," said Dr. Tubojola.

"Fine," said Jim, nodding toward Mr. Smythe.

"Mr. Smythe's experience as an accountant has apparently served him well this morning, Mr. Henderson. He and Mobutu have been busy reviewing your discoveries of last evening."

"I see you've brought some of them up here," said Jim.

"First, let me congratulate you on your efforts. What you found is most interesting, Mr. Henderson, most interesting, indeed. Oh, please take a seat. This is not a court proceeding or an inquisition. There is no judge or jury to impress here. We have no court reporter here to catch your every word," said Dr. Tubojola.

Jim continued standing while he finished buttoning the last button on his shirt. Jim's legal training warned him to stand and not take a subordinate position in any confrontation. He followed his instinct and training. There was no jury, but Dr. Tubojola was certainly acting and sounding a bit like both prosecutor and judge. Jim sensed he was on the defensive side of whatever issue was being discussed.

"Mr. Smythe, as I said, has been busy collecting, assembling, and cataloging the items you found in the finish tent last evening. Before we get to our primary exhibit this morning, I thought, perhaps, Mr. Smythe, we might start with that pen and bottle of ink you brought up from the site," said Dr. Tubojola, as he turned and addressed Mr. Smythe.

"Yes, of course," said Mr. Smythe, busying himself with the exhibits on the table.

"Oh, I should say, Mr. Henderson, that everything was assembled, labeled, and brought up here with both Ms. Bronston and Mobutu, members of your team, as witnesses to the entire process. I believe we have maintained a good evidentiary trail should we need to substantiate our exhibits," said Dr. Tubojola.

Jim stared at the skull. It was just as impressive in the daylight as it had been in the tent the night before. He had hardly noticed that Mr.

Smythe held up the bottle of ink and pen that Nancy had found on the table in the tent the night before.

"I don't suppose you remember these items; this bottle of ink and this pen, do you, Mr. Henderson?" asked Dr. Tubojola.

"They look like the ones Nancy found on her father's work table," Jim responded, casually.

"Good. I think they will provide us a good place to begin," said Dr. Tubojola.

"Fine," said Jim, totally at a loss as to why Dr. Tubojola was not focusing on the skull.

"Do you remember the label on this ink bottle?"

"It looks like the same bottle we saw on the table last night," Jim repeated, anxious to move on to something important.

"Ah, yes, but what I was hoping for was that you would recognize it as India ink."

"I didn't check the label. I only saw it from a distance," said Jim.

"Of course, but we can read and identify it. Perhaps we can agree that it is rather permanent stuff, India ink, is it not?"

"I'm familiar with India ink," said Jim.

"Certainly, it is a far cry from using pencil, wouldn't you agree? What I mean is, a person doesn't use India ink unless they are pretty sure of the permanent nature of what they are doing."

Jim felt more than ever he was in a legal proceeding. Yet he had no idea what or who was on trial or what the charges were. His real problem was that he had no idea where Dr. Tubojola was heading with his questions.

"All I am trying to get at, Mr. Henderson, is that all records at this site have been written very carefully in pen and ink. There are no pencil entries, nor is there any evidence of alterations or attempts to change any of the entries. I would say that Dr. Bronston was a man of conviction when he wrote down his notes. He was very sure of his facts before he put things down in permanent ink. A look at these entries tells me he was very deliberate and precise in what he was doing. Wouldn't you agree?" asked Dr. Tubojola.

"Yes. I remember the entries were all completed in ink," said Jim. "I only looked at them briefly last night, but I would agree."

"Thank you for your cooperation. Mr. Smythe, and I should add, Mobutu, have spent a lively morning counting the pieces that were glued together to make our primary exhibit which I'll simply refer to as Exhibit A," said Dr. Tubojola.

The greatest discovery of all time had been summarily reduced to Exhibit A. Clearly, Jim thought, Dr. Tubojola is in charge. Jim decided that he would say as little as possible since he had no idea what Dr. Tubojola's objective was or where his questions were leading.

"You have seen Exhibit A before, have you not?" asked Dr. Tubojola.

"Yes. The hominid skull is the one we found last night in the assembly tent. The box was labeled Box 01 of HO-011," said Jim.

"Yes. Well, as I was saying, they have painstakingly counted each and every separate piece that was used in the reconstruction of Exhibit A," said Dr. Tubojola.

"I'm sure that wasn't easy," said Jim.

"Incredible as it may seem, Mr. Henderson, they each came up with the same number. Quite extraordinary, don't you think?"

Jim said nothing. The question was stated in such a way that no answer was required or expected.

"The count, please," asked Dr. Tubojola, looking down at Mr. Smythe.

Mr. Smythe smiled briefly before he answered the question. "One hundred ninety three," Mr. Smythe responded, looking directly at Jim.

Jim detected a bit of arrogant self-confidence in Mr. Smythe's voice that he did not like.

Dr. Tubojola continued, "And you, Mobutu, do you agree with this figure?" Dr. Tubojola looked sternly at Mobutu.

"Yes, sir," said Mobutu, quietly. "One hundred ninety three. That was the number."

"There you have it, Mr. Henderson, a total of one hundred ninety three bits and pieces. A figure everyone here agrees on. Oh, if you want, after we are through, you can have a few minutes to count them for yourself. We can make the exhibit available, under supervision, of course. I'm sure you can understand, we must maintain our evidentiary trail."

"I'll agree to the figure. If Mobutu has checked it, I agree," said Jim.

"Good. Mr. Smythe has been busy this morning, Mr. Henderson. He has been earning his keep, so to speak. He has reviewed the entries in the site log," said Dr. Tubojola, nodding over to Mr. Smythe. Smythe then picked up the large binder and turned it around so Jim could come forward and examine it closely.

"I remember the book," said Jim, not approaching the table, but remaining where he stood.

"Well, you'll be excited to know Mr. Smythe has made a discovery of his own, Mr. Henderson. Oh, but let's back up for a moment. Can we agree to take judicial notice of the fact that this binder is the official record book for this site? I think we should start with that," said Dr. Tubojola.

"Yes," said Jim. "It's the book we found, and it looks like it was intended to be the official record book Dr. Bronston maintained for the site."

"For the record then," said Dr. Tubojola. "This official site log book was brought from the table in the tent by Mr. Smythe under the observation of your witnesses. I am sure they can reassure you that it has not been tampered with in the process of moving it. We do have a solid evidentiary chain, I believe," he said, looking over at Mobutu.

Mobutu said nothing, but Jim noticed that Mobutu nodded in agreement, very quietly.

"I agree that it is the official record book," said Jim, thinking the process at this point was silly. No one was challenging the records.

"Then we agree, Mr. Henderson, this book is the official, permanent record for this site."

Jim just nodded. Dr. Tubojola was being repetitive. Jim was beginning to get annoyed.

"For your information, we have marked this book as Exhibit B. The pen and ink are indexed as exhibit C."

"Fine," said Jim.

"The book is open to page 129. Is this the page where you made your discovery, Mr. Smythe?"

"Yes," said Mr. Smythe firmly, staring at Jim again.

"I was wondering, Mr. Smythe, if you could share with Mr. Henderson, first what the entries on this page are all about? Then, if you would, tell us what you showed me this morning?" asked Dr. Tubojola.

"Well, yes," said Mr. Smythe, clearing his throat, then looking first at Jim, then down at the open book. "This page is labeled Hominid HO-011. The entry describes each of the pieces of fossilized bone assigned to that hominid."

"And that is the hominid identified with our Exhibit A here before us, is it not?" asked Dr. Tubojola, continuing to address Mr. Smythe.

"Yes," said Mr. Smythe. "The box in which it was found was labeled H0-011. Yes, sir. All the post cranial bones identified and assigned to this hominid are in box 02 under the same identification system. The skull, Exhibit A, was found by itself in box 01 and was recovered on the table this morning."

"Please go on," said Dr. Tubojola.

Mr. Smythe cleared his throat again and then continued.

"Everything is carefully set out. What I mentioned this morning is right here on this page, where it says the skull was assembled using one hundred thirty nine pieces."

Mr. Smythe paused, as if waiting for the approval by Dr. Tubojola.

"Thank you, Mr. Smythe. Now, Mr. Henderson, can we agree once again that these are the official site records, one more time, if you will?"

Jim just nodded. Dr. Tubojola was repeating himself again.

"This book is the documentary foundation with all entries very carefully penned in ink, India ink. I think we can agree, a great deal of care was taken in the preparation of each page in this book. Of course, we have already addressed the importance of this binder, I believe."

"Yes we have," said Jim, becoming more than a little annoyed at Dr. Tubojola's repetition.

"Good. Then there it is, Mr. Henderson, right before us."

"You lost me," said Jim. "What is right before us?"

Dr. Tubojola paused for a moment, scowled briefly at Jim, then continued to explain. "A total of one hundred ninety three pieces were used in the reconstruction we call Exhibit A, and one hundred thirty nine is written down in the official records," said Dr. Tubojola. "Now, the difference between one hundred ninety three and one hundred thirty nine is quite significant, wouldn't you say, Mr. Henderson?"

"But it's obviously just a mistake in transposition when the numbers were written down," said Jim. "I don't see the problem."

"That's your assumption, Mr. Henderson. You understand, you are already attacking what we agreed on. You say we are looking at a mistake, a simple error in transposition, but you must admit the possibility exists that perhaps there is something more sinister here."

"How so?" asked Jim, as he began to realize the trap he had been caught in.

"If the records are correct, and the count this morning is also correct, I hesitate to say this, but we could have a modern Piltdown, a fraud, a forgery of horrendous proportions. We could be facing the addition of non-associated pieces to this rendition, just enough, in my humble opinion, to change this reconstruction from that of a normal *Homo erectus* to this exhibit we have before us. Could such an undertaking have been intentional?"

"That's a pretty big assumption," said Jim.

"No more so than yours," answered Dr. Tubojola.

Jim was beginning to feel a little anger at the trap Dr. Tubojola had cleverly lured him into. If this was a trial, he was losing quickly. Dr. Bronston was not here to defend himself. The Bokuru hominid had been extinct for almost two million years. Jim simply had no client and no witnesses. In addition, he was not prepared to defend anyone. He did not know the facts.

"Perhaps I can help you see my point by casting a little doubt on the issue," said Dr. Tubojola.

"Please do," said Jim, hoping for a break.

"Mr. Smythe, can you please turn to that other page you mentioned?"

"Page one hundred twenty seven?" asked Mr. Smythe.

"Yes. I believe that's the one," said Dr. Tubojola. "This, I believe, is the page, Mr. Henderson, that describes the hominid found in association with Hominid HO-011, is it not, Mr. Smythe?" asked Dr. Tubojola.

"Yes," quipped Mr. Smythe. "This page is labeled HO-010. It was the closest one to HO-011. It was nearby."

Jim was at a loss because he had not looked at the book the night before. Nancy had only seen it briefly. He was totally unprepared to discuss any details.

"Now, Mr. Smythe, perhaps you can tell us about the hominid on this page. I assume, Mr. Henderson, we can agree about the meaning of in association, and that these two hominids were found, basically, together, perhaps so much so that it was hard to differentiate the bones of one from the other."

"It was the closest one," repeated Mr. Smythe, softly this time.

"How far apart, exactly, Mr. Smythe?" Jim asked.

"Thirty six centimeters at the closest point," said Smythe, weakly.

"That's almost three feet," said Jim.

"Yes," said Smythe, turning the book around and looking at the entries.

"Then they are not in association," said Jim. "They are some distance apart. Thirty six centimeters is not what I would call in association."

"I will take it under advisement that they may not be commingled," said Dr. Tubojola.

"To be in association they must be found in the exact same location," said Jim. "I know that much about archaeology. Mr. Smythe has done no more than tell us they were near each other. For a distance he mentioned, they cannot be confused with each other."

"I will concede your point," said Dr. Tubojola. "My only concern, Mr. Henderson, is that we have our own version of the story of Humpty Dumpty."

"Humpty Dumpty?" asked Jim.

"Yes. It seems that your hominid had quite a fall over the cliff into the dark void of two million years of natural history. Now, all the king's men can't seem to put the poor fellow back together again, at least correctly."

"I see no more than an error in writing down the records," said Jim. "The other skull you mentioned wasn't close enough to be confused with it."

"Ancient skulls are not puzzles, Mr. Henderson. They are no longer made up of carefully cut pieces. The pieces have been separated for almost two million years and have suffered a bit of wear and tear in the process."

"We can agree on that," said Jim.

"We have to acknowledge that there is a lot of intuition, conjecture, and I might add, pure guesswork in such an assembly. Let me ask you, Mr. Smythe, where is the reconstructed skull HO-010?" asked Dr. Tubojola.

"We found none, and the records note that none has been undertaken. In fact, none of the others have been reconstructed either," said Mr. Smythe, no longer looking so self-assured.

"A smoking gun, Mr. Henderson. I still see the possibility of an oversized reconstruction using pieces of one skull for the reconstruction of this unusually interesting rendition before us."

"You're stretching," said Jim. "Mr. Smythe just said we don't know anything about any other hominids." Jim didn't know what else to say. He knew nothing of the other hominids, although the reference to HO-011 created at least an inference that they had identified 10 other ones.

"So you see, Mr. Henderson, in a state of exhaustion late last night, when you thought you found the greatest archaeological discovery of all time, in your euphoria, you jumped to a wild conclusion based on an assumption. Then you came tearing up to camp to radio me about your great conclusion, arousing me in the middle of the night, I might add. Now, in a moment of more rational calm, it seems you really didn't do your homework in spite of having an archaeological background," said Dr. Tubojola.

"We decided to call you right away, as soon as we found the discovery," said Jim.

"I think you now know your error. Thankfully you did not run to the nearest media source. The damage could have been catastrophic. Any announcement would have made headlines around the world within hours."

"I still can't believe it's anything but a mistake in the transposition of the numbers," said Jim.

"I see that you like your assumption, Mr. Henderson, don't you? Unfortunately, we have to be realistic. We have to deal with the possibility that we have a fraud, and a skillful one at that. Piltdown was that way. It took years to unravel the mess and undo the damage it caused."

"I don't see a Piltdown here," said Jim. "At worst, I see an honest error."

"Ask yourself, Mr. Henderson, why did David Johannson kill Dr, Bronston? And, why did he try to kill you and Miss Bronston? Those shots this morning were too close to be an accident, if I understand the facts correctly. Miss Bronston was kind enough to share your rather harrowing adventure with us just before you joined us. Certainly, you must have thought about that incident?" asked Dr. Tubojola.

"I have," said Jim.

"I'm anxious to hear your theory of the event," said Dr. Tubojola.

"David wanted to shut down the site," said Jim. "It's as simple as that."

"So, he was not just a crazed lunatic fighting with some inner devil, and shot at you in an attempt to exorcise his demons?"

"No, he saw a demon, but I believe it was an external one. We spoke to Eric, his big brother at the temple. He explained that David believed the site itself was evil. As a result, David was driven to kill the serpent. I interpreted this as a need to shut down the site, stopping the excavation work. That was his real objective. I don't believe he had any personal animosity against anyone," said Jim.

"So, no petty personal vendettas or feuds?"

"No. I don't see evidence of that. I believe what Eric said," said Jim.

"It may surprise you, but we are not so far apart in our hypotheses. I, also, agree with your summary."

"I'm surprised we agree on anything," said Jim, bewildered.

"So, it's entirely possible that David was on a noble mission, and he may, in fact, be a hero?"

"A hero?" asked Jim. "He tried to kill us."

"His goal, we agree, was not personal. I think we should consider that he was seeking justice," said Dr. Tubojola.

"Justice? You must be kidding. For what?" asked Jim.

"Let me ask you a question. You claim to be a man of details, do you not?"

"I am a commercial litigator. I deal with evidence," said Jim.

"Then perhaps your notes will tell you how far it was from his tent to the latrine?"

"The latrine? What has that go to do with anything?" asked Jim.

"Bear with me for a moment. Let's assume that Dr. Bronston was, in fact, a mere mortal and, from time to time, perhaps two or three times a day, he had to, shall we say, answer nature's call."

"Yes," said Jim. "I'm sure he did."

"Then, let's say that it took him an average of twenty minutes to make a round trip from his work table and back," said Dr. Tubojola.

"That sounds reasonable," Jim added.

"Good. Then over the period of a few days, David would have regular periods of unsupervised time to make a pretty thorough examination of Dr. Bronston's work and his records, wouldn't you say?"

"Yes," said Jim. "He would have had time to look around. They both worked in a small tent."

"Then, we may also assume that he could have made the same discovery Mr. Smythe did this morning. Perhaps, David found the same discrepancy in the numbers. You must at least admit the possibility, Mr. Henderson."

"That is possible, but there is another theory," said Jim.

"Please proceed. I'm all ears, Mr. Henderson."

"He could have realized the Bokuru hominid was real. He could have concluded that it was not faked. His decision to kill could have been stimulated by a direct and immediate threat to his personal beliefs," said Jim. "He was raised in a fundamentalist Bible background."

"I don't think you are looking at David carefully when you make him appear so devout. I have some knowledge of this temple he came from. They recognize a divine presence, but I'm afraid it is not perceived to be in the shape of a man. They have no objection to the discovery of ancient creatures on this earth. I would not expect any reaction from them regarding the discovery of Exhibit A, assuming, for the moment, it is accurate. I think they would simply shrug it off as of little importance, no more significant than any other ancient creature Dr. Bronston found," said Dr. Tubojola.

"But David was not a true believer in the temple. He was not here by choice," said Jim. "He brought his beliefs with him when he came to Africa."

"The point, Mr. Henderson, is that he could leave the temple at any time by choice. If his religious beliefs were so conventional, so strong as you seem to suggest, he would have left this temple long ago. No, Mr.

Henderson, I think your case is weak. I see a noble purpose in his acts. In fact, we may all owe him a great deal."

"How?"

"What he did was save us from a modern Piltdown, the consequences of which would have made the original one seem rather trivial."

"That's just your theory," said Jim.

"We haven't addressed the possibility that, perhaps, it was the other way around. Heaven forbid, Mr. Henderson, they could have been colluding together, and one tried to back out. With both of them dead, we must consider all of the possible scenarios. You must have enough of an open mind to admit that," said Dr. Tubojola.

"Assuming you are right, that Dr. Bronston faked HO-011, then you have to address the issue of motive. Why would he do it?" Jim asked. "Why would he sacrifice his name and reputation to commit a fraud?"

"I could see a man grabbing at his fifteen minutes of fame. Perhaps he saw this as his last act before bowing out into the anonymity of retirement," said Dr. Tubojola.

"That doesn't work," said Jim. "He was already world famous."

"Perhaps he sought another fifteen minutes, a final grand finale. My observation of human nature is that fame is habit forming, Mr. Henderson. Once you have tasted it, you develop an appetite for more," said Dr. Tubojola.

"He was a private man," said Jim. "He only used the press to generate funds for his excavations. If he was ready to retire, there was no need for additional public exposure. Besides, he was keeping Bokuru a secret, even from you."

"Yes. I fear, however, he was simply biding his time until he was ready to spring it on an unsuspecting public."

"Now I think you are the one who is stretching it," said Jim.

"I admit that you made some points that must be considered, Mr. Henderson. The fact is, we do not know with any degree of certainty, what really happened."

"That is precisely my point," said Jim. "There could have been a simple mistake."

"We agree, Mr. Henderson. It is, however, the very lack of knowledge of the truth that creates the real problem I have to deal with. No one knows or ever will know what happened here at Bokuru."

"That's the precise issue I was trying to raise," said Jim. "We have to take our time. We must study everything very carefully before we act or jump to any conclusions."

"Ah, but, Mr. Henderson, I am an administrator. I am not a detective. I'm not here to solve a murder mystery. I simply don't care what the facts really are."

CHAPTER TWENTY: *THE POISONOUS TREE*

"I think I'm confused," said Jim. "This is not a court of law. In fact, I'm not sure what it is."

"Well, technically, I suppose it's an administrative hearing of sorts. You could call it that. You did take a course in administrative law in school, didn't you?"

"Yes," said Jim. "It was a requirement."

"Good. Let me remind you, just for the record, that I am a citizen of Uhuru. I live and work in Elizabethtown. As you know, my primary responsibility is that of Minister of the Interior, which also includes acting as head of the Department of Antiquities, which to you means I am charged with the implementation and carrying out of the administrative rules and regulations relating to archaeology in Uhuru."

"I understand," said Jim.

"I have the power to act as needed in implementing and enforcing the law. I have chosen to act informally this morning in furtherance of my obligations. I do, however, understand that you should be somewhat confused. You do not handle the issues of archaeology in your country the same way as we do here in Uhuru. Of course, we also need to recognize that you are just waking up, and your full thought processes are apt to be a bit slow and possibly foggy," said Dr. Tubojola.

"No one woke me," said Jim. "I didn't even hear your helicopter land."

"Jet lag, Mr. Henderson, jet lag. You are not immune. You have been maintaining a blistering pace since you got here. We are in awe of your stamina. We wanted to let you catch up on some well deserved rest this morning."

"Well, I haven't had time to dress, but I'm up now. My mind may not be too sharp yet, but I'm up," said Jim.

"So you are. You have made your appearance known. I think your mental faculties are with us. You have handled yourself quite well for one who just woke up."

"Thank you," said Jim.

"We owe you an apology. We have been a bit uncivilized. We haven't even offered you a cup of coffee yet, never mind breakfast. I'm afraid the rest of us are a bit ahead of you."

"That's fine," said Jim. "I really don't need anything. I'm stepping into the middle of your meeting. I don't want to hold anyone up."

"Please, relax, Mr. Henderson. You are not on trial here. You are not representing those who are not with us and unable to defend themselves or whom you cannot consult. I'm not here to attack your exhibits or your presentation."

"Somehow, I've gotten a different impression," said Jim. "I thought what you have labeled Exhibit A is very much the issue."

"Quite the contrary. Oh, I admit that superficially it looks rather incredible. Anyone could be drawn in on a first glance, but cooler heads must prevail. Our little exercise this morning has a different objective. I already know what I must do. That is not the issue."

"I thought you were trying to decide what to do about the hominid skull on the table?"

"No. I've already made up my mind about that. My goal is to convince you that what I am going to do is the right thing. I need the cooperation and understanding of everyone here in this tent. You do not need me this morning. You would have been content to sleep in. No, I am the one who needs you, and my success depends in no small way on your understanding of what I have decided to do and more importantly, why I am doing it," said Dr. Tubojola.

"I see," said Jim, although he was still puzzled about Dr. Tubojola's objectives.

"Please, let me assure you that we should not take much longer," said Dr. Tubojola. "I much prefer the air conditioning of my office in the museum in Elizabethtown to the blistering heat of this dusty canvas oven."

Detecting a more relaxed atmosphere, M'Bee brought both a coffee pot and a cup and placed them on the table next to where Jim was standing.

"Thank you," said Jim, looking over at M'Bee, who smiled wanly and then returned to his seat.

"The matter before us is quite simple, actually," continued Dr. Tubojola. "Unfortunately, of all of us here, you are the only one we still need to convince. I have simply tried to illustrate, in a way you would understand, why we are in the position where we have to undertake the action I have chosen to take. I can only hope that you will understand the need to act decisively, and why time is of the essence. As an attorney, you, of all people, should be able to comprehend my dilemma."

"Well, I appreciate your confidence in me. Thank you," said Jim. "I'll do my best to stay with you." Feeling more relaxed; Jim sat down and took a sip of coffee.

"Good," said Dr. Tubojola. "I'm glad you have taken a seat. There is no need to stand. You were beginning to make even me nervous." He paused for a moment to take a sip from his own coffee cup, before continuing in a more subdued voice.

M'Bee rose and refilled Dr. Tubojola's cup with coffee.

"You do understand the doctrine used in criminal cases in your country which is referred to as the 'fruit of the poisonous tree'?" asked Dr. Tubojola.

"Yes. Of course," said Jim.

"I am no authority on American jurisprudence, especially your criminal justice system, but we do have a similar law adopted here in Uhuru that may also be applied in the archeological arena. This law applies to me directly, since I am the one who must enforce it in such matters. In the end, it dictates what we must do here this morning."

"I am not familiar with your version of the rule," said Jim.

"I understand, but I am sure you know your own rule," said Dr. Tubojola. "There is a strong similarity between them. In your criminal cases, you are so concerned with the rights of the accused that you go to great lengths to protect those rights. The law says that if the evidence being used to convict someone of a crime was obtained illegally, as opposed to the definition of what is legal, then all the evidence obtained through the search is illegal as well. The result is that all such evidence obtained illegally is repressed and rejected."

"Yes," said Jim. "That is how our rule works."

"To say it another way, if the tree is poisonous, then the fruit of that tree is tainted and poisonous as well. You call it the 'fruit of the poisonous tree.' Am I sort of on track, Mr. Henderson? Please correct me if I'm off base."

"You are doing fine," said Jim.

"I am impressed, Mr. Henderson. I should say most of us in the third world are impressed with the tenacity with which this rule is enforced in your country. I was reading in the papers recently about a case in your country involving a serial killer whose conviction was overturned. The defendant was freed and killed again. He obtained his freedom solely because the proof that supported the original conviction depended on an illegal search."

"That's how our law works," said Jim.

"The rest of the world is in awe of your steadfast belief in your rule."

"You are right," said Jim. "We do take the rule seriously."

"Good. Then perhaps you can understand how we have adopted a similar law of our own that we apply to archaeology."

"You lost me," said Jim. "I don't see how you would apply that rule to archaeology."

"Our concept is that, if anything found at a site is incorrect, whether due to negligence, fraud, or any other reason, then the entire site is tainted such that it becomes a case of 'the fruit of the poisonous tree.' The result in our country is similar to yours."

"Your rule is the reverse. You are saying that if some one fruit on a remote branch is poisonous then the whole tree must be poisonous?" asked Jim.

"Yes, that is our rule. It is our twist of your rule. I knew you would understand."

"I think your rule is a bit bizarre," said Jim.

"Yes, perhaps, but my point is that here at Bokuru we have the fruit of a poisonous tree, Mr. Henderson. Perhaps, if you had a better grasp of our history, you would see the reasoning behind this archaeological rule."

"I admit I know little of your country," said Jim, taking a sip of coffee.

"Geographically, we are small. We have few natural resources. We are familiar with the colonial past of most of Africa. The one thing that best describes not only Uhuru, but our neighbors, as well, is the stark reality of poverty and an ever-expanding human population. To compensate for what we saw happening elsewhere, all resources under the earth's surface were made the property of the nation in our constitution, and our definition of property includes archeological artifacts and fossils."

"I see," said Jim, as he remembered their discussion at the museum.

"I am digressing. This special rule about the poisonous tree comes into play if we have a problem with a particular excavation site. We designed the rule to protect the integrity of the national effort and our hard earned reputation. We can simply squash the specific project or site that is tainted to protect our desired goal of a rapidly recognized international scientific center of effort here in Uhuru. We cannot take risks, Mr. Henderson. Just stop for a moment and think about this so-called discovery we have labeled Exhibit A this morning," said Dr. Tubojola.

"I can't get it out of my mind," said Jim.

"Dr. Bronston was a man of world wide reputation. His every find drew international exposure. Normally, what he did brought great prestige to our humble efforts."

"He was recognized as the best," said Jim.

"Good. You understand. Now, in this particular case, we have what you are trying to argue is the most important discovery in human history."

"It would change the scientific thinking about a lot of things," said Jim. "It is very significant."

"To put it mildly, Mr. Henderson. I agree. The fact is, even if the data was totally accurate, the discovery would not be a welcome event in some quarters. I should add that, by itself, controversy is no great burden. Certainly, we are always at odds with many a vested interest in our line of endeavor, but you must admit this one exhibit in particular would be even more strongly opposed and challenged by reputable sources," said Dr. Tubojola.

"I'm sure it would," said Jim. "I have to agree."

"It is that challenge that we must be able to meet on absolutely sure footing. You see, extraordinary discoveries require extraordinary proof, if you will. That, Mr. Henderson, is our problem here this morning. I don't mind facing a few vested interests and a little adversity. They provide some spice to our lives. That is the nature of our business. Even the scientific community could use a little shaking up now and then to loosen up the cobwebs. Sometimes it is actually entertaining to step on a few sanctimonious toes, but only, Mr. Henderson, if we are absolutely sure of our facts; only if we are squeaky clean as to our science," said Dr. Tubojola.

"I understand your point," said Jim.

"I'm not sure you do. Let me say it this way. I cannot afford to have egg on my face, Mr. Henderson. Let's face it, not only will the world wide press be here, but it's representatives accompanied by the mainstream scientific establishment will be on our doorstep with microscopes. Our protractors will arrive on the next flight with the express purpose of looking for cracks in our armor," said Dr. Tubojola.

"The press is a serious issue," said Jim.

"Many of the reporters in the international press are very well informed. They ask the right questions. I fear them far more than the reactionary fringe."

"Yes," said Jim. "I can imagine."

"Good. Then, understand, I am not here to argue the case one way or the other. I will even concede the possibility of your position to some degree. That, however, is not my job this morning."

"Go on," said Jim. "You already said you didn't care about the facts."

"What I am asking is that you understand my position. If we cannot put up a united front, if we cannot provide a solid stance and defend our position, we are doomed. The potential for damage will far outweigh the loss of any discovery such as this one site," said Dr. Tubojola.

"I'm sure there would be a lot more questions here than with other discoveries," said Jim. "I can agree with that."

"Good. Put yourself on the stage with me as the questions start to fly. I think you will agree that we could not weather a long, lively inquiry. What I hope I have demonstrated here this morning is that we cannot withstand even a superficial inquiry. That, Mr. Henderson, is the problem. The truth of what was found here is not the issue. We have only been here a couple of hours. Already, key elements such as the inconsistency between the numbers in the book and those in Exhibit A, have been easily exposed. Who knows what else our antagonists would find on a more thorough analysis. Any crack in our armor, and we will face a challenge that will make Piltdown look like child's play," said Dr. Tubojola.

"You have made your point," said Jim.

"I don't know whether we face fraud, simple gross negligence, or a stupid mistake. In fact, it doesn't matter which it actually is, Mr. Henderson. Our little country cannot afford the attack. Our economy depends on archeologists and tourists coming here and spending their time and money to fortify our economy. Our goal is to provide a topnotch arena for study and observation of the ancient human past. We are rich with events from our archaeological history. My obligation is easy, if you understand that our rule makes sense."

"I understand what you are saying," said Jim.

"Good. I'm beginning to think you do," said Dr. Tubojola, smiling for the first time.

"We need to take the time to analyze everything that we found very carefully so that, when the announcement is made, we have done everything properly," said Jim.

"I would like to agree with you, Mr. Henderson. In fact, normally I would, but we do not have the luxury of time. I am forced to agree with the late Dr. Bronston that premature disclosure is our primary concern. We are here this morning, with a heavy heart, but time itself requires that we act swiftly to enforce the rule. Enforcement is my responsibility and my burden. I fully understand the implications of what we do, but the clock forces the application of the rule."

"Your concern is about premature disclosure," said Jim. "I understand that."

"Precisely. You know, I would like to stop for a minute and compliment both you and Miss Bronston on how you handled last evening," said Dr. Tubojola.

"Compliment us?" asked Jim.

"Yes. I shudder to think what damage would have been done if you had gone to the press or virtually anyone else. Within days there would have been an overflow of people from radio, television, and the press in my office from all corners of the globe pressing microphones in my face, but this did not happen. Your training stood you well. You saw the danger. The first thing you did was to contact me. In spite of the fact I may bemoan the hour you radioed, all of Uhuru is eternally grateful that you did."

"It seemed like the right thing to do," said Jim.

"It was. I did not mean to leave Mobutu out when I complimented you on your actions, but he is a professional. He knows the rules well. He knows when we speak out, and when we do not. He is blessed by years of training under Dr. Bronston, something I am just now beginning to understand and appreciate."

"When we first met back in the museum, you were right. Dr. Bronston was holding back," said Jim.

"Yes, and in this case, his actions were more than justified. He was right. I was wrong." Dr. Tubojola paused for a moment. "We are losing valuable time. I have no choice but to invoke the administrative regulation we discussed in this situation."

"You are going to destroy Exhibit A," said Jim.

"More than that, Mr. Henderson, we are not going to just set Exhibit A aside. We are going to put it back."

"Put it back?" asked Jim.

"Yes. We are going to return the skull back into the pit, along with the inkbottle, the site logbook and all other artifacts and fossils that have been taken out of the excavation. They are all going back into the pit. When we have done that, the excavation is going to be back filled. We are going to bury Bokuru, Mr. Henderson, and contour the terrain so that it will never be found again," said Dr. Tubojola.

"Bury everything?" Jim asked.

"Yes, Mr. Henderson, everything. We do not have time to do anything else. That is what our law requires us to do."

"Oh," said Jim, momentarily at a loss for words.

"I have a plan to take care of everyone. These two loyal laborers have worked well with Mobutu since Bokuru first opened. I think you'd agree that the three of them make a very good team."

317

"Yes. You're right," said Jim. "I have seen them in action."

"Good. I see no reason to interfere. I will arrange for both of them to be transferred to work for Mobutu at the north basin giraffe excavation site. We need a good professional team there. We do have some time pressures as you and I discussed previously."

"Yes, I remember," said Jim.

"The giraffe site must be defined so we can finish the lake contours and release the equipment back to the road project," said Dr. Tubojola.

"Yes. You told me about the problem," said Jim.

"The best thing I can do is put in a seasoned team."

"Yes. I agree."

"Mobutu will be in charge of the site as resident archaeologist. He is certainly qualified for his own site. He has extensive first class experience, perhaps the best in Uhuru. He will be the first native African in Uhuru to act as resident archaeologist. He is deserving of this honor," said Dr. Tubojola.

"I certainly agree," said Jim.

"I have recommended that the Bureau of Education of Uhuru award the late Dr. Bronston with a special, honorary degree as Professor of Archaeology. This award will be retroactive so we can qualify Mobutu's fieldwork and study program under Dr. Bronston as fully qualified credits towards his four-year degree. Frankly, Mr. Henderson, we should have done this a long time ago."

"There is nothing wrong with the present," said Jim.

"I cannot, of course, address the acceptability of a degree from Uhuru in other jurisdictions, but at least Mobutu will be recognized and assured of employment here."

"This is a great promotion for him," said Jim.

"I want to correct an obvious inequity. M'Bee is well known to us for his culinary and kitchen managerial skills. He is a true team player. We have offered to bring him into Elizabethtown to run the kitchen operations for the cafeteria at the museum."

"That will be a great opportunity for him," said Jim.

"I'm proud to inform you that he has graciously accepted our offer. He will be relocated as soon as we can complete the arrangements," said Dr. Tubojola, who paused for a moment. He then looked over at Nancy. "This now brings me to Miss Bronston. You will be happy to know that we reached an agreement with her as well."

"You have been busy this morning," said Jim.

"Yes. Unless I am a poor judge of character and human relations, Miss Bronston is being groomed for the top position at the Chicago museum. I don't know what they call the position these days, Curator or President, or whatever, but I want to let them know how greatly we appreciate the time she spent helping us heal an open wound here in Africa. We look forward to working closely with her throughout her career with the museum. A couple of letters showing that she has the support of Uhuru sent to the right people should help supplement her personnel file," said Dr. Tubojola.

"That would be very considerate," said Jim.

"We also need to protect her father's reputation. We will set up a plaque and a bronze bust in the museum in appreciation for his contributions to many of our exhibits. He will have, at our expense of course, a new headstone in the cemetery. Miss Bronston has provided assistance with the epitaph this morning. We have also agreed to donate a surplus stone obelisk, currently in our possession, to be erected at this very spot where we are standing now. This will be a monument to Dr. Bronston's life work and to mark this place as the location of his last site."

"That's great, but the excavation is over a mile away," said Jim. "This is just the camp."

"Precisely, Mr. Henderson, precisely. That is why the monument will be here. The site and all it's artifacts and records will be buried under tons of rocks and soil so that there is no way anyone will find it. If any curiosity seeker decides to dig here where the monument is located, they will find nothing, absolutely nothing. The actual site will be hidden forever."

"What about the site location in your computer? The site is registered there," said Jim.

"I am surprised, Mr. Henderson. Don't you remember? Garbage in, garbage out. I think I can make the appropriate corrections of the coordinates right at my keyboard when I get back, don't you agree? That is one of the advantages of the computer. Errors are easily corrected."

"Oh," said Jim, at a loss of words.

"After all, what are a few numbers? At least they are not written in pen and permanent ink."

"But...."

"I regret that I have to leave this morning. I have other matters needing my attention that are on my regular schedule. In my absence, Mr. Smythe will be in charge of the burial operation. He will be sure that all evidence of the excavation is buried, and that the landscaping will prevent identification of the exact location of the original excavation site.

Oh, Mr. Smythe," he said, turning to address his associate. "Please be sure we plant a lot of Sansavaria around the area."

"Yes, sir," said Smythe.

"I understand it is a good soil stabilizer. We wouldn't want the area to erode any further."

"Yes, sir," said Smythe, smiling wryly at Jim.

"So there we have it, Mr. Henderson, all wrapped up, that is, except for you."

"Me?" Jim asked.

"I will personally provide letters of commendation to your client, the Museum in Chicago and to your employer as well. We will inform the museum that we do not need Miss Bronston or you any further since the site is barren. I will let them know we can clean things up ourselves with no cost to them. I feel I can assure you that there will be an inquest on Dr. Bronston's death, and the actual facts will come out. There should be a new death certificate shortly so your client will have coverage under the life insurance policy," said Dr. Tubojola.

"Will you need my testimony for that?" asked Jim.

"Thank you for offering, but I believe we can handle the matter here ourselves. I am sure the Chicago museum will be interested to know the crime was discovered and solved, in no small way, directly due to your efforts. We will also let them know that you played a valiant role in protecting Miss Bronston in the attempt on her life."

"My role was not as significant as you make it appear," said Jim.

"Where would we be if you had not come here to Uhuru, Mr. Henderson? I am always facing crises. I have tried to address all the issues that we face this morning. I prefer to take care of everything at once, so there are no loose ends."

"I'm still concerned that the Bokuru hominid has to be lost just because the site is tainted," said Jim.

"Let me ask you a simple question, Mr. Henderson. I am no philosopher, but what difference would it make?"

"Well....."

"We look forward to a long, fruitful, and I might add, mutually rewarding relationship with the museum in Chicago and Miss Bronston as its representative. In the end, isn't that more important in the real world than writing some learned treatise that winds up in some old archaeological library? Who will really care a year from now how one person reconstructed the pieces of some remote skull that dates back millions of years? I think there are more important things to deal with. Tomorrow morning millions of people will get up and go about their daily lives, just as they always have. Do you really think their lives would change, if you are right?" asked Dr. Tubojola.

"The public should know the truth," said Jim.

"You will have to file a report. I would recommend that it be simple and limited to the relevant facts. By now, you now know how to align it with my activities here."

"Yes," said Jim.

"I think it would be wise if you stick to the issue at hand and simply let it go at that. It would, I think, be most unwise to digress into collateral matters. Besides, what happened here is beyond your responsibility. Your task was to find the cause of death of Dr. Bronston. You are a lawyer, not a professional archaeologist."

"You're right. My report will be focused," said Jim.

"Good. I'm glad we see eye to eye on what could be a delicate situation."

"I guess I should thank you," said Jim. "You seem to have addressed everything."

"No, Mr. Henderson. It is I who owes you a debt of gratitude. Oh, and before I forget, I have made arrangements for both you and Miss Bronston to be on a flight together out of Uhuru. It is scheduled for tomorrow, early in the afternoon. The flight will put you back in Chicago as expeditiously as possible, at our expense, of course. Oh, and Mr. Henderson…"

"Yes?" asked Jim.

"Please. If there are any expenses you incur that are not reimbursed by your employer or the museum in Chicago, just send the bills to my office. We do have some room for legal expenses. We would be most happy to pay any uncovered invoices you may have."

"I'm sure I'm covered, but thank you for the offer," said Jim.

"Then I believe this meeting is adjourned. I trust I have everyone's confidence to say no more of the matter. I trust everyone understands that everything relating to this site must remain here. Take nothing of this place with you. There is no recorder here. There will be no record that this meeting ever took place. Are there any final questions?"

No one spoke.

"Good, said Dr. Tubojola. "I believe M'Bee is prepared to put together some lunch for everyone before we all go our separate ways. I'm sorry, Mr. Henderson."

"Sorry?" asked Jim.

"Yes. You seem to have missed breakfast."

CHAPTER TWENTY-ONE: *SECOND THOUGHTS*

Nancy drove because she knew the road. They left right after lunch. At the camp, everyone had eaten lunch in silence. Once they were on the way back to Elizabethtown, Jim and Nancy barely spoke to each other. Thankfully, the trip across the savannah was uneventful. Dr. Tubojola and Dr. Umbawi flew back in the helicopter. Mobutu and both laborers stayed with M'Bee to help Mr. Smythe clean up, bury the excavation site, and dismantle the camp. Dr. Tubojola had given them two days to complete the work before a truck would be sent out to move the camp to the north basin excavation site where Mobutu would set up camp. Once the move was completed, the truck was scheduled to bring M'Bee back to the museum where he would take over management of the cafeteria.

That evening, Jim and Nancy had an early dinner together in the dining room at the Grand Hotel in Elizabethtown.

"This was a wonderful dinner, Jim. I've had a very nice time."

"Don't thank me," said Jim. "All meals here at the hotel are charged to my room which, as you know, is paid for by the museum. If you want to thank someone, you should thank your boss, Mr. Kendall," said Jim.

"Well, it was a nice thought. I had no idea we would drink a whole bottle of wine. In any case, all good things have to come to an end. I've got to make it back to Nairobi tonight. I have a lot to do if I'm going to make that flight tomorrow afternoon."

"You know, I've been thinking," said Jim, slowly.

"A penny for your thoughts. So far, your thinking here in Africa has been pretty good."

"I've decided I have to go back," he said, seriously.

"We're both going back tomorrow afternoon. We need to start thinking about Chicago."

"No. I mean I have to go back to Bokuru," said Jim, a little dismayed that he had not been clear so she understood what he meant.

"Why? We just came from there. Did you forget something important, like your brain? It's one hundred fifty miles round trip, and we just got here. I thought that was all behind us. Now, you want to go back?" she asked, sounding a bit confused.

"I just can't do it," he said.

"Can't do what?" she asked.

"I know what we agreed to. I know the Bokuru excavation site has to be closed down. I agree with that," he said.

"Then what's the problem?" she asked.

"I still have to go back," he said.

"Then spare me the mystery. Why do you need to go back? What is it that you have to do?"

"I can't just walk away from the Bokuru hominid. It's real Nancy. The site has to be abandoned, and I understand why, but the Bokuru hominid is a new species that lived on this earth two million years ago. I know it was far more intelligent than *Homo sapiens*. I just can't walk away from that. The world needs to know about the most important event in the natural history of the earth," said Jim.

"Tell, me, Jim, just how is going back out to Bokuru going to help?"

"Don't you see? No one would listen if we tried to tell the story of the Bokuru hominid without some proof," said Jim.

"What you are saying is that if you had some token, some real physical artifact that could prove its existence, you could hold the interest of some recognized archaeologist back home and induce him to come to the Bokuru River Valley and start a new site to prove the existence of the hominid," Nancy replied wryly.

"Yes. I just can't let the Bokuru hominid be lost to the ages because of an error at this one site. The hominid is too important. Human history can't be allowed to hang on the simple transposition of two numbers. The public has to know about it, Nancy."

"So you propose to drive back out there in the wee hours of the night, grab some artifact before it is buried, and dash back here with your loot. Then, somehow, you plan to sneak your evidence out of the country so you can tell the world about the Bokuru hominid using that token as proof?" she asked.

"Yes, something like that. I don't have all the details worked out, but that's the general idea."

"You know, I can't be involved in this. I believe in the hominid, too. I really do, but I've made a commitment that I plan to honor. I'm not going to get into any crazy, wild goose chase. Do you have any idea what could happen if you were caught plundering an archaeological site in Uhuru? I've never seen their jails, and I'm sure I don't want to."

"It's a calculated risk. Due to the significance of the hominid, I'm willing to take the chance. It's something I have to do," Jim was emphatic.

"I understand your concern for the hominid. I share your interest. I'm just not wild about your means to find a way to tell the world about it," she said.

"I have to live with myself. I just can't leave Africa without doing something. It's all I can think of," said Jim.

"What do you expect me to do?" she asked. "Do you expect me to give you my blessing? A kiss on the cheek? Turn over the keys to the Jeep and sit here getting silly on a bottle of wine while you are out on your crazy caper? I can't do that Jim, and you know it."

"I can rent a vehicle. The front desk will make the arrangements for me," said Jim.

"No. You can't do that. If you go alone out there, you'll either get lost and never be found or you'll slip into soft sand and be discovered the next day. In which case, you'll be arrested on the spot and charged with goodness knows what crimes. I'm not going back to Chicago on that plane without you. I went to great expense to bring you here to Africa so I have an obligation to be sure you're on that flight."

"I can still make the flight. There's time," said Jim.

"I have this sinking feeling that I'm sliding down a slippery slope, but if you absolutely insist on this hair-brained scheme of going back out there, then I'm going with you."

"I don't want you to do that," said Jim. "You'd be putting yourself at risk."

"That's not your call. Besides, I have the keys to the Jeep. I don't believe in your plan, but I'm worried about you. The only way I would feel comfortable about this is to be the driver both out and back. The African savannah is not a Sunday drive along Lake Shore Drive in Chicago."

"This isn't your issue. It's too risky for you," said Jim.

"It's the only deal that will keep me from calling the territorial police and having you arrested before you start," she said.

"No choice?" he asked

"No choice," she said. "If you go out there, you're not going alone."

"If you're the designated driver, you know what that means."

"No. What?" she asked.

"No more wine. We're going in the dark. All I need is something I can use as proof of the hominid's existence, enough to reach the right people. Without some hard evidence, Nancy, no one will ever believe that such a creature existed so long ago," said Jim.

"You're fooling yourself if you think some evidence means anything other than the skull of hominid H0-011," she said. "Nothing else will work. The record books and the post cranium skeleton would not mean a thing without that skull, and you know the problem with the log. You are going out there on the assumption the skull has been returned to the site away from the camp, yet it still hasn't been destroyed or buried."

"You're right," said Jim. "I know it's a long shot, but I need that skull."

"Your plan has a chance of one in a million in my opinion," she said.

"Yes, maybe, but I've got to try," said Jim.

"Then we leave at midnight. At least we'll have moonlight."

Nancy's final consent to go with him had been partially based on the remote hope that he would fall asleep before it was time to leave, and the venture would be forgotten.

However, Jim remained alert all evening, and he was ready to go when the time came. The final thirty minutes of the trip was difficult and slow because they traveled without headlights to avoid being detected by anyone at the camp. Thankfully, the moon was almost full, hidden only occasionally by thin scattered clouds that raced silently across the night sky. By 2:00 AM they were up in the rocks on the south side of the Bokuru River, not far downstream from the camp. They had avoided the last stretch of road that led to the ford across the stream to avoid being heard or seen. Moonlight helped them see their way up through the rocks. Clouds blocked out the moonlight for a few brief moments at a time, but otherwise its soft light gave them a clear view of their surroundings. Each time the moon was blocked by a passing cloud, they paused and waited for the moonlight to reappear. Eventually, they reached the top of the riverbank without incident.

Jim stood partially hidden behind a large rock and adjusted the binoculars so he could look up at the bluff on the opposite side of the river. After a few moments squinting through the lenses, he found the camp. The white mess tent stood out. The lantern that was usually hanging from a hook in the interior was now hanging from a pole rigged high outside the front of the tent. He could not see the bunk tent because it was directly behind the mess tent, but he remembered that it had no lantern. It looked as if they were in luck and everyone was asleep. There was no sign of activity.

He watched for some time, panning the glasses back and forth over the terrain west of the camp, then swept his sights down to the river and back again to the camp.

"What can you see?" Nancy whispered from behind him.

For a moment, he did not answer. Finally he stepped back, lowered the glasses, and handed them to her where she remained hidden behind the rock.

"It's over," he said, in a soft whisper.

"What is?" she asked, accepting the binoculars, as she slipped around in front of him where she had a better view.

"Look for yourself. It's all gone," he said, stepping aside so she had a clear view across the river.

"What is?" she asked, as she took her turn to squint through the binoculars. "I don't see anything."

"Look a little lower to your left," said Jim, reaching out to help her aim the binoculars in the right direction.

"Oh, yes, I see it. There's the tent. I can see a lantern," she said.

"Yes," said Jim. "Can you see that light hanging on the pole outside the tent?"

"Yes. I can see the lantern," she said.

"Doesn't that bother you?" he asked.

"Why should it?" she asked.

"Who needs a lantern hanging on a post outside the tent? I don't think anyone is up," Jim added. "No one would benefit by putting the lantern up outside, over the tent. Everything is quiet. They've gone to sleep. There's no need for that lantern."

"I give up," she answered. "Why is the lamp out side the tent? They can't see inside with it out there. It's never been out there before that I can remember."

"It's not for them," he said.

"It's not?" she asked.

"No. It's for us."

"I don't get it, Jim?"

"It's a warning."

"A warning? What do you mean?" she asked.

"It's there to warn us to stay away. Smythe knew we would come back. The light is to let us know they are aware we are coming and to tell us to go back. We were supposed to see the light from back out on the savannah, but we were too busy navigating through the moonlight. We were supposed to see the light from a distance and think they were still up. They hoped we would turn around and go back to Elizabethtown. They didn't think we would come this far."

"We did though," she whispered. "We're here."

"Yes, but we're too late. Pan the glasses down along the trail and look for the excavation site."

"I am, but all I can see is the mess tent. The tent stands out in the moonlight and the light of the lantern," she said. "I can't see the site at all."

"Look further to your left. Can you see the dirt trail that leads down to the site?"

"I don't think so. I'm not sure," she said, looking intently through the field glasses.

"Well, try to follow where you remember it was, along the top of the ridge, then turn down where you think the site should be," said Jim.

"I can't find it. I'm trying, but I still don't see the site."

"The moon is out," said Jim. "Look again closely."

"Yes. I can see the moon is out, but it's not helping me."

"The moonlight should reflect off the white supply tent as well as the sun awning stretched over the excavation pit. They are both bright white. They should stand out like the mess tent," said Jim.

"Yes, I agree," she said, concentrating on the view through the glasses.

"Let me give you a hint," he said. "Both white canvases should be almost directly across the river from here, maybe just a little further up stream."

"I'm looking there, but I don't see anything," she said.

"If you look closer, you will see the tractor that was parked up by the camp this morning when we left. It's not bright white, but it's right where the excavation should be. You may not be able to see it clearly, but it's there."

"I still don't see a thing, Jim. I'm sorry I'm having so much trouble. Maybe it's the way I'm holding these binoculars," she said.

"You're doing fine. You saw the mess tent at the camp?"

"Yes," she said.

"You don't see anything at the site because there is nothing to see," said Jim. "There's nothing there except the tractor. The tents and the sun tarp are gone."

"Gone?" Nancy gasped.

"Don't you see? They have already plowed in the excavation pit. They must have filled it in this afternoon, right after we left, while we were on our way back to Elizabethtown."

"I'll have to take your word about the tractor. I can't see it. I agree the tarp and the tent should stand out, but there's nothing there," she said.

"Everything has been buried, Nancy. Smythe wasted no time. He could not take the chance that we would come back."

"Do you really think they anticipated we would come back out here tonight?" she asked.

"Not they, Smythe and Tubojola. Absolutely. That's why Dr. Tubojola put Smythe in charge, and left him out here. Mobutu could have done the job, but he would have taken a couple of days to do it. I think Tubojola was also concerned that Mobutu might have assisted us if we had reached him in time," said Jim.

"I see what you mean."

"Dr. Tubojola gave Smythe instructions to do what had to be done quickly just in case we had second thoughts and decided to come back this evening," said Jim. "The whole plan of hustling us out of camp and then onto the plane tomorrow was all designed to get us out of the country quickly. He wanted to be sure we didn't have second thoughts and try to come back out here to save something," said Jim. "He was steps ahead of us."

"He probably knows we are here now."

"Exactly," said Jim.

"So, there's no chance the skull might still be up at the camp?"

"No way. That was the most important evidence. They would have put it at the bottom of the pit just before they started to fill it in. The skull and the logbook and all the other boxes of fossils would have been in the bottom of the pit before they did anything else. Everything is buried, Nancy. Dr. Tubojola knew what he was doing when he put Smythe in charge. He was way ahead of us."

"How can you get any evidence of the hominid now?" she asked.

"I can't. It's too late. I've brought you out here for nothing. Returning to Bokuru wasn't your idea. It was mine. This whole trip was a mistake. It was a knee jerk reaction on my part. I gambled that Smythe wouldn't start to fill in the excavation pit until tomorrow," said Jim.

"You didn't know. Your idea was good," she said, as she lowered the binoculars.

"I let you down. You brought me here to Africa to think, not to do foolish things like sneaking out here in the dark."

"Your concern about recovering some evidence was not foolish. If you want to tell the story of the Bokuru hominid, you have to prove it existed with hard evidence. If you don't have proof, no one will believe you. You're right about that."

"Look," he said, "Point the binoculars down toward the river."

"I can see the river without them," she protested. "I don't need the binoculars to see the river."

She handed the binoculars back to Jim, but he pushed them back to her. She used them to take a quick look where he was pointing.

"I can see the river. It's right where it should be," she said, sarcastically.

"So," he said, "How were we going to get across? We can't drive across the ford in the Jeep because we would wake someone up."

"That's why we are down here, away from the road," she answered.

"We can't wade across, up by the camp, because we would most likely be seen. Down here, the river is narrower, but the current is too strong, and it's deep," he added.

"There was an old boat right by the ford," she said. "You could have used that."

"If you looked at that boat closely when we drove across before, it was full of water. I think it's sitting on the bottom of the riverbed," said Jim.

"Oh, I forgot. You're right. I told you they had to fix it," said Nancy.

"Yes, and we both forgot about your crocodile. Don't you see, I didn't even think about how we were going to cross the river? Coming out here was just a stupid reaction."

"Well, I didn't think about it either. You're not alone," said Nancy.

"I don't know what really happened in that finish tent when your father was alive, but I don't believe the Bokuru hominid is a fake, Nancy. I believe it's real. Bokuru was no Piltdown."

"I agree. I know my father would not fabricate such a thing," she said. "I also understand why Dr. Tubojola made the decision he did."

"I'm not questioning his conclusions. It is the existence of the hominid that needs to be told to modern science. Now, without proof, there is nothing we can do. There is no story to tell," said Jim.

"If my father did not destroy the scientific integrity of this site, Dr. Tubojola and his assistant did this morning," said Nancy. "This site is dead, no matter how you look at it. All you could ever do is stir up enough interest for other archaeologists to look for other sites on the slight chance of finding another Bokuru hominid," said Nancy.

"Unfortunately, our trip out here was a waste of time. The Bokuru hominid is lost forever. We are at risk if someone sees us," he said.

"Look, I came here with you voluntarily. You had a simple objective of bringing back some evidence of the existence of the hominid. You can't do that now, but someone else will come out here someday," she said. "They'll find a new site."

"You forget that all the permits and licenses are controlled by Dr. Tubojola."

"I think there have to be other sites along the river. Other archaeologists will look for other new sites. You're right; Dr. Tubojola won't let anyone dig up Bokuru, but there must be other locations where remains of the hominid may be found."

"You sound confident of that," said Jim.

"There have to be more sites in the river valley. The population in this one cave could not survive alone. Our knowledge of genetics tells me that the dangers of inbreeding alone indicate that there are many other sites along the river somewhere."

"First, someone has to have a license to come out here just to look around. Then they have to find evidence of another site. If they are lucky in that, then they have to obtain another license as an archaeologist to obtain a permit to dig. Personally, I think Dr. Tubojola wouldn't let anyone near the Bokuru River Valley again," said Jim.

She handed him back the binoculars.

"I could not sit idly by after luring you to Africa, then wait for you to return from a dangerous mission out here by yourself. I cannot sit around worrying about you, but I also have some concerns about the Bokuru hominid, too. I'm not sure I agree with you about Dr. Tubojola possibly blocking others from looking for other, future sites. He's a scientist."

"No, he's a politician. I think this was the one and only chance to save the Bokuru hominid. The battle had to be won at the hearing in the tent. Dr. Tubojola won more than just closing the site. He closed the door to the scientific existence of the Bokuru hominid. From the moment he decided to bury the site, there was nothing more we could do. You should have made me listen to reason before we came back out here," said Jim.

"I knew better than to argue with you. Your mind was set. You would not have listened to me. The decision to return was something you had to do. You had to make your own decisions and come to your own conclusions," said Nancy.

"You're probably right, but I'm still not so sure I share your enthusiasm about other sites," said Jim. "Unless I miss my guess about Dr. Tubojola, he will block any effort for anyone else to come out here," said Jim.

"Why do you say that?" she asked.

"Like I said, Dr. Tubojola controls all licenses and permits."

"So?" she asked.

"I don't know what really makes him tick. In the end, the decision to issue new licenses will depend on his inner beliefs," said Jim. "I think the question will be whether his beliefs override an open mind to factual scientific inquiry. Personally, I don't know where he stands on that issue. I really don't. Maybe he could not accept what the Bokuru hominid represents."

"He was quite convincing to me. He did what he had to do," she said. "I understand his decision. I think any one of us in his position would have done the same thing."

"Maybe, but we still do not know his inner beliefs. The key to future exploration and excavations out here hinges on his deeper beliefs. He will issue or deny future licensing based on those beliefs."

"The eternal question, belief versus science," she said in resignation.

"Yes, you've got it. That's not our issue. The future here is in Dr. Tubojola's hands. Right now it's time for us to get out of here before anyone discovers we are here," he said, leading her back down through the boulders.

"If you are ready to give up, then I am, too," Nancy responded seriously. "We are both in danger being here. The sooner we get out of here, the better."

"Okay, we're on our way," he said.

"Just because you can't do anything here, it's not the end of the world. You must find another way to get the message out," she said, following him back to the Jeep.

"There's nothing I can do now," he said

"Then Dr. Tubojola was right," she said.

"How's that?" he asked.

"We'd better be on that plane."

CHAPTER TWENTY-TWO: *THE EXAM*

When they finally arrived back in Elizabethtown, it was still dark. Nancy did not stay. She dropped Jim off at his hotel, then continued alone back to Nairobi. There was, she said, not enough time to get ready to make their flight that afternoon unless she left immediately. She had a lot to do to get ready to leave Africa. She told him she would meet him at the airline gate.

Jim finished packing his clothes and gear into his two duffle bags. He'd had very little sleep, but he was wide-awake when the alarm went off at 8:30 AM. He found the hotel daily circular protruding under the door. The flier posted the bus schedule to the airport in Nairobi. He would have to make the 10:00 AM bus departure to be sure of making the airline flight scheduled by Dr. Tubojola out of Uhuru.

At 9:30 AM the phone rang. He anticipated the front desk would want to confirm his check out time and baggage pick up. Instead, he was informed that Dr. Umbawi was in the lobby ready to take him to the airport. This change, he had not anticipated. He was not aware of any plans for Dr. Umbawi to pick him up. After the events of the day before, Jim was convinced that he would never see Dr. Umbawi again. Dr. Umbawi had barely looked at Jim during the "trial" at Bokuru. In fact, Jim was convinced that Dr. Umbawi had intentionally avoided him.

Now, suddenly, Dr. Umbawi was here to personally pick Jim up, without any advance notice. That meant Dr. Umbawi had driven all the way from Nairobi to escort Jim back to the airport, a round trip of over 90 kilometers. Such an undertaking, Jim thought, was strange. He checked the room one more time to be sure he had not forgotten anything when he packed. He called the front desk to pick up his bags, then grabbed his briefcase, and went down the two flights of stairs to the lobby. Somehow he felt awkward wearing a suit and tie again.

Dr. Umbawi was seated in one of the big, overstuffed chairs in the lobby. The hotel staff had set up a continental buffet table with a complementary pot of fresh coffee and rolls next to his seat. Jim took the chair opposite him. At first, Dr. Umbawi did not look up. He was engrossed in a Nairobi newspaper.

"Good morning," said Jim, as he eased into the chair.

"Oh, Jim, good morning," said Dr. Umbawi casually, looking over the top of the paper. "Please help yourself to some coffee. It's self-serve this morning. You'll need the coffee. We have a long trip back to Nairobi. There's not enough time for a full breakfast, I'm afraid."

"Thanks," said Jim, putting down his briefcase. He went over to the small service table where he poured himself a cup of coffee, spread cream cheese onto a roll and balanced the roll on his saucer while returning to his seat.

"I know you are surprised at my being here, Jim, but there are some things I would like to go over with you before you leave Africa."

Jim settled into his chair, being careful not to spill his coffee.

"Well, frankly, I thought I would never hear from you or see you again after yesterday. I thought you had disowned me," said Jim.

"Give me some time, and I will explain," said Dr. Umbawi, putting his newspaper down momentarily. "I know showing up here this morning without calling you is a bit presumptuous of me, but I was concerned you would talk to Nancy. She's a good woman, Jim. If I told her I was coming to pick you up, she might have wanted to come along for the ride. She doesn't know I'm here. In fact, no one does, including my wife."

"Sounds a little mysterious," said Jim, taking a sip of coffee.

Dr. Umbawi paused for a couple of moments while he took a black pen out of his shirt pocket and circled two articles on the front page of the paper. When he had finished, he looked up at Jim, smiled, and then handed Jim the newspaper. "Have you had a chance to read the paper this morning?" Dr. Umbawi asked.

"No," said Jim. "I just got up."

"Keep this one. In fact, take it with you. There is a reason for my cloak and dagger routine this morning. I don't want to sound melodramatic or anything, but I think what I have to say is best done in confidence. The events of yesterday morning upset my plans. Then, suddenly this morning, I realized we were out of time."

"Well, yes. Dr. Tubojola has whisked me out of Africa without much notice and with barely enough time to pack," said Jim. "He did the same to Nancy."

"You know," said Dr. Umbawi, changing the subject. "I do like the ambiance of this old hotel. I've come here for years. It's become like a second home for me."

"Yes. It is very nice," said Jim. "I have the feeling of being whisked back a hundred years in time."

"I genuinely like the place, Jim, but it has a problem."

"A problem? You said you eat here all the time. The food has been good while I've been here, and the service was good, too," said Jim.

333

"Oh, yes, the service is excellent as is the food. I agree, but unfortunately, even the walls in this place have ears. You must be careful of what you say."

"So, you are saying we can't talk here, which means you are ready to go right away," said Jim, gulping down the rest of his coffee. He noticed that Dr. Umbawi's cup was empty and had already been returned to the service table before Jim arrived.

"Well, if you're going to make that flight with Nancy, and I think it's important that you do, we need to be on the road," said Dr. Umbawi. "Bring that roll with you. You can finish it on the way. It's a long ride."

"I'm ready," said Jim, as he rose to put his cup back on the service table.

"My Land Rover is right out front. Your bags will already be in the back. Don't forget that newspaper. You can look at it while we are on our way. You don't have to read the whole thing. Just don't miss the articles I marked on the front page," said Dr. Umbawi.

"I'll bring it," said Jim, as he picked up the paper, folded it, and put it into his briefcase.

"Sign out at the front desk on your way out. They've already prepared your bill. Once you sign it, they'll fax it to the museum in Chicago. Your signature is authorization for the museum to pay it. There is nothing else for you to do."

"No problem," said Jim. "I think I saw the porter going up for my bags when I came downstairs."

"Yes. Well, good. He knows me, and he knows my Land Rover. I'm sure your bags will already be in the back ready to go. They're very efficient here."

Within a few minutes they were on their way out of Elizabethtown, traveling on the Outer Territories Road, on the way to Nairobi. Until they reached the outskirts of town Dr. Umbawi drove in silence.

"Someday this won't be necessary," he said looking over at Jim.

"How is that?" Jim asked.

"They'll have commuter plane service from Elizabethtown to the airport in Nairobi."

"That would be convenient," said Jim.

"Yes, but it won't be available for a few years," said Dr. Umbawi.

"What's the delay? Couldn't they use it now?" Jim asked.

"Elizabethtown has no airport to speak of. All they have is a dirt strip for private planes. If they want the tourists to travel by air, they are going to have to upgrade the runway and pave it for commercial planes," said Dr. Umbawi.

"Dr. Tubojola may have mentioned the airport was a future project," said Jim.

"Yes, but I'll bet he didn't say how far into the future, did he?"

"No, he didn't," said Jim.

"I wanted to apologize again for my behavior yesterday, Jim, and my arrogance for simply showing up this morning."

"That's all right," said Jim. "I wasn't looking forward to riding in the hotel bus. Your Land Rover is much more comfortable. Besides, this way I have someone to talk to. Your company will make the trip seem shorter."

"Good. If you remember, I told you to watch carefully who people were to determine how they would act in certain situations."

"Yes, you did," said Jim. "I remember your comment."

"Then you will also recall that I am merely a guest here in Uhuru, just like you. I am an outside consultant to Dr. Tubojola's department. I just happened to be in the museum in Elizabethtown yesterday morning for an early meeting of the Antiquities Department. During the excavation of a lake for the north basin project in Karanga National Park, the construction crew inadvertently stumbled onto some fossilized bones of what the museum people initially thought might be a rare extinct giraffe."

"Dr. Tubojola told me about the discovery," said Jim.

"Good. I was brought in to confirm the identification of the fossils discovered. Anyway, Dr. Tubojola found me in the museum lobby early yesterday morning. I was drafted on the spot for the trip to Bokuru. All Dr. Tubojola told me was there was an emergency meeting at Bokuru. I had no warning of what had happened, or what to expect."

"So, he didn't tell you about the Bokuru hominid in advance?"

"No, and he made it clear that he brought me along as merely an observer, a witness, not as a participant," said Dr. Umbawi.

"I can believe that," said Jim. "He would not want anyone to upstage him."

"I have known Dr. Tubojola for many years, Jim. I have learned when to express an opinion and when to remain silent. Besides, there was little I could add. It seemed to me you were doing quite well on your own."

"Dr. Tubojola did all the talking. It was hard to get a word in edgewise. It was all his show," said Jim.

"So you do understand," said Dr. Umbawi. "Dr. Tubojola is one of the top three administrators in Uhuru, and he is very opinionated. You don't win many arguments against people in those kinds of positions and authority, at least not in a direct confrontation."

"You're right about that."

"I know my appearance this morning was a surprise. I had to make an emergency change in my plans for the day. Have you had time to look at the newspaper I gave you?"

"No. I was just finishing my roll, but I have the paper right here. I see the two articles you circled on the first page. The top one addresses a bombing in Jerusalem, and the second one describes a mobbing at an archaeological dig in southern Israel," said Jim, as he quickly scanned the front page.

"Yes. Good," said Dr. Umbawi. "Middle East unrest is a world away from Uhuru, but it is, never the less, directly related to what we do, even in this remote part of Africa."

"How so? I don't see any correlation," asked Jim, puzzled.

"Modern archaeology has its roots in the Middle East where, some time ago, a handful of self-declared experts showed up. They had a Bible in one hand and mason's trowel in the other. They brought with them the assumption they could find God in the dirt, and prove his existence to everyone else by validating the early biblical stories with archaeological evidence."

"That doesn't sound very scientific," said Jim.

"What they did wasn't science then any more than it is today. They called themselves archaeologists and showed up with a self-imposed directive to prove the biblical stories were true."

"Where did they get the money?" asked Jim.

"The cash came from many vested interests in Europe. No one wanted to know the facts for what they really were. The financiers wanted the researchers to come up with the results that supported their position. My point is that the early archaeologists gave their sponsors exactly what they wanted, which of course was no surprise to anyone."

"You don't sound like you think much of early archaeology," said Jim.

"Unfortunately, that is how modern archaeology was born. The early researchers had to produce or lose their funding, so it was easy to simply distort the facts to show the sponsors the results they desired," said Dr. Umbawi. "Politically correct results would assure a continued flow of funding. Unfortunately, even today, archaeologists often lock into set positions of what they believe is correct for all sorts of reasons, sometimes even in defiance of the evidence they find. I might add, they either do not see or simply do not want to see the truth."

"Are you trying to say things are no better now?" asked Jim.

"In some ways, we could even say things are worse," said Dr. Umbawi. "Sometimes, I think archaeology in the Middle East is almost a misnomer. The political pressure is too great because everything is at stake. We have a clash of two widely different cultural groups. After World War II, the allies had this enormous problem of cultural refugees. Their first concern was to avoid another holocaust."

"How could they be sure of that?" asked Jim.

"They couldn't, so they decided the best solution was to relocate the refugees to what we now call Israel. The general public was convinced Israel was the land of the biblical stories, which people argued, gave them historical rights to the land."

"Are you saying they could have been wrong?" asked Jim.

"The problem was, no one paid attention to the fact that this solution caused another problem."

"Another problem?' asked Jim.

"Where do you relocate the inhabitants of that land who were already there?" asked Dr. Umbawi.

"That's why the violence goes on," Jim observed.

"Some say the land is theirs by historical right, citing the old biblical stories, and others want their homes back because they were physically there first. Your country was one of those that came up with the present solution, and had the clout to enforce it. Now, as a result, America is the target of extremists. I digress, forgive me," said Dr. Umbawi.

"But archaeology is important. It is now a true science," said Jim.

"Yes, but you must look at the details of what is done in the name of science very carefully. Please go on to the second article."

"You mean this one, about the desecration of the archaeological site in Israel?"

"Yes. That activity is not new either. If a real discovery is not, shall we say, politically correct at the moment, people will deny its validity. In the right political environment, they will even destroy the site."

"That sounds harsh," said Jim.

"I could give you many examples in human history where such acts have been undertaken. What I'm trying to say, Jim, is that human beings don't necessarily like or want to know the truth. The science of archaeology has been struggling with this problem from its inception. All too often, science has to pay the price. Humanity doesn't always like facts, Jim, unless the facts are politically acceptable at the time."

"Yes, I remember the story of the brontosaurus in our country where the first major find had no head, so someone added one they thought was appropriate from another totally unrelated site, and everyone adopted it as truth. The head in fact, had no real scientific relationship with the body. That error took years to straighten out," said Jim. "They are still struggling to correct the proper stance of several dinosaurs after initial assumptions have been found to be incorrect. They have to keep changing the museum displays. Look at Tyrannosaurus Rex."

"Precisely, Jim. Scientists are no different from any other human beings. They try, but they often suffer from the same human frailties and misconceptions as everyone else. The Middle East with it's volatile political situation often shows the bad side of archaeology where those in favor of one side press on to find verification of the biblical stories, while the other side challenges any discovery and will desecrate or destroy it if it gives any substance to political views other than their own," said Dr. Umbawi.

"The Middle East is a morass," said Jim. "It's been a mess for a long time."

"Look at it this way, Israel would be in serious trouble if the stories aren't true. If the biblical stories are fiction, the original decision could have involved a relocation of the Jewish nation somewhere else. Did you know that one of the other alternatives considered was farther away on the island of Madagascar?"

"I never heard that before," said Jim. "Aren't you being a bit extreme?"

"Perhaps. Try to understand, Jim. The articles are there in your newspaper, but my editorial comments are not being expressed for their truth."

"They're not?" asked Jim.

"No. I'm trying to open your mind to other views, right or wrong, that are different from your preconceived notions. I'm trying to shock you into thinking. Good students consider all the alternatives."

"I see," said Jim.

"That is why I came to pick you up. I was afraid you would leave Africa with a closed mind."

"So, you didn't come all the way to Elizabethtown to tell me about the Middle East?" asked Jim.

"No, certainly not. I just wanted to show you how the science of archaeology is often compromised by political pressures, and how, in the end, the advancement of science often suffers. The Middle East is a problem. It's a big problem, but it is not our problem this morning."

"You're trying to tell me that I don't have an open mind," said Jim.

"You need to look at the big picture. You need to be more observant of what is really going on. Yesterday, I was brought out to Bokuru to give some psychological support to what Dr. Tubojola did."

"To support Dr. Tubojola? You didn't say anything," said Jim.

"He knew you would respect me. He hoped my appearance on his side of the table would impress you."

"I'm not sure you had any effect," said Jim.

"Dr. Tubojola is a strong force in reality, Jim. In your training for your profession, you had to learn to stand up and speak for yourself. You have to deal with the real world and all the people like Dr. Tubojola who reside there. Don't forget, I'm just an educator and a consultant. My position is never to speak up unless asked to do so. I have attended many meetings where my presence is required, but my opinions are not requested, simply ignored, or specifically silenced."

"Yesterday, I felt abandoned," said Jim.

"Of course. That was Dr. Tubojola's objective. Try to understand Dr. Tubojola. He is an administrator. He is Minister of the Interior. His responsibilities include the Department of Antiquities, the Department of Natural Resources, and the Department of Wildlife."

"Yes, I know," said Jim.

"He is building one of the largest wildlife parks in this part of the continent. It is impossible for him to handle all these responsibilities unless he is organized and knows how to prioritize."

"Okay," said Jim. "He discussed his managerial style with me when I first met and interviewed him."

"He has to make a list each day of the most important outstanding issues requiring action and then reduce things down to the bare essentials so he can make the right decision on them, and then move on to the next item on his agenda. He has to be quick and decisive, Jim. He's a busy man."

"Yes. I agree those are characteristics are required for someone in his position," said Jim.

"Remember, I told you Dr. Tubojola is primarily a politician. I think I told you the other evening that politics and archaeology are strange bedfellows, Jim, even in the best of times. To be honest, they don't mix, but that is where Dr. Tubojola resides all day, every day. Then, do not expect people to act out of character. What he did was entirely predictable."

"He was very convincing about what he had to do," said Jim.

"He is a very intelligent man. He does have a point, and we should respect his views."

"But, you didn't come all the way out here to pick me up, just to tell me to accept the views of Dr. Tubojola," said Jim.

"No, hardly," said Dr. Umbawi. "Nor did I come out here to lecture you about the Middle East. My objective is to get you to think. All a teacher can do is to induce the student to look at a problem with different perspectives. I know you have been deeply concerned about the Bokuru hominid. Yet, I ask that you accept Dr. Tubojola's arguments. You will not gain any satisfaction by fighting him or going against his decisions. You will have no success if you try to go out into the world in a futile effort to prove that the hominid existed."

"Then what do you want from me?" asked Jim.

"What I'm trying to do is to light a fire. What I am trying to do is get you to recognize that your future does not lie in that direction. Your destiny is elsewhere. What I am trying to say is, even if you could get the attention of anyone to consider the possibility of the past existence of the Bokuru hominid, you are likely to ruffle a few too many feathers and find yourself on the defensive without any evidence to support your position. If that happens, the focus of attention will be lost and the real issues will be missed."

"I think I understand," said Jim.

"I think you have a pretty good understanding of the issues raised by the Bokuru hominid. The reason you are upset is that there has been a wrong committed here that affects not only you but also everyone else in the world, as well. Dr. Tubojola has effectively muzzled you. You know you can tell the Bokuru story because you have lived through it. Your conscience will not allow you to leave it buried beneath the sands of Uhuru. I know you are deeply troubled by the loss of the Bokuru hominid. I know you must do something, but I want you to be effective in what you do and not a target for overwhelming criticism," said Dr. Umbawi.

"You're right. I can't just walk away and I can't go back on my word to Dr. Tubojola and the others."

"Of course. You know the story, so you must tell it. To keep the story from the public is immoral."

"I fear that no one will believe me no matter what I do," said Jim.

"To tell the story you will have to be brave, perhaps more so than you ever have been in your life. Don't underestimate your mission."

"If I only understood how I am supposed to tell the story," said Jim.

"Look, Jim. There was a time before you were here on this earth."

"Yes, I understand the earth was here long before I was born."

"Good. Then understand that there will be a time after you are gone. Life is the fleeting moment between those events. Rejoice in it, but make your time meaningful. People fear death because they are afraid of the unknown, but if death is just a big nothing, Jim, then there is nothing to fear. Life is a privilege, a gift, no matter how brief, no matter how painful, no matter how we screw it up, and no matter how unfair it is. Who are we to ask for more than what we get?"

"You're right," said Jim.

"Oh, we are about to reach the border. You'll need your visa."

Jim's visa was a bit of a problem. It was not in his briefcase as he thought. They were delayed while he rummaged through his duffle bags until he found it. When they were underway again, they were behind schedule. For some time, Dr. Umbawi drove on in silence, concentrating on the road, leaving Jim alone with his thoughts.

"We have a road block ahead. It's just around the bend," said Dr. Umbawi, as he slowed down in anticipation of a delay.

"A road block?" asked Jim, looking up from the paper. "Why?"

"It seems a fellow is moving his herd of cattle across the road. We're going to have to wait for him. We have no choice."

Dr. Umbawi stopped the Land Rover, and they both got out to watch the Masai use a short stick to prod his herd of cattle across the road.

"Do you remember I asked you the other evening if you believed in an ultimate being?" asked Dr. Umbawi.

"Yes. I remember. You didn't give me time to answer the question," said Jim.

"It all comes down to the 'R' word, Jim."

"The 'R' word? You mean religion?" asked Jim.

"No. The 'R' word is random, Jim."

"Random?"

"Yes, random. You told me Eric and David worked at Bokuru because, in spite of their beliefs, they had made peace with science and archaeology. They thought both concepts were compatible."

"Yes. That's what they implied," said Jim.

"In their case, I think it's sloppy thinking, Jim. On one side, there are the creationists. You don't have to believe there is an elderly, white Anglo-Saxon grandfather type floating around on a cloud to fall in that classification."

"Oh?" asked Jim.

"You don't have to believe in a place where you go when you die so you can sit around for eternity playing a golden harp, either. It's not that simple," said Dr. Umbawi.

"It's not?" Jim asked, no knowing where Dr. Umbawi was leading him now.

"Creationists are those who believe there is some ultimate, intelligent force that, at least initially, put things in motion and spent time and energy to make things happen. There are as many opinions of the degree to which there is personal involvement by the supreme being in our individual lives on a daily basis as there are creationists, but they all agree about divine creation at the beginning of the universe. That's what identifies them," said Dr. Umbawi.

"Okay," said Jim. "I'm with you on that."

"On the other side is the application of the 'R' word. The true scientist says everything that happens in the universe, including its own existence, is random. The world of true science is cold and uncaring, and is governed by events that are explainable but ultimately have a random source. In an ultimate sense, science and religion are opposites, Jim."

"So the temple is out in left field?"

"When you dig in, you find there are different degrees of both creationism and science in the minds of men. You cannot simply apply a label and hope to understand people."

"So there is no absolute answer as to which is right?" asked Jim.

"It is like me asking you if you believe in a creator. Remember, I am a teacher, and that question is not for me to answer. I present an opportunity for you to think for yourself. It is up to you to find the answer that suits you. I simply suggest that there are different views of science and religion. There are different shades of gray and no absolutes when it comes to asking people what they believe. Everyone has different thoughts and opinions," said Dr. Umbawi.

"But we are discussing truth. Opinions have nothing to do with truth."

"Sometimes truth is in the eyes of the beholder. Belief is the acceptance of something as a fundamental truth upon which you will adjust your behavior, without any factual proof. Science involves the application of proof to determine something fundamental, but let me muddy the waters a bit."

"I think you already have," said Jim.

"My observation is that every human mind is split into two distinct areas."

"They are, Dr. Umbawi. The human brain has been dissected. It has two separate, distinctly different halves," said Jim. "That is common knowledge."

"I don't mean in a physical sense, Jim. I mean that each human mind has two totally different ways in which it perceives and reacts to the world in which it exists. One part demands strict proof, the second part houses belief where no facts are involved. I'm not trying to criticize, only make an observation of human behavior. Everyone functions daily using both concepts. Both functions are required for the individual to survive."

"I don't understand. I thought we could not have two opposite ideas in our minds at the same time," said Jim.

"You do not get on an airplane unless you are sure of your facts. You want to know that flying is safe; that science can put the plane up in the sky; maintain it up there; and land it safely. If the mechanic comes out of the hanger, religious documents in hand, and said he has done nothing and all passengers should board based on their faith, no one would get on the plane. You accept the fact that sometimes planes do fall out of the sky, but you have this inner belief that it will happen to the other person, not you. If your plane has even a hint of trouble you pray, not to the pilot or the mechanic but to your individual perception of the ultimate creator," said Dr. Umbawi.

"You think we should be praying to the pilot and the mechanic?" said Jim.

"To them, or perhaps for them. Certainly, yes."

"Is that the only way we use two opposite sides of our brains?" asked Jim.

"We all put every issue we encounter into one category or the other, science or belief. People differ in that each of us puts different issues into different categories, so that the mix for use in survival differs in the combinations of the two."

"Do you think religion evolved with man?" asked Jim.

"At some time in our remote past, the concept of the self came into being, and with it the awareness of the concept of death. At the same time, we could not understand the natural world around us, so we put the unknown things we could not control into the realm of religion or superstition, which fits into the belief side of the brain. I can say the single deity concept is fairly recent in our history. I think some concept of religion evolved with us to give meaning to the death of the individual, just as being left or right handed has evolved. Specific religions come and go, but the concept of a religious belief is, I think, a part of us as thinking human beings."

"You do look at things in a different way," said Jim.

"Anyway, enough philosophy, Jim. Let's get going. We are already running too late for me to meet with Nancy. We'll make your flight, but you'll have to say goodbye to her for me. She'll be past security and at the gate ready to board before we get there."

They rode on in silence until Dr. Umbawi drove through the airport entrance.

"You didn't say why you didn't tell Nancy you were coming to pick me up," said Jim.

"Because the story of the Bokuru hominid must be told," said Dr. Umbawi.

"But I agreed to accept Dr. Tubojola's dictate of silence and say nothing about Bokuru?"

"Yes, but think of it this way. The existence of the hominid is important, and that story needs be told. You are the only one to do it. Nancy can't be involved because of where she works. I can't do it either, because I, too, am compromised. You, and you alone, are free to tell the story. All I can say is, if you are going to tell the story of the Bokuru hominid, however you do it, you need to look at things from a different point of view than from your cultural perspective," said Dr. Umbawi.

"Okay, but how?" asked Jim.

"Does it surprise you that Dr. Bronston was a religious man?"

"You said that before, but yes, it does," said Jim. "You just convinced me that science and religion are completely incompatible opposites. I cannot see the areas of gray that you talk about."

"Dr. Bronston did not believe in the conventional man on a cloud concept, nor did he believe there was a heaven as a place where everyone sits around for eternity on the right hand of the creator. In fact, Jim, he told me once that if that picture was real, he didn't want to go there," said Dr. Umbawi.

"You're kidding," said Jim.

"No. He said life on this earth was interesting and exciting. Heaven, he said, sounded dull and boring. He kept asking what were we going to do when we got there. He told me that if I got there first, to tell the creator to leave him out, that he was quite content to die here on earth and let it go at that."

"He said that?" asked Jim.

"Yes. Yet, at the same time, he said he did believe in an ultimate being that put the forces in motion that created the universe, but he did not have a picture of what that meant."

"What else did he say? I'm confused about his views," said Jim.

"He remembered visiting a cathedral in France while he was there for a European archaeological conference several years ago. He told me that he sat in on a Sunday sermon in one of the churches there. He remembered the awesome architecture, the sun streaking through the stained glass windows, the choir, the people in attendance."

"That's a human created environment," said Jim.

"Yes. I agree, but what he said was that he could feel the presence of the Creator, but he could not define it. He told me that he simply did not have the words to express what he felt."

"That's strange. It's hard to believe a scientist who spent his life using rational analysis could not describe what he meant, never mind have a strong religious belief," said Jim.

"I would agree with you, but he said he felt like a small child who was asked to draw a picture of the sun."

"The sun?" asked Jim.

"He said when asked to draw the sun, a young child will draw a circle, color it yellow, then add two eyes, a nose, and a mouth. He said he felt like that child. Adults are like children, he said. They can only see the creator in terms of themselves. That's why children draw faces on their sketches of the sun."

"Well, that is a good point. I don't think he is alone in that observation. He is a bit vague about what he means though. In my opinion, a scientist should be more specific," said Jim.

"We have seen terrorists kill in the name of God, Jim. Are they praying to a different God than the one their victims believe in?"

"I think I'm getting more confused," said Jim. "I still don't understand Dr. Bronston's beliefs."

"Let me share another conversation I had with Dr. Bronston. Perhaps it will help."

"Go ahead," said Jim.

"He asked me if I had ever been to Las Vegas."

"What has that got to do with religion?"

"Everything. He said that the average person who flies there for a long week end of gambling will allocate around $2,000.00 for gambling."

"I think I read that statistic somewhere," said Jim.

"His point was, that, at the end of the trip, when they get on the plane to go home the money is gone. That, he said, is what makes Las Vegas work. They call it the five percent factor, because the odds are stacked with a five percent bias in favor of the house."

"I've read that too, but only in the context of gambling," said Jim.

"Dr. Bronston said the world of science is correct in painting the universe as a cold place of random events. He could see how there were galaxies and stars and planets, but he could not see how life could exist anywhere. Life, he said, was something more than physical events. He said life could not exist without the five percent bias in its favor. Without a bias in favor of life, there would be no living things. He believed in the process of evolution, but without that bias, there would be no life to evolve. He called that bias the 'Creator.' I'm afraid he did not have any more of a definition than that," said Dr. Umbawi.

"That's it? That's your story?" asked Jim.

"No, not mine, Dr. Bronston's."

"I'm not sure it helps me," said Jim.

"There are a lot of rail splitters, Jim, who say they would like to accept evolution, but they see humanity as too intelligent."

"Too intelligent?" asked Jim.

"They say we are smarter than we need to be to survive on a day to day basis. They say that the concept of evolution does not allow for such an excess of intelligence. For that reason, they say, creation makes more sense than evolution."

"So, how do you explain our intelligence?" asked Jim.

"Those who see us as having extra intelligence are not looking at humanity very carefully. In fact, I think they could see the error of their ways if they watched the baboons more carefully before they turned their observations to mankind."

"How so? You lost me," said Jim.

"It all comes down to tools, Jim."

"Tools?"

"The key for survival of a species is for males impregnate as many females as they can, and for females to bring up as many successful children as they can. That's the bottom line. It is all that is of value in an evolutionary sense."

"But those people you were talking about believe we have more intelligence than we need," said Jim.

"Yes, and they say they do not see how altruism, love, affection, care for others can have any evolutionary value. They are wrong, Jim. We are not more intelligent than we need to be. We barely have enough to survive as it is."

"You lost me again. What were you saying about tools?"

"The key is to understand the ultimate tool."

"The ultimate tool?" asked Jim. "What is the ultimate tool?"

"The most successful people from an evolutionary sense are those who can produce the most successful offspring. The male must be able to obtain those things necessary for the female and her offspring to survive. The key is not the use of physical tools that we create with our hands. The fact is that we are social animals. We use others of our own kind to help us meet our needs. To say it another way, social connections are what we develop as tools to obtain our goals."

"Networks," said Jim.

"Precisely. That is the key to our survival. The most important survival characteristic is that we have a conscience. We are both aware of ourselves as individuals and we are aware of our neighbors and how our neighbors think. In addition, we can understand how those who are opposed to us think, as well. We can anticipate the reactions of others to the actions we take. This social awareness is a skill that has a survival advantage from an evolutionary standpoint. Human life is a world of ever changing interpersonal connections. We are constantly maneuvering for our own evolutionary advantage. Social success is a tool. The individuals who use it the best have the best survival potential. To succeed, social interaction skills are the most important tools you have."

"I never thought about intelligence that way before," said Jim.

"The ultimate key to the ability to understand your neighbor and how your neighbor will react is manipulation," said Dr. Umbawi.

"Manipulation?"

"Yes, the ability not only to understand how your neighbor will react to a set of circumstances, but to be able to set up a false set of circumstances to induce behavior that you know will benefit your own objectives is the most advanced of interpersonal interactions. That is something that *Homo sapiens* is very good at. Manipulation and control of others are the highest form of the skill of social communication."

"We are certainly good at deceiving others," said Jim. "I have to agree with that."

"You know, you may not realize it, Jim, but I was a student once, too. I particularly remember one exam I took back when I was in college at the university in Nairobi."

"You remember an exam from that long ago?" asked Jim.

"Yes. The professor even said we would never forget the exam, and he was right."

"What course was it?" asked Jim.

"Philosophy."

"It's amazing that you can still remember the exam so many years later."

347

"Yes. Not only was he a good teacher, but he was also an innovative one. He told us the exam would be three hours long. Then he told us we would each get three blue books for our answers."

"Oh, yes, I remember those blue books from law school," said Jim. "I don't have any good memories about blue books."

"He limited us to three books, nothing more and nothing less. He then told us he would entertain no questions about the exam. He assigned a proctor to the room and gave the gentleman a metronome."

"I had a metronome when I took take piano lessons," said Jim. "I tried to be a musician, but I was tone deaf. Anyway a metronome maintains a steady click at different set time intervals to set the pace of the music you are playing."

"Good. I remember its loud ticking. The exam was written on one sheet of paper, which the professor had placed inside the first blue book. When he left the exam room, he told the proctor the clock on the wall was to be used to time the exam, but the metronome was to run during the entire exam."

"That was a unique approach for an exam," said Jim.

"I'll never forget when the professor left the room and the proctor said we could begin. When I opened my first blue book and looked at the exam the single sheet of paper, I thought, this would not be too bad. You cannot imagine my reaction, Jim, when I turned that sheet over."

"I remember some law school exams and the bar exam that had me traumatized, too," said Jim. "Those memories stay with you."

"My heart skipped a beat."

"Why? Was it that bad?" Jim asked.

"It was worse. The backside was just like the front."

"I thought you said the front side was blank?"

"Both sides were blank, Jim. Here was the ultimate test. In addition, I had both time and space limitations to deal with."

"So, what did you do?" asked Jim.

"That was the hardest exam I ever took. For the first time in my life, I had to really think and plan what my response was going to be. I was constantly reminded of the time factor, because always there was the sound of the clicking metronome."

"How did you handle it?" Jim asked.

"There are always questions, especially in philosophy. The questions were not the problem. The issues are always the answers, Jim. The exam was like life."

"Like life?"

"There are no answers. There are no easy answers in life. The answers are always specific to the individual who has to struggle to find them."

"I see why you remember the exam so well," said Jim.

"I have digressed. It is time to drop you off and send you out into the real world," said Dr. Umbawi, as he drove up to the curb.

"You're right. We're already at the terminal," said Jim. "The drive went very quickly."

"Personally, I don't think you need an exam. We can save you the terror of what I went through. Just remember to recognize that the world is full of questions, not answers. All I can say is that the story of the Bokuru hominid must be told, and you are the only one who can do it. That, my friend, is my message this morning. It is time for me to leave you here at the gate."

Dr. Umbawi stopped outside the front entrance to the departure terminal. "I appreciate everything you have done for me, Dr. Umbawi. You have been a great guide and teacher. I don't know how to thank you."

They shook hands. Dr. Umbawi stared at Jim intensely. He squeezed Jim's hand hard for a moment. "I'm sure you will tell the story, Jim. It will give your life some real meaning. Just remember that mankind is just now grappling with the concept that our origins may be the result of random, not preordained, events. You cannot just charge out onto the world stage proclaiming the possibility that our cherished idea of our place in the natural world may not be what we believe it to be. The thin veneer of what we refer to as civilization may disintegrate before our eyes if the Bokuru hominid is what you and I would like to think it is. That is why I suggested there must be another way."

"But you never told me what that direction is," said Jim.

"If you take away all our beliefs, what will be left? What new social structure will you offer as a substitute?"

"All I'm looking for is a way to tell the story," said Jim.

"You cannot just pull the rug out from under humanity's feet and leave the public bruised and hurt lying on the street. You have a moral obligation to do more," said Dr. Umbawi.

"What you are saying is that part of my mission is to help humanity get back up," said Jim.

"See, there is hope for you after all. I had the feeling you would understand. You really are ready to take the first step in what may be a long journey."

Jim stepped out of the Land Rover, opened the back door and retrieved his duffle bags from the back seat.

"Oh, Jim, just in case I haven't given you enough to think about for your mission, just remember one more thing," said Dr. Umbawi leaning toward the open passenger window so Jim could hear him.

Jim approached the open window.

"What's your last suggestion, Dr. Umbawi?"

"Jim, just remember, it is entirely possible that all God's children are dead."

Within moments, Dr. Umbawi was gone. Jim stood at the curb watching the Land Rover disappear into the traffic. Jim remained motionless, knowing he had heard that statement before, but for a moment he was unable to make the connection. Suddenly he remembered. "Son of a gun," he said out loud. "Son of a gun. You've been using me all this time."

No one heard him. Dr. Umbawi was gone.

That phase was in the first letter Dr. Bronston had written to his deceased wife, the letter that Mobutu had shown Jim in the supply tent. Dr. Umbawi had never seen that letter. He must have picked the phrase up when talking to Dr. Bronston over dinner at the restaurant in the hotel. Dr. Bronston must have shared the discovery of the Bokuru hominid with Dr. Umbawi, otherwise Dr. Umbawi's parting use of the phrase made no sense. When Dr. Bronston died, Dr. Umbawi must have realized that now there was no one to tell the story until he saw Jim's resume.

Everything Dr. Umbawi had said and done since Jim arrived in Africa had been to prepare and motivate Jim to tell the story. Jim laughed lightly. No matter how deceptive Dr. Umbawi had been, he was right. The story had to be told, and Jim was the only one who could do it. Now, Jim had his answer. He knew how he would carry out his mission. He turned from the traffic and walked briskly into the terminal.

Nancy was waiting. They had a plane to catch. Besides, he thought, if he made this flight he would be assured of getting back to Chicago in time to sail with Sonny Chesterson this weekend. If he missed the last race of the season, he was sure Sonny would drop him from the crew list for the following year. No matter what else happened, it was important that he was on that list.

CHAPTER TWENTY-THREE: *THE ESSEX*

Jim worked his way down the aisle of the African Air Boeing 737, his boarding pass in his hand, looking for row 27. Nancy was seated in Seat 27B. At first she did not see him, but she smiled warmly as soon as he reached her seat. Thankfully, he thought, Dr. Tubojola had arranged for them to sit next to each other on both legs of the flight, first to Lagos, Nigeria, where they would change planes, and then on the long direct flight back to Chicago.

"Good afternoon, Nancy," he said, as he put his briefcase down in front of his aisle seat.

"Good afternoon, Jim. You're late," she said. "I was beginning to worry if you were staying over for another day or two on some wild plan to save the Bokuru hominid. I thought maybe you met with Dr. Umbawi."

"Dr. Umbawi?" he asked, wondering how she knew about his trip to the airport.

"Yes. I called his office this morning to say goodbye, and he wasn't there. In fact, no one seemed to know where he was. I called your hotel, but you had already checked out. Finally, I called his home and talked to his wife. All she knew about his whereabouts was that he left very early this morning. She said when he left that early it was usually because he was on his way to Elizabethtown. I just guessed he was with you."

"Well, you're right," said Jim. "Dr. Umbawi picked me up at the hotel this morning and drove me here to the airport. We were late, so he just dropped me off in front of the terminal. It looks like I just made it."

"You mean, he got up this morning and drove from his home in Nairobi all the way to Elizabethtown just to pick you up and drive you back here to the airport?" asked Nancy, stunned.

"Yes. He wanted to share some thoughts with me before I left Africa," said Jim.

Jim took off his suit coat and put it in the overhead bin, before taking his seat next to her. As soon as he was seated, he fastened his seat belt.

"You have been smiling like the cat that ate the canary," she said. "What is it that you're not telling me?"

"Dr. Umbawi helped me a lot. He wanted to say goodbye to you too, but he said what he had to say was for my ears only. He said he did not want to compromise you since you have a conflict of interest, but you should not take it personally," said Jim, grinning.

"That's a strange comment," she said.

"He said you should not get upset because he has the same problem. I know your families have been friends for many years, but he said he wanted to talk to me alone and time was limited to accomplish what he wanted to do. He was quite anxious to meet with me, but he does send his best regards. Frankly, I was intrigued, to say the least, because of the way he cold-shouldered us out at Bokuru, yesterday. He never spoke to us, and he barely acknowledged our presence. Yesterday, I was upset about it. If you remember, all we got from him was a cursory hello and farewell. Dr. Tubojola was the only one who spoke all morning. The whole time we were there Dr. Umbawi said nothing of substance to anyone," said Jim.

"I know. I thought he acted rather odd while we were out there. Dr. Tubojola did all the talking," she said. "I think Dr. Umbawi was there solely at Dr. Tubojola's request. He was just window dressing."

"You're right. Dr. Tubojola knew all about our discovery of the Bokuru hominid because you told him the night before. Anyway, Dr. Umbawi met me at the hotel this morning, totally unannounced," said Jim.

"That still seems a bit strange," she said.

"In all honesty, I was happy to see a familiar face. I was relieved to know I would be traveling with someone I knew on the way to the airport. Besides, his behavior was a real contrast to the day before."

"What did he say on the way here?" she asked. "What was so important that he drove all the way to Elizabethtown just to pick you up?"

Jim opened the fold out table from the seat back in front of him and placed his briefcase on it. He opened the case, took out a pen and legal pad, then closed the case and placed it under the seat in front of him.

"Dr. Umbawi said he was simply Dr. Tubojola's guest yesterday. He was instructed to say nothing to anyone. It was Dr. Tubojola's show. He said we should understand, and we should recognize he has to stay here in Africa where he lives and teaches. He reminded me that he has to continue to work with Dr. Tubojola for the rest of his professional life, Nancy. Much of his career and income is based on his business relationship with Dr. Tubojola. He said that you also have to work with them in your professional capacity at the museum in Chicago," said Jim.

"He's right," she said. "We both have professional relationships with Dr. Tubojola."

"However, he said my situation is different. When I leave Africa, he said I am gone forever," said Jim.

"Is that all he said?" she asked.

"Oh, no, not at all. He said I should understand that Dr. Tubojola was right in what he said and did yesterday, and that I should be sensitive to his position. Dr. Umbawi was concerned that I would leave Africa feeling upset about what had happened. He knew exactly what I was thinking," said Jim.

"That's nice, but what did he offer to help you? He must have had something more to say than that? Besides, I can tell by your behavior, there is something more you haven't told me. Yesterday you were upset and depressed. Now, today, you are almost jubilant. There is something more," said Nancy.

"He told me that it was up to me to tell the story of the Bokuru hominid," said Jim.

"Did you tell him about our little escapade last night?" she asked.

"Of course not. He just said I was the only one who could tell the story."

"That's amazing. You have no professional standing and no proof. What does he expect you to do?" she asked, frowning.

"Dr. Umbawi knows my shortcomings, but he still insisted I was the one to tell the story. He just didn't say how I was supposed to do it. He left that up to me," said Jim.

"You mean he told you to tell the story, and didn't give you a clue how to do it?"

"Yes, in a nutshell, that's what he said. He went so far as to call it my mission," said Jim.

"A mission?" she asked. "That sounds a bit like a crusade."

"Yes. Well, he said the mission he had in mind required someone who was not directly involved in the professional archaeological world, but someone who had knowledge of what was involved. He said I fit all the requirements perfectly for the mission. He said the mission was mine and mine alone," said Jim.

"Well. Dr. Umbawi is an amazing man. The more I think about it, the more I think he is right. The rest of us are too involved. You are the only one who is free from direct conflicts, and still knows about the Bokuru hominid," she said. "My greatest concern is our promise to Dr. Tubojola to say nothing about Bokuru."

"Dr. Umbawi was aware of that," said Jim. "I think he hinted at what I had to do without violating our agreement with Dr. Tubojola."

"He gave you a hint, after all?" she asked.

"In fact, he said it was probably better this way."

"What is better this way?" she asked.

"He said it was probably better for me to tell the story precisely because I could not prove that the Bokuru hominid ever existed, and I had no evidence to prove it. Dr. Umbawi said that if I had some evidence, then the whole world would focus its attention on the facts I used, and that would destroy my mission."

"I am interested in knowing just exactly what you think your mission really is," she said.

"Well," said Jim, "Dr. Umbawi didn't say. He left that entirely up to me."

"If I read the smile on your face when you got here, you have solved that problem," said Nancy.

"I have. I'm going to write a book," said Jim.

"But Jim, that's why we went back out there last night, to obtain some evidence so you would have something to back you up. If you write a book without proof, no one will read it," she said. "No one will ever believe you."

"You don't understand. I figured it out. I'm not going to write about facts. I'm going to write a book of fiction," said Jim.

"Fiction!" she exclaimed, her voice sounding surprised.

"Yes, Dr. Umbawi said that you have to look closely at who people are to understand them. Just now, out on the curb, I realized who he was. I mean, he kept telling me, but it didn't sink in. Finally, it dawned on me that he was not just any teacher, he was my teacher. Ever since I landed here in Africa, I have been in school. He said all a teacher can do is help students learn to think. He would never give me the answer. He could motivate me, but I had to figure out how to tell the story. Maybe it was something he said. It just hit me while I was standing on the curb watching him drive away. The way to tell the story and not stir up all sorts of opposition is fiction," said Jim.

"Well, that makes sense," she said. "The only problem I have with what you're saying is that fiction is like fairy tales and make believe. We both know that the Bokuru hominid is real."

"Nancy, we have no evidence. Fiction is the only medium left to tell the story and avoid tremendous resistance and criticism."

As the plane backed away from the gate and made it's way across the tarmac to the runway, they sat for a few minutes in silence.

"You know, Jim, Dr. Umbawi is right," she said. "This discovery would never have been accepted." She paused and looked at him in a strange way, as the plane started down the runway. "Jim, forget everything I just said about fiction. Dr. Umbawi is right on the money, more than he knew. He is amazing. He could see that we were going to lose, and the site had to be buried for all time, but he wanted the world to know about the hominid, so he turned to you. He could see that you were upset enough with how Dr. Tubojola handled things yesterday that you would be motivated to do something. That was why he didn't say anything at the camp. He didn't need to. Dr. Tubojola was a pawn in his game. He's a genius, Jim."

"He's smart. I'm not sure he's a genius though," Jim answered.

"Perhaps, you are right. He probably didn't know how accurate he was about you, Jim."

"What are you trying to say?"

"Do you remember how you and I first met?" she asked.

"Sure. It was back in college," said Jim.

"Yes. We met in a class we were both taking. Don't you remember?" she asked.

"Yes, it was our senior year. The course was sophomore level. We both took it because we were short on English credits and needed a few, easy elective credits to graduate," said Jim. "Of course, I remember."

"Great. More specifically, Jim, we were in a class on American Literature," she said.

"Yes, I remember the class," he said. "Herman Melville, Walt Whitman, and Edgar Allen Poe."

"Ahab and the white whale," said Nancy. "We studied the story of Moby Dick. I remember you got the highest grade and some sort of special commendation from the English department."

"Yes, I remember," Jim repeated, laughing lightly. "The head of the English department wanted me to give up on my dreams of going to law school and enroll in graduate school in English. They even had a scholarship for me. I don't remember all the details. But, I was committed to go to law school. I had promised my mother that I would stay on that course."

"Well, I remember the details of your paper. You analyzed Moby Dick. You did a thorough study on the biography and personal background of Herman Melville. You pointed out that he actually spent time on whaling ships with whaling people, so he had first hand knowledge of the environment on a whaling ship. Anyway, even though the story of Moby Dick was written as fiction, it actually was based closely on the real story of a whaling ship named the Essex, which, as I recall, was the only whaling vessel ever known to have been sunk by a whale. Look, you know this story better than I do. You should be telling me about this. Anyway, the story was in the headlines of all the papers for a long time, but that's not my point," she said.

"It isn't?" he asked.

"No, the point is that Herman Melville wrote his book as fiction. Since everyone at that time knew the story from the newspaper headlines, it did not sell well. When the book was first published, it failed miserably because it was seen as nothing more than a rewrite of the real story of the <u>Essex</u>. The public was tired of the <u>Essex</u> story from reading about it in the newspapers. They weren't interested in another version of what they saw as the same old story again. It took a long time for the true story to die away before people began to read the book and see the story of Ahab and the whale. Finally, after the real story was forgotten, <u>Moby Dick</u> became popular, and in time, an American classic," said Nancy. "Your conclusion then was that fiction was more powerful than fact, and that is what is relevant to your life now, Jim. Dr. Umbawi knew fiction as a story with real issues is far more important than reality and fact. You had to realize for yourself that the true facts of Bokuru will be long forgotten, and buried forever, but the fictional story and what it represents can last forever. That," she said, "is the true story of <u>Moby Dick</u> and it is the same for the true story of Bokuru."

"Wow, you're ahead of me," said Jim.

"You may not be Herman Melville, but Dr. Umbawi is right. You cannot write about the Bokuru hominid as a book of nonfiction. Everyone would attack you, no matter whether it was truth or fiction. You are the right one to write a book of fiction. The English professor was right about you. You do have a special skill. You chose to ignore your special talent and go on to law school instead. Didn't you tell me once that they told you the decision would haunt you, and someday you would have to write?"

"I'm not sure. I may have," said Jim.

"You walked away from your true destiny back then. Now, here it is back to haunt you."

"But I'm not a published author," he said.

"No, but history says that if you have a good story and the issues are real, you'll find a publisher. You are the only one who can write it. The important thing now is that you also have the writing skills to succeed."

"I'm flattered by the faith you have in my untested ability to write a book," said Jim.

"I know you will succeed," she said. "So tell me, Jim, if I want to read this book how will I find it? How will I look it up? What will you call it?"

He folded up the table into the seatback, lifted up the pad on which he had written one word. Nancy looked down at the note pad and read the word as Jim spoke, "Bokuru, Nancy. I'm going to call it Bokuru."

CHAPTER TWENTY-FOUR: *NO REGRETS*

When Nancy Bronston returned to her apartment from work two days after her return to Chicago, she collected her mail from her box in the lobby. She caught the elevator up to her apartment on the 11th floor and checked for messages on her answering machine. There were three. Two were from friends welcoming her back from her trip, and the third was from Jim Henderson inviting her to go sailing. According to his message, they would be guests on the last sail of the season. The afternoon event was called the 'Frostbite', which he described as little more than a casual afternoon on the water. She smiled at the invitation. He had never asked her to go sailing before.

She put her mail down on the coffee table and started to go through what she expected to be bills that had piled up while she was overseas. In the middle of the parcel of mail was a letter personally addressed to her in an envelope from a store bought stationary note set. The postmark was stamped Elizabethtown, Uhuru. However, the return address was carefully penned in permanent ink as Cape Town, South Africa.

Goose bumps ran down her spine as she recognized her father's distinctive handwriting on the envelope. With shaking hands, she opened the envelope. Inside she found a handwritten letter from her father. As she opened it, a business card slipped out and fluttered down onto the coffee table. She bent over and picked up the business card. It was embossed with the name Stephen Browning. She did not recognize the name, but, yet, it seemed somehow familiar. The address on the business card was from Phoenix, Arizona.

She looked at the postmark on the envelope once again, puzzled. The postmarked date was stamped five days earlier, while she had still been in Africa. There was no date written in the body of the letter. Slowly, she read the letter.

Dear Nancy,

I placed this letter with a service agent in Elizabethtown with instructions to mail it to you on a predetermined date. By now, you will know that I have taken my retirement. I am informing you by mail after the fact because I did not want to start another debate with you on the subject. St. Louis and Chicago are nice places, but my heart lies here in Africa.

I have taken a position with the College of Surgeons in Cape Town, South Africa. As you may recall, we visited Cape

Town and the campus when you were a little girl. You may also remember the college is located on the high slope of Mount Kimonju, facing southeast. I will be staying at the Village Inn right on campus where most of the senior faculty members reside. My time teaching should roughly offset my housing costs. The college is known for sponsoring well known, but controversial, figures in anthropology and medicine, so I'll fit right in.

Before I leave Uhuru, I will have completed the preliminary report on Bokuru and turned it in to Dr. Tubojola. Initially I wanted to wait until all the field work was done and all the fossilized bones reconstructed, but my fear of early unauthorized disclosure and my decision to retire soon pushed me to make what I would normally call a premature report. I have completed only one restoration, that of HO-011.

Bokuru is not only unique, but it will be extremely controversial. The post cranium anatomy is clearly that of our direct ancestor, *Homo erectus*, but the head is unusual enough that at the risk of being called a splitter I have concluded that I have found a new species. The lower and upper denture is clearly that of *Homo erectus*, but that is where the similarities end. The cranium is twice the size of modern man, and the eye apertures are expanded, indicating a specimen of a creature far more advanced than us. The implications are mind boggling, and, if the discovery holds up, it will be the most significant archaeological find in human history. This discovery challenges all our preconceived notions of human history and deeply held beliefs about ourselves and our ancestry.

I am not new to controversy. I have been down this road before, but for the first time in my life I am not as sure of the science behind what I have done, and that is really why I am writing this letter. I completed the field notes in permanent ink as I always do, and I had finished my reconstruction of the skeletal bones and the skull for HO-011 using the new super glue that makes a bond as strong as the pieces of fossilized bone it is holding. I thus found myself locked into the position that I had taken. The problem of the science did not come up until Mobutu, who has never seen my reconstruction, was reviewing our field data. He noticed that we were not watching our facts as carefully as we should. He suggested that we had been using the assumption that five meters below the datum plane was the flat bottom of the cave, which we called the datum base plane or occupation level. He noted that some bone fragments had been found 10 centimeters below the base plane. While we did have bones from over 12 different species of animals, it was only the bits of hominid bone that were found at the 10-centimeter depth.

I do not want to be too technical, but his thinking was that this exclusion of the other bone fragments indicated a possible hominid burial in a depression in the cave floor at some date prior to the time the cave filled in. Mobutu's comment introduced the issue that there could have been another crushed skull, the pieces of which I may have included in my reconstruction of HO-011. This new unidentified burial was located directly below HO-011. Any combination of pieces would have a very serious impact on all my conclusions.

Because I did not have enough pieces to lump together as a separate individual burial, I shrugged off Mobutu's comments. However, I was still concerned. It appears that I was slipping in my old age. I had not been as careful as I should have been. I knew then it was time for me to toss in the towel.

I reviewed everything with the one professional I could trust, Dr. Umbawi. He convinced me that I had done everything according to professional standards and practices, and my conclusions were within the normal range of professional discretion. Ancient skulls are not easy to work with. Over time the broken pieces are worn and distorted so that any reassembly is often no more than a professional hunch. Dr. Umbawi suggested that I shouldn't change anything and go ahead with my report. He suggested I rely on my professional reputation and stand pat. After thinking about it for a couple of days, I have decided to rely on his good advice.

Since the Bokuru hominid is not a usual discovery, the attack by vested interests will be especially virulent, and our weakness as pointed out by Mobutu may be discovered. I can predict how extremists will yell fraud and even allege a new Piltdown. If we do incur that type of muckraking by our antagonists, it may seriously affect you and your position with the Chicago museum. Frankly, the Bronston name could become a liability instead of an asset.

Perhaps you remember our old neighbor from St. Louis? Thinking he heard a prowler late one evening, he took his gun and mistakenly killed his wife those many years ago. He now has a successful insurance agency in Phoenix. We both agree your work experience would make you a good prospect for taking over so he can retire. He anticipates your call. I have included his business card with this letter.

My decision to retire before any public announcements are made about Bokuru was planned to give me a new base from which I could respond, a place where no one had any leverage over me, unlike Uhuru where all my licenses and permits are in the hands of the strongest anticipated antagonists.

Dr. Umbawi said it best. If my life goal was to bring awareness to the general public about our human past so that humanity would be in a better position to deal with the future, then certainly the announcement of this discovery would assure the accomplishment of my objective. He said the real issue for me was whether I was willing to risk my reputation to reach my goal. I made my decision with a full understanding of the consequences. If you remember that visit to South Africa so long ago, perhaps you will remember the veranda outside the small restaurant next to the main library on campus. Think of me sitting there on that patio looking out over the wonderful view of Table Mountain, the city below, and the sea in the hazy distance. Whatever you do, don't worry about me. I will be sitting at one of the tables sipping an iced tea, smiling, secure in the knowledge that the name 'Bokuru' will, for better or worse, become a household name. As Dr. Umbawi said, it makes no difference whether I am right or wrong. The issues raised as a result of this discovery will be on the world stage. He always was, first and foremost, an educator. As for me, I am satisfied. I have no regrets.

With all my love,

Your father.

Nancy read the letter again slowly. After a moment, she smiled, then took the letter over to her home office worktable and fed it carefully through her paper shredder. She picked up the phone and returned Jim's call. He was not in, so she left a message on his answering machine, "Jim, this is Nancy. I got your message. I'd love to go, but I have never gone sailing before, so I have two questions. First, what do I wear? It's got to be cold and wet out on the water. Send me a fax with particulars.

Second, exactly what is 'ballast'? It sounds sort of submissive to me. I assume you will at least bring a large thermos of hot coffee. I'll rely on you for that."

ABOUT THE AUTHOR

Jon C. Hall is a graduate of Purdue University and Indian University School of Law- Indianapolis. He was admitted to the Indiana Bar, the Illinois Bar, and the Florida Bar.

He retired from the active practice of law in 2000. He has had a life long amateur interest in archaeology and is a former member of the South Florida Archaeology Association. He is a member of the Florida Anthropological Society and the Roebling Chapter of the national Society for Industrial Archaeology.

Printed in the United States
32160LVS00005B/40-279